Holiday In Your Heart

Books by Susan Fox

Caribou Crossing Romances

"Caribou Crossing" novella

Home On the Range

Gentle On My Mind

"Stand By Your Man" novella

Love Me Tender

Love Somebody Like You

Ring of Fire

Holiday In Your Heart

Wild Ride to Love Series

His, Unexpectedly

Love, Unexpectedly

Yours, Unexpectedly

Also by Susan Fox

Body Heat

Writing as Susan Lyons

Sex Drive

She's On Top

Touch Me

Hot In Here

Champagne Rules

Anthologies

The Naughty List

Some Like It Rough

Men On Fire

Unwrap Me

The Firefighter

Holiday In Your Heart

SUSAN FOX

ZEBRA BOOKS
KENSINGTON PUBLISHING CORP.
http://www.kensingtonbooks.com

ZEBRA BOOKS are published by

Kensington Publishing Corp.
119 West 40th Street
New York, NY 10018

First Printing: October 2016
ISBN-13: 978-1-4201-4028-6
ISBN-10: 1-4201-4028-0

eISBN-13: 978-1-4201-4029-3
eISBN-10: 1-4201-4029-9

10 9 8 7 6 5 4 3 2 1

Printed in the United States of America

Author's Note

It's with some sadness that I tell you that *Holiday In Your Heart* is the final (eighth) title in the Caribou Crossing Romances series. But I'm delighted to finish the series with a holiday book and a message that redemption, hope, and love are possible for even a seriously troubled soul. When I introduced Mo Kincaid at the beginning of the series as Brooke's ex-husband and Evan's father, the man who had abused and abandoned them, little did I know that he'd be a hard man to get out of my mind. And so I thought . . . Brooke was a bad mom and a bad wife, and in her thirties she completely turned her life around. Why couldn't the same thing be possible for Mo?

Well, that was my challenge, and of course when I got to know the man Mo had turned into over the years, I fell head over heels for him. No wonder Maribeth Scott can't resist him, even though he shows up at the absolute worst—or is it the absolute best?—time in her life. I hope you enjoy their rocky progress toward their own special happy ending.

Domestic abuse is a pervasive and widespread problem. It does not discriminate by gender, age, education, occupation, race, religion, or sexuality. It can take many forms, from emotional/psychological abuse (such as belittling and controlling) all the way to murder (of the victim or of the abuser). Domestic abuse has had a powerful impact on a number of the characters in the Caribou Crossing series. Former rodeo champion Sally Ryland, fire chief

Lark Cantrell and her mother, and investment counselor Evan Kincaid were all victims of abuse. Brooke Kincaid was both a victim and an abuser. Mo Kincaid was an abuser.

If domestic abuse has touched your life, or that of a friend or family member, please know that there are many, many resources available to assist. In an emergency situation, call 9-1-1 or any other local emergency service. Otherwise, good places to start are with the HelpGuide.org website and that of The National Domestic Violence Hotline (thehotline.org; or loveisrespect.org for teens). There are resources including shelters, support groups, and counselors in most communities. You can search on the Internet using terms such as *domestic abuse* (or *violence*) *services* (or *resources* or *shelters*) plus your geographic location.

I believe in rehabilitation and redemption, but I know it's a tough road and takes a strong and committed person—people like Mo and Brooke. It also most often takes professional help. For domestic abusers, the best source of help is a batterer intervention program. These can also be located through an Internet search. Other resources such as counseling and A.A. may also be useful.

If a former abuser has reformed and apologized, it is up to the former victim whether to offer forgiveness. A person should never feel pressured or obligated to forgive, although forgiveness that is genuinely given can be a part of an individual's healing process.

To turn to a more cheerful topic, I am so grateful to everyone who has supported the Caribou Crossing series. Thank you to all the readers who have taken the time to contact me, write reviews, or tell their friends and family about my books. Thank you to my publisher, Kensington, and my fabulous editor, Martin Biro, for believing in this series, helping me make the books as good as they can be, and giving them such gorgeous covers and marketing support. Thanks also to my wonderful agent, Emily Sylvan Kim of Prospect Agency, for being my cheerleader and business partner. And for *Holiday In Your Heart*, special thanks to the following people who provided valuable critiques: Nazima Ali, Rosalind Villers, and Alaura Ross.

I've been asked if people need to read the Caribou Crossing Romances in order. No, not at all. Each is a stand-alone story. You can dive in at any point. A complete list of titles (in order) is available on my website.

The Caribou Crossing Romances may have come to an end, but **I'm delighted to announce that I am now writing a new series for Kensington titled Blue Moon Harbor.** Set on a quirky made-up island in the Pacific Northwest, the stories will include romance, challenges, humor, eccentric characters, and a gorgeous natural setting. **The first book, *Fly Away With Me*, will be published in the summer of 2017!**

I love sharing my stories with my readers and I love hearing from you. I write under the pen names Susan Fox, Savanna Fox, and Susan Lyons. You can e-mail me at susan@susanlyons.ca or contact me through my website at www.susanfox.ca, where you'll also find excerpts, behind-the-scenes notes, recipes, a monthly contest, the sign-up for my newsletter, and other goodies. You can also find me on Facebook at facebook.com/SusanLyonsFox.

Chapter One

Outside the window of the bus, Mo Kincaid saw a sign with a stylized caribou and the message WELCOME TO CARIBOU CROSSING. It was a fancier sign than the faded one he had walked past when he left almost twenty years ago. Seemed the town had changed. Well, so had he.

He figured he'd be about as welcome here as a dead car battery in the middle of a mid-January snowstorm, but here he was all the same. Compelled, driven, maybe obsessed. Selfish or honorable? Hell if he knew.

Unable to sit still now, he rose, grabbed the battered backpack that contained all his worldly goods, and made his way up front. "Can you let me off here?" he asked the stocky, middle-aged female driver.

"Don't want to go all the way downtown?"

"No, ma'am." Not quite yet. He'd left Caribou Crossing on foot, his thumb out, hoping for a ride. Somehow it felt right to reenter town striding along the dusty shoulder of the road, one purposeful step at a time.

"It's against the rules to make an unscheduled stop."

She cocked a bushy brown eyebrow, waiting to see if he'd try to persuade her.

He gave her the lazy smile that women seemed to like. "Aw now, what's the fun in always following the rules?" He'd never had much time for rules. When he was younger, there'd been plenty of women willing to break theirs for him, and he guessed not much had changed because the driver's foot shifted over to the brake.

She grinned, the mirth in it lending her face an unexpected beauty. "Good point, mister." With a wink, she added, "Promise you won't tell on me."

"I surely won't. Much obliged." He tipped his head to her and went down the steps.

When both feet were planted on the ground, he stood there as the driver waved and drove away. The bus disappeared and still Mo stood, alone on a nondescript country road in the middle of British Columbia, wondering if he was a damn fool. He could cross the narrow two lanes, stick out his thumb. No one would know that he'd almost come to town, but had turned around before getting anywhere near his ex-wife or his son.

Mo would know, and he'd beat himself up for it. He'd already debated this trip for a good two years before quitting a decent job in Regina, shoving his belongings in his pack, and heading to the bus depot. Real men were supposed to be decisive, but then real men didn't let booze get the best of them; they controlled their anger; they didn't hit women or kids. It had been a very long time since he'd done any of those bad things, but they still weighed on his conscience. The doing, and the weighing, those were the reasons he would not cross that road. He couldn't change the past, but he could, at long last, stop running from it and try to make amends.

He buttoned his heavy denim jacket against the chilly, early November air, hoisted his pack, and set out along the broad shoulder of the road into town. A sullen gray sky threatened snow, but so far the ground was clear. Beyond a wooden fence lay ranch land scattered with grazing cattle. After a passing glance, Mo's focus wasn't on the scenery but on his thoughts.

He'd never liked Caribou Crossing. Never liked any of the dusty dots on the map that he and Brooke and Evan had lived in back in the old days. But then he hadn't liked much of anything. He'd been too damned pissed off at the world and at how his life had turned out.

He had fumed every step of the way out of town until he'd hit the highway and a trucker picked him up. It was one thing to skip town as a matter of choice. But when the police had showed up at his and Brooke's door that day, he'd figured he had no choice but to leave.

Mo hated the man he'd been back then. An asshole who, when he was pissed off, got drunk and riled up. There were no excuses for the things he'd done. It didn't matter that his young, pretty wife drank too much herself and ragged on him for ruining her life. It didn't matter that she spent much of her time either partying herself senseless at the Gold Nugget Saloon, or holed up in bed with the covers over her head, or engaged in screaming matches with him.

Whatever the folks around him did, a man was responsible for his own actions. Way too late in life, Mo had come to that realization.

So now here he was, dragging his sorry ass back to the town his wife and kid had called Hicksville, to apologize. Much too little, much too late, and they would probably—

and deservedly—want to plant a boot square on his backside and kick him straight back out of town.

If they did, maybe he'd go. But maybe he wouldn't. He used to walk away when the going got tough. But taking responsibility meant not taking the easy way out.

When the compulsion had hit him to reconnect with Brooke and Evan, he'd wondered if he would even be able to locate them. Caribou Crossing was the only place he'd known to start, and the online *Caribou Crossing Gazette* had given him the surprising news that both were still in town.

Brooke was married again, to a man named Jake Brannon. When Mo'd seen the guy's occupation, he'd done a double take. Brannon was the Royal Canadian Mounted Police detachment commander for Caribou Crossing. Did that mean Brooke had stopped drinking and causing a ruckus?

As for Evan, the boy had been smart as a whip and always insisted he was going to go to some fancy college and build a successful career in a high-powered place like New York City. He'd had the dreams, the smarts, the drive, yet now he was a small-town investment counselor. Poor kid; having parents like Mo and Brooke had probably doomed him.

Traffic had increased enough—meaning three or four cars and trucks in succession—to make Mo refocus on his surroundings. He'd reached the outskirts of town. A nicely maintained barn, paddock, and hitching rails belonged to a business called Westward Ho! It advertised trail rides and horse boarding both long term and short. It seemed Caribou Crossing was still all about horses.

Him, he was better with machines than with animals. Not that he didn't like animals. It was just easier to understand machinery and to fix whatever went wrong. And when it came to people . . . Well, it was ironic that he could repair anything with an engine, but had almost destroyed the lives of the two people he cared about the most.

In an odd counterpoint to his thoughts, a medium-sized light brown animal ran around a corner and headed straight for him. At first he thought it was a fox, but when it pulled up a couple of feet short of him, he saw it was a dog with a broad, wedge-shaped head. It didn't bare its teeth in a threat nor wag its tail, just stood there watching him.

A dark-haired girl, late teens maybe, burst around the same corner, and then slowed when she saw the dog. Panting for breath, she approached slowly. Above the collar of a puffy green jacket, her cheeks were pink from exertion. "There you are," she said to the animal.

It edged a foot closer to Mo, making him wonder if the creature had been abused. God knew, Mo had reason to recognize that kind of wariness.

The girl stood back a few feet, tugging a striped toque more securely down over her shoulder-length hair. "I'm from the animal shelter," she told Mo, "and he's our resident escape artist."

"He was abused?"

"We don't think so. There were no physical signs of it. He'd been well looked after, he's definitely been trained, and we found him with his leash tied to the railing by the shelter's door. We figure he was abandoned because he wasn't the kind of pet the owner wanted."

Mo glanced again at the dog, which was staring up at him with its ears cocked forward. The whitish face and chest contrasted nicely with the pale reddish-brown coat. The dog's body was lean and fit, and it had a bushy, longish tail. For some reason, Mo felt defensive on the animal's behalf. "What's wrong with him? He looks fine to me."

"Want to adopt him?" she asked promptly.

He grinned at her. "Nice try. No, thanks. But seriously, why wouldn't someone want him?"

"He's a New Guinea singing dog." The girl inched closer to the animal. "The first one any of us had ever seen. We had to look him up. They're called singing dogs because they have a unique kind of howl. They're a lot like the Australian dingo. A wild dog, though the ones that are bred in captivity can be trained." She glanced at Mo, her expression earnest. "Like, a wild dog would naturally prey on cats, but Caruso's been trained to leave them alone. All the same, singers aren't your typical pet dog. They're, like, total free spirits. Independent. More like cats. If someone wants a dog that fawns all over them, a singing dog isn't right for them."

Mo was liking the creature more and more.

The dog had moved to sit on his left, about ten inches from his well-worn work boot. Mo squatted. "Hey, Caruso. I've never heard a dog sing. Want to give me a demonstration?"

As he spoke, the girl moved closer. While the dog gazed at Mo, not opening its mouth, she clipped the leash to its collar. Caruso shot both of them a dirty look. Mo tried not to feel guilty.

"Come on, Caruso," the girl said. "It's time to go home."

Home. An animal shelter. Well, at least the creature would have food and be warm and dry. Seemed it didn't want anything more than that—like affection—anyway. Mo and Caruso did have a lot in common.

"You sure you don't want to adopt him?" the girl tried again.

Mo shook his head. "I'm a wanderer."

"So's Caruso. You're perfect for each other."

"Nope. Not happening. I've got enough on my plate."

As she led the dog away, it cast a glance at Mo over its shoulder. Not begging, not hopeful, not even blaming this time. Just a glance.

Mo resumed his own walk, knowing exactly where he was headed. Thanks to the Internet, he knew that Hank Hennessey still ran his vehicle and farm equipment repair shop, and it was still the only one in town. Hank would be getting on now, in his midsixties. He must have an assistant or two. Likely he didn't need Mo's help—and wouldn't take him back even if he did—but what the hell, a guy had to start somewhere.

As he covered the few blocks, Mo noted changes. When he'd lived here, the town had a used-up feel. Way back in the 1860s, the gold rush had made it a boomtown. After a few years, the gold ran out and the place almost became a ghost town, but a few ranchers kept it going and it slowly grew into a little community. Back in Mo's day, it was a backwoods off the main highway that meandered the interior of British Columbia in a rough vertical line.

Since then, Caribou Crossing had obviously gone through a revival. Even on a chilly, gray Monday afternoon, people bustled around looking cheerful. Businesses and homes were spruced up and old buildings had been restored. There were picturesque touches like bright awnings, planters full of bronze and yellow chrysanthemums, and stylized wire-frame animals that he figured were supposed to be caribou.

Hennessey Auto Repair, when he reached it, looked much the same. There wasn't a lot you could do to make an automotive repair shop look picturesque. As usual, the parking area held a motley assortment of cars, trucks, and farm equipment. One of the doors to the service bays was partially open. The whirr of a drill sounded from inside, competing with Johnny Cash on the radio singing "Folsom Prison Blues." Nope, not much had changed here.

Mo followed the whine of the drill to find a stocky, overall-clad back bent over a workbench. No one else appeared to be around. The drill shut off. Johnny Cash finished up the song, wishing for a train whistle to rid him of his blues.

Mo said, "Mr. Hennessey?"

The man turned, shoving protective goggles up over thin, gray hair. "Yeah?"

"Wondered if—"

"Mo Kincaid?" Hank asked, stepping toward him and narrowing his eyes. "That really you?"

"You recognize me?" He'd worked for Hank for not much more than a year and it had been a long time ago. But Mo's looks were distinctive, his blue-green eyes a contrast to his brownish skin and black hair. His birth name was Mohinder McKeen, the first part coming from his South Asian mother and the second from his Irish-American dad.

"You were a good mechanic." The shorter man studied Mo's face.

"You fired me." After Mo showed up late for work, hungover, one too many times.

"I'm a businessman."

"I know." Hank had been a fair employer and a decent man. While Mo had faced some small-town racism, there'd never been a hint of that from Hank. "And that means you don't likely want to give me another chance,"

Mo continued. He'd known this was a long shot, but he'd worked out what he wanted to say to this man.

"You're looking for a job?" Hank asked disbelievingly.

"I am. I used to be a good mechanic, and I'm better now. And I'm a changed man, Mr. Hennessey. I can't promise I'll stay for long because my plans are, uh, a little uncertain. But as long as I'm in town, I'll work hard and I'll show up on time. You don't have to pay me much, only enough to cover rent and groceries." Mo had saved money over the years, and this was less about earning a salary than about his desire to keep regular work hours and do something useful with his time.

The older man's blue eyes were faded, but still piercing as he kept them on Mo's face.

Mo went on. "I used to have a drinking problem, but that's a long ways in the past." At one point, he'd gone to some A.A. meetings. He'd realized he wasn't an alcoholic, but at those meetings he'd figured out that he was a bitter, angry man who was weak enough to seek solace in alcohol. He'd seen that booze never offered a solution; as with the alcoholics, drinking made his problems worse. Blaming fate or other people wasn't constructive, and he'd managed to let go of his anger and make peace with the world he lived in. He'd also decided that, even if he wasn't an alcoholic, it was safest to stay away from booze. "I haven't had a drink in years. For the last five years, I managed an auto repair business in Regina. I can give you a phone number and you can check with them."

"Uh-huh. Well, I just fired an assistant last month. Idiot couldn't be bothered with diagnostics, just threw parts at the problem." Hank's gaze remained steady on Mo's face. "You say your plans are uncertain. Mind sharing those plans?"

Mo swallowed. He wasn't a guy who opened up to anyone about his personal shit. But it was a fair question, given how he was asking Hank to take a chance on him. "I hope to see my ex-wife and my son. I know I can't make things right, but I owe them an apology."

"Yeah, you do. But they've built good lives for themselves. What if they don't want to see you?"

And there it was. The worry that kept Mo awake at night.

Was he here for Brooke and Evan, as the honorable, responsible thing to do, or was he being selfish? He kept telling himself he had to own up to his sins, offer a sincere apology, and see if there was any way he could make amends. But he had no right to mess up their lives just because he wanted to make peace with himself and feel a little less of a shit. "I don't know. I honestly don't know. Maybe this is a bad idea."

"But?"

"But for the past two or three years, I've had this compulsion. I can't ignore it any longer."

"Your gut talking to you," Hank said.

More like his conscience, but he'd said enough already.

"My gut talks to me," the other man went on. "Now it's telling me to hire you." He held out his hand. "Don't make me regret listening to it."

"Aside from your age, you're an ideal candidate," Dr. LaTisha Jones told Maribeth Scott on Wednesday afternoon. "The lab test results are all great. You're healthy and physically active. And thirty-nine really isn't all that old these days."

"Thanks for that," Maribeth said dryly to the petite

younger woman with her neatly cornrowed black hair. It was in fact Maribeth's age and her insistent biological clock that had brought her to the women's health clinic to discuss artificial insemination. As far back as she could remember, she'd known she was destined to be a mom. It was part of her identity, even more than her red hair.

She'd assumed she would meet the love of her life and everything would fall into place: marriage, building a happy home, having a handful of kids. But, to her bafflement and frustration, she'd never even reached the first step. Though she'd dated tons of men, most of them pretty great guys, she'd yet to feel that magical "click" and know that this was the person she wanted to build a future with. And no way would she settle for anything less than true love.

Next year she'd turn forty. The longer she waited, the lower her chance of getting pregnant and the higher the risks. It was time to pursue a different route. Although her social conscience nagged that she should adopt an underprivileged baby or child, her dream had always been the full experience: carrying a baby within her body, giving birth, holding that warm, sweet little body in her arms moments after he or she first emerged into the world. Of course in that dream, there'd been a loving man at her side through every—

"You've already gone off birth control." Dr. Jones's voice interrupted Maribeth's musing. "Eat healthily, take the prenatal vitamins, cut down on or even better eliminate alcohol and caffeine, and keep up with your yoga and other exercise. This first time, we won't use ovulation stimulation medication. We'll see how you do without it. Your period started on Sunday, so come back next Monday and we'll check for signs of ovulation, but more likely it won't occur for another week after that. Most women ovulate around day fourteen of their cycle." The doctor flashed a saucy grin. "And most important, find that perfect sperm donor."

"I can't wait to start looking through the profiles." Maribeth had thought seriously about the men she knew, some of whom were really quite wonderful. But it was such a huge thing to ask of a friend, and then what if he wanted to be involved in the baby's life? That definitely wasn't her dream, raising a child together with a man she didn't love and didn't live with. Besides, one day Mr. Right would come along, they'd get married, and he'd step into the role of dad.

So she would do her shopping online and find a donor who'd remain anonymous. Dr. Jones had given her a code to access the online site for a sperm bank the women's clinic was affiliated with.

"Let me know as soon as you decide on a donor," the doctor said, "so we can order the sperm and have it ready for you when you're ovulating. But remember, if you're not ready this month, we'll do it in January. This is a decision you don't want to rush into."

Dr. Jones was so right. Maribeth felt the weight of the responsibility. She'd be choosing the biological father of her child. Yet now that she'd made the decision to proceed, she was eager to get on with it. If insemination worked this month, she would be pregnant at Christmas. It would be such an amazing gift. Of course, even if she got pregnant in the next two or three months, there'd still be a little one sharing the next Christmas with her. And then Maribeth would probably have—or maybe this time adopt—a second baby. Being an only child was lonely, as she well knew. Of course, it was possible that her first pregnancy would result in twins, and wouldn't that be a blessing?

As she closed the clinic door behind her, a twinge of regret slowed her steps. She'd been dating since she was thirteen. Though her friends teased that she was super picky, that wasn't true. Falling in love wasn't a rational decision; it was about that gut-level, heart-level certainty that this was the one person you were destined to be with. Your happily-ever-after person with whom you'd create babies the good old-fashioned way.

She shook her head, deliberately shoving the regret from her mind. When she was a little girl longing for a sibling, her mom had told her it wasn't going to happen. When she was orphaned at the age of nineteen, she'd had to come to terms with the fact that she'd never be able to hug her parents again or hear them tell her they loved her. She couldn't have a brother or sister and she couldn't have her parents. She *could* still have love, and one day the right man would come along.

But for now, if she didn't move quickly, having a baby would fall into the "can't have" side of the equation—and no way was she letting that happen. It was time to stop waiting and wishing, and to start being proactive. She *was* going to be a mom and give her child—children, hopefully—the best, most loving, happiest life that she possibly could.

Checking her watch, she saw that it was past five. There wasn't much point heading back to Days of Your. Running her own business, a thrift shop, gave her flexibility in terms of setting her hours, though she generally tried to keep regular ones: ten until six, Tuesday through Saturday. It was a rare occasion when she shut early, as she'd done this afternoon.

She was eager to get home and start checking out sperm donor profiles, but first she had to walk over to Hennessey's and pick up her car. She had dropped it off first thing that morning for an oil change and tune-up, and to get snow tires put on.

Maribeth turned up the collar of her tweedy black-and-white coat against the brisk November air, put on red leather gloves, and hitched her Kate Spade tote over her shoulder. With the two-inch heels of her leather ankle boots clicking on the sidewalk, she set off toward the garage. She loved pretty clothes, and running a thrift shop gave her first pick from a wide selection of items. It was amazing how many nearly new clothes, shoes, and bags, some with designer labels, were donated.

As she walked, she exchanged greetings with a few townspeople. Caribou Crossing was small and she'd lived there all her life, which meant she had at least a passing acquaintance with many of the residents. Once she got pregnant, there would be gossip, but she'd ride it out. Folks liked her and they'd be sympathetic. Her child wouldn't suffer as a result of her decision to be a single parent. As for male companionship and role models for her little one, she knew loads of great guys, some of them married to good friends of hers, who'd provide that.

Hennessey Auto Repair, on the outskirts of town, had the usual half-dozen cars parked outside, including her red-and-white Mini Cooper. The doors of the auto bays were closed against the cold, but light shone through the windows. As she approached the building, a cinnamon-brown dog skittered away and ran under one of the parked cars. Unleashed; maybe a runaway? If it was still there when she came out again, she'd call the shelter. The temperature was dipping below freezing these nights, and the animal shouldn't be fending for itself.

Maribeth went in the front door to the office and reception area, which was deserted. No surprise. Like her, Hank ran his business single-handedly much of the time. His two kids had chosen other careers, and though he sometimes hired an assistant, things never worked out for long. She had to wonder what the town would do when the aging mechanic decided to retire, since his was the only repair shop in town.

Knowing Hank would be in the auto bays working on a car, she went on through. That distinctive machine-shop scent of oil and metal filled her nostrils, and as usual the radio was playing. Jason Aldean was telling his lady friend that they were just getting started. Raising her voice so it would carry over the music, she said, "Hank?"

A muffled grunt was her response.

Following the sound, and unbuttoning her heavy coat, she stepped carefully around a big-wheeled truck to see overall-clad legs protruding from under a green car so ancient that it had fins. A couple of clangs came from under the car, and then the man began to slide out on one of those roller-tray thingies.

But was that Hank? The legs were awfully long and the waist very lean for the stocky mechanic. A torso in grimy overalls slid into sight, and then finally—no, that definitely wasn't Hank. Maribeth stared at a strikingly handsome face framed with longish, wavy, black hair.

"Hey," the man said, swinging up from the rolling mechanic's board and getting lithely to his feet, giving her a slow-breaking smile that flashed white against brown skin.

Wow. That smile scored higher on "dazzle factor" than Tom Cruise's. "Hi. So Hank has a new assistant."

"Just started today. I'm Mo."

She read male appreciation in his eyes, which wasn't the least bit unusual. What was less common was the responding ripple of heat through her blood. The man truly was hot. "Maribeth," she said. "Also known as MB. So, where's Hank?" Had he left a brand-new assistant in charge of the shop?

"Some family thing came up and he was needed at his daughter's house. What can I do for you, Maribeth?"

His voice was purely masculine with a slight rough edge like callus on fingertips. It distracted her so that she barely caught his actual words. "I came to pick up my car. It's the Mini parked outside."

"Sure. Let's see if we can find your keys and an invoice." He gestured toward the office.

She walked ahead of him and rounded the counter to stand on the customer side.

He took a small key ring from his pocket, unlocked a cabinet behind the counter, and rummaged inside. "This'll be yours." He produced her spare key.

As she took it from him, she studied him more closely. Normally, Hank's assistants were young guys, but this man was at least her age. Maybe that was why he'd made her think of Tom Cruise. A few strands of silver threaded that wavy, black hair, and lines cut lightly into the skin around his eyes and between his nose and mouth. His skin was medium brown, something other than a suntan left over from summer. She guessed he was mixed race, maybe part South Asian or Native Canadian. His eyes were unexpected, a mix of blue and green that was stunning against that darkish skin. Black stubble shadowed his jaw, and a smudge of grease on one strong cheekbone made her finger itch to smooth it away. To be honest, her fingers, her entire body, itched to touch him all over, even though he was greasy and smelled like a machine shop.

She'd dated a lot of good-looking guys, but had she ever felt this kind of immediate chemistry?

It seemed as if the feeling might be mutual, because he'd more or less frozen, staring at her face. She smiled, flexing her feminine power. Guys had always been drawn to her red hair, sparkling green eyes, and full lips.

He grinned back, the lines running from his nose to his lips turning into dimpled clefts.

Maribeth liked men. Always had; probably always would. Just because she'd decided to become a single parent, that was no reason not to enjoy being with a particularly attractive guy. One who drew her with an almost magnetic appeal. "You're new in town," she said.

"That's not a question," he noted.

"A guy like you, if you'd been in Caribou Crossing long, I'd have known." The words themselves were neutral, but the way she said them wasn't. She was flirting and making no bones about it.

He laughed. "You're not shy, are you?"

"Not for a single day of my life. Seems to me it's a waste of time."

The humor faded from his face, leaving him looking older. "Since you don't like wasting your time, I should tell you that I'm not, you know, looking to date."

Her eyes widened with surprise. Well, that certainly told her where she stood. Except that she could have sworn he was attracted to her. "Married?" she guessed. "Or involved?"

He shook his head. "And don't want to be."

The hottest guy she'd met in forever, and he was turning her down. She shouldn't feel such a jolt of disappointment. After all, she had better plans for the evening anyhow: shopping for a sperm donor. "I should pay my bill."

"Sure. Let me see if I can find it on the computer." He jiggled the mouse, clicked some keys, and asked, "Last name?"

"Scott."

A moment later, he said, "Got it." Another click, and a printer hummed to life. He took the page and handed it over. "Look about right?"

She leaned over the invoice and curls tumbled into her face. Her hair, thick and wavy down past her shoulders, was getting unruly. Shoving it back with an impatient "pfft," she muttered to herself, "I need to call Brooke and make a hair appointment." She scrutinized the bill and then took a credit card from her wallet. "This looks fine."

Mo didn't seem to notice the card. He was staring at her face. "Brooke?" His voice croaked. "Brooke, uh, Brannon?"

She nodded. "Do you know her?"

"Do you?" he countered.

Frowning in puzzlement, she said, "She's a good friend as well as being my hairstylist. How do you know her?"

"I, uh . . ." He finally took the credit card she'd been holding out and ran it through Hank's machine, taking more time than the task required. And not answering her question.

Weird.

Mo handed the card and two copies of the receipt to her. "Sign this one, please. So, do you know her son, too? Evan?"

"Sure." She signed the merchant copy and handed it

back. "He manages my money." When Maribeth's parents had been killed in a bus crash during a holiday in Austria, she'd been shattered, but had found herself quite well off, financially. Still in her teens, she'd inherited not only the family home but also her parents' fair-sized investment portfolio and the proceeds of their life insurance policies. When Evan Kincaid had opened his business in Caribou Crossing a few years back, Maribeth had transferred her portfolio to him, and he'd done exceedingly well for her. "Why are you asking about Brooke and Evan?"

Mo's handsome face was marred by a frown and he didn't answer for a minute or two. Then he said, "I wonder if I could talk to you."

"I thought we *were* talking." This guy might be gorgeous and sexy, but he was getting annoying.

"Sorry. I mean about, uh, something private."

"Something that involves Brooke and Evan?"

He nodded.

"I guess so," she said slowly. "But this is all very mysterious."

"I'm sorry. Let me buy you a drink and I'll explain."

This man, a stranger to town, didn't want to date her, but he wanted to buy her a drink and talk about two of her friends. Well, there was only one way to find out what was going on. "Okay," she agreed. "Do you want to meet somewhere later?" Though she had no reason to trust the guy, no harm would come to her if they met up at one of the town's bars. She'd be bound to know at least half the people in the room, and they'd watch out for her.

He glanced at his watch. "It's time to close up. Could you give me five minutes, and I'll be ready to go?"

"Why not?" Too warm in her coat, she shrugged out of it and tossed it on one of the guest chairs.

Mo's eyes widened. Her figure—unfashionably curvy, but she was happy with it—tended to have that effect on guys.

She tugged down the hem of the long, emerald sweater-top she wore over thick, black leggings, and sank down in the other chair. Crossing one leg over the other, she swung a booted foot back and forth. "Five minutes," she reminded the glazed-eyed man.

Chapter Two

Oh, man, that was one sexy woman. Every single thing about her was smoking, from those gleaming red curls to the dainty feet in black leather boots. She knew it, too, the way she flaunted her curvy breasts and hips in those clingy clothes. Not that Mo was complaining. He couldn't remember when last he'd felt such pure pleasure just looking at a woman.

But she'd given him five minutes, and he must've used up one already, drooling. He tore his fascinated gaze away from her and strode back into the shop. Fortunately, Hank's small bathroom included a shower.

As Mo washed his hair and scrubbed his body under steaming water, he thought about Maribeth Scott. It wasn't the first time a woman had let him know she was interested. Actually, it happened a lot—all due to the way his mom's and dad's genes had combined. Superficial shit, but when he'd been young, he'd exploited that lucky coincidence when he could, just as he'd fought back against the occasional racist who found his mere existence offensive. Now the racial slurs were fewer, but the female interest continued. Mostly, he pretended not to notice either one.

Having royally screwed up his marriage to Brooke all those years ago, he'd learned his lesson and had since avoided anything that smacked of being a relationship. It was tough, because he was a healthy guy with a strong libido. Sometimes he gave into the need for a night's hot sex, but even that could lead to complications. A woman might say that all she wanted was a hookup, but too often afterward she tried to mess around in his life and build herself a place there.

Tempting as Maribeth was, those womanly curves and dazzling green eyes could get a guy into trouble quicker than using a grinder without wearing protective goggles. All he should be wanting from the flirtatious redhead was information about his ex and his kid, something that might help him decide how best to approach them.

He dried himself on a questionable-looking towel and made a mental note to buy a couple of cheap towels for the shop. After dressing in the jeans and pullover he'd worn to work, Mo tugged a comb through his hair. For the first time in a long while, he wished for a razor to get rid of his five o'clock shadow.

He made sure the shop doors were locked, turned off the lights, and rejoined Maribeth. She sure did brighten up the messy office.

She rose, picked up her coat, held it out to him, and turned her back.

He had to grin. The woman had expectations, and no thought that he wouldn't meet them. He stepped closer, opening the coat so she could slide her arms into the sleeves. Even in those heeled boots, she was several inches shorter than his five feet eleven. Such a feminine package. He tugged the coat up around her neck and shoulders and couldn't resist breathing her in, a scent with a hint of spice like an exotic flower. He wanted to bury his face in her hair so that its softness tickled his nose and brushed his cheeks. To immerse himself in her sensual femininity.

Instead, he forced himself to step back as she buttoned her coat and took red gloves from a big purse patterned with black and white flowers.

He did up his own well-worn jacket, opened the door for her, and clicked off the office light as she stepped outside. He followed her into the darkness of a November late afternoon, locking the door and checking that it fastened securely. It blew him away that Hank Hennessey had trusted him to hold down the fort and to lock up, especially on his first day of work. It was probably a testament to what Mo's old boss in Regina had said when Hank phoned him that morning.

"Where should we go?" Mo asked Maribeth. "Is there a place, uh . . ." He searched for the right words to suggest an out-of-the-way coffee shop or bar. He doubted there'd be many people in Caribou Crossing who would recognize him after all this time, but still he didn't want word of his arrival reaching Brooke or Evan before he'd decided how to approach them. While he was deliberating, a dog emerged from the dark lot where several vehicles were parked. It approached them, but stopped several feet away.

"You again," Mo said. It was Caruso.

"That dog was here when I came," Maribeth said. "Is it yours?"

"No, he's from the animal shelter. Apparently he keeps escaping."

"Poor guy." Maribeth squatted down and held out her

gloved hand. "Hey there, buddy. You're just looking for a good home, aren't you?"

The dog studied her, but maintained his distance.

"His name's Caruso," Mo said. "He sings, or some such thing."

Maribeth tilted her head up to him. "He what?"

Mo shrugged. "That's what the girl from the shelter said." He took a couple of slow steps toward the animal. "If I can catch him, I'll take him back there. It's too cold for him to be spending the night outside."

The dog plunked down on his ass, lifted his head, and let out a warbling kind of howl.

"He's singing to you," Maribeth said, sounding charmed. "Why don't you adopt him?"

"Last thing I need's a dog." Mo held out his bare hand toward Caruso, who eyed it warily. "Why don't you take him, Maribeth?"

"I work long hours. I own my own business, a thrift shop."

"If it's your business, you could take him to work with you." For some reason, Mo wanted to find this dog a good home.

"Too many people have allergies. It's not a good idea to have an animal in the shop."

"Maybe he's hypoallergenic. Some dogs are, aren't they?"

"Yes. Poodles, for one. But even if he is, it's not the right time for me to be getting a dog. I have other priorities."

The dog sniffed Mo's hand. Mo stroked his head and Caruso accepted the gesture with what looked like tolerance more than enjoyment. Casually, Mo gripped the dog's collar. "Where's the animal shelter?" he asked Maribeth.

"On the other side of town. You'll have to drive him."

"I don't have a car."

"Really? Okay, we'll take him in mine. Can you get him into it?" She walked toward her Mini Cooper, taking her key ring from her purse.

"We'll see." He tugged gently on the collar. "Come on, Caruso. Bet you could use some dinner."

The dog balked for a long moment and then made the decision to go along.

Maribeth had the back door open and Mo urged the dog to jump into the small backseat. He and Maribeth were both cautious with the doors when they climbed into the front, but for the moment the dog didn't seem inclined to escape. Mo had the sense the creature was giving them a chance to prove something to him, though Mo wasn't sure what that might be.

"Here," Maribeth said, handing Mo her purse. "I don't want to put it in the back with Caruso. He might chew on it."

Not about to sit there with a big, flower-patterned purse on his lap, Mo put it on the floor by his feet.

The car was tiny, making him totally aware of Maribeth. Even bundled up as she was, doing something as prosaic as putting a key in the ignition and starting the car, there was no denying the powerful impact of her sheer femininity. He couldn't remember the last time he'd felt such a compulsion to touch a woman, to smell her, to even just be close to her. Arousal stirred under his fly and he was tempted to test out how serious she'd been about that flirtation. But she knew Brooke and Evan, and he had to remember his mission.

He was curious about Maribeth, though. "You own a thrift store?" he asked as she backed her car out of the parking lot—doing it the girlie way, craning over her shoulder rather than using the mirrors. "From the way you dress, I'd have guessed you ran a fancy boutique."

"My parents taught me the value of money. Why waste it on new clothes when you can get nice ones secondhand? I like recycling clothes so they go from people who don't need them anymore to folks who like to dress well on a tight budget. Including me."

"Huh." There was more to this woman than met the eye. "Guess that makes sense. Does your business do okay?"

"Well enough."

The route she drove took them down the main street of Caribou Crossing. It was after six and most of the businesses were closed now, the storefronts dark. Bare-branched trees were strung with sparkly white lights, and welcoming golden light came from the windows of a few restaurants and bars. The Gold Nugget Saloon was still there, but it had been modernized and didn't bear much resemblance to the tacky dive where he and Brooke had spent many the drunken night—and afternoon.

Brooke Kincaid, married to the police commander. He shook his head in wonderment. Seemed like Mo wasn't the only one who'd stopped being an asshole and got their life sorted out. Interesting that his ex had taken another chance on love and marriage. It was also odd that she'd stayed in Caribou Crossing after all the times she'd bitched about the place being Hicksville. It must have grown on her over the years.

In the backseat, the dog moved around restlessly, obviously having second thoughts about his decision to enter the car.

"Almost there, Caruso," Maribeth murmured soothingly. "Soon you'll be nice and warm and have a good meal."

The dog would also be in a prison cell, albeit a more pleasant one than Johnny Cash's Folsom Prison. Mo could relate to Caruso's dislike of confinement. Still, November was no time for an animal to be fending for itself at night.

Maribeth pulled into the driveway of a rancher-style building that bore the sign HAPPY PAWS ANIMAL SHELTER.

"How about you go in," Mo suggested, "and find someone who has a leash?"

"Good idea." She slid out of the car and hurried to the door.

A couple of minutes later, she was back with a youngish man wearing low-slung jeans and a gray hoodie with the hood pulled up over a baseball cap. A leash dangled from the guy's hand.

Mo climbed out of the car and, as the young man reached for the back door handle, said, "Be careful. The dog may try—"

Too late.

The moment the door opened a few inches, Caruso was out like a shot.

"Shit," the kid said ruefully.

The dog raced across the street—thankfully, there was no traffic—aiming for a sturdy, bare-branched tree on the boulevard. The lowest branches were about four feet off the ground, and with a leap, the dog launched himself from the ground. He landed in a crook of the tree. A quick scramble and he had climbed up a few more branches, to perch like a cat and peer down at them. In the muted light from streetlights, the dog's eyes glowed an eerie green.

Mo, Maribeth, and the kid all gaped back at the dog. That was one pretty amazing animal.

"Caruso climbed that tree." Maribeth sounded dumbfounded. "I've never seen a dog do anything like that."

"You'd think he was half cat," the staffer muttered. "He's, like, boneless. He can squeeze through cracks that you'd swear a rat couldn't get through."

That had to be an exaggeration, but it did get the point across and also make Mo wonder why the boy hadn't been more careful when opening the car door. "What are we going to do about him?" Mo asked.

The kid shrugged. "I'll put some food at the bottom of the tree. He won't starve."

"But he'll be cold," Maribeth said. "He should be inside. We should try to get him out of the tree."

"Know what?" the boy said. "If he's cold, he can get back inside the same way he got out. Or go to the door and bark. It's his choice."

"I guess," Maribeth said, sounding uncertain.

"Lady, you can't help an animal unless it wants your help."

Just like people. Mo nodded at the truth of that statement. "He's right," he said to Maribeth. "Seems to me that dog knows what he wants. He's healthy and he's survived up until now, so he must know what he's doing. Come on and I'll buy you that drink." He took her elbow. It was an automatic gesture, but suddenly his bare palm tingled as if he'd touched the heat of her skin rather than the thick wool of her coat. Static electricity? Had to be. Still, he felt disconcerted as he urged her back to her car.

When they'd both climbed in again and she started the engine, he said, "Here's the thing. Would you mind if we didn't go to a coffee shop or bar? I'd invite you back to my apartment, but I just moved in and the cupboards are bare. Any chance we could go to your place?"

As she turned to stare at him, he held up both hands. "I know it sounds weird. Honest, I'm not trying to pull anything. It's just that I, uh, don't exactly want to publicize my presence in town. Not until . . . Well, that's what I want to talk to you about."

She hadn't backed down the driveway. Instead, with the engine still running, she took her gloved hands off the steering wheel and crossed her arms over her chest. "Yes, it sounds weird. What's going on, Mo with no last name, who's only just come to town? Why should I trust you?"

"To start with, my last name's Kincaid."

Maribeth gaped at the damp-haired, strikingly handsome man who sat in the passenger seat of her little car. Kincaid?

"That's Evan's surname," she said slowly. "It was Brooke's before she married Jake." Earlier, she'd seen how Mo reacted when she mentioned Brooke, and she'd seen the give-nothing-away expression he'd put on when he asked about Brooke and her son. "Are you related to them?"

"I was." He swallowed, and it looked painful. "I'm Evan's father."

Her mouth fell open. When she and Brooke had gotten to be friends, Brooke had confessed that she'd been a terrible mother. Maribeth knew that Evan had left town right after high school and hadn't talked to his mom until he returned a few years ago and they reunited. All Maribeth knew about Evan's father was that he'd run out on his wife and son when Evan was still in elementary school. This man, Mo Kincaid, was the deadbeat dad?

He'd wanted to find shelter for a homeless dog, and yet he'd abandoned his own family? Normally she was a good judge of character, and she'd thought this man was a decent guy. One she'd like to know more intimately, in every sense of that word. More fool her.

She shook her head. "No. You aren't coming to my house. Get out of my car."

"Wait, Maribeth. Whatever you've heard about me, it's true, and worse. I was a shit. A total shit. But I'm a changed man. That's why I need to talk to you."

She scowled at him. Was he telling the truth? She always wanted to believe the best about people. Even the worst sinners could reform. Brooke herself was a perfect example. Yet Brooke and Evan were Maribeth's friends, and she was fiercely loyal. To talk to Mo felt like a betrayal of those friendships. "Why do you *need* to talk to me? What do you hope to gain?" Was there anything he could possibly say that would stop her from kicking him out of her Mini?

"Perspective. Wisdom." The streetlights didn't give the brightest illumination, but as best she could tell he looked sincere.

Okay, he'd managed to say something that intrigued her. She tipped her chin, challenging him. "Go on."

"I want to apologize to them. If there's any way to make amends, I want to do it."

This was starting to make sense. "You're in A.A.?" Brooke was, and had been sober for many years.

"No. I don't drink anymore, but I'm not an alcoholic. I didn't even have the excuse of being an alcoholic. I was just a shit."

Despite herself, her lips twitched. "So you said." She liked how frank he was and that he didn't make excuses. "Okay, so what kind of perspective are you looking for from me?"

"I want to know if it's the right thing to do."

"How could an apology and amends ever be wrong?" But even as she framed the question, she knew the answer. "If it would hurt Brooke and Evan more than it would help."

He nodded. "Exactly. I hurt them both so much. Apologizing feels like the right thing to do. There's something inside me that's driving me to do it, like I can't live with myself any longer if I don't."

She narrowed her eyes. What did he mean by that?

He held up a hand. "No, I'm not saying I'm going to off myself if I can't do it. Maybe I'm just being selfish, trying to salve my conscience. What I need to do is think about Brooke and Evan, not about me. I want to make things better, to maybe give them some resolution. But if I'd only mess up their lives, then—"

A knock on the car window beside her made Maribeth jump and Mo stop talking. She lowered the window to see the puzzled face of the shelter employee. "Everything okay here?" he asked.

"Yes, it's fine. Thank you." She raised the window again and backed out of the driveway. To Mo, she said, "I'm going to take a chance on you. You can come back to my place and we'll talk."

"Thank you. Thank you for trusting me."

"An inch," she specified. "That's how far I trust you. And if you betray my trust, I'll . . . Well, you'll be in deep trouble, mister." All it'd take would be one call to Brooke's husband, Jake, the local RCMP commander.

Having gotten what he wanted from her, Mo kept his mouth shut as she drove toward the residential neighborhood where she lived. On the radio, Sam Hunt was singing that he didn't want the woman's heart, just some of her time.

It struck her that the singer had something in common with Mo Kincaid.

Why was she letting this stranger, this self-proclaimed "shit," take her time on a Wednesday night when she'd planned to check out sperm donor profiles? Too late now. She'd already agreed, and she honored her promises.

She drove up to the two-story house with the dormer windows and big front porch that had always been home. With its four bedrooms, it was way too big for one person, but she'd always believed she would share it with a husband and children. The garden, which she devoted a lot of effort to during three seasons of the year, was dormant now. It looked a little stark as her headlights played over it before she turned into the driveway and hit the remote control to open the roll-up garage door. Oh well, in less than a month she'd be hanging her colorful Christmas lights, and then the house would have a sparkly, festive façade.

After parking, she ushered Mo through the door from the garage into the house and down the hallway to the kitchen. She clicked on the track lighting so the room was bright and cheery. It was warm, too. The heating was on a timer, set to turn on twenty minutes before she normally arrived home. She put her bag and keys on the counter and tossed her coat over a chair.

"Nice," Mo said, glancing around.

"Thanks." She'd kept the same basic layout she'd grown up with, but over the years had done some upgrading. Now the floor had terra-cotta tile, the counters were peach-colored granite, the composite sink was a copper color, and the appliances were white and shiny. Dark colors and stainless steel didn't belong in her kitchen. On the walls hung a couple of paintings, cheap, colorful ones of a village in Crete that she'd picked up on her last holiday.

Her favorite thing in the kitchen was the table, the same battered wooden one her parents had found at a garage sale when they were newlyweds. Maribeth would never, ever replace it. Her own child—children?—would grow up eating meals, doing homework, and sharing confidences at that table, just as she had.

"Sit." She cocked her head toward the table. She wasn't going to take this man any farther into her house. "What do you want to drink? I have milk, tea, coffee."

"I don't need a drink. I just want to talk." He took off his denim jacket and hung it over the back of a chair. Clad in a navy pullover and jeans, he had a rangy build: broad shoulders, narrow hips, long legs. Most definitely an attractive man with that same kind of sexy charisma that Hugh Jackman and Brad Pitt had. Normally, she'd have been pretty happy to have such a hot guy hanging out in her kitchen.

Mo sat down, not settling in but kind of perching. Like he was as restless and wary as that crazy singing dog up in the tree.

The man unsettled her, and few things in life unsettled Maribeth. She didn't like it one bit. "Well, I could use a drink," she said. "It's been a long day." She opened the fridge, which was covered with photos: friends' weddings and children, her with various friends, her on holiday in exciting places. About to pull out a beer for herself, she changed her mind. Dr. Jones had said it was best to avoid alcohol. She made a mental note to buy some fruit drinks and decaf coffee and tea.

She grasped the milk jug. "I'm going to make hot chocolate." The drink was soothing and homey, which appealed to her right now. If there was a little caffeine in the cocoa powder, surely it was negligible.

"That sounds great, if you're offering."

As she took cocoa and sugar from the cupboard, she felt his gaze on her. Unsettling. Yes, that was the right word for Mo Kincaid. She flicked on the radio, wanting something else familiar to ease her nerves. Vince Vance & the Valiants were singing "All I Want for Christmas Is You."

"I wish they wouldn't start with Christmas music until December," Maribeth complained as she stirred warm milk in a pot on the stove.

"Yeah? Why?"

"So it doesn't get overdone. Like, every year, come December first, it should be this special treat. And it should last through Christmas, and then be put away again for a year."

"Huh. And turkey's only for Thanksgiving and Christmas, and you should only eat hot cross buns at Easter?"

"Pretty much." She shrugged. "Anything wrong with that?"

"You know what you like. Nothing wrong with that, not at all."

She finished up the cocoa and poured it into two large mugs. Though she'd have liked a puffy marshmallow on top, she wasn't giving Mo any special treats. When she sat down across from him, he said, "How come you're not married?"

She blew out a puff of air. "Never met the right man. Why?"

"Just"—he shrugged—"you seem like you should be. Pretty woman. Smart. Nice cozy house with a big kitchen. I'd picture you with a husband and two or three rug rats."

So would I. But she wasn't about to share that bit of

personal information with him. "Maybe one day. Now, you wanted to talk about Brooke and Evan."

He blew on his cocoa, took a sip. "This is good. Thanks. Hmm, I'm not sure where to start."

"Call me conventional, but I like stories that start at the beginning."

"You won't like this one." Another sip. "Like I said, I was a shit. A rebellious teenager, pissed off at the world. Brooke was a few years younger. So pretty and sweet, like a blond princess."

Maribeth knew that Brooke was in her midforties, so Mo had to be approaching fifty. Ten years older than Maribeth. Like his ex, he didn't look his age.

"I was like a boy staring in the window of a candy store," he said. "And I guess she was dumb enough to fall for the bad boy on the motorbike. We probably wouldn't have lasted long, except that she got pregnant. There was parental pressure on both sides. We got married." He raked a well-shaped hand through his almost-dry hair, dragging curls back from his face. "We were both immature and we had lots of problems."

Maribeth sipped her cocoa, trying to focus on his words rather than on how good he looked. "Go on."

"I'm not even sure why we stayed together. I guess in some muddled way, we thought it was the right thing to do. There was Evan, and both of us cared about him even if we did a piss-poor job of showing it. We were both really unhappy. We drank; we fought. Sometimes it, uh, got physical."

Maribeth caught her breath. She'd guessed this, as much from what Brooke hadn't said as from what she had, but it still set her pulse racing. "Physical?" she asked quietly.

"Sometimes I hit her. Not really hard, but enough to bruise."

She swallowed. It hurt to ask this question about her friend, but she had to know. "Did Brooke hit you?"

For a moment, he didn't answer, and then he said, "Yeah. She slapped and punched." He squeezed his eyes shut. When he finally opened them, he said, "It gets worse. Sometimes Evan got in the way. He took a few knocks." He gazed straight into Maribeth's eyes. "There's no excuse for what I did, and I know it."

Maribeth pressed her lips together, trying to settle her nerves and think straight. She agreed that there was no excuse, and knew Brooke did as well. "Brooke drank, too," she said.

"Yeah." He scrubbed a hand across his stubbled jaw. "Have to say, when I saw in the *Gazette* that she was married to the RCMP commander, it was a real surprise."

"She doesn't drink anymore. At all."

His eyes widened, and then slowly narrowed. "Earlier, you mentioned A.A. Is Brooke doing that?"

It was hardly a secret in Caribou Crossing, so Maribeth nodded. "She's been sober for years now."

"Good for her." A touch of humor flickered across his face, making him look even more irresistible. Maribeth could certainly understand why Brooke had been drawn to the guy. "Must make her a hell of a lot easier to live with," he added.

"She was moody," Maribeth said. She knew about that from Brooke as well.

"Sure as hell was. Especially after Evan was born. When she sparkled, there was no one like her. But it was almost, like, over the top. Like she was burning too bright. Sure enough, one day it would all fizzle. She'd be depressed, pissed off. And I was always mad at the world, so we'd drink, we'd fight." He cocked his head. "Is she happy now?"

"Definitely. She's a happy, serene, wonderful woman." A woman who'd been diagnosed with bipolar disorder at the same time she'd figured out she was an alcoholic. Brooke had been on bipolar medication ever since, and it worked well for her. But that information was too personal to share.

"I'm glad for her." His mouth softened with what looked like genuine affection, or at least the memory of it. It suited him. "I don't want to mess with that."

Maribeth nodded. "I hear you."

They were both quiet. Maribeth savored the delicious aroma of chocolate and listened to the song on the radio. This wasn't a Christmas one, but the upbeat "Any Man of Mine" by Shania Twain. Another woman who knew just how she liked things. The familiar words made Maribeth reflect on Mo. Yes, he was, quite literally, a breathtaking guy. But the quality that mattered most in a man was the way he treated people. Mo said he'd changed, and the frank way he talked about himself made her inclined to think he spoke the truth. That he had redeemed himself just as much as Brooke had. Sitting here alone with him in her house, Maribeth's instincts—which rarely led her wrong—didn't tell her to feel anxious. Instead, she actually felt comfortable with Mo.

People deserved second chances. Maribeth believed that, and she knew Brooke did, too.

She took another sip of cocoa. "Brooke's strong. She's gone through a long process of building a new life. I know that meant coming to terms with her past. It also meant her own set of apologies and amends. To Evan, for example. But they worked through it and reconciled, and—"

"Reconciled?" he broke in. "They were, what, estranged?"

"Oh, right, I guess you wouldn't know. Yes, for ten years. Evan left town the moment he graduated from high school. He ended up building a successful career in New York City."

Mo let out an admiring whistle. "He was always a bright, determined kid. God knows where he got those qualities."

She ventured a teasing comment. "Brooke's no dummy."

His lips quirked. "Ha. I'm wounded."

She smiled. "Anyhow, Evan came back to Caribou Crossing a few years ago. He's married, with a little boy and an adolescent stepdaughter. And he and Brooke are very close. But I'm sure that didn't come easily for either of them."

When she revealed that he had grandkids, Mo blinked and looked a little stunned. But when he spoke, he didn't mention them. "You're saying I should talk to Brooke and Evan."

"I'm thinking out loud," she corrected. "I'm saying that they're both strong and they're capable of dealing with crap from the past."

Mo barked out a wry laugh. "That'd be me. Crap from the past."

"I didn't mean . . . Okay, yeah, I guess that's true. If you asked Brooke and Evan about their relationship now, I'm positive they'd both say it was totally worth the pain, the bad memories, and the awkwardness it took to get there."

"You think that could be the same with me?" She saw hope in his eyes, and vulnerability.

Her tender heart throbbed, but she was also a practical

woman. "Maybe. But that depends on you, Mo Kincaid. Brooke and Evan are good people. They're my friends. If you mess up their lives, don't make things right, and run out on them again, then . . ." She didn't know how to finish that sentence. Setting Jake Brannon, Brooke's husband, on Mo could never make up for any pain suffered by Brooke and Evan.

Mo said quietly, "Then it'd be bad. Really bad."

She nodded. "What kind of man are you?" Sexy, and too handsome for his own good, but those things didn't count. "You say you've changed, but how much have you changed? You may no longer drink a lot or get violent, but are you going to treat Brooke and Evan right? Are you going to stick around?"

He swallowed.

She went on. "Do you have the guts to hear what they need to say, to not argue with them, to accept the blame? To persist, even if they don't want to accept you into their lives?" As she spoke, he nodded a couple of times, looking increasingly determined. She went on. "To prove to them that you're a man worth knowing?" She peered into those fascinating blue-green eyes. "*Are* you a man worth knowing?"

Her question surprised him; that was evident from the way his eyes widened. His shoulders rose and then fell, and the look of determination faded. When he spoke, he sounded discouraged. "When you put it that way, I guess the best I can say for myself is that I try to tread lightly on the earth."

"What do you mean?"

"I did a lot of harm in my youth. Now I try not to. I fix vehicles and I try not to break anything." His mouth tightened. "Guess that's not much to show for fifty years on this planet."

She watched him, not speaking.

"But," he went on, squaring his shoulders, "it's a hell of a lot better than the man I was in my twenties and thirties."

Slowly, she nodded. "That sounds . . . good." Commendable, yes. But also sad, if that was all his life was about.

Chapter Three

Maribeth's gaze was assessing, making him want to squirm, but he managed to keep his shoulders squared and hold her gaze. She'd been more than fair with him, and he would answer every question she asked.

"You never remarried?" she said.

"God, no. Inflict myself on another woman? I'm not relationship material. And I'm sure not having any more kids."

Two or three years after he'd run from the police and left Caribou Crossing, he'd sent divorce papers to Brooke. It had seemed crazy to stay married when he figured they'd never see each other again. He hadn't asked for visitation rights with Evan, and—asshole that he'd been—hadn't offered child support. He'd kind of figured that once Brooke had his address, she'd go after him for money, but she didn't. She just returned the signed forms, no doubt relieved to be rid of him. A clean break; obviously, it was what they'd both wanted.

It was probably still what she wanted.

"Do you have friends?" Maribeth's voice cut through his thoughts. "Male or female?"

He shrugged. “I’m not much of a people person. Yeah, I’ve hung out with some folks now and then, to shoot some pool or whatever. But that’s it.”

Her nicely shaped eyebrows, darker than her red hair, pulled together. “What’s the longest you’ve stayed in one place?”

“Five years, in Regina. That’s where I lived last. I managed an auto repair shop.”

“So you’re capable of staying in one place and holding down a responsible job.”

“I guess.” It wasn’t that he’d had any particular love for Regina, but the job was a good one and he’d grown tired of drifting around. He’d have still been there if the regret about Brooke and Evan, and the desire to see them again, hadn’t become a compulsion as persistent and nagging as an engine tick that defied diagnosis.

“Hmm.”

He’d asked for Maribeth’s wisdom and perspective. She was weighing him and finding him lacking, and there wasn’t a damn thing he could do about it. Mo drank the remaining hot chocolate, cold now and more bitter than sweet.

“If you’re not a people person,” she asked, “what is it that you want from Brooke and Evan?”

“To let them know that I’m sorry. I want them to know that I realize what a shit I was. If I could change the past, I would. But I can’t.”

“Do you want their forgiveness?”

He wrinkled his nose. “That’d be a lot to ask for.”

“What, then? You apologize and then you go away again?”

“I don’t know,” he admitted. “I haven’t really thought past the point of me apologizing. If there’s some way of making amends, I'd do that, but . . ." He shrugged. "Guess I don't know if that's possible."

She gave a soft huff. "That's it? That's your whole plan?"

Anger stirred, but he tamped it down and admitted, "I didn't exactly come with a plan. I just found myself thinking about them this past couple years. I wondered how they were doing, if they were still in Caribou Crossing. I found the *Gazette* online, and from time to time there'd be something about them. Once I started, I couldn't get them out of my mind. I felt . . . I guess driven is the right word. Driven to see them again and, uh . . ."

"Prostrate yourself at their feet and tell them you know you were a shit?"

Damn, he liked this woman even if she didn't think much of him. "Pretty much."

She crossed her arms over her curvy chest. "You're kind of a mess, aren't you, Mo Kincaid?"

There was only one honest answer to that question. "Yes, ma'am."

"You really don't have a best-case scenario in your mind?"

He blinked, not sure what she meant.

"Think about it," she said. "You see them and apologize. After that, what's the best thing you could imagine happening?"

He closed his eyes and concentrated, but nothing came to mind. Shaking his head, he opened his eyes again.

Maribeth was gazing at him, her green eyes kind of misty and soft. God, but she was one beautiful woman. "Do you ever let yourself dream?" she asked quietly.

Dream? Tonight he might well have steamy dreams about a green-eyed redhead. But he figured that wasn't what she was talking about. "You mean, not when I'm asleep but about the future?"

"Exactly. Do you dream about what you'd like your life to look like?"

"I think I gave up the right to do that," he said gruffly.

She leaned forward, resting her elbows on the table. "And I think that you're not as bad a person as you think you are."

His eyes widened in surprise. So she hadn't completely written him off? "You're a generous woman."

"I'm an optimist."

Which made her his opposite. Not that he didn't already know that. She was vibrant, caring, domestic—qualities that put her on the opposite end of the spectrum from him. Although it still surprised him that she wasn't married with kids, he'd noticed those photos on the fridge. She had a bunch of friends, close ones. He'd also bet a month's pay that she'd have a pack of guys chasing after her. Which made it all the more strange that she'd flirted with him.

But his purpose in being here tonight wasn't about flirtation, as appealing a prospect as that might be. "Does that mean you think it'd be okay for me to contact Brooke and Evan?"

Her eyes narrowed in thought. "It means . . . how about this? Let me sound Brooke out."

"You mean tell her I'm in town and see if she's willing to see me?"

"Something like that, I guess. I need to make a hair appointment anyway."

Her hair looked awfully pretty to him, but women had their own ideas about that kind of stuff. "I'd be much obliged," he said. "You can reach me at Hennessey's." No point in owning a phone; the only people who wanted to talk to him were telemarketers.

He stood. "I'll be on my way now." He didn't belong in

this homey room, with all those photos on the fridge. He didn't belong with this woman who was so generous and beautiful, who had a full life that was the opposite of his.

She remained seated. "Where do you live?"

"Over on Cottonwood Drive." Hank had told him about a pair of eightysomething women, a married couple, who had a studio apartment in their house. Mo'd been skeptical that they'd want to rent to a guy like him, but Ms. Haldenby and Ms. Peabody had checked his references, laid down some rules, and then welcomed him.

"That's a ways." Maribeth rose. "I'll give you a ride."

He shook his head. "Thanks, but I won't take any more of your time. I'm used to walking. I like it."

She studied him. "You're a mechanic and you once had a motorbike, and now you don't have any kind of car?"

"Don't need one." He'd always loved the feeling of a powerful machine, whether it was a Harley, a sports car, or a Jeep. But he didn't need one, and so he didn't have one. "It's part of that treading lightly thing."

She muttered something under her breath. He thought he caught "doing penance," but he wasn't sure. If that was what she believed, maybe she wasn't so far wrong. He had a lot to atone for.

He shrugged into his jacket. "Maribeth, just one thing? If you could see Brooke sooner rather than later, that'd be good. If anyone who knew me back in the day comes into Hennessey's and recognizes me, it'd likely get back to her."

She folded her arms across her chest. "I know. It's a small town. I'll make an appointment as soon as I can."

"Thanks."

"You can go out the front door." She walked out of the kitchen and he followed her down the hallway, past a dark room at the front of the house.

She stepped back, letting him open the door. "Good night, Mo. I'll call you."

"Thanks for everything." He stepped out onto the front porch and went down a half dozen steps. Those sullen gray clouds had finally fulfilled their promise. Snow dusted the ground and small, crisp flakes nipped his face. He resisted looking back until he got to the street. When he turned, she was there, standing in the doorway, framed by light behind her. He raised his arm in a wave.

She returned the gesture, then stepped inside and the door closed—a warm, kind woman retreating into her cozy home. Leaving him alone out here on the sidewalk on a snowy November night, with nothing to go home to but a lonely one-room apartment. And the hope that his ex-wife would agree to talk to him.

The next morning, Maribeth hung the clock sign on the door of Days of Your, indicating that she'd be back in an hour. Last night, she'd checked the online appointment calendar for Beauty Is You. Brooke only worked part-time now that she and Jake had little Nicki. Fortunately, Brooke had had a slot open at 10:30. Kate, the owner and other stylist at the salon, was booked at that time doing a perm with Carlotta Bowden. Elderly Mrs. Bowden was such a talker, there was no chance she and Kate would pay any attention if Maribeth talked to Brooke about Mo Kincaid.

As she walked the three blocks to the salon, she wondered how her friend would react to the news about her ex-husband. She didn't want to upset Brooke, and yet that was almost guaranteed to happen.

The man had even messed up Maribeth's own evening. She'd anticipated spending engrossing hours poring through online profiles and studying pictures of sperm donors. Instead, each time she gazed at a new photo, into her mind popped the image of a brown-skinned man with blue-green eyes that reminded her of river water. Somehow, none of the guys on the screen came close in terms of physical attractiveness and appeal.

Not that her baby's father had to be handsome, but Maribeth knew that looks mattered. If she could stack the deck in favor of having a boy or girl who was good-looking as well as healthy and intelligent, of course she'd do it.

Maribeth pushed open the door to Beauty Is You, and the bell jingled. She pulled off her gloves and undid her coat.

Brooke came toward her. "Good morning, Maribeth." Brooke was in her midforties, but dressed in charcoal pants and a mauve sweater, with her wavy hair shining and a smile on her face, she looked easily ten years younger. Sobriety certainly suited her, as did having a sexy new husband and an adorable toddler. "Time for a trim?"

They exchanged hugs.

"Hi, Brooke." Maribeth smiled back, guessing that Brooke wouldn't look so cheerful after hearing her news. "Yes, it's getting heavy and flyaway."

"It's always a pleasure working with your lovely hair."

Brooke ushered her to a sink at the back, and Maribeth waved a greeting to Kate Patterson and Mrs. Bowden. The older woman was nattering on about her grandchildren while Kate wrapped her thinning white hair on rollers.

Brooke enveloped Maribeth in a navy cape and tested the water temperature. Maribeth closed her eyes, luxuriating in sensations: the scent of lemongrass shampoo, Brooke's deft fingers massaging her scalp, warm water pouring through her hair, and then a delicate whiff of coconut. "Bliss," she murmured.

"We all deserve a little spoiling every now and then," Brooke said as she wrapped a towel around Maribeth's hair and urged her to sit up.

"So true." She stood and followed Brooke to her station. Her friend was lucky to have a devoted husband who no doubt spoiled her more than every now and then—as, Maribeth was equally certain, Brooke also spoiled him. Life was supposed to be lived in pairs. Maribeth's parents had been so happy together, and she'd always assumed that she'd find the same kind of deep, committed love.

And she still would, one of these days. For now, she was taking charge of her own life and moving forward. An idea struck her. If she created a short list of potential sperm donors, she'd love to get her girlfriends' input. So far, she hadn't told any of them what she was thinking of doing, but now that she'd actually made the decision, it was time.

"We haven't had a ladies' night in a while," she said to Brooke, who had run a comb through Maribeth's thick hair and was now wielding scissors. "I'd love to have everyone over to my place. You, Jess, Cassidy, Sally, Corrie." They'd become a tight-knit group. She had other girlfriends, too, ones she'd known longer—some dating back to elementary school—but she would invite them on a different night rather than have one huge "pick my baby-daddy" party. Another person occurred to her for this first group. "Lark Cantrell, too, I think." After all, a conversation with Lark had helped her arrive at her decision.

"Sounds like fun, MB. I'm in." Brooke didn't look up from her work. Wisps of Maribeth's hair were hitting the floor and tumbling down over the navy cape.

"I'll e-mail everyone and try to find an evening that

works." Over at Kate's station, which was some distance away, the stylist and her customer were still engrossed in conversation. Gazing in the mirror at her own reflection and Brooke's, Maribeth said, "There's something else I wanted to ask you."

"Shoot."

"You believe in redemption, right?" she asked quietly. "That people can change."

Now Brooke did pause, and her gaze met Maribeth's in the mirror. The stylist's eyes were blue green, but more like the Caribbean, while Mo's reminded Maribeth of a fresh mountain stream. After a moment, Brooke said, "You know that I do. That's the story of my life."

"So if a person had gone through that process and wanted to apologize to people they'd hurt, you think that would be a good thing?"

"It's one of the basic tenets of A.A. I did it myself."

"Was everyone receptive?"

Brooke tilted her head, considering. "Pretty much. With some, it took time. I needed to convince people I really had changed. It was tough for my parents and sister down in California. I'd hurt them badly. Evan, too, of course, but he was so generous."

"He's a good guy."

"The best."

"You got in touch with everyone you'd hurt?"

Brooke's gaze dropped. She studied the top of Maribeth's head. "Except for one person," she said so softly that it was barely more than a whisper. "My ex-husband."

"Why didn't you?"

"I didn't know where he was." And then Brooke's gaze rose again. "And I didn't look all that hard to find him." Maribeth knew that Brooke, now that she was sober, hated to lie. She rarely even allowed herself a white lie. "The two of us, we weren't good for each other."

"And yet something drew you together in the beginning."

Brooke's face brightened, and for a moment Maribeth felt as if she were looking at a teenage girl. "Oh, he was something," her friend said. "Long, black hair, ripped jeans, leather jacket, and a motorcycle. When he walked, he had a swagger. He was older. A man, or so I thought. I'd matured early and I lied about my age so he'd go out with me." She shook her head and grinned wryly. "I swear, Mohinder McKeen was the sexiest thing I'd ever laid eyes on."

Maribeth could believe it. Even at fifty, the man was damned hot. So, Mo was short for Mohinder. But . . . "McKeen? I thought his name was Kincaid?"

Brooke blinked. "Long story, and not mine to tell."

Respecting her privacy, Maribeth returned to the main subject. "So if you could see Mo again, you would?"

Brooke began to snip hair again. After a moment, she said, "It would be hard, but yes. There are so many things I'd like to apologize for. And I'd like to see if there's any way of making amends."

Knowing that the words she was about to say would change her friend's life forever, Maribeth took a deep breath. It was the right thing to do. Wasn't it? "He's in town. Mo."

The scissors dropped, clattering on the floor.

Kate and Mrs. Bowden glanced over as Brooke bent and fumbled to pick them up. "Sorry," she called. She stood, holding the scissors awkwardly, her face white and drawn. "He is?"

"He just started work at Hennessey's garage. I met him yesterday when I went to pick up my car."

Brooke plunged the scissors into a jar of liquid and swished them around. Under her breath, she said, "How did you know who he was?"

"I happened to mention your name, and he told me. Brooke, he came to town because he wants to do exactly what you said. Apologize and make amends. To you, and to Evan."

Brooke's hand flew to her chest, where Maribeth guessed her heart must be racing. "Evan," she whispered. "Oh my God, Evan."

Chapter Four

Thursday, the night after Mo had left Maribeth's house, he was again stepping outside into the cold as a beautiful woman stood in the doorway of her cozy home.

"Thank you, Brooke," he said. "I appreciate, well, everything." He felt like an old rust bucket that's been driven over a hundred miles of potholed dirt road but managed, somehow, to come out the other side still on four tires.

Maybe she felt the same because when she smiled, she looked tired and yet serene. "I'm glad you came back, Mo. I'm glad we could talk and both own up to our failures."

Anxiety stirred. That sounded pretty final. "But, uh, we'll talk again, won't we?"

Her smile faded and now all he saw on her face was tiredness and worry. "I'll think about Evan, I promise. I'll call and let you know."

She had told Mo she wasn't sure whether it would be good for Evan to meet his father, and she needed to reflect on it. Evan was a grown man and Mo didn't need his ex's permission to see him, but he wanted to do the right thing, not cause his son more pain. He figured Brooke was the best judge. Still, she needed to do her reflecting fairly quickly, or Evan might find out on his own that his father was in town. But Mo didn't say that; Brooke knew it as well as he did.

He moistened dry lips. "It's not just about Evan. I mean, I'd kind of like to see you again. To talk some more." She'd matured so much, and though they'd only spent an hour together, he thought he would like the woman she'd turned into. Besides, there were so many topics they'd barely skimmed over. To him, tonight felt more like a start than a conclusion.

Her lips trembled. "I think I'd like that, too. But tonight . . . it's been a lot. I need to think. To talk to Jake."

Mo felt a moment's anger. Evan, Jake, why did his own future depend on these men? But he stifled the frustration. The answer to that question was obvious: because he'd fucked up so badly in the past. "Let me know," he said, discouraged.

It seemed she read his feelings, a more sensitive and compassionate woman than she used to be, because she reached out and touched his shoulder. It was only the briefest brush of her fingers, but it was the first time she'd touched him at all. "Mo, I do want to see you again. I just need some time."

Hope filled him. "Thanks, Brooke," he said, finding that his voice came out a little ragged. He gave her a nod and then turned and strode toward the Hennessey Auto Repair truck Hank had loaned him.

As he drove back to town, the night was dark and drizzly, so he focused his attention on the road. There'd be time later to process his first meeting with Brooke in almost two decades.

As he pulled into the parking lot of the garage, the

truck's headlights illuminated Caruso lurking by the closed doors of the service bays.

"Good God, dog," he said when he climbed out of the truck. "You could be somewhere warm and dry."

He'd found Caruso waiting there when he came to work at seven in the morning, and then the animal had disappeared on his own business. Now, as Mo walked closer, Caruso regarded him warily.

"Guess there's no point trying to take you back to the shelter, is there? You'd just go climb a tree again." He shook his head, having to admit that Caruso intrigued him.

The dog didn't retreat, but held his ground until Mo stood beside him. The creature tossed his head, rotating it up and back as if he were looking over his shoulder. Then he gazed up at Mo. The dog didn't have that pleading "puppy-dog eyes" expression common to so many dogs. Instead, his brown eyes held a question, maybe a challenge.

Mo bent to run a hand over the animal's head, surprised and pleased when Caruso welcomed the gesture. "I live in a tiny apartment. Even if I had the slightest inclination to adopt a dog, and even if my landladies agreed, you'd hate it."

Caruso cocked his head and made that warbly howling sound, kind of like a coyote or wolf call combined with whale song. This was one strange animal.

Mo sighed. "Hang on a minute."

He unlocked the shop door, went inside, and hunted around for an old wooden box and some clean rags. He took them out and around to the side of the shop where the roof's overhang created a dry space underneath. The dog followed and, when Mo stepped back, went to sniff the box.

"If Hank fires me for this, I'm going to be royally pissed at you," Mo said gruffly.

Caruso hopped into the makeshift bed and again gazed at Mo.

"If that's a thank-you, then I guess you're welcome." Should he feed the beast? No, as resourceful as that dog was and as healthy as he looked, Mo guessed he was proficient at finding food. As he turned to go, he found himself saying, "See you in the morning," and he was actually looking forward to it.

He went into the office to lock up the keys for the truck Hank had let him borrow. A phone sat on top of the counter. Mo stared at it, thinking *Maribeth*.

That was ridiculous. He wasn't a guy who had people in his life to phone at nine o'clock on a night when a bunch of confusing stuff was going on. Mind you, last night he had asked Maribeth for assistance, and she'd offered exactly what he'd requested. She'd given him perspective and wisdom, and then spoken to Brooke on his behalf.

He could sure use some more perspective and wisdom. Not to mention a big mug of hot chocolate. Most especially not to mention big, expressive green eyes and a face and body that were pure pleasure to look at.

Okay, so that was what *he'd* like. But how about her? The woman had better things to do with her time than listen to him blather. Though when she'd phoned him at Hank's around noon to tell him that Brooke had agreed to see him, she had said that she hoped things went well. Maybe she'd be curious.

Hell, if he phoned, she could always tell him she was busy.

Would it be stalkerish to look up her phone number in the customer file? Yeah, maybe. Instead, he trusted his fate to the Caribou Crossing Phone Directory that resided on a shelf in the office. Sure enough, she was listed.

Feeling more awkward than he had in a long time, he dialed her number and listened to the phone ring. When she said hello, he said, "Maribeth? It's Mo Kincaid. I, uh, looked your number up in the phone book."

"Mo?" She didn't sound pissed off, and that was something. "Are you back from Brooke's? How did it go?" In fact, she did sound curious, and almost . . . caring.

"It went okay." He paused. "I wondered if maybe I could come by and tell you about it." Quickly, he added, "Though you're probably busy."

"I was just, um, doing some research on the computer. It can wait. Sure, come on over."

"I could pick something up. Bottle of wine?" He had no problem being around people who were drinking.

"Thanks, but don't bother."

"Okay. I'm at the garage. I'll walk over now."

"See you soon."

Walking was good. Mo'd always been a physical guy, and he tended to walk a lot of miles every day. Tonight, striding along the drizzly, almost-deserted streets got his blood flowing. Not wanting to show up empty-handed, he stopped at a corner store that was still open and picked up a bunch of brightly colored flowers that reminded him of Maribeth.

Yesterday, she'd taken him into her house through the garage. Tonight, he went up the front walk, thinking how appealing her house looked with light glowing out an uncurtained front window and smoke rising from the chimney. It wasn't just a house, it was a home, and again it struck him as strange that Maribeth didn't have a husband and two or three kids sharing it with her.

On the porch, he shook like a dog, trying to rid his

hair and jacket of some of the dampness before ringing the bell.

The door opened and Maribeth stood there like a vision of . . . well, of something he didn't even recognize. Something warm and welcoming, like maybe the home that as a boy he used to dream about. A home that his ever-bickering, ever-demanding parents sure hadn't provided.

Maribeth's red hair gleamed, a coral zip-front top hugged her generous breasts, and gray leggings showcased her curvy hips and shapely legs. Sliding his gaze down all this perfection, he reached her feet and had to grin. The sexy, stylish woman wore fluffy slippers with puppy-dog faces. "Nice slippers," he commented.

She stepped back, ushering him inside. "I love them. I wore them as a kid, and one of my old, good friends gives me a new pair every Christmas."

"What do you give her?"

"Pajamas with moo-cows."

He laughed, feeling almost lighthearted for the first time in forever. Optimism filled him in a tingly surge. Things with Brooke had gone as well as he could reasonably have wished. He and his ex had a long way to go—and she'd yet to agree to see him again, much less tell him she thought it was okay to contact Evan—but he was hopeful. And now here he was with one of the most attractive women he'd ever seen, who was ushering him into her home with a big smile and a pair of puppy-dog slippers.

"You're all wet," she commented. "Honestly, I don't know what men have against umbrellas."

"They're not manly. We guys have to be macho," he joked as he put down the flowers and peeled off his wet jacket.

"Pfft." She rolled her eyes and took the jacket from him

gingerly. "Look up macho in a thesaurus. The synonym's 'stupid.'"

"I believe you."

Taking a hanger from the hall closet, she put his jacket on it and hung the hanger on the doorknob, not in the closet where it would get her clothes wet. "Come on in and get warm."

He picked up the flowers and handed them to her. "These are for you."

"I kind of figured." She took them. "They're beautiful, but . . ." She tilted her head to look up at him. "Flowers seem kind of like a 'date' thing, and you don't date, right?"

If he were going to date, she was the woman he'd want to go out with. He was in a new place, maybe building a new life. Why shouldn't he have more than a one-nighter? Why shouldn't he actually date a woman if he wanted to? If *she* wanted to, knowing that he wasn't a guy who believed in long-term commitment? "I might be reconsidering that," he said, letting a little of the old Mo show in his eyes and his slow smile.

Her face lit, warming until those green eyes danced. "I might be in favor of you reconsidering that."

She walked off with the flowers and he followed her to the kitchen. She opened a big, pantry-type cupboard, went in, and emerged with a ceramic vase. Deftly, she arranged the flowers in it. "Thank you for these. Now, what can I get you to drink?"

"I wouldn't turn down more hot chocolate, if you felt like making it. Seems to suit the night."

As she took out the ingredients, he studied the photos on the fridge. She sure was one active, popular woman. Glancing at a picture of a man and woman with a pony-haired girl and a big black poodle, he commented idly, "That singing dog's still hanging around."

"Caruso?" She glanced over her shoulder. "Hanging around where?"

"The garage. Since he seemed determined to stay, I put a wooden box outside in a sheltered spot, with some rags in it to keep him warm."

"You're a soft touch."

"Tell me you'd have done any different."

"Nope. But then I don't pretend to be macho."

Damn, but the woman made him smile. "Just hope the stupid dog doesn't get me fired. Can't imagine Hank's going to be too happy about having some stray hanging around the shop."

"Tell him Caruso will be good for business. He can sing to the customers."

She poured hot chocolate into two big mugs and held up a bag of fluffy marshmallows. "Want one?"

"Please."

She popped a marshmallow onto the top of each drink and picked up the vase. "Come on into the sitting room. I have a fire going."

Carrying both mugs, he followed her to a room at the front of the house, with a sofa, love seat, recliner chair, and a bunch of bookcases full of books and knickknacks. The base colors were neutral—pale gold walls and oak furniture—but there were lots of vivid accents: pillows and rugs, a multicolored blanket over the back of a chair, lush green plants. On the walls, framed color photographs looked like they'd been taken in Greece, Italy, maybe Spain, for all that he knew anything about Europe. They were a contrast to the music that was playing: Loretta Lynn's "Coal Miner's Daughter."

The fireplace was a big old brick one, but a black insert

had been added, and the burning wood generated real heat. A framed photo on the mantel showed an attractive young couple with a redheaded girl maybe two or three years old, all of them sprawled on the floor beside a decorated Christmas tree and surrounded by gifts and wrapping paper. A portion of that very same mantel showed in a top corner of the photo.

"Nice room," Mo commented, sitting on the sofa and putting the mugs on coasters on the coffee table. She'd put the vase down there, beside a closed laptop computer. "You take those pictures on the wall?"

"Yes. Every two or three years, I go for a holiday someplace special."

"You must be doing well with that thrift shop to afford a nice house like this and take fancy holidays." Then he said, "Sorry. I'm not so good with the social graces. Guess that wasn't the most polite thing to say."

"It's okay." She pulled up the chair so it was across the coffee table from where he sat and then took off her slippers. Before she tucked her bare feet up under her, he caught a glimpse of sexy red toenails, painted to match her fingernails.

Cradling her own mug in both hands, she said, "Actually, I don't take much money for myself from Days of Your. I have enough money to get by nicely, thanks to my folks. Dad was a civil engineer and Mom was a dentist, and they were both great with money management and financial planning. Sadly, they died when I was nineteen. I'm an only child and I inherited everything."

She sighed and glanced at the family photo on the mantel. "Of course, I'd rather have them still alive, living in this house, with me coming over for Sunday dinner every week." Her tone was utterly sincere.

"I can tell they were good people."

"Oh? How?"

"Because of you. I mean, because you're a good person." Unlike him, who'd never been very nice. Nor had his parents, who'd cared more about appearances than about his or his sister's happiness.

"That's a sweet thing to say, Mo."

He shrugged.

"So, tell me," she said. "You saw Brooke."

"Hank loaned me the truck and I drove out to her place." He closed his eyes, remembering. "It was weird, walking through the gate in the white picket fence and up the walk to the front door of that immaculate little house in the country. Wondering what to expect. How she'd look. How she'd act. But it was a man who opened the door. Her husband, Jake." Humor twitched his mouth. "In his RCMP uniform."

"Oh, my. Was he on duty, or just being unsubtle?"

"The latter." He opened his eyes and grinned. "Can't say I blame the guy. He was looking out for his wife. I respect that. Anyhow, we introduced ourselves, he did some glaring and said he wasn't so sure this was a good idea, but it was what Brooke wanted. I pretty much kept quiet. Then he said he'd leave us alone, but he'd be in the back of the house with their little girl." It was still hard to believe that Brooke, who'd had Evan when she was in high school, had given birth to a second child when she was forty-three.

"And then you saw Brooke. Doesn't she look fantastic?"

"Oh, man. Yeah, she sure does. She was one pretty girl, and now she's a really lovely woman."

Brooke Brannon *was* a lovely woman. It was crazy for Maribeth to feel a pang of jealousy when Mo commented on it. Holding on to her half-full mug with one hand, she uncurled her legs from underneath her and shifted to curl them up the other way.

Mo's gaze didn't follow her movement. He had picked up his mug and was staring into it, like he saw something in there other than a marshmallow melting on top of hot chocolate. "One thing I could see," he said slowly, "was that even though she was tense about seeing me again, she was happy. I mean she's happy with her life." He glanced up, at Maribeth. "That's the first time I've seen her like that." A sense of wonder gave a softness to his rough-edged voice.

"Seriously?"

He nodded. "When we first started to date, she was, you know, excited. Happy in that keyed-up kind of way. She was dating this older guy, making her girlfriends jealous."

Maribeth held back a grin. Mo would always be the kind of guy who drew female attention.

"Then she got pregnant and we got married. And again, she was excited, like suddenly she was a grown-up. But then she had the baby, and he was"—he shook his head—"I guess Evan wasn't what she expected. She'd played with dolls not all that many years before. But a real baby, one who cried all the time and pooped just after you changed his diaper, well, that wasn't so much fun."

"And she was so young. Barely more than a child herself."

"And I was no help. I was pissed off about suddenly being tied down, and I pretty much ignored the fact that I was a husband and father. I had too high an opinion of myself, but when it came to acting like an adult, taking on responsibility, I couldn't cut it. I hung out with my old friends, cheated on Brooke, avoided looking after Evan." He shrugged. "Like I said, I was a shit. And that kid, man, he was one unhappy, demanding baby. Maybe he knew he was a mistake."

"Poor Evan."

"I know." His jaw tightened. "That's something Brooke and I admitted tonight. We made no bones about letting that poor kid know that he'd ruined our lives. He shaped up real quick: being quiet, trying to please us. Doing well in school, once he reached that age. But Brooke and I were both so immature and miserable, we took our unhappiness out on him as well as on each other."

Maribeth stared at him. "I don't know what to say. It seems so inconceivable to me when parents don't love their children."

He sighed. "I think we both did, in some place in our hearts, but instead of showing it, we screwed him over. Brooke told me tonight that she'd never stopped loving Evan." He met her gaze. "She told me other stuff, too. Not just her alcoholism, but that she has bipolar disorder. She said you know about that. She appreciated that you didn't tell me."

Maribeth nodded.

"See, she had excuses," Mo said. "Excuses for being a crappy mother and, as she said herself tonight, a crappy wife." He leaned forward to put his mug on the coffee table. "I didn't."

"Living with a wife who was bipolar and alcoholic couldn't have been easy. Nor was having your own life turn out so differently from what you'd expected."

The shadow of a smile played around his mouth, drawing her attention to the sensuality of his lips. "Aw, you're being nice. Like I said, you're a nice woman, Maribeth. But the truth is, I had no expectations about what my life would turn out like. I'd already dropped out of high school by the time I met Brooke. Did some drugs, shoplifted, even stole a couple cars and was lucky enough not to get caught. If there hadn't been Brooke and Evan, I'd have found some other path that I'd surely have messed up. I was a loser. There's no two ways about it."

"What were your parents like?"

His eyebrows lifted. "Blame it on the parents? Nah, that's not gonna wash. Look at Evan. Two shitty parents, and he turned out successful and well-balanced."

"I'm not talking about blame. There's no point to blame. I just wondered what it was like for you, growing up."

He leaned back and rotated his neck as if he was trying to loosen tight, achy muscles. "We lived in Los Angeles. My dad was an Irish-American kid from a family of cops who broke family tradition and became a baker instead. Amma's—that's Hindi for mom—anyhow, her parents had come from India when she was in her teens. Her dad was a microbiologist who got a job with a company in L.A. They expected her to go along with an arranged marriage with a man back in India. Instead, my parents met, fell in love, and got married. Both their families were mad at them and pretty much disowned them."

"That's harsh."

"Yeah, but their parents were right that they weren't a good match. Oil and water. Or more like corned beef and cabbage versus saag paneer." He added, "That's a vegetarian dish, spinach and cheese."

"I know. I've had it."

"Anyhow, there was lots of squabbling. They were both very demanding of me and my sister, but what they demanded never matched up. Dad wanted to raise us Catholic; Amma wanted us to be Hindu. Dad wanted me to be a baker; Amma wanted me to get a professional degree."

"That must have been horrible for you and your sister."

And so different from the way Maribeth had been raised, with parents who respected and truly communicated with each other and with her.

"My sister Kaitlin," he went on, "who's four years older than me, was a good girl who walked the fence between our parents, trying to make both of them happy. Me, I wasn't going to twist myself out of shape like that. They didn't want to see who I really was and they didn't care what I wanted. So why should I care what they thought? I rebelled and went my own way." He shook his head. "How did I get onto this? I was gonna tell you about Brooke."

"We did kind of get off track," she agreed. Still, she'd found this glimpse into his past fascinating.

Mo rested his hands on his jean-clad thighs. "First thing Brooke did, which blew me away, was apologize. So then"—the humor was back, around his mouth and eyes—"we kind of had this competition over who could apologize the most."

"I guess that's better than railing at each other."

"Yeah, for sure. There was a point where she started to laugh. It caught me off guard, but then I saw that she was right, we were being ridiculous. So I laughed, too."

"That sounds good. You cleared the air between you?"

"We made a start. An awkward one. I asked if we could talk some more and she said she wanted to, but she needed a little time. She didn't just, you know, listen to my apology and then tell me to get out of her life. So that's good."

"It is." Maribeth hoped Brooke and Mo could find a resolution that was comfortable for both of them. But there was a third party to consider. "What about Evan?"

He sighed. "Brooke said she needs to think about that. Whether it'd be good for him to see me or not."

If it was good for Brooke, why wouldn't it be good for Evan? Maribeth frowned slightly. "It's not up to her to decide," she said gently, feeling a tug of disloyalty to Brooke. But Evan and Mo had rights, too. As far as Maribeth could tell, Mo had been doing penance for years and years—far longer than if he'd actually been convicted of an offense and sent to jail. He had earned a second chance. And Evan had a right to hear his father's apology and learn what kind of man he'd become. "Evan's an adult," she pointed out.

"I know. But I don't want to hurt him any more than I already have. And I figure his mom's probably the best judge of how he'd react."

"The longer you're in town, the more chance he'll find out anyway. And if he does, and you haven't been in touch, he might think you don't want to see him."

His mouth tightened. "I know. But I gotta trust Brooke on this."

Maribeth tried to be optimistic. "She loves Evan. She'll do what's best for him." And if Brooke didn't do it soon, Maribeth might have another chat with her. Sometimes people benefited from an outside perspective, and Maribeth had never been shy about giving her friends advice.

"I'm going to believe that. Tonight was good. A good start." Mo smiled across at her. "And this is good. Thanks for letting me come over. I hope I didn't interrupt anything important."

Only hunting for a sperm donor. She glanced at her computer, waved a hand, and said, with a private grin, "Just some online shopping." In fact, she'd been happy to get Mo's call, and when she'd opened the door to the wet man holding a bunch of flowers, her heart had given a jump of pleasure. Sitting here watching his attractive, expressive face, listening as he revealed himself to her, she felt so drawn to him.

How did he feel? He'd made that comment about "reconsidering" dating. Was he serious? She decided to test him out with a little flirtation.

She uncurled her legs slowly and sensually, and this time his gaze did hook onto her. She slipped out of the chair and, barefoot, went to the fireplace and tossed in another chunk of wood. Returning, she ran a finger over the orange petals of a gerbera daisy. The bouquet he'd brought was nothing fancy, just a plastic-wrapped one from a grocery store, but she loved that he'd chosen vividly colored flowers. She'd never been much of a one for pastels.

"How are you coming on that decision?" she asked, dropping down to the sofa beside Mo. She wanted to touch him, and the wanting was almost irresistible. But something held her back. Maybe she hoped that the first touch would come from him, to prove that he was as drawn to her as she was to him.

"Which decision?" he asked.

"About reconsidering dating."

He turned sideways and looked at her, deliberately casting his gaze from the top of her head down her body. "I can't believe you're not already dating someone."

She shrugged. "Not at the moment. It's a small town. I've gone out with most of the eligible guys, and many of us are still friends."

"You're not looking to get married?"

"I'd like to, but not until I meet the right person."

"Man, you're choosy."

"I'm not. Really, I'm not." It always rankled when someone made that accusation. "It's not that I'm looking for anything so special or that I think I'm too good for these men. I've dated lots of really nice, smart guys, starting back when I was thirteen."

"But?"

She shrugged. "We have fun for a while, but that's it. I don't need to be married. I'm not going to get serious about a man unless—" She bit off her next words as a realization stunned her and her comfortable little world tilted on its axis.

"Unless what?"

There was no reason not to tell him, so she said slowly, "Unless there's a click." She didn't go on to reveal the rest. What she felt with Mo . . . well, it bore a strong resemblance to a click.

"Click? You've lost me."

Mouth dry, she swallowed and tried to gather her thoughts. "To start with, a special chemistry. Something, and maybe it's pheromones, that draws you, physically, to another person. Lust, but more than that, because lust is pretty common. More, um . . ." She studied him, feeling the itch to touch him, flesh to flesh. "Like a magnetic, undeniable attraction."

A knowing gleam lit his eyes. "Got it."

"But that's only part of it. It's not just physical, not solely chemistry. There's also a recognition of . . . who they really are, I guess. That they're someone who—" Thinking of how she felt about Mo, she tried to put it into words. "Someone who's different from you, and not perfect, but you can relate to them. You want to understand them. You want to make them happy, help them find what they're looking for." Frustrated, she shook her head. "But it's more than that, too." She often felt that way about people, just not with the same intensity as she did with Mo.

"Like all that 'two halves of a whole' or 'you complete me' romantic shit?"

"Not exactly. I don't believe that stuff. I think people should be self-sufficient, not need someone else to complete them. Sorry, I honestly don't know how better to describe it except to say that there's this click inside you, like tectonic plates shifted and the world rearranged itself in a different way, and you know you're supposed to be with this person for the rest of your life." Which was insane, because she barely knew him. He was Brooke's ex, Evan's father. He had been, as he labeled himself, a loser and a shit.

But if she could believe him—if she could trust in his words and what she heard in his voice, trust her own instincts—he was also a redeemed man, a careworn guy who was struggling to make things right. A man worth loving. Staring into those river-water eyes, Maribeth did indeed feel as if her world had shifted on its axis. Now, what was she going to do about it?

She needed to be patient and not get ahead of herself. She barely knew this man. Quite possibly, at some point his actions would belie his words. Or there'd be something about him that totally put her off. Or he'd turn out to be lousy in bed. Sometimes the hottest-looking guys proved to be duds between the sheets, men who didn't have a clue how to look after a woman.

On the other hand, if Mo truly was the one man for her, before long everything would start to fall into place. How amazing if that happened at the very moment she'd decided to move ahead as a single parent. Maybe she should stop shopping for a sperm donor? But no, that would be short-sighted. Right now, she needed to keep all her options open.

Chapter Five

Mo grinned at the beautiful redhead who was such an intriguing combination of practical and romantic. "Tectonic plates?" he queried with amusement. "Is that the same thing as 'the earth moved'?"

"Don't knock it until you've tried it," she said saucily. A few moments ago, she had looked a little dazed, but now she'd recovered her sass.

The only thing he wanted to *try* right now was to touch her. He'd told her about when he'd first met Brooke when they were teens, how he'd felt like a kid staring in the window of a candy shop. It was the same with Maribeth, except more potent because he definitely wasn't a kid and he knew exactly what, as a man, he wanted from the irresistible redhead. Sex, yeah. But also he wanted to know if her hair felt as springy and silky as it looked. If her cheek was as soft yet resilient as it appeared. If those lush reddish lips tasted of strawberries, lipstick, or chocolate. Whether the tantalizing flowery scent came from her hair or from perfume.

There was so much more to a woman than just sex.

Tentatively, he reached a hand toward her face, then

saw how rough his skin was and noticed the grease that lurked under his nails no matter how hard he scrubbed. She was so clean, so sweet-smelling, so perfectly feminine. It seemed almost like a profanity to touch her with this hand—and yet she was leaning forward as if she wanted him to do it.

What had she been talking about with that romantic tectonic plates stuff? Should he be worried? No, he'd told her he didn't get involved in relationships. Besides, despite her earlier denial, she obviously was choosy. If all those guys she'd dated before him didn't measure up to her standards, no way would she get serious about a man like him.

Which meant he needn't have qualms about accepting her body-language invitation. As gently as he could, he ran a couple of fingers down her cheek, feeling warm skin, not makeup. That delicate paleness tinted by a slight rosy blush, it was all Maribeth, which made it even sexier. And so did the fact that her color deepened as he caressed her skin.

Such a simple touch, and yet it affected her.

Him, too. It was no surprise that arousal surged through him, but it did startle him to see that his fingers trembled as they slid along her cheek and down to cup her jaw. A strong, determined jaw for a woman who knew her own mind. Maribeth was a grown-up, that was for sure, and he liked it. Liked her. Liked everything about her.

Liked the way her lips parted slightly as he leaned closer, angling his face to hers.

And then there was the soft brush of her warm, chocolate-scented breath against his skin. A moment later, his lips touched hers. A sound—a rough moan—escaped him.

So sweet, her lips, chocolate and sugar and woman.

So eager, in the way they met his. So intoxicating that the world spun around him and he was dizzy, lost, wanting only to kiss her and kiss her and kiss her. And so he did, with his lips, with his tongue, even with little nips like he was testing to make sure she was really there. Which she was, kissing him back just as urgently.

He held her face in both hands, her hair like curly, living silk tumbling over his skin. Her fingers twined in his hair, then rubbed over his shoulders like she wasn't happy to find a sweater rather than bare flesh. God, he wished they were both naked. He couldn't wait to unzip that tantalizing silver line down the front of her top, to undo her bra, to see her full breasts, and to feel them against his chest. To taste them, and every other inch of her lush body.

There was another sound, a groan, and then Maribeth's hands were on his shoulders, pushing him away. "Oh God, Mo," she gasped. Her cheeks blazed now and her breath came in sighing pants between her parted lips.

He struggled for breath, too. "Oh man, I'm sorry. I didn't mean to take it that far. You're just . . . so amazing. I got carried away." Under his fly, a throbbing, single-minded hard-on urged him to surrender again to his need for her.

"You're amazing, too." Her eyes were huge, feverishly bright emeralds. "But then it hit me." She was still trying to catch her breath. "What about Brooke?"

Brooke? At this moment, he had trouble remembering who Brooke was. He struggled to collect his thoughts and control his lust-crazed body. "You mean, she might be upset if we . . . ?"

Maribeth ran her hands through her hair, messing it up and making herself look even sexier, if such a thing were possible. "Yes. I didn't think before." Her speech sounded disjointed, like she, too, was having trouble pulling her thoughts together. "The girlfriend thing."

He frowned slightly, trying to figure out what she meant. "You mean like the female equivalent of how a guy's not supposed to hit on a buddy's girlfriend? But Brooke and I have been divorced for decades."

"I know." She breathed in and out, more slowly now, and when she went on she sounded calmer. "And this is such a small town that a lot of women have dated their girlfriends' exes. If we didn't, there'd be no one to go out with. It's kind of understood that if one woman's finished with a guy, he's fair game." She sighed. "But maybe this is a different situation."

"I can guarantee Brooke's finished with me. And vice versa." As lovely as Brooke was, he no longer felt even a tug of attraction to her.

A smile flickered on Maribeth's face. "I got that. But you two have so much history. And you were away for all those years, and now you're back and trying to resolve things, maybe find a way to be friends."

Friends? Could he and Brooke ever be friends? Could he and Evan ever be . . . what? Father and son? That seemed pretty much impossible.

Maribeth had at least distracted him from his painful arousal.

"I need to talk to her," she said.

"I guess I get what you're saying," he said. Or at least he realized it was some kind of female thing he would never truly understand. Reflecting, he went on. "Maybe it's what I deserve for what I did to her. Now it's in her hands whether I see Evan and whether you and I can, uh, date."

Date seemed like a high-school word for what he wanted to do with Maribeth. And yet he not only wanted to have steaming hot sex with her, he also wanted to sit and chat while they drank hot chocolate. Maybe take her out to one of the Western bars and dance with her. *Date*. Seemed that was what he wanted to do after all. "Will you talk to her soon?" he asked.

Maribeth fussed with her hair again, trying to tidy it. "She and some other friends are coming over tomorrow night. I'll find a private moment to talk to her."

He sure hoped his ex-wife, who had no reason to think kindly of him, would be generous. "I'd better be going, then."

"Yes." She picked up her cell phone, which lay on the coffee table. "Give me your phone number."

"Don't have a phone."

"Seriously?"

"I do have e-mail." The only device he owned was a tablet. It provided him with everything he needed: e-mail, banking, music, books, news, movies. He gave Maribeth his e-mail address and she input it into her phone.

"Okay," she said, "I'll e-mail you and let you know what Brooke says."

The women on Maribeth's list—with the exception of Corrie, who spent much of her spare time with her new boyfriend—had all been happy to come over to her place at eight o'clock on Friday. She'd offered dessert, a raisin pie that she'd made before work that morning. There was a lot to be said for a job that started at ten o'clock, as she had time for yoga, a relaxing breakfast, and a chore or two.

Now several of her girlfriends curled up on various seats in Maribeth's sitting room, casual in sweaters, jeans or winter leggings, and socks. Each had a plate of pie topped with cinnamon-sprinkled whipped cream, and a mug of coffee or tea. The fire blazed cheerily, and Maribeth pulled the curtains against the sound of sleet hitting the window. She spared a thought for Caruso, glad that Mo had provided shelter for the independent dog.

So far tonight, she hadn't had a chance to speak to Brooke alone. The blonde looked tired and a little stressed. Maribeth only hoped that Mo's return to Caribou Crossing would prove in the long run to be a good thing for all concerned.

Maribeth glanced at Cassidy Esperanza, who sat in the recliner with her feet up. The younger woman was as lovely as always, with her black hair in the pixie cut that drew attention to her half-Latina features and smoky blue eyes, but she'd said her bad leg was bothering her. "You're sure you're okay?" Maribeth asked her. "There's nothing else I can get you?"

Cassidy wrinkled her nose. "I'm good, MB. It's just been a long week and my stupid MS won't cut me a break." She'd been diagnosed with multiple sclerosis last year, and though mostly she was doing really well, she did suffer from symptoms when she got too tired. "Tonight is exactly what I need—delicious food and girl talk. I promised Dave I'd stay off my feet except for hobbling to and from Jess's van."

It was terrific the way that Dave Cousins's ex-wife, Jess, and his new wife, Cassidy, got along. Of course, it didn't hurt that Jess was very happily remarried, too—to Brooke's son, Evan. Ah, the joys of a small town. Rather than six degrees of separation, it tended to be more like one or two.

So much had happened since Mo left town almost

twenty years ago. He not only had an ex-wife and son, he had a daughter-in-law and grandchildren. If the self-confessed loner could examine his heart of hearts—something that, unfortunately, he didn't seem inclined to do—what role might he see himself playing in the lives of his family? Not to mention, in Maribeth's life.

Cassidy's bright voice interrupted her thoughts, saying, "On a much more interesting subject, I have great news. My parents and my brother and sister-in-law are ditching rainy Victoria to come to Caribou Crossing for a proper white Christmas! We've reserved rooms for them at the Wild Rose, which means the inn is now full for the holidays." Dave owned the Wild Rose Inn, a beautifully restored historic hotel, and he and Cassidy ran it.

"We're all looking forward to seeing them again," Jess said, her chestnut ponytail bobbing as she nodded. "It's going to be a huge family Christmas this year." Her eyes widened suddenly, and she glanced at Brooke.

That glance spoke volumes, making it clear that Brooke had told her son and daughter-in-law about Mo's presence in town. What had they decided to do? Automatically, Maribeth ate a forkful of pie, but didn't really taste it.

Lark Cantrell, a striking, six-foot-tall brunette who was the town's fire chief, spoke from her easy chair at one side of the fireplace. "It's sure going to be a different holiday for my family, with Eric there." Her happy smile left no doubt that "different" meant "wonderful." She'd recently fallen for a soldier who'd lost a leg in Afghanistan, and he was in the process of leaving the army and moving to Caribou Crossing. Prior to that, her family had consisted of Lark, her mom, and Lark's nine-year old son.

Maribeth was happy for her friends, with all their holiday plans, but more than a little envious. It had been twenty years since she'd had a real family Christmas. Each year over the holidays, she spent some volunteer time at a church soup kitchen and at the women's shelter. She held an early December open house. Friends invited her to join them for Christmas Eve carol singing, midnight Mass, present opening with kids, and turkey dinners. But nothing was the same as being with her own family. Of course, she could have visited her grandparents in Vancouver, but she loved the small-town warmth and color of Christmas in Caribou Crossing, and besides, her store was always so busy. It had become tradition to make her trip to Vancouver in mid-January instead.

Next year, would she be enjoying Christmas with her own baby girl or boy? Or, if the click she felt with Mo Kincaid proved to be the real thing, would the two of them be married and starting a family in the good old-fashioned way? So many possibilities ahead, and how wonderful they were to contemplate!

Smiling to herself, she tuned into the conversation again. Sally Ryland, an attractive strawberry-blonde in her early thirties, was talking about her holiday plans with her sexy fiancé, Ben.

"Wait a minute." Maribeth snapped her fingers. "Sally, the big rodeo finals are coming up, right?"

"Next weekend." Sally put down her coffee mug and twisted her fingers together. "The CFR—Canadian Finals Rodeo. In Edmonton. Ben and his partner, Dusty, qualified for the finals in team roping, and Ben also qualified in saddle bronc. Corrie persuaded me to go, and she'll hold down the fort at Ryland Riding." Corrie was Sally's assistant.

"That'll be so exciting," Maribeth said.

"Exciting?" Sally groaned. "Try nerve-wracking. Watching the love of my life climb onto the back of a bronc whose sole goal is to toss him off? I swear, it was easier competing myself." She'd once been a champion barrel racer.

They all offered words of sympathy and encouragement, though Jess seemed a little distracted, not her usual bubbly self.

Maribeth wasn't the only one who noticed because Cassidy asked, "Is everything okay with you, Jess?"

"Yes, sure." Jess glanced at Brooke, who'd been quiet, too.

Brooke said, "MB, it's your turn. What's new in your life?"

"That's actually why I invited all of you tonight. Well, partly just to get together before it's officially the holiday season and everyone gets crazy-busy. But also because I want your advice on something." Maribeth stood. "First, does anyone want another slice of pie?"

"Oh my God, I couldn't," Cassidy said. "It's amazing, but man is it rich! Who knew the plain old raisin could make such a decadent dessert? And I love the hint of orange."

"I'll take a small slice," Sally said. "It's pure heaven, and I only had time to grab a snack for dinner."

She was the only taker for more pie. Maribeth asked, "More tea or coffee, ladies? Maybe a liqueur? I have Baileys, Grand Marnier, and Kahlúa."

"Ooh, yum!" Cassidy said promptly. "Grand Marnier for me, please."

Sally said, "Better not, since I'm driving."

"Me, too," Jess said regretfully. "Though I do love Baileys."

"Go ahead," Brooke, who'd also come with Jess, said. "I'll drive us home." She and her husband and little girl lived down the road from Jess's family.

"Best mother-in-law in the world," Jess said. "Yes please to a Baileys, MB."

"Lark?" Maribeth asked, beginning to gather the empty plates.

"Thanks, but I can't. I'm on call tonight." Although the fire chief worked regular weekday hours, she and the other firefighters were on call most evenings and weekends.

Brooke had risen and was collecting the mugs. The two women went into the kitchen where Maribeth put the kettle on to boil and set the coffeemaker to brew another pot.

After glancing around to make sure the others were still in the front room, Maribeth said, "Brooke, there's something I need to ask you."

The blonde leaned a hip against the kitchen table. "Yes, I told Evan and Jess." She sounded weary. "Evan said he didn't want to see Mo. Ever."

"Oh God. I'd hoped—"

Brooke held up a hand, stopping her. "When Evan first came back to Caribou Crossing, he refused to see me. Jess tried to talk him into it, but he was adamant. Eventually he changed his mind, thank God."

Maribeth, standing by the coffeemaker, nodded.

"Mo says he's a changed man," Brooke went on, "and I find myself believing him. If I could change so drastically, why couldn't he? Maribeth, I *want* to believe him, but how can I know for sure? How can I *know* he's trustworthy? For me personally, it's not such a big deal. I have a whole wonderful life now, with the best family in the world. Mo has no power over me."

Her face tightened and her blue-green eyes, normally so gentle and warm, glittered. "But I don't think the same is true for Evan. Mo is still his father. Even though Evan is close to Wade Bly, a father-in-law isn't the same thing.

Mo is the dad who hurt him and abandoned him. So when Evan says he doesn't want to see Mo, I'm not so sure he's wrong."

Maribeth's heart ached for all of them, yet to her the path seemed so obvious. "Evan had similar issues with you, but I know he's so happy that the two of you reconciled."

A tired smile warmed Brooke's face. "Yes, he really is. But this thing with his father needs to be Evan's decision. Or at least I want it to be. I hope Mo will respect that. If he forces a meeting, it could go badly."

Maribeth chewed her bottom lip. "They might run into each other by chance. I mean, if Mo stays." If Evan remained adamant, would Mo leave town?

"I know."

Their gazes held for a long moment. Then Maribeth said slowly, "There was actually something else I wanted to talk to you about." It was a difficult subject to raise. Was she absolutely sure she wanted to see more of Mo, given all the complications surrounding him?

Yes, because of that click, the feeling of a true connection with him. She'd never felt that before, so how could she not explore it? At least if it wouldn't upset Brooke. "Do you still have feelings for Mo?"

Brooke's fair eyebrows arched. "You're kidding, right? I love Jake. Totally, exclusively, madly."

"I know." And how Maribeth longed to love and be loved exactly that way. Could Mo be the one? "It's just . . . Well, how would you feel if someone went out with Mo?" She swallowed. What a coward she was. "If I went out with Mo?"

Brooke's brows went even higher. "You? You and Mo?"

"Is it so unbelievable?"

"I . . . Uh, well . . ." She stopped and considered.

"Believe me, I know he can be appealing. But, Maribeth . . ." She trailed off, shaking her head.

Suddenly, Maribeth was almost hyperventilating. Brooke had to say yes. Until that moment, Maribeth hadn't realized how crucial it was that Brooke agreed. But now there was only one thought in her head, an echo of something Sally Ryland had just said. *What if he's the love of my life?* What else was the click, the one she'd been waiting for all her life, about? If Mo was the one man for her, she had to find out. She had to make Brooke see.

Maribeth was almost ready to speak the scary words aloud—*What if he's the love of my life?*—when her girlfriend spoke again, her words coming slowly.

"There's the age thing—ten years between you and Mo. But then again, Jake taught me that age doesn't matter." Her husband was several years younger than Brooke.

Maribeth nodded. Age was just a number. What mattered was staying fit, physically and mentally.

"You're just so . . . so everything he isn't," Brooke said. "Vivacious, upbeat, outgoing. Generous, sweet-natured. Even if I give Mo the benefit of the doubt and believe that he's a reformed man, it strikes me that he's—oh, what do they call it in the movies?"

"A bad boy?"

Brooke gave a surprised chuckle. "He sure used to be. But what I was thinking was a lost soul. I can see why he'd be drawn to you—why so many men are drawn to you—but I'd worry that he might . . ." She trailed off, her expression troubled.

"Hurt me?" Maribeth asked quietly.

Brooke's lips pressed together. "Do you mean hit you? Well, he does have a history, but then so do I. I hope he's as far past it as I am—and if he ever tried anything, I know you're strong enough to deal with it. You'd have him behind bars in an instant. No, I was thinking more that he might, uh, drag you down. That his angst might dim that lovely warm flame of yours." She blinked. "But on the other hand, I've rarely met a woman who knew herself so well and was so self-confident. How many men have you dated? And none of them has changed you yet. No, I can't see you giving any man that kind of power."

Was there something a bit odd about that endorsement? Maybe at some point Maribeth would revisit Brooke's words and try to sort out what bothered her about them. But for now, the kettle was boiling, the coffee was ready, and the women in the living room would be wondering what was taking so long. Not to mention, her heart was still racing, hopeful about where Brooke was heading but needing that final confirmation. "Are you saying it wouldn't bother you if I dated Mo?"

Brooke shook her head. "No, it wouldn't. I think you'd be good for him. God knows, I'm not sure the poor man has ever been with a woman who's been good for him. I only hope that he's good for you, too, Maribeth. But that's for you to say, not me."

Maribeth crossed over to her and squeezed her hand. "Thanks." She hoped so, too. It was so disconcerting, experiencing the magical click for the first time in her life at the identical time she was shopping for a sperm donor. If Mo wasn't Mr. Right, hopefully they'd be friends and she would go ahead as planned with insemination. If he was, then she'd have an even more exciting "happily ever after."

She put a couple of Earl Grey tea bags into the teapot and a decaf peach ginger one into her own mug and poured boiling water into both. "Brooke, could you serve the tea and coffee? I'll get the liqueurs and Sally's pie."

When the two of them returned to the living room, the

others were speculating about just how snowy a Christmas it would be.

After everyone had been served, Maribeth took her seat on the sofa and said, "I have an announcement and a request."

"Shoot," Cassidy said cheerfully.

"I'm thirty-nine and obviously not getting any younger. I'd always hoped to fall in love, marry, and have children. Love and marriage can come along at any stage of life, but my biological clock's running out on having a baby, and that's the thing I want most in life."

"I can relate to that," Sally said quietly.

"Me, too," Lark put in. "Having done it once, I have to say it was the most incredible experience, and I can't imagine my life without Jayden. I sure wouldn't mind giving him a little sister or brother."

Cassidy was silent. Multiple sclerosis ran in her family, and Maribeth knew that it would be a tough decision for her and Dave, whether they should have a baby.

"Anyhow," Maribeth said, "I've been dating since I was thirteen and—"

A splutter of laughter escaped Lark. When they all turned to her, she said, "Sorry, but I was remembering that 'men, men, men' rant you went on one day, MB. How did it go? Tall ones, short ones, black ones, white ones?"

Maribeth chuckled. "Doctors, lawyers, Indian chiefs. Yes, something like that. I've dated them all. Sweet ones and spicy ones, rich ones and poor ones, science nerds and jocks. And there's not a single one that I fell in love with. I'm not going to marry a guy just for the sake of getting married and having a baby."

"That would be a huge mistake," Lark agreed firmly.

"And I don't need a man," Maribeth went on. "Except

for the biological contribution. So I'm thinking seriously about using a sperm donor. I've put together a short list of men and I'm looking for input."

Her last words were swallowed up by a flurry of exclamations and comments, as well as a pair of arched eyebrows from Brooke, who obviously thought it odd that Maribeth would date a new guy and shop for a sperm donor at the same time.

When the noise settled down, Maribeth told them about her visit to the women's clinic and her online shopping. She did not mention Mo; if things worked out with him, her friends would know soon enough. "I've chosen six prospects. Come on into the dining room and let me show you."

The women gathered up their mugs and liqueur glasses and followed Maribeth.

Earlier, she'd moved the big flat-screen monitor from her home office upstairs and hooked it up to her laptop, along with the wireless keyboard and mouse. Now, after making sure Cassidy was seated in a comfortable chair with her leg up, Maribeth logged onto the website and navigated to the page of options she'd set up, the product of hours of browsing. It showed six head shots, along with brief biographical data: age, height, weight, race, religion, education, and occupation.

Her friends studied the screen avidly. Cassidy pointed. "I'd pick that one. He reminds me of Dave."

The man was handsome, with medium brown hair and gray eyes, but his outstanding feature was the sense of warmth and compassion in his expression. It matched perfectly with his occupation as a family practice doctor. "Me, too," Maribeth admitted. "That's why he's on the list."

"This one's hot, though," Jess said. "I mean if you like

the type." She nudged her mother-in-law. "Which you do, right, Brooke?"

The guy did look a lot like Brooke's husband, Jake, with his black hair, five o'clock shadow, and rakish grin. He was listed as a pilot.

"That one's hot, too," Sally said, pointing to a man with beautiful near-black skin, strong features, and close-cropped black hair. "And he's a veterinarian. He loves animals, so he's got to be a good guy."

"What about this one?" Lark asked, indicating the one redhead in the bunch. "He's not that great-looking, he's short, and he's a dentist. Nothing against any of that, but what made him stand out for you, MB?"

"Don't knock dentists," Maribeth said. "My mom was one. The other reason I put him on the list was his red hair. Women often aren't that attracted to redheaded guys, and as a 'ginger' myself, I wanted to at least short-list one."

"So if you two have a son," Cassidy joked, "women won't want to date him?"

They all laughed and Maribeth said, "Okay, you're right." She clicked her mouse on the man's face and, feeling a pang of guilt at rejecting a fellow redhead, deleted him. "There are more detailed profiles on all of them. I'll show you."

For the next half hour, they read, commented, and debated the pros and cons of each man. "I don't want to make a final decision tonight," Maribeth said. "I'm having my old school friends over on Monday and I'll get their input, too. But it seems to me we're leaning toward the doctor or the vet."

"They both sound like a good match for you, MB," Sally said. "You're such a generous, compassionate person."

"But remember she's not dating them," Lark said. "This

isn't about finding the most compatible guy to date, it's about finding the best genetic match."

"I do keep losing sight of that," Sally admitted. "It's just that I'd so love it if Maribeth did find the perfect man and they fell madly in love and had kids of their own."

"Believe me, I'd love it, too," Maribeth said. While Mo wasn't exactly "perfect," could he be the man to make her dreams come true?

"Then shouldn't we be looking at an online dating site instead of a sperm donor one?" Jess asked.

"I'm not willing to waste any more time," Maribeth said. "Remember the men, men, men thing? I've been there, done that, didn't find the man who clicked." Until now.

"I take it that you plan to keep dating while you carry on with the sperm donor thing," Brooke asked. Not waiting for Maribeth's answer—which, obviously, she already knew—she went on. "So would you tell your date about your sperm donor plans?" Her curious expression suggested that she didn't even consider the possibility that Maribeth might view Mo as being anything more than another in her long string of "men, men, men."

"Uh, no," Maribeth said slowly. "Not until . . . well, I guess until I make a final decision."

A shiver tickled her spine. Was she fooling herself to think that Mo might be her true love and that their lives and dreams could magically align? Given his track record and the things he'd said about himself, he wasn't the most likely prospect for the husband-and-father role. And yet there was that click. It had to mean something. She'd only find out what that something was by dating the man. If he truly was the love of her life, then somehow things would work out. Wouldn't they?

Chapter Six

After a Sunday lunch of canned tomato soup and a grilled cheese sandwich made in a frying pan, Mo walked from his apartment to Maribeth's house. He wasn't surprised to find Caruso on his heels. The animal seemed to have developed a sixth sense that led him to Mo. At nights, the dog slept in the rag-padded box Mo had set up for him under the overhang at the garage. Hank Hennessey had accepted his presence with a grumble, but last night at closing time Mo had caught the man tossing the animal half a roast beef sandwich, left over or saved from Hank's lunch.

During the day, Caruso went off on his own business, but he usually turned up to accompany Mo on his walks. He chased an occasional squirrel or bird—the dog's curiosity and energy both ran high—but mostly he paced easily along at Mo's left side. Mo'd had a couple of people politely inform him of the town's regulations about leashing and poop-and-scoop, and he had replied, "He's not my dog." Occasionally, a dog lover tried to stroke Caruso, but the animal usually backed off.

Now Mo spoke to Caruso. "We're going to Maribeth's.

You remember her. The pretty redhead." For some reason, he'd taken to talking to the animal, at least when no one was watching. It almost seemed rude to stay silent, like he was shunning his unasked-for companion.

"You can't go out with us, though." He reconsidered. "Or can you? Probably best not. She wants to go riding." Saturday morning, when Mo had woken and checked his tablet, he'd found e-mail from Maribeth. She said she'd spoken to Brooke, and the other woman had no problems with the idea of Maribeth and Mo seeing each other.

Mo'd been happy about that, for more reasons than he could count. When he'd e-mailed back to ask when they could get together, Maribeth had said she was babysitting for friends on Saturday night. She'd proposed that, since she and Mo both had Sundays off work, they go riding in the afternoon.

"Riding," he said to Caruso. "Can't say that was what I expected. She seems like such a, you know, feminine type of woman. Well, not that feminine women don't ride, but she's so . . . groomed. Soft. Sweet-smelling. Didn't take her for the outdoorsy type."

The dog trotted along, looking up at Mo periodically as if he understood what he was saying.

"Lucky for me, I guess. I like being outside, being active. And it makes it easier to spend time with someone. Sitting in a bar or a restaurant across the table from a woman, there's a lot of pressure. When they talk about themselves, you have to say the right things back. Then they go and ask questions about you, and it's hard to know how to answer."

Mo stopped talking as a woman and a little boy, holding mittened hands, approached. The woman gave him a bright "Good afternoon," and he returned the greeting.

The boy said, "Pretty doggy," and no one mentioned the absence of a leash.

After the pair had walked on, Mo returned to musing to the dog. "You know something, though? It hasn't been so awkward, talking to Maribeth. She's . . . well, different, I guess. Different from other women. Easier to be around, for all that she's so damned sexy."

He glanced down to see Caruso peering up inquisitively.

"Yeah, 'different' is a cop-out word, isn't it? Too vague." He tried to clarify his thoughts. "She's not judgmental. Oh, she asks tough questions all right, like whether I'm a man worth knowing. Maybe I even like that about her, how she makes me think. But what I like most is that she seems to accept me for who I am."

They were walking down the block where Maribeth lived, on a well-weathered sidewalk that took them past a variety of houses: contemporary ones that hadn't yet settled into their surroundings, ranchers from the sixties, and older places like the one where she lived. Two-story wooden homes with well-established gardens, homes that looked like families laughed together in them and played in the yards. The kind of house that didn't fit a loner like him.

The kind of house that seemed made for Maribeth, to share with a husband and two or three kids. Yeah, she was sexy and flirtatious, but he got the sense that there was a much deeper, more emotional core to her. The kind of core that spoke to him—even inexperienced with such things as he was—of hearth and home and family. But likely he was wrong, or, as practical and desirable as she was, she would already have all those things. And that meant that Mo could date her and she wouldn't have crazy expectations that she'd somehow domesticate him and turn him marriage-minded.

As he and Caruso approached the house, her red-and-white Mini was backing out of the garage. She climbed out of the driver's seat, turned, and raised a hand in greeting as she saw them. Today, she did look more outdoorsy, in heavy jeans, boots, and a sheepskin jacket over a blue turtleneck. A red knitted hat was pulled down to cover her ears, and her hair—a different but equally vivid shade of red—spilled brightly out beneath it. The clothing suited her just as nicely as everything else he'd seen her wear.

He walked toward her as she came to meet him. "Hey," he said.

"Hi, Mo. Did you know that not only do you get those deep dimple-groove things when you smile, but your eyes crinkle up at the corners?"

"Didn't know that." He hadn't even realized he was smiling.

"So," she said. "Are we calling this our first date?"

"Guess we are." And didn't that sound fine? "In which case, I figure the right way to start it is like this." He reached out with both hands to capture her head, leaning down as she came up on her booted toes. Her cheeks were pink and so were her lips, all rosy and glossy. All warm and soft when they met his.

He took his time with that kiss, making it gentle but thorough, not going deep or intense. Not yet. If the afternoon went well, the time for passion would come later. He knew it was there, had felt the blaze when they kissed the other night. Stoking it would be worth a few hours' wait.

For now, Maribeth met him and matched him, resting her gloved hands on his shoulders and not trying to change the pace or up the ante. Content, it seemed, to treat this as a hint of things to come.

When the two of them finally separated, she tipped her

head down toward the dog that sat patiently beside him. "You brought a friend. Hi, Caruso."

"The crazy animal's turned into my shadow."

"Aw, that's so sweet. But what's he going to do while we go riding?"

"Guess he can't go?"

"Uh . . ." She considered the dog, who stared up at her with that blank "I'm not asking any favors" look of his. "Well, maybe. I'd have to ask Sally if it's okay. You aren't afraid he'd run away?"

"If he wanted to run away, nothing's stopping him from doing it now."

"True."

"We've gone for walks on a country road and passed riders, and he's been fine with the horses. He does like to chase squirrels and so on, but somehow he always ends up back at my side."

"Let me call and see what Sally says." She took her phone from her jacket pocket, scrolled, and a moment later said, "Corrie? Hi, it's Maribeth. You know that I booked two horses for a friend and me? Well, I was calling to ask you and Sally what you'd think about us bringing a dog along."

She listened, and then said, "Yes, my friend has a dog." She grinned at Mo, who mouthed, "He's not my dog."

Another pause as she listened, then she asked Mo, "Do you think he's been trained?"

"The girl from the shelter said yes, and it sure looks like it to me. His biggest issues are being shy with strangers, liking to explore, and escaping confinement."

Maribeth passed that on to the person at the other end of the line, along with what Mo had said about Caruso being fine with horses. She listened, and then said, "Sounds good. Thanks, Corrie."

Stowing her phone again, she said, "That was Sally's assistant. She says they have a couple of clients who bring dogs along, but they need to be careful in the beginning to make sure the dog is okay with the horses as well as with the kids and adults who ride there."

"Sure." He glanced from Maribeth to her Mini, and then at Caruso. "Next question is, can we get him in the car?"

Maribeth squatted down and gazed into Caruso's eyes. She didn't try to pet him or grab his collar. "Caruso, we won't take you to the shelter. We won't ever take you anyplace where you'd be shut up. We're going to go riding in the country, where it's all wide-open space."

As she spoke, the dog cocked his head, clearly listening. Now Caruso shifted his gaze up at Mo.

"I think you'll like it," Mo told him.

Caruso seemed to be thinking, and then he let out that warbling song.

Mo laughed. "Seems to me that's a yes." Between the dog and the woman, he'd laughed more this past week than he could remember doing in the last year or so.

Maribeth rose and opened the back door of her car. After the dog hopped in, Mo climbed in the passenger side. Maribeth didn't ask him if he wanted to drive, as women often did. He kind of liked her assumption that since it was her car, she'd drive.

"We going to that place on the edge of town?" he asked as she backed out into the street. "Westward Ho!? Caruso and I've walked past it a couple times, heading out into the country."

"No. It's good and I used to ride there, but then I made friends with Sally Ryland. She has a place in the country, about a fifteen-minute drive, where she rents horses, boards horses, and teaches riding. She just got engaged to a rodeo rider, and next year they're going to add a rodeo school."

"This is still horse country," he commented, "even if the town has spiffed itself up since I was last here."

"Horse country and tourist country." She turned the car onto a road that led out of town. "There's Gold Rush Days Park, the Crazy Horse Guest Ranch, and lots of other attractions. Another friend and her family run Riders Boot Camp, an intensive riding program for people who come and live on-site for a week or two." She flicked him a glance. "You do ride, don't you? I never thought to ask. I just assumed."

"I didn't ride when I lived here before, but I've done some now and then over the years. I enjoy it." Like long walks, it was a good pursuit for a loner. "You go riding a lot?" He glanced out the window, noting how cold and crisp the ranch land looked under a brooding gray sky. It wouldn't surprise him if it snowed.

"In the summer, I usually go out a couple of times a week—evenings or on a day off. Sometimes alone, sometimes with friends. I go less often in winter due to the short days."

She gestured to a couple of thick-coated horses gazing over a fence. "I was horse-crazy when I was a girl. Nagged my parents to buy me a horse." She gave a soft laugh. "They said I'd grow out of it, and I said I never would, but then I discovered boys. After that, horses didn't seem quite so important."

"You don't own one now?"

"No. I wouldn't have enough time to commit, and owning one isn't important to me now. I even ride different horses, to get to know them and have some variety."

The heater in the car was pumping and Mo unbuttoned his denim jacket. Maribeth pulled off her hat and reached over to turn the heat down. He caught a whiff of her scent, a different one yet again, not flowery or spicy but more herbal. Outdoorsy, like her clothes. Seemed she liked variety in more than just horses.

Maybe that was what had kept her single. Even though she'd said she might get married one day, her behavior suggested that at heart she had no desire to settle down with one man. If so, that was good for him. It meant she wouldn't put pressure on him. Wouldn't get hurt when inevitably they broke up. In fact, odds were that she'd be the one doing the breaking up, once the novelty wore off and she found a better man. That thought made him vow to enjoy every precious moment she shared with him.

Best to clarify the situation, though, rather than make assumptions. "So, this dating thing," he said. "I take it you're no more into finding a serious relationship than I am." He watched her profile as he spoke.

Her eyes widened for a moment. Then they narrowed and her lips pressed together. Finally, she said, "I start every relationship without expectations. I take it as it comes, see where it goes." Another lip press, and then, "To be honest, I would like to fall in love with a wonderful man who's crazy about me. I'd like us to get married and have children."

He swallowed hard. If that was what she wanted, she shouldn't waste her time with him.

Maybe that gulp was audible, or maybe she read his mind, because she flicked him a glance and said drily, "Don't panic, Mo. I've been dating for twenty-six years and I've dated at least twice that many men."

"Did you fall in love with any of them?" He remembered her talking about that click, the tectonic plates thing.

She shook her head. "Nope. If I had, I'm sure things would have worked out for us and we'd be married now and have two or three children." She shot him a quick sideways glance. "How about you? Have you been in love? Did you love Brooke?"

With some regret, he said, "No, I'm afraid not. I was hot for her, but we'd never have lasted more than a few months if she hadn't got pregnant."

"You don't think she loved you either?"

"Only in the way teenage girls fall for guys in boy bands, or older dudes on motorbikes. But not once she got to know me and found out what a shit I was."

"Why did the two of you stay together?"

He'd asked himself that question more than once over the years. He hoped he got another chance to talk to Brooke, because he'd like to hear her perspective. "Looking back, I don't really know. It's hard to understand the things you did when you were a kid. Maybe in our own misguided way, we both figured it was the right thing to do. We were married and had a baby. And then, well, circumstances built upon each other and it seemed like we were bound together. You know how they say in weddings 'for better or worse'? We got the 'for worse' part."

"That's sad."

"Long time ago." Curious, he asked, "Brooke ever talk to you about our marriage?"

"Not much. Except to take her own share of the blame for things being so bad."

"That's good of her. I'm glad she got herself sorted around. Found herself a new life." He reflected. "I've never seen her like that before. It's like she's calm inside herself."

"She's found love, peace, joy."

Those were three mighty big words. Ones that Mo never expected to apply to himself. Yet Maribeth tossed them out as if they were no big thing. As if they were achievable.

Brooke had achieved them. Back when he'd known her, Mo would have said that was impossible.

"You didn't answer my other question," Maribeth said. "Have you ever been in love?"

"Brooke was the closest. And that taught me my lesson." He knew he wasn't cut out for love, and in fact it was pretty amazing to even be dating. His life had sure changed since he walked back into Caribou Crossing.

"Hmm." Maribeth turned onto a smaller road marked by a wooden sign with horses on it that read RYLAND RIDING.

Mo glanced back at the dog, who sat on the seat with his nose pressed up against the window. "Caruso, I figure it's best that we leave you in the car until we get the lay of the land. Then when we head off for a ride, we'll let you out and you can come with us. That sound okay?"

The dog flicked him a glance that clearly conveyed skepticism.

To Maribeth, Mo said, "When we get out, let's be careful so he doesn't escape. I don't want to have to talk him down out of a tree."

She pulled the car into a parking lot and Mo gazed around, noting several other vehicles, mostly minivans and SUVs. Past the parking area were a couple of outdoor rings. One was empty, but in the other a barrel racing course was set up and a woman on horseback was rounding the barrels while another watched. Mo saw a large barn and, behind it, a big wooden structure. "Indoor arena?" he guessed.

"Yes. Corrie's probably teaching a children's class in there now."

They both slipped out of the Mini and Caruso shot them a soulful gaze through the window.

As Mo and Maribeth walked toward the barn, the woman who'd been racing around the barrels rode over to the fence. "Hey, MB," she called.

"Hi, Sally. This is my friend Mo."

He exchanged hellos with the pretty blonde who wore a cowboy hat and a denim jacket that was heavier than his. Her gaze was curious, but only mildly so. Probably she was used to Maribeth bringing male friends out to enjoy a ride.

"Corrie told me you have a dog," she said to Mo.

"He's in the car. I think he's okay with horses. I figure Maribeth and I could ride out along the road we came in on and pick him up along the way. He knows both of us, so that'll likely keep him calmer."

"Sounds like a plan," Sally said. "Corrie and I got the horses ready for you." She turned to Maribeth. "It's Campion and Daybreak. They're in stalls in the barn. You'll just need to tighten their cinches." Addressing Mo again, she said, "You've ridden before?"

"Yeah, a number of times."

"There's a waiver of liability we ask people to sign the first time they come here. I left one in the office—Maribeth knows where that is—so please read it over and let me know if you have any questions."

"Sure. Thanks."

He and Maribeth went to the barn and he breathed in the combined scents of hay, alfalfa, and horses. Much as Mo thrived on the machine-shop aroma he was familiar with, he had to admit that a well-maintained barn smelled pretty good, too.

In the small office, he skimmed over a standard waiver form, and scrawled his signature and the date. Then he and Maribeth went to find their horses.

The one he'd be riding, Daybreak, was a sturdy palomino

gelding. Maribeth's, called Campion, was a bay gelding. Maribeth greeted both horses by name and crooned to them as she stroked them. To Mo, she said, "They're even-tempered. They won't kick up a fuss as long as Caruso behaves himself."

Mo held out his hand to Daybreak, let the horse nose it, and then stroked him. "Hey there, fellow."

He and Maribeth led the horses out of the barn, tightened their cinches, and then mounted. It wasn't half-bad being on top of a well-mannered horse, out in the country on a November afternoon, in the company of a fine-looking woman.

They rode across the yard and through the parking lot. Caruso's bright eyes peered at them through the back window of the Mini and he did that weird head-toss thing, looking eager and impatient. Mo swung out of the saddle and handed Daybreak's reins to Maribeth. "How about you hold on to my horse while I get the dog out."

She took her keys from her jacket pocket and handed them over.

Rather than press the button that would sound a beep, Mo unlocked the door manually. He eased it open a crack and Caruso's nose was immediately there, scenting the air. "Remember, you gotta behave yourself," Mo warned him.

Really, what made him think that the dog would? He barely knew the creature, and singing dogs were, according to the girl from the shelter, a semi-wild breed, not one that had been domesticated for centuries. Knowing this could be a very big mistake, and yet also guessing that Caruso would consider the wide-open countryside to be the next thing to heaven, Mo eased the door farther open.

The dog was out in one bound, but then he stopped, staring at the two horses. His furry, pointed ears cocked forward and then rotated, taking in the sounds in all directions.

The horses stood still, their heads slightly down and their own ears cocked as they assessed Caruso. "He may look like a fox," Maribeth murmured soothingly to the horses, "but he's really a dog. You've seen lots of dogs before. You know they're nothing to worry about."

To the dog, Mo said, "They won't hurt you if you don't yap at them or snap at their heels. Maybe best not to sing to them either, at least not until they get to know you. Come on over and meet them." Mo took a step forward and tapped his left leg with his hand, encouraging Caruso to fall into place at his heel.

Maribeth sat atop Campion, keeping one firm hand on her horse's reins and the other on Daybreak's, but neither animal seemed inclined to startle. Caruso stuck obediently to Mo as the man and dog approached the horses.

The only quickened pulse here was her own. Mo Kincaid had that effect on her. Partly, of course, it was his looks: the rangy body in casual outdoors clothes; the silver-shot black hair that despite its length and waviness looked 100 percent masculine; the gorgeous brown skin; and those stunning river-water eyes. Also, it was the way he related to that wary, abandoned dog, like the two of them were soul mates. Brooke had called Mo a lost soul, and that was a dangerous kind of man to get involved with. But yet this was the man—the one man in her entire life—who'd ever had this effect on her.

Like her, he'd never fallen in love. Unlike her, it sounded as if he didn't want to. Was she utterly insane to think that their relationship might go somewhere?

She watched the dog and horses check each other out

using their eyes and noses and ears. When none of them seemed fussed, Mo mounted Daybreak again and took the palomino's reins from her. "Lead on, Maribeth."

She urged Campion forward, onto the road they'd driven in on.

Mo brought his horse alongside, patting his left leg again and saying, "Here, Caruso. Stay with us as long as we're on the road." He glanced at Maribeth. "His training must have included traffic. In town he knows to stay clear of it."

A short distance down the road, a wide trail branched away, and Maribeth took it. "There's a network of trails and farm roads," she told Mo. "You can ride for miles, and the scenery's wonderful." Here the trees were deciduous, with leaves that unfurled jewel green in spring and turned vivid gold in fall. Right now, the branches were bare, stark against the gray sky, beautiful in a different way than during other seasons. Though there had been snow three or four times so far this year, the snowfall had been light and hadn't stuck for more than a day or two.

Mo said to Caruso, "You can go explore, but remember that we're your ride home."

The dog gave a quick warble and then darted off, tail waving. He wove here and there through the trees, following intriguing smells or sounds.

"In a month's time," Maribeth said, "the ranch land and hills will be white. Many of us still go riding, and there's cross-country skiing as well."

"When I lived here before, I never much appreciated the scenery. Didn't see myself as a country boy."

"You were from Los Angeles? Yes, that'd be a lot different from Caribou Crossing. What brought you and Brooke to our little town?"

"I don't remember. We moved around quite a bit. I

wasn't good at holding a job. Didn't like taking orders, didn't like showing up on time, drank too much. Brooke got part-time jobs sometimes, but her work record was no better than mine. We didn't like any of the places we lived, so if we ran out of work or got restless, we'd up and move on."

"Why not go back to L.A.? And now that I think of it, how did you even get permits to work in Canada?"

He didn't answer for a moment. Finally, he said gruffly, "Long story, and not a nice one. If I tell you, our first date may end up being our last."

Startled, Maribeth gazed over at him to see him looking at her with a wry expression.

"But yeah," he went on. "You have a right to know."

A right? He must mean because they were dating.

They came out of the trees and Maribeth leaned down from the saddle to open a latched wooden gate. "Caruso!" she called as she rode through.

Mo followed her and bent to refasten the gate. "If the gaps between the bars aren't wide enough for him to get through, he'll just climb it."

Sure enough, as they started down a dirt-and-grass farm road that ran alongside a wooden fence, the dog bounded up to join them. On either side of the fence was rolling grassland, a bleached-out yellow. Maribeth had chosen a route where there wouldn't be cattle or sheep in the fields, not wanting the dog to harass them.

Caruso belted down the track ahead of them, scared a red-winged blackbird perched on a fence post, and then tried to chase it when it flew away. Maribeth smiled at the dog's exuberance and then turned again to Mo, about to prompt him to share his story.

Before she spoke, Mo said, "Want to pick up the pace?"

Was she willing to give him a few minutes' grace?

"Sure." She urged Campion on, into an easy lope. The brisk air nipped her cheeks and she was glad of the wool hat that covered her ears. Still, it was invigorating being out on a day like this.

Mo was bareheaded but showed no sign of feeling the cold. Rather than huddling into the upturned collar of his jacket, he held his head high as if he was savoring the wintry air. He looked comfortable in the saddle even if he hadn't done a lot of riding. She got the sense that he was not only a physically attractive man, but a physically competent one, too. And from the way he kissed, she guessed he was more than merely competent in bed.

Would she find out tonight? He'd said that if he told her the truth about how he came to Canada, this might be their last date. She already knew his history with his ex-wife and son. What could he possibly say that would be worse than that?

Caruso ran back to them, like he was checking on them or reporting in, and then took off again.

Maribeth slowed her horse and Mo did the same. When they were walking again, she said, "That's not going to get you out of telling the story."

"I figured you weren't a woman who gave up easily." He ran a hand through his wind-tousled hair. "Okay, so when Brooke and I got married, I moved in with her family. But we both pretty much still lived the lives we'd lived before. She hung out with her girlfriends. I hung out with guy friends, didn't hold a job, drank too much. Screwed around on her. Brooke and I fought, especially when I'd been drinking. She slapped me once and I grabbed her arm, twisted it, hurt her enough to leave bruises."

Maribeth stroked Campion's neck and kept quiet.

"Her dad gave me a talking-to. He drank, too. We even

drank together. It was our common interest, beer and a game on TV. But he'd never hurt a woman. He told me that if I was going to live under his roof, I had to grow up and shape up."

"So you left and came to Canada?"

He gave a rough laugh. "I left and joined the army."

"The army?" It was the last thing she'd expected him to say. "Seriously? I thought you didn't like taking orders."

"Yeah, well I was too dumb to realize how much of that there'd be. I thought it'd be exciting, edgy. There'd be weapons. Physical challenges. I was even crazy enough to think it'd be cool to see action overseas. Anyhow, I did make it through basic training, though it was touch and go. Meanwhile, Brooke had the baby and then she went back to school. Her mom looked after Evan." He broke off and glanced around. "Where's that damned dog?"

Maribeth had been so caught up in his story, she'd lost track of the animal.

"Caruso!" Mo called. A few seconds later, the dog bounded into sight and came to join them.

Maribeth gestured to another gate in the fence. "Let's go that way. It leads to Eagle Bluff. There's a nice view."

The two riders and the dog went through, and then she said, "Go on. What happened next?"

"There was this lieutenant. He was an asshole, and he was always in my face about something. Maybe I didn't bootlick enough for him, or maybe it was a racial thing, me being half Indo-American. I was chafing under all that discipline anyhow. Feeling resentful about the whole mess my life had turned into: a wife, a baby, the army. So I was like a powder keg ready to blow."

"And you did?"

He nodded. "One night at a bar. The lieutenant and me, we'd both been drinking. A lot. He pushed me around.

I pushed back. He called me a . . . well, it was a racist slur. That's when I snapped. I was holding a beer bottle and I whacked it against a table and threatened him with the broken bottle. It was stupid. Totally stupid. A couple guys grabbed me, pulled me away. I don't know whether I'd have cut the LT or not."

"My God, Mo." It was horrible, and thank heavens those two men had stopped him before it got even worse. "You were arrested?"

"I got loose from the two guys, and I ran. That sobered me up quick and I figured I'd be arrested, kicked out of the army, sent to jail."

"So what did you do?"

"Went to L.A. and got Brooke and Evan, which in hindsight was the worst thing I could've done for them. We ran some more. I found this group of anti-war activists. Talked to a woman there and spun her a story about how I'd enlisted and then seen the error of my ways and deserted. She got fake IDs and other documentation for us so we could come to Canada. She changed my name from Mohinder McKeen to Mo Kincaid. Through her contacts, she even found me a job in Red Deer, Alberta, in an auto repair shop."

"Wow." Maribeth knew her eyes must be round as saucers. "That's quite the story."

"The activist woman recommended that Brooke and I be careful about getting in touch with our families because Uncle Sam and the police would be looking for me. That didn't prove to be very hard because once our parents found out what I'd done, they didn't want anything to do with us."

"You were what, twenty-one then?"

He nodded.

"And Brooke was even younger. The two of you had

a baby and you were living in a strange place, a whole different country, with no family support. That must have been incredibly hard."

"Yeah, it was hard. Brooke was royally pissed off, and rightfully so."

"But she didn't leave you. And you didn't leave her."

"Guess we had some misguided sense of duty, of being a family."

Maribeth felt so blessed to have had such wonderful parents, even if they'd been taken from her far too early.

"Anyhow," Mo said, "to finish the story. Seven or eight years ago, I found a lawyer on the Internet and said I wanted to turn myself in. She represented me, contacted the military authorities, and negotiated a kind of plea bargain. I had to pay a fine and I got an administrative discharge."

Past mistakes could never be undone, but Mo had done the right thing in the end, as he was trying to do with Brooke and Evan.

They'd reached the foot of Eagle Bluff, and Maribeth turned Campion onto the zigzag trail that led up the increasingly rocky incline. The dirt-and-rock path through scrubby trees was narrow and they had to ride single file. Mo brought Daybreak in behind her and Caruso ran ahead. They didn't talk for the five minutes it took to ride to the top of the bluff. Maribeth thought about the young couple: the pretty, immature blond girl who had within her the seeds of alcoholism and bipolar disorder; the unhappy, rebellious boy who hadn't found a place in the world where he fit. If they'd been more careful about contraception, who knew what their lives might have been? But then there wouldn't have been Evan.

When they reached the summit, Maribeth dismounted,

tied the bay's reins to one of the scraggly trees, and patted the horse's neck.

Mo, still quiet, did the same with Daybreak, and Caruso ran off to wherever his nose led him.

Maribeth walked to the edge of the bluff and gazed out at the view. It always reminded her of a crazy quilt. Each time she saw it, the patterns and shades were different. Today, under a snow-cloud sky, the colors were saturated and intense. The wooded areas were a particularly dark green, the lakes and streams held the charcoal gleam of graphite, and the dried-out grasslands had the burnished glow of old gold.

Mo had come up beside her and she was aware of him standing there, silent, staring out at that same view. She wondered how he saw it. This was probably the first time he'd viewed the region from this perspective.

Perspective. So much in life depended on the perspective from which you viewed it. And depended also on the crazy quilt of circumstances that brought you to a particular moment in time.

When Mo turned to face her, she turned, too.

Grim-faced, he said, "Now you know the worst about me. I wasn't just an abusive husband and father, but an army deserter and fugitive." One corner of his mouth curled downward in a self-disparaging expression. "What do you think of me so far?"

"I was thinking that life's such a combination of circumstances."

"Huh?"

"I started dating when I was thirteen. I first had sex when I was sixteen. We used condoms, but they're not one hundred percent reliable, right? What would my life have been like if I'd gotten pregnant?" Now it was what she wanted most in the world, but in her teens she'd been nowhere near ready.

"What would the baby's father and I have done?" she went on. "Get married or break up? If we'd married, what chance would we have had of being happy? Of growing to love each other and building a good marriage, good careers, a happy family?" She waved a hand. "Yes, it can happen. But it seems to me, you and Brooke had the odds stacked against you. One stupid mistake, and the consequences were huge."

"Really huge," he said grimly. "But that didn't mean I had to be such a shit."

"No, it didn't. You didn't react well. But you were a kid, and it sounds to me like you didn't have a whole lot of helpful adult guidance."

He snorted. "Sounds like you've met my parents." Then he quickly added, "And that's blaming, which is wrong. I guess they tried their best, they were just such different people and had conflicting ideas of who they wanted me to be. None of which had anything to do with who I was and what I wanted. So I acted out. They tried to crack down harder and I rebelled even more."

She'd suspected something like that. "My parents were wonderful. That was a lucky circumstance for me." Reflecting, she said, "And sometimes even the unlucky ones result in amazing things."

"In my case, not so much."

She gazed into his eyes, which looked more jade than blue today, under that sullen sky. "Evan. He's an amazing man."

He swallowed. "Despite me."

"Perhaps. Still, he wouldn't exist but for you. And maybe he wouldn't have had the same drive and worked so hard if you and Brooke had been better parents."

"I hope I get to meet him. I hope he'll let me apologize."

"I hope so, too."

Mo reached a gloved hand toward her shoulder, and then let it fall again. "How about you, Maribeth? Now that you know all my dirty secrets, do you still want to spend time with me?"

"No one's perfect."

"Yeah, but I'm less so than most."

She considered. "Actually, I've dated worse."

"Jesus!" The exclamation burst out of him. "Like what, a sociopath?"

She gave a surprised laugh, and then sobered again. "No, but I've dated people who weren't honest. Who shaded their stories to always put themselves in the best light." She certainly couldn't accuse Mo of doing that.

"That's human nature, isn't it?"

"It's a natural instinct, I guess. We all want people to like and respect us. But I'm not a fan of 'little white lie' dishonesty."

"You never tell little white lies? Never tell a customer that she looks good in a dress when in fact it makes her look fat?"

"No, that would be wrong. Unfair to her, and bad business as well because she'd eventually figure it out herself. Oh, I'm polite. Like if a woman asks, and the dress actually does make her look fat, I'll say it's not the most flattering style or color for her, and I'll find something that suits her better." She considered. "Okay, I'm not totally opposed to the tiny deceptions that we use to make someone else feel better about themselves. What I don't like is when someone uses deception to make himself look better than he really is. Besides, it's a sign of low self-esteem. It means he thinks that the real him isn't good enough."

"In my case, that'd be the truth."

"Don't confuse the old you and the new you," she said, a touch of impatience in her voice. "You said you've changed." Her instincts told her it was true, and every hour she spent with him confirmed it. "If you'd gone to jail, you'd have been out years and years ago. Free to make a new start, to be a better person. Well, you didn't go to jail, but all the same you learned your lesson and have become a better person. Right?"

"Yeah," he agreed quietly.

She tilted her head up to him, seeing him against a backdrop of winter sky and thinking how ruggedly handsome he looked in that denim jacket, his hair stirring in the slight breeze. She'd ridden out here a number of times, sometimes with girlfriends, sometimes with friends' children, sometimes with boyfriends. With some of the adults, even the kids, she'd had some reasonably heavy conversations. There was something about horses and the outdoors that seemed to free constraints so people opened up.

But today felt different. Being with Mo made the familiar sights even more special, the same way the November lighting made the colors more intense. As for Mo opening up, he'd pretty much done that from the beginning, and this afternoon's revelation was the backstory to give context to the rest. Why had he told her?

"When you've been interested in other women," she said, "did you give them your whole history right up front?"

"Uh, no. But this is different."

"You mean because I know Brooke and Evan, and already knew a bit about their history?"

"Well, yeah, but . . ." He frowned.

"But what?"

His brow was still furrowed. "There's something different about you. About you and me."

Yes, there was. She was so relieved that he felt it, too. She cocked her head, the gesture asking him to go on.

"Before, it's been, like, I'll meet a woman in a bar. Maybe she's alone. Lonely, horny, just looking for a night's company. Or she's with a pack of girlfriends and they're all hustling guys, chalking up notches on their belts."

She knew what he was talking about, but she'd never done either of those things herself. For her it was never just about one night; it was always about getting to know a guy and see where things went. With some men, she ended up having sex. With others, the relationship never went there.

"It's like that two ships passing in the night thing," Mo said. "A little company, a little fun, then go our separate ways. No harm, no foul. I make it clear up front that that's how it's gonna be, and if somewhere along the line the woman starts trying to change the rules, I break it off."

"You don't date those women, you just hook up."

He nodded.

"When you first met me at the garage and flirted, you told me you didn't want to date. Then you brought flowers and when I said that it seemed like a date kind of thing, you said you might be reconsidering. And we both called this afternoon a date."

"I like spending time with you." He studied her, making her feel self-conscious. When she was cold, her cheeks always went pink, which was fine, but so did her nose, and she looked a little like Rudolph.

That didn't seem to put Mo off, though, because he said, "Yeah, I'm pretty sure we'd be hot in bed, but I like this, too. Going riding with you. I like drinking hot chocolate by the fire."

Trying to get a better understanding of how he felt

about her, she said, "Maybe you'd have liked doing those things with other women, too, if you'd given it a chance."

"Maybe. But nothing made me want to."

"And now?"

"You make me want to."

Ah, yes. The answer she'd been hoping for. His admission was a definite step in the right direction. She smiled up at him. "Good."

Earlier, he'd started to touch her, but then dropped his hand. Now he reached out to capture her shoulders in his gloved hands.

She stepped closer, putting a flirtatious gleam in her eye and a sexy tease in her voice when she asked, "What else do you want to do that I might like?"

Mo's face, so solemn and almost tortured when he'd been talking about his past, had lightened and now he grinned at her. "How about I show you?"

He kissed her, cold lips against cold lips, but warming so quickly. She sensed a new confidence in him. Maybe it came from having cleared his conscience by telling her his worst stories and finding that she accepted him. That she wanted him.

Which she most definitely did. She wrapped her arms around him and kissed him back without hesitation. When he probed the crease between her lips with his tongue, she opened and let him in. She met his tongue with her own, and the sexy dance made her moan.

She darted her tongue into his mouth, where the moist heat was such a sweet contrast to the crisp chill of the afternoon. Passion blazed through her, making her wish they were somewhere sheltered where they could rip off their coats and keep stripping off layers until they were naked.

Something brushed her face, tickling, but she didn't lift

a hand from his back to wipe it away. More tickles, and then Caruso's warbling howl cut the air.

Startled, she pulled away, feeling dazed.

Mo, running a hand through his hair, looked just as stunned.

She saw white splotches in his hair and she realized what had tickled her. "It's snowing!" A few small flakes drifted down, and even as she gazed up the flakes got bigger and more numerous.

Caruso howled again. The dog sat on his haunches a few feet away, muzzle lifted as he sang to the falling snow.

Maribeth caught a few lacy flakes on her tongue and laughed. "I love the snow, but we don't want to get caught out in a snowstorm. We'd better head back."

As they walked toward the horses, Mo slung his arm around her shoulders, making her feel feminine and protected. "I can think of other reasons for going back." His tone was suggestive. "Like a snow check on what we just got started. Unless, that is, you have plans for tonight."

"I have a big pan of lasagna in the fridge, all ready to bake." She'd made it that morning in hopes that the afternoon would go well.

"If that's an invitation, I won't say no." He hugged her closer. "I'm sure we can find some way of passing the time while it cooks."

Chapter Seven

When Maribeth pulled her car into her garage, what Mo wanted most was to be alone with her. And yet there was Caruso to deal with. Glancing at the dog, who sat in the back looking out, he saw that the animal's coat was dry. Outside, it was still snowing, quite heavily now. "I'd hate to see Caruso go running off in the snow."

"Oh no, he shouldn't be out in this," Maribeth agreed. "Do you think he'd come in the house?"

"That'd be okay with you?"

"I like Caruso, and he seems to have good manners. We could keep him in the kitchen."

He had his doubts that the dog would be amenable, but he said, "Let's give it a try. But roll down the garage door before we let him out."

She used the remote to do so, and then they both climbed out of the car and Mo let the dog out. Caruso sniffed his way around the garage, which was neatly organized. Shelving along one side held lidded plastic tubs with labels, the other side had folded-up garden furniture as well as a cord or so of split-up firewood, and at the end opposite the roll-up door there were tools and gardening stuff.

Maribeth opened the door that led into the house. "Come on in, you two."

Mo accepted the offer, but Caruso came only as far as the doorway. He glanced inside, then up at Mo and Maribeth, and then he backed away.

"Maybe we could make him a bed in the garage," Maribeth suggested. "I could leave the door open enough that he could get out."

In the car, she'd pulled off her hat and run a hand through her hair, getting rid of hat-hair and tousling the glossy red waves. She looked mussed, flushed, gorgeous, and desirable—but at the moment more concerned about the singing dog than interested in flirting with Mo. Somehow that made her even more appealing.

"It's nice of you to want to look after him."

"Of course I do. He's your dog." Humor gleamed in her eyes. "Don't bother denying it."

"We're . . ." He hunted for the right word. The concept of ownership likely wouldn't sit any better with Caruso than it did with Mo. "Kind of pals, I guess."

"You know, I may have a better idea for your pal. There's a sun porch out back that would be cozier."

Mo wasn't so sure that "cozy" was what Caruso was looking for, but the dog could make up his own mind. "Let's see if we can get him to give it a try." He'd like to get the dog safely settled and be free to enjoy some one-on-one time with Maribeth.

She stepped through the door into the house and went down the hall, where she opened another door and clicked on a light. "Come on, Caruso, see what you think."

The dog stared toward her, and then up at Mo.

Leaving him there, with the door to the garage open,

Mo followed Maribeth. The sun porch was a glassed-in room running the length of the back of the house. A rattan couch and chairs had tie-on cushions upholstered in a faded green-and-purple striped fabric. He imagined Maribeth sitting here on a sunny day, maybe reading a book, drinking some girlie drink. Even with the snow coming down outside, the room looked welcoming. “Okay if we open the outside door a crack?” he asked.

“Good idea.” She stepped over to do it.

Mo turned back to the dog, who hadn’t budged from his spot in the garage. “It’s nice. Come take a look.”

Body radiating skepticism, Caruso stepped cautiously down the hall and into the sunroom. He went immediately to the door leading outside and stuck his head through the crack. Apparently satisfied that he could get out if he wanted to, he pulled his head back and explored the room. As he did, Maribeth took a colorful cotton blanket out of a rattan cabinet. She tucked it into one of the chairs and patted the seat. “How’s that look, Caruso?”

The dog came over, sniffed the blanket, and then hopped onto the chair and curled up.

Maribeth beamed. “Good boy. Wait a minute and I’ll bring you some water and food.”

In the hall, she closed the door to the sunroom, hung her and Mo’s coats—dry now, thanks to the car heater—in a closet, and set her boots on a mat.

Mo pulled off his boots, too, and put them beside hers. Sock-footed, he followed her to the kitchen.

“I roasted a chicken yesterday,” she said, opening the fridge, “thinking it’d give me leftovers for lunch salads and sandwiches. Do you think he’d like chicken?”

“I’d bet on it.”

Working together, they filled one bowl with water

and another with scraps of chicken. The meat smelled so delicious, Mo couldn't resist sneaking a few bites himself.

When they took the meal out to the sunroom, Caruso first lapped water eagerly and then set in to devour the chicken.

Mo looked from the dog to Maribeth, who leaned against the door frame smiling at the animal.

She caught Mo looking and turned her smile on him. "He can stay here tonight if he wants." She took a step toward him. "It's shaping up to be nasty out there."

Listening to the snow—more like sleet now—rattling against the roof, he said, "It is."

"Seems like a pity for any warm-blooded creature to go out in it." There was a sexy purr in her voice. "If he doesn't have to."

Did she mean him? Was that an invitation to spend the night? Throat dry, he said, "It does seem like a pity." It wasn't so much the thought of walking home through a snowstorm that was on his mind, but the image of curling up in bed next to Maribeth's warm curves. Of waking in the middle of the night to the sound of sleet against the window, and rolling into her for some slow, thorough lovemaking.

He wasn't a guy who spent the night. He was always out of bed and on his way long before dawn. It avoided giving the wrong impression; avoided complications. But like he'd told her earlier, with Maribeth everything was different.

She captured his hand and tugged him out of the sunroom, closing the door behind them. "I turned the stove on. I'll put the lasagna in, and then I'm going to swap my outdoor clothes for something more comfortable."

Lingerie? That was often what women meant when they said "something comfortable." The red-blooded male part of Mo hoped it'd be lingerie, but to his surprise another part of him vetoed the idea. For once, he wasn't in a blazing hurry to skip the obligatory chitchat and get to the sex. With Maribeth, he found something appealing about anticipation—about having dinner, conversation, and then some lazy foreplay, perhaps in front of the fire-place. "How about I get a fire going?" he asked.

"That would be great." Standing in the hallway, she squeezed his hand. "I have a sense that you're pretty good at lighting fires, Mo Kincaid."

Taking that as a hint, he leaned down and kissed her, tasting welcome and eagerness on her full lips. Heat surged through his blood, a dark urge to abandon any thought of anticipation and to drive toward the goal, right here and now in this hallway. He forced himself to pull away and say lightly, "I'll give it my best shot, Ms. Scott."

Laughing, she walked down the hall and turned into the kitchen.

With a grin on his face, he headed down the hall in the opposite direction, passing a half-open door to the dining room and a couple of closed doors.

"Oh," her voice followed him, "I forgot to say, there's a powder room off the hall."

"Thanks."

In the living room, he saw the flowers he'd brought over a few nights ago sitting in pride of place on the center of the coffee table, holding up pretty well. Maribeth had filled the wood box on the hearth, so it was an easy matter to set a fire and get it going. He brought in more wood, then washed up in the powder room and pulled off the heavy navy sweater he wore over a plaid shirt made of lightweight flannel.

He was checking out the books on her shelves—mostly romance novels and travel stories—when she returned.

No, she wasn't wearing lingerie, but she looked plenty sexy in clingy black leggings with a slim-fitting shirt worn loose over them. The shirt was a deep purple, shiny and silky-looking. Her dangly gold earrings had sparkly purple stones. On her feet were the puppy-dog slippers.

"Would you like a drink?" she asked. "There's a sparkling orange drink that I find really refreshing."

"That sounds good. By the way, if you want to drink beer or wine, don't stop on my behalf." Any time he craved the taste of an ice-cold beer, he remembered all the times that drinking had been coupled with anger and violence, and that killed the urge.

"Thanks, but I don't." She returned with two glasses of something orange and fizzy, and handed him one.

He took a swallow. "This is good."

She kicked off her slippers and curled up on the sofa beside him. The polish on her toenails and fingernails was pink today.

For the next little while, they talked about how the town had changed over the past couple of decades. It seemed that she, like him, was in no hurry to push things along. If she'd meant what she'd hinted, about him staying the night, they had hours and hours to work their way toward the endgame.

Still, he was totally aware of her. Of each time she shifted position, of the way her shirt draped her breasts, of that row of buttons down the front, of the fresh, herbal scent that drifted his way.

When a timer went off down the hall, she gracefully unfolded her legs and stood, sliding into her slippers again. "I'll take the lasagna out, and it should sit for a few minutes. That'll give us time to throw together a salad."

Clearly she expected him to help. He had no issue with that. It was the least he could do, considering that she'd prepared the lasagna that scented the kitchen with a rich, meaty aroma.

Following instructions, he ripped lettuce and chopped tomatoes and yellow peppers while she put oil, vinegar, and dried herbs in a bottle and shook them up. She snipped some leaves from a basil plant growing on the windowsill and cut them up into the salad.

"We could eat in the kitchen or dining room," she said, "but it's so nice by the fire."

"Sounds good to me."

They set everything out on the coffee table, and while he put another log on the fire, she turned on some music. When he heard instrumental light jazz, he said, "I was expecting country music."

She shrugged. "I like—"

He held up a hand, cutting her off. "Variety. Yeah, I get it."

They sat side by side on the sofa and dished out the food.

They didn't talk a lot while they ate, which was fine with Mo. He'd never been a big conversationalist, and he was busy enjoying the wonderful food. Riding in the snow had whetted his appetite. He liked it that Maribeth seemed content with his company and didn't feel the need to babble about herself or to probe him with questions. The jazz felt a little sophisticated for him, like it should be playing in a club where people were dressed up, drinking fancy drinks. All the same, it danced seductively in his ears, kind of intriguing compared to the country music and classic rock he was more familiar with.

After he had seconds of the lasagna and Maribeth finished off the salad, they put the leftovers in the fridge and the dishes in the dishwasher.

"Raisin pie?" she asked.

"Thanks, but I'm stuffed."

She refreshed their drinks and then they settled back on the sofa. He put his arm around her shoulders and she leaned into him. Her head on his shoulder felt so good, as did her hand on his thigh. She'd turned the lights off, and firelight flickered off the glass of the framed photographs.

"You take holidays to all those places," he said, "and you read travel stories. Yet you seem happy living here in Caribou Crossing."

"I am. I was born here and have never wanted to live anywhere else."

"Your parents were natives, too?"

"No. Mom was from Vancouver and Dad from Victoria. They met at university and dated while she studied dentistry and he got his doctorate in civil engineering. They got married, looked for jobs, and he got an offer with the township of Caribou Crossing. They moved here, she set up a practice, and they fell in love with the place."

"Why do you enjoy travel? Is it your thing about liking variety?"

"I guess. It's fun to see other places and learn about them. To get a different, broader perspective. I learned that from my parents."

"You go to those places alone?"

"Sometimes alone, sometimes with a friend."

A man friend? That idea shouldn't bother him, yet somehow it did.

"Are you into travel?" she asked. "You said that when you and Brooke were married, you moved around a lot."

"I had a restless nature and Brooke complained about every place we lived. I'd lose a job or we'd get kicked out of a rental place, or the police would nab us for being drunk and disorderly, and it'd be time to move on. Since then . . ." He tilted his head, gazing at the fire and reflecting.

"I wouldn't say I have the travel bug. I've never been anywhere other than L.A. and Canada. I wouldn't mind, but I never felt the need. But I also never lived in a place that I really liked. The longest I've stayed anywhere was in Regina, and that was because I had a good job."

"How long were you in Caribou Crossing, before?"

He thought back. "Three or four years. That was a record for us, and it happened because of Brooke. The first year Evan was in school, we moved a couple times. Then Brooke said he needed stability. We couldn't keep picking up and leaving whenever the fancy took us. She was a better parent than me." He shook his head, remembering. "It sure wasn't that she liked the town. Called it Hicksville. Evan picked that up from her. I still find it hard to believe that she stayed here."

"It grew on her, I guess." Maribeth leaned back slightly, tipping her head up to look at him. "How long do you see yourself staying this time, Mo? If things work out with Brooke and Evan . . ."

"That's a big *if*, given that Evan hasn't even agreed to see me."

"If he doesn't agree in a week or so, are you going to pack up and leave?"

"No." He stroked her shoulder, liking the silky slide of her shirt over the warm skin beneath. "That first time I talked to you, if you'd said it would be a terrible idea for me to approach Brooke and Evan, I might have listened to you and gone. Might have. I needed to figure out what was the decent, responsible thing to do. But now I've talked to Brooke, and it seems to me that turned out to be a good thing for both of us. We'll see each other again, I hope. Take it slow."

"And Evan?"

"I'll wait for a while. See what happens." He gave a wry smile. "He'll get curious."

"How do you feel about having a couple of grandchildren?"

"Can't really get my head around that one," he confessed. "The years I've been away, fixing cars, moving from place to place, it doesn't feel like enough time for me to get old enough to have a grown-up son and grandkids. It's like, I'd have to see them to believe it." A sour pang twitched his gut. "And even if Evan does bring himself to talk to me, I can't see him allowing me to meet his kids. Not after the crap I threw his way."

She gazed steadily into his eyes. "He had some pretty harsh feelings about Brooke, too. It took him a while to trust her, but now she's always babysitting the grandchildren."

Having met the new Brooke, Mo could picture that.

After a moment, Maribeth leaned her head back on his shoulder. "Do you like children, Mo?"

"Oh, man." She did ask some humdinger questions. "I haven't had much to do with them. Guess I've avoided it, since Evan." The truth was, he'd avoided relationships, period. He'd become closer to Maribeth—and even old Hank at the garage—in the week he'd been in Caribou Crossing than he'd gotten to anyone in his five years in Regina.

"But you're not the same man," she said. "You wouldn't hit a child now." She paused. "Would you?"

"God, no. Never. But that doesn't mean I'd be good with kids. Or relate to them."

She made one of those confusing female sounds that could have been "mmm" or "hmm." After a swallow of her orange drink, she said, "But you'd like to meet your grandchildren if you could."

"I guess," he admitted slowly. "Like I said about Evan, I'm curious. Tempted, even. But what's the point of feeling that way when it's not likely to happen?"

"It might."

A remote possibility, and he wasn't going to waste energy thinking about it. He had hoped that tonight would involve more kisses, maybe even sex, and this conversation sure wasn't getting them there. "How about," he said, "we stop talking about my failings and things that aren't likely to happen." Casting about for a change of subject, his gaze lit again on her photographs. "Why don't you tell me about one of those places you've been and what you liked about it?"

"Or," she said.

"Or what?"

"Or I could tell you what I like about you."

"That's going to be a short conversation," he said wryly.

Chuckling, she pulled away and shifted position to kneel on the couch, resting her hands on his shoulders as she gazed into his face. "I like your eyes, which right now are glinting with blue and green flecks like a stream in dappled sunshine."

Figured she'd pick a physical attribute. Women had always liked how he looked. Still, he wasn't about to complain when Maribeth was all but in his lap.

She ran her fingers through his hair. "I like your hair, so black and glossy like a raven's wings, with those silver threads for contrast, and I like how long and curly it is. It makes your face look even more masculine in comparison. And speaking of masculine"—she gripped his shoulders more tightly—"I like all the muscles. I like how tall you are—"

"I'm not that tall." Only five feet eleven.

"To a woman who exaggerates when she says she's

five-four, you're tall." Her gaze roamed over his face. "Yes, I definitely like the way you look, Mo. But that's only part of it. I like how you are with Caruso. You're patient and you respect him. You care about him."

"Crazy dog seems to have adopted me," he grumbled.

Her lips twitched. "And vice versa. I also like how . . . earnest you are."

"Earnest? What the hell does that mean?" No one had ever called him earnest before.

"You don't know all the answers and—"

"You can say that again."

"But you admit it, and you're trying. You've already come so far in redeeming yourself, but you know there's more you want to do. You're trying to figure out how to do it."

He frowned, puzzled. "Yeah, but I can't see why you'd like that. I mean, as compared to a guy who's got everything figured out and is a success."

"I've dated that kind of man. You're more interesting."

"Huh." Who'd have guessed?

She shifted so that now she straddled his thighs. "Now tell me what you like about me."

He should've known that one was coming. How was he supposed to think with her firm, warm, curvy body in such an intimate position? But he tried, and after a moment, said, "I like how you see me. How you give me the benefit of the doubt. I like how confident you are. You know what you like, you know what you want, and I respect that. I like how smart you are, and how you care about people." He smiled a little. "And about dogs."

He settled his hands on her waist, feeling the flare of her hips. "And yeah, I sure like how you look. I like how you smell and how feminine you are. I like that you go riding in the snow and that you make terrific lasagna."

Gazing at her beautiful face, he said, "I like your eyes. Green like springtime. And your nose, with that uptilt at the end. And your lips. Man, I dream about those lips." Not to mention about her breasts and hips, but maybe better not to say that. "I dream about kissing those lips."

He made his dream come true by urging her closer until their lips touched.

He knew the shape of her mouth now, though each time he kissed her, her taste was different. That afternoon, she'd tasted of fresh air, and now her flavor was oranges combined with Italian seasonings.

Arousal, desire, need, they all pulsed through him. Beneath his fly, he hardened, and it was all he could do to keep from pulling her forward that extra couple of inches to rub against him. He wanted Maribeth. Wanted sex with her. But even more than that, he wanted to give her pleasure.

He eased away from the kiss and studied her. Red waves of hair tumbled around her face and onto the shoulders of her shirt. The top two or three buttons were undone, and her skin looked so creamy against the deep purple fabric. He touched his finger to that smooth skin, knowing that his fingertip must feel rough to her. But then a little bit of rough wasn't always a bad thing.

She didn't seem to think so because she arched into him as he caressed her chest. Her full breasts thrust forward, a temptation no man in his right mind could resist. Mo slipped the next button free from its hole and spread her shirt open wider to reveal a shadowed line of cleavage.

Another button. Curves of creamy skin decorated with a band of pink lace. He traced the line where her bra touched her flesh, and she gave a murmur of approval.

"You're two buttons ahead," she said.

He glanced from her breasts to her face and saw mischief glint in her eyes.

"Didn't think you were shy," he teased back. "But if you need an invitation, I'm issuing one."

She let out a throaty chuckle and then applied her pink-tipped fingers to the buttons of his shirt. When she spread the top of his shirt, she didn't run a gentle, exploring finger over him the way he'd done with her. Instead, she touched his chest with both hands, fingers spread wide and palms pressing into him like she wanted to encompass as much of him as her small hands were capable of.

Oh my, he feels good. Maribeth didn't move her hands. She left them where she'd first spread them, and catalogued each sensation. Skin so hot it almost scorched her flesh, carrying the hint of a soapy scent. Crisp curls of hair. Solid muscle beneath. Under her right palm, the racing thud of his heart.

Her own was zipping along just as fast, and need pulsed in her feminine core. She wanted this man, the one whose solid jean-clad thighs she straddled. It almost scared her how much she wanted him. Was the "click" she felt just hormones, maybe crying out that this was her last chance at finding a non-sperm-donor father for her baby? Or just maybe, was Mo the love of her life?

Was he Mr. Right, or all wrong for her? He said he didn't want marriage and kids, the things she most desired. But she sensed that he was partway stuck in the past, still thinking of himself as the man who trod lightly, when really he was a guy who truly wanted to connect: with his ex, his son, his grandkids; with a singing dog and old Hank Hennessey. With her. After all, they were dating, and he'd admitted it was a first for him.

She took a deep breath. Since when was Maribeth Scott scared of anything?

Her philosophy on relationships was to never look too far ahead, to never guess the ending because that could not only ruin the fun but also turn into a self-fulfilling prophecy. She shouldn't act any differently with Mo.

And so she took what she wanted and ripped into the rest of his buttons, then tugged his shirt out of his jeans—sucking in a heated breath when she took in the size of the erection that pressed against the denim—and then she tried to pull his shirt off his shoulders. His arms were trapped in the sleeves, but she succeeded in baring his shoulders, chest, and rippled abs. Murmuring approval, she saw that his body was beautiful in a purely masculine way that attested to not only great genes but hard physical labor. So much more appealing than the gym rats she'd dated on occasion, the ones who were more concerned about their own physical appearance than hers.

Mo, on the other hand, seemed very interested in her body. While she ran her hands over him, marveling at the strength of his shoulders and the firmness of his pecs, he undid the rest of her buttons, spread her shirt, and gazed at the plump mounds of her breasts as they strained against her pink satin-and-lace bra.

"My God, woman," he said roughly. "You're one fine sight."

"You could try touching them, too," she said, aiming for saucy but finding that her breath caught when she imagined his deft, rough-skinned hands teasing her nipples.

"Oh, I plan to. And tasting them as well. All in good time."

She wanted that time to come *soon*, please.

As if he'd heard her silent plea, he cupped one of her breasts, squeezing it gently through her bra, molding it until the nipple peaked and pressed painfully against the satin. He did the same with the other breast. Voice scraping, he said, "I need to see you."

He reached under the back of her shirt, found the clasp of her bra, and unfastened it. Her breasts were large enough, firm enough, to hold the sagging fabric in place.

Maribeth took her hands off his chest long enough to free herself from her shirt and then her bra, tossing them aside to land wherever they might. When she straightened, Mo's eyes were huge, staring at her naked breasts.

"Wow," he said reverently. "You are so damned beautiful." He reached out, but to her surprise he didn't clasp her breast. Instead, he fingered the wavy hair that tumbled across the top of her chest. He stroked the red curls aside, his fingertips sensually abrasive, like a cat's tongue but far sexier. His fingers drifted down, across the upper curve of her breast, into the cleavage, down around the bottom curve where she knew he'd find a dew of sweat. And then those provocative fingers came up to circle her areola and brush her budded nipple.

She gasped at the pleasure and arched, offering more, asking for more.

He took his time with one breast, and the tingly ache in her nipple was echoed between her legs. When he moved to her other breast, she couldn't stop herself from squirming needily against him.

"I want you," she said, as if her movements didn't make it entirely obvious. She wanted everything. Wanted his erotic touch, everywhere. Wanted to explore every inch of his naked body. Wanted him inside her, driving the ache even higher and then taking her over the top all the way to release. She was full of hunger, of greed. She wanted it now, all at once. But that was impossible, and so she groaned in frustration.

His hands caught her waist, holding her firmly. He urged her to her feet, and her legs were almost too wobbly to hold her upright. But it didn't matter. He shrugged his shirt all the way off and then hooked one arm around her back and the other under her knees and lifted her. Was he going to carry her all the way upstairs to the bedroom?

But no, he walked only a few steps, to the abstract-patterned area rug in front of the fire. He bent, lay her down, and kneeled beside her. Hooking his hands in the hip-hugging waistband of her leggings, he asked, "Okay?"

"Oh, yes," she said gratefully, knowing that what she was really saying yes to was sex.

He peeled the leggings down, leaving her clad only in a pink thong.

He was staring at her body, which left her free to study his face. His expression was intent, all hard lines except for his sensual lips, which were parted. A flush burned on his dark cheekbones, and his eyes glittered fiercely.

Without taking his eyes off her, he undid his brown leather belt. The fastenings of his jeans came next and she waited, breathless, her sex throbbing.

He paused to pull a condom packet from his jeans and tossed it on the rug, and then yanked the jeans down his hips. Taking his underwear—if he'd been wearing any—with them.

She'd never seen anything as sexy as Mo Kincaid naked in the firelight. He had a stunning body. Broad shoulders, slim hips, long legs, everything perfectly muscled in a lean, rangy way she found very appealing. He was the yang to her soft, curvy yin.

As for his impressive erection, it made her mouth water and her sex weep with need.

Mo took a green throw pillow from the couch and came down beside her on the rug, tucking the pillow under her head. He leaned over to kiss her and she raised her arms, looping them around his neck.

The kiss was slow and seductive, and when it ended she said, "Well, here we are."

"There's no place in the world I'd rather be," he said a little gruffly, as if it was a difficult thing to admit.

"Me either."

He raised himself a little, causing her arms to drop, and then he leaned over, curving his hand around her breast and plumping it up as he put his lips to her nipple. With flicks of his tongue and gentle sucks, he had her squirming with pleasure.

After taking his time with both breasts, he moved down her body, touching and tasting, finding the places that made her gasp or moan. When she spread her legs for him, she knew he'd discover that the crotch of her thong was soaked.

He stroked it with firm fingers and licked through it, adding his dampness to hers and pulling more from her body as she pressed against him seeking release.

Without even removing her thong, he used his fingers and mouth to take her to the peak, and then he tipped her over into a shuddering orgasm.

Only then did he pull the final garment from her body.

When he reached out for the condom packet, she found the energy to force her quivering body to sit up. She took the condom from him. "Let me."

She curled one hand around his shaft and he groaned. "Don't mess with me, Maribeth. I've waited long enough."

Hearing the need in his ragged voice, she relented. "Okay, but I reserve the right to mess with you later." She smoothed on the condom. "No more waiting, Mo." She lay back on the rug, raising her knees and opening them in an age-old invitation.

He came down between her legs, capturing her hands in his and stretching over her, lowering their clasped hands to the rug behind her head. The front of his body brushed hers, his hard pecs pressing into the softness of her breasts and his hips seeking the cradle of hers. The tip of his penis brushed her entrance, and even though she'd just climaxed, arousal coursed through her again.

Mo pushed into her slowly, giving her time to adjust. Her body stretched, encompassing him eagerly. She thrust her hips forward, wanting more. He gave it to her, inch by inch, until their bodies were fully merged.

He kissed her then, hungrily, his lips taking hers as her body strained upward, into him, urging him to pump his hips. She nipped his bottom lip and he gave a rough laugh. And then, finally, he began to thrust in and out, long strokes that made her wrap her legs around him, lifting her lower body higher, clinging to him and crying, "Oh God, yes, Mo."

His movements quickened and she felt tension in every part of him, from the strong hands that clasped hers to the lean hips that jerked forward, back, and forward again. The fact of their stretched arms and clasped hands somehow heightened the focus on where their bodies joined, and on each intense movement.

"So good," he muttered. "So damn good."

She rocked against him so that, with his every stroke, his shaft nudged her clit. Tension mounted inside, so delicious, almost unbearably delicious. She couldn't stand it any longer, not without breaking. And then everything came together exactly right and she did break, giving a high, wordless cry of pure physical pleasure as her body spasmed around him.

Mo groaned, a guttural, wrenching sound, and then he was coming, too, his forceful strokes prolonging her orgasm.

As the spasms faded, their bodies softened into each other, melding in a different way as he sank down on top of her. For long minutes they simply breathed, chests pressing together, breath whispering against each other's cheeks.

He released her hands and she hugged her arms around him, stroking down his back, curving one hand around a firm butt cheek.

When she felt his muscles gather as he started to raise himself off her, she tightened her hold on him. "Don't go."

"Don't want to crush you."

"You won't. I'm stronger than I look."

He chuckled, his body relaxing again. "I felt that when you locked your legs around me."

"Yoga," she said smugly. "Works wonders for muscle tone, strength, and flexibility."

"If that's a commercial, you're selling me."

She chuckled. "I'd love to see you in yoga pants."

His body shook with laughter. "You see me like that, I might have to kill you."

"I think you just did. The little death, isn't that what the French call it?"

"I dunno, but what a way to go." He lifted himself up on his elbows. "Seriously, Maribeth, I need to get up and deal with the condom."

"Oh, right." She released him so he could pull out and roll off her. Usually, she was a practical woman, but tonight she'd forgotten all about that detail. An especially critical detail now, since she was no longer on birth control. After all, she thought wryly, she wouldn't want to get pregnant—even though having a baby was the one thing she most desired, and she was sure she and Mo would make an amazing one. But it wouldn't be right. She'd never do that to a guy.

"Fire's burned down," he pointed out. "Want me to put more wood on it, or . . . ?"

"What's the weather doing?" she asked, sitting up.

He walked to the window, unself-conscious in his nakedness, moving with easy masculine grace. When he pulled back the edge of the curtain, he said, "Snowing heavily. Rough guess, there's a good eight inches so far."

"Snowed in," she said. "You should stay. You and Caruso. Maybe you should check on him, Mo."

"Good idea."

As he left the room, she rose, took the multicolored afghan from the back of a chair and wrapped it around herself, and then went to look out the window. The falling snow was thick enough that she could barely see the street-lights, but they did add a golden glow that gave the scene a sense of serenity.

She was still by the window, smiling as she watched the snow come down, when Mo returned. "Is Caruso okay?" she asked.

"Curled up all warm in his bed. And speaking of warm, you never answered my question about the fire."

"Yes, let's get it going again, and I'll make hot chocolate. This is the first big snowfall of the year, and snuggling up in front of the fire seems like exactly the right way to celebrate it."

"But no Christmas music, right?" he teased. "Because it's not December yet."

"Laugh all you want," she said without rancor. "My way makes sense." She poked her feet into her slippers and, clad only in them and the afghan, went down the hall.

Peeking into the sunroom, she saw Caruso just where

Mo had said he was. The dog raised his head, saw her, and rested his chin back down on his paws.

"Sleep tight," she murmured.

In the kitchen, she hummed as she set about making the drinks. Riding, brisk air, a hearty meal, the fire, and fantastic lovemaking had conspired to make her feel tired yet very content. What a lovely day, and Mo was a huge part of it. Being with him was invigorating and satisfying, and felt just plain right.

But that was dangerous thinking. She didn't want to get ahead of herself.

At least no further than spending the night together and waking up together in the morning.

Chapter Eight

Mo felt surprisingly at home on Monday morning, wearing yesterday's clothes and pouring orange juice in Maribeth's kitchen. She, looking cute in a forest-green bathrobe, wearing glasses, her hair skewered into a messy pile atop her head, cracked eggs into a bowl. It had stopped snowing sometime in the night after having deposited several inches, and the white world outside was dazzling in the sunshine.

He'd spent the night. After hot chocolate and fire watching, he and Maribeth had made love on the rug again, under the afghan. They'd checked on Caruso and then gone upstairs to spend the night in her comfy queen-sized bed. There'd been more lovemaking in the middle of the night, and then lazy, laughing wake-up sex before they got up.

"Coffee ready?" Maribeth asked.

He checked the machine. "Yup. If you can call that stuff coffee." She'd insisted on making decaf.

"Feel free to brew yourself a separate pot of regular coffee if you need the caffeine."

Pouring two mugs, he said, "After last night, I almost

do. But I guess bacon and eggs will get me going." She had a big pan of bacon cooking, too. "What do you take in your coffee?"

"A splash of milk. I need some for the scrambled eggs, too."

He doctored her coffee and then handed her the milk jug. She added some to the eggs, whisked, and then poured the mixture into a frying pan.

She looked like every guy's fantasy of a sexy librarian or schoolmistress in those glasses. After the number of orgasms he'd had in the past twelve hours, he'd have thought his body was immune to arousal, but now it proved him wrong, stirring to life.

"You're giving me that slow, lazy grin," she said.

"That what?"

"That utterly devastating smile. Don't tell me you don't know when you're doing it and don't know the effect it has."

He bit back another grin. Mostly, he didn't think about it; he just smiled when he felt like it—which, until he'd met her, hadn't been often. But yeah, he'd been known to use a smile deliberately, like when he'd asked the lady bus driver to make an unscheduled stop.

"So, what're you smiling about this time?" she asked.

"I'm not used to you in glasses."

"I don't put in my contacts until my eyes are awake. What, you don't like glasses?"

"I do. They're sexy." Behind the lenses, those stunning green eyes looked even larger.

She rolled her eyes and then turned her attention back to the eggs and bacon.

Watching her cook, Mo felt something more than arousal. Something deep in his bones—contentment, maybe?—that he didn't recall ever feeling before. Almost like he was a man who had the capacity to be happy. It was a feeling he didn't quite trust. After all, what right did a guy like him have to happiness?

"There's bread in the bread box," she said over her shoulder. "Can you get some toast going? I'll dish out Caruso's breakfast and you can put it in the sunroom." When they'd checked earlier, he'd still been curled contentedly in his blanket nest.

By the time Mo had put a couple of slices of seed-studded bread into the toaster, Maribeth had a bowl full of scrambled eggs and crumbled bacon ready. "Maybe the snow will turn Caruso into a homebody," she said, handing it to Mo.

"Guess we'll see." He couldn't resist brushing a kiss against her delicate ear, exposed by her upswept hairdo. One day, he wanted to make love to her when she was dressed exactly like this. He wanted to kiss her ears and nape before freeing her hair to tumble down, and then he'd unwrap that body-concealing robe to reveal the beauty beneath. But he'd leave her glasses on and gaze at those huge green eyes as he thrust deep inside her.

Those eyes stared into his right now, glittering, and the flush on her cheeks suggested she might be thinking something similar.

The toaster popped with a ping. Maribeth gave a sort of shiver-shrug and said, "Breakfast's ready."

Mo hurried to take the food to the sunroom, where he found the door open a wider crack and no sign of Caruso but for a haphazard path in the snow.

Leaving the food, Mo returned to the kitchen, where Maribeth had served up two plates of eggs and crisply fried strips of bacon and was buttering the toast. After she seated herself at the kitchen table, Mo sat across from her. The table was wooden, maybe oak, and battered enough to have character. On it were bright woven place mats and pots of jam and honey. It was homey, which was a rare and unexpectedly pleasant experience for Mo.

He spread blackberry jam on his toast and dug into the meal. After a few delicious bites, he said, "I'll shovel your driveway and front walk so you can get out."

"That would be very nice. Not that I couldn't do it myself, of course."

"Yeah, yeah. I know. You're . . . what was it? Strong and toned and flexible? Of course, if you want to prove it by doing the shoveling yourself—"

He broke off, laughing, when she reached across the table to swat his arm.

"It would be a big help if you did it," she said. "Days of Your is closed on Mondays, which means it's chore day, and I have a bunch of things to get done."

"Will the roads be plowed?"

"Yes. We're used to snow here, even if this is the first biggie of the year. The main roads will be plowed by now and they'll be working on the residential streets so everyone can get to work and school. Are you working today?"

"Hank's open six days a week and he said he'd take Saturdays and Sundays off if I took Sundays and Mondays. So technically, no. But I'm guessing the garage will be busy after the snow. Folks who haven't got their snow tires on yet, cars that won't start, a fender bender or two. Thought I'd drop over and offer him a hand."

"That's nice of you." She smiled at him and rose. "More toast?"

"Please. This sure is a fine breakfast."

She put more bread in the toaster, refilled their coffee mugs, and then brought two slices of toast to him along with the butter dish.

Once she was seated, finishing her breakfast, Mo asked, "So, uh, when will I see you again?"

"Not tired of me yet?"

"Nowhere near." Right now, it was difficult to imagine ever being tired of the multifaceted redhead.

"Well, I have plans tonight. At least if there isn't another dump of snow to clog up the roads."

"Oh?" It was none of his business.

"A few girlfriends are coming over." Her smile was gone and something tugged at the corner of her mouth: a hint of uncertainty, perhaps.

"Sounds like fun," he ventured.

"It will be." Her noncommittal tone didn't match up with her words. She picked up her juice glass and took a long swallow. "Then tomorrow night I'm babysitting for friends. You could come along, the kids are fun."

"Doesn't sound like my kind of thing."

She frowned slightly. "Okay."

They both ate in silence for a few minutes, and then he asked, "So maybe Wednesday night? I could take you out for dinner."

"I'd like that," she said quietly. Gazing across at him, she added, "We'll take it one day at a time, right? Our relationship, I mean."

"You mean no expectations? No, uh, specific goal in mind?"

"That's what you want, isn't it?"

It was his turn to frown. "You're okay with that, aren't you? I mean, I told you up front that I'm a 'tread lightly' kind of guy. I'm not good at relationships and I'm not looking for anything serious."

"That's what you said." Again she sounded noncommittal. "And yet you came to Caribou Crossing to see Brooke and Evan." She captured a wayward curl and tucked it back in the messy pile atop her head. "Speaking of which, have you arranged to see Brooke again?"

Had Maribeth just changed the subject? Well, at least he had made himself clear about not looking for anything serious, so he moved on and answered her question. "I called her and we talked about getting together for lunch one day this week. She said she'd check her schedule and e-mail me. I should drop by my apartment so I can check e-mail on my tablet." He should also shovel snow there, since his landladies were both in their eighties.

"If you got a phone, you could check e-mail on it."

"When I had a phone, the only people who ever called were telemarketers."

"Hank might need to get in touch," she said. Then her eyes crinkled. "Or who knows, someone might want to call you at night for phone sex."

He grinned. "Someone might?"

"You'll never know until you get a phone."

"I'll buy one today and let you know the number."

She put on an innocent expression, but her tone was teasing when she said, "You thought I was referring to myself?"

"You'd rather someone else called me for phone sex?"

She chuckled and then said, "Just to be clear. One day at a time and one partner at a time. Understood?"

"Works for me." Why would he want to be with another woman if he had Maribeth? Breakfast finished, he stood and went around the table, where he bent to kiss her soft temple. "If you do the dishes, I'll get going with the snow shovel."

She put her arm around his waist, holding him at her side as she looked up at him. "What are you going to do about Caruso? He can't sleep outside at the garage, not in the snow. I don't mind leaving the sunroom door open for him, but I'm guessing he'd rather be with you."

Mo scratched his head. "Crazy dog. Wish he'd just stay at the shelter."

"No, you don't."

"Maybe not," he admitted. "He does seem okay inside if the door's open a crack. Guess I could talk to my landladies, but I can't see them wanting a half-wild dog in their house."

"Landladies? House?" She cocked her head. "I assumed you were in an apartment building."

"No. It's a house owned by a couple of women in their eighties."

"Ms. Haldenby and her wife?"

Mo raised his eyebrows, and then said, "Small town, eh?"

"Ms. Haldenby was my fourth-grade teacher. She was everyone's fourth-grade teacher until she retired. She's, hmm . . ."

"Hmm?"

"When I was her student, I thought she was pretty strict, but later I realized how much I'd learned from her. Not just academically, but things about being a decent, productive person. She was, uh . . . principled, is a good word for it. But I admit that, even now that I'm an adult, she kind of scares me. She seems so starchy."

"She was a little starchy when they interviewed me," he agreed. "Ms. Peabody was more laid-back."

"A friend of mine, Cassidy, rented that apartment when she first came to Caribou Crossing. Now she's good friends with both the women. She says Ms. Haldenby is a compassionate woman who doesn't suffer fools gladly."

"Caruso may be crazy, but he's no fool. I wonder what the ladies would say about him?"

"You don't know until you ask. Take him over with you this morning and let them see how handsome he is. Maybe he'll sing for them and charm them." Her lips curved. "His singing tends to have the same effect as your smile. You and Caruso might want to go for a double whammy."

He chuckled. "Thanks for the advice." It seemed that whether he'd intended to or not, he'd acquired a dog and the responsibilities that went along with that. "Well, there's lots to do before I head over to the garage. I'd best get my butt in gear."

"Nice butt." She squeezed his jean-clad ass.

"Keep that up and your snow will never get shoveled."

Laughing, she pushed her chair back. "Just don't forget, in that long list of things to do today, that you need to buy a phone."

With phone sex as motivation, that was one task he wasn't likely to forget.

Late Wednesday afternoon, Maribeth primped in the bathroom at the back of Days of Your. Mo was taking her out for dinner and they'd decided that rather than both go home after work, he'd shower at Hennessey's and then come to her shop. This would be his first time here, and she'd spent almost as much time fussing over the displays of clothing, shoes, and jewelry as she had on figuring out what to wear. Not that Mo was even likely to notice the finer touches of a thrift shop, but Days of Your was her creation, and pride urged her to make it perfect—at least in her own eyes.

He would, however, definitely notice her. She'd made sure of that, changing from her more casual work garb into ivory-colored dress pants, cinnamon-colored boots, and a scoop-neck leopard print top that not only hugged her ample breasts but showed off her cleavage. She'd added dangly copper earrings and a wide copper bracelet, and painted her fingernails a deep, shimmery nutmeg brown.

Twenty minutes ago, she'd turned the sign on the shop door to the CLOSED side, so when she heard a firm knock on the glass, she figured it would be Mo.

Her heart raced as she hurried toward the door. She'd barely talked to him since Monday morning. Though he had bought a phone, the promised phone sex had yet to come about. Last night, she'd babysat until late, and with a couple of little kids asleep upstairs she hadn't felt right about calling Mo for sex.

And Monday night she'd been up late with her old girlfriends, gorging on her homemade brownies, catching up on everyone's news, and discussing the merits of various sperm donors. After much deliberation, Maribeth had decided that if she did proceed with insemination, the baby's biological father would be the family practitioner. He had all the good stuff—education, intelligence, health, physical attractiveness, and lack of medical problems—but in the end it was the warmth and compassion in his eyes that had tipped the scales over the extremely hot veterinarian. Dr. Jones had said that once Maribeth selected the donor, the clinic could put a rush order on the sperm, in hopes it would be there when she next ovulated.

Maribeth had instead, after considerable reflection, chosen to hold off for a month and see what happened between her and Mo. Although she hated to put off the opportunity to get pregnant, how could she opt for an anonymous donor when she felt so drawn to Mo? Even though at the moment, having another child seemed to be the last thing he wanted—or, at least, that he thought he wanted. Not to mention, she didn't yet know whether that magic click really did mean he was the love of her life. How, in such a short period of time, had her life become so complicated?

When she unlocked the door, Mo said, "Everything okay? You're frowning."

"Oh, sorry. Just . . . something on my mind." She shook her head, trying to rid it of her dilemma and to focus on the moment. And the man.

"Want to talk about it?" he asked, stepping inside and shrugging out of his denim jacket.

And have him turn tail and run? "No, thanks. It's, uh, female stuff."

"Okay. And wow, you look terrific."

He wore jeans, but not faded blue jeans; these were slim-fitting black ones. His blue cotton shirt looked crisp and new. The color contrasted well with his dark skin and brought out the blue in his multicolored eyes. No tie, but that was fine with her because she much preferred seeing the vee of firm chest. The belt was his usual brown leather one, but he'd traded his heavy work shoes for brown boots. She noticed something else different, too. "Did you get a haircut?" His hair was still long and wavy, but it looked even nicer than usual.

"Brooke."

He'd gone to the salon where anyone in town might see him and his ex together?

Reading her thought, he said, "Not where she works. At her house, in her kitchen. She said she'd rather not talk in public so she asked me over today, which was one of her days off." His mouth twisted with wry humor. "She served me a meat loaf sandwich, and when I thanked her, she said it was no big deal, just leftovers. Don't think she remembered, or maybe I never told her, but I like leftover meat loaf better than straight out of the oven."

"Why did she cut your hair?"

"She said it relaxed her."

That was probably true, but no doubt Brooke also knew that there was something about sitting in a chair while someone moved around you, snipping at your hair, that loosened minds and lips. Studying him again, Maribeth said, "She left it pretty long."

"Said it suits me that way. I figure she's the expert."

"I happen to think she's right." She stepped closer, bringing the front of her body almost up against his. "By the way, hi."

"Hi to you, too. Did I tell you how great you look?"

"So do you."

He put his arms around her then, and kissed her.

She melted into him, kissing him back and raising her hands to thread her fingers through his newly styled curls.

From outside the door came a familiar warbling howl.

"You brought Caruso."

"It's not like he gives me much choice."

"He's okay? You found a place for him—" She broke off. "So much to catch up on, and it's only been two days. I want to hear all about your conversation with Brooke, and how things are going with Caruso. But let's do it over dinner."

"Sounds good." He stepped away from her, moving farther into her store. "But first, let me take a look at this place." He glanced around, walking toward the back.

She followed.

"You said it's a thrift shop?" he commented. "I was expecting something more, oh, like what you'd find in a church basement."

"Just because clothing's secondhand, that doesn't mean it's second-rate. Whether it's once-worn designer fashion or well-used jeans for a growing kid, it has value and it deserves to be displayed that way."

He turned to her. "It's a great store. Next time I need something, I know where to come."

"Ooh, I'd have so much fun dressing you!" He was so handsome and had such a great body, she could turn him out as anything, from a *GQ* cover model to a businessman to a cowboy.

"Personally, I'd rather you were undressing me, Maribeth. But that's just me."

Laughing, she said, "No, it's definitely not just you. As I'll demonstrate if you come back to my place after dinner. By the way, I notice you call me Maribeth. Most of my friends call me MB. Feel free."

"No, thanks. Maribeth is such a pretty name, and it suits you."

"I like that. Thank you, Mo. Now, where shall we go to eat? What appeals to you? I'm sure you've walked past most of the restaurants and bars by now."

"I guess anywhere we go, that small-town thing's gonna happen, right? You know everyone, and folks will be coming over to say hi and find out who I am."

"At the Gold Pan, yes." The diner was informal and popular. "And at the bar at the Wild Rose Inn." Not in the dining room at the restored inn owned by her friends Dave and Cassidy. There, people would be more circumspect, but the restaurant was pricy. "Arigata is quieter." And reasonable, for a man who'd just started a job as an auto mechanic. "Do you like Japanese food?"

"Sushi?"

"They have it, but lots of other things, too. Like tempura prawns, chicken karaage, and the most amazing marinated, grilled steak."

"I could go for steak. And by the way, I'm okay with sushi, but I'd rather have it in summer than winter."

"Arigata it is. I'll get my coat and purse from the back room."

When she returned, she found that Mo had gone out, closing the door behind him. She followed, pulling a red woolen scarf off a shelf before turning off the lights and locking up. Mo and the dog were keeping each other company on the sidewalk.

"Hi, Caruso," she said, squatting. When the dog didn't back away, she held out her bare hand toward him. "How are you liking the snow?"

He stepped forward and nosed her hand as Mo said, "He's figured out it's something he can play with."

Not pushing her luck, Maribeth didn't try to stroke the dog's head. She straightened and reached up to drape the scarf around Mo's neck. "I want you to stay warm."

"Being with you should take care of that."

"But you're not with me all the time." She adjusted the scarf to her liking.

"Okay then. Thanks. How much do I owe you?"

"Pfft. It's a gift."

"Thanks again."

She pulled on her gloves and then hooked her hand through Mo's arm. "What'll Caruso do while we have dinner? He'll freeze if he hangs out on the sidewalk outside."

"He's got places to go."

Knowing how much Mo cared about the dog even if he didn't want to admit it, she stopped worrying. She also took encouragement from the way his actions belied his words, because the same could well prove true when it came to the subject of children. Once Mo reconciled with Evan and met his grandkids—both of which things she was positive would happen soon—he'd warm to the idea of having children.

As she and Mo headed down the sidewalk, he said, "What about your car?"

"We'll leave it here. Arigata's only a block and a half's walk."

As they set off, their breath made puffs of fog in the near-freezing air. It had only snowed lightly since the big snowfall on Sunday night, and the sidewalks and roads were mostly clear. The layer of white that clung to the trees sparkled, illuminated by street lamps, decorative strings of little white bulbs, and the colored Christmas lights that were already starting to go up.

"It's wrong," she said, "putting up Christmas decorations in the middle of November."

"Same rule as with carols? No earlier than December first?"

"Don't you agree?"

"Uh, I never thought about it. Truth is, I don't think much about Christmas. Usually all it means is a couple days off work."

That didn't surprise her, but it was a strange coincidence that his conscience had led him back to Caribou Crossing just before the start of the most family-oriented holiday of the year. "So you just hang around your apartment by yourself?" That sounded so lonely, on such a special holiday.

"I go volunteer at a soup kitchen or something like that."

"So do I!" Along with doing lots of social things with her friends.

Caruso whuffled into a snow-coated planter box full of shrubs, came up with a snoutful of snow, and sneezed, making Maribeth and Mo laugh.

Arigata had a narrow storefront, partially screened by bamboo through which welcoming light beckoned.

Mo bent and rested his hand on Caruso's head. "We're going inside and we'll be a while. Don't hang around waiting."

The dog gazed up at him and then turned and loped away.

"Smart boy, isn't he?" Maribeth said. "Now that you've admitted he's yours, what are you going to do about the town bylaws?"

Mo pulled a plastic bag from his pocket. "I'm carrying this, but he's pretty discreet about wherever he goes to do his business."

"How about putting him on a leash?"

"Oh man, I hate to do that to him. Doesn't seem right."

It struck her that Mo probably felt the same way about the idea of a wedding ring on his own finger. Not that Maribeth was obsessed with the formalities. Though she wanted a lifelong commitment, she could be flexible about the form it took. But so far, Mo didn't seem amenable to the idea of anything more than casual dating. She reminded herself that he'd only arrived in Caribou Crossing last week, they barely knew each other, and he had a lot of heavy stuff on his mind. Being impatient wouldn't do her any good.

Focusing on the Caruso issue, she said, "Maybe you could dangle a leash at your side. People would assume it was attached to his collar unless they looked closely. Or, of course, unless he took off after a bird or something."

"He's pretty good about knowing how to behave in the city versus out in the country. That's a good idea, Maribeth. We'll give it a try."

Mo opened the restaurant door for her and she preceded him inside to the melody of muted wind chimes.

From the back of the long, narrow room, Keiko Nomura came toward them. The slim, elegant woman wore a kimono with stylized pine trees against a silvery-gray background. The kimono wasn't one of the elaborate ones with huge hanging sleeves but a simpler, more practical design. Keiko's shiny black hair was pulled up in a sleek twist decorated with a flower ornament.

The Japanese woman gave a small bow and then lifted her head, smiling. "Welcome, Maribeth-san. How are you this evening?" Away from the restaurant, Keiko was completely Western and would have said, "Hi, MB," but at work she maintained as Japanese an ambience as possible.

Maribeth returned the bow and smile. "Hi, Keiko. I'm great. I'd like you to meet my friend, Mo. Mo, Keiko and her husband own Arigata, and he's the chef."

When Keiko again bowed and said, "Welcome, Mo-san," he mirrored the bow and said, "Thank you. It's a pleasure to meet you. I hope you have room for two for dinner. We don't have a reservation."

"For Maribeth-san and her friend, there is always room," the woman replied. As she reached out for Maribeth's coat, there was only a tiny hint of curiosity in her black eyes. She'd seen Maribeth here many times over the years, sometimes with dates and sometimes with friends, male and female.

After hanging the coats in an alcove near the door, Keiko led Maribeth and Mo through the restaurant. Rice paper screens painted with Japanese scenes divided the tables, offering the illusion of privacy, and Japanese flute music played a gentle, haunting melody. A few people who Maribeth knew glanced up, and they exchanged nods of greeting. Female gazes lingered on Mo with appreciation.

Keiko seated Maribeth and Mo at an enameled black

table with two place mats of woven straw, ivory chopsticks, and a stem of purple orchid blossoms in a crackle-glazed vase. She left for a moment and returned with menus and small towels, hot and damp so they could clean their hands.

When Keiko had taken their drink orders—a Japanese fruit drink for Mo and a pot of jasmine tea for Maribeth—Maribeth smiled across the table at Mo. "What do you think?"

"I'm a little out of my element," he admitted. "But it's nice. Simple, not fussy. I like the music, too."

"No country and western here."

"Nor too-early-in-the-season Christmas songs," he teased.

They studied the menu and decided to start by sharing an edamame and shitake salad and sweet potato gyoza dumplings. For the main course, Maribeth chose miso prawns with soba noodles. Mo, as she'd figured he might, went with the marinated, grilled steak.

Although another waitress was working tonight, it was Keiko who came to serve their drinks and take their orders. Once she'd gone, Mo sipped his drink and said, "That's certainly different." Another sip. "I like it, though."

"Good. Now tell me about Caruso. You said he has somewhere safe to go?"

"A couple of places. At the garage, we rigged him up a better spot. A well-padded box, outside but in a very sheltered location. And if he wants to be inside, he can get into my apartment."

"Your landladies said it was okay?"

"I talked to them Monday morning, after helping Ms. Peabody's son and his husband, who came over to shovel their snow. I told them what the girl from the shelter had said about Caruso, that he'd been trained. I said I'd never seen him act aggressive to anything other than a squirrel or bird—and then he just chases them, doesn't ever catch them. He did his thing, singing. I could see he was winning them over, but they said they needed to research the breed first, and then they'd get back to me." He made a wry face. "Ms. Haldenby told me I needed to get a phone."

"And you did."

He leaned forward, lowering his voice. "Not that it's gotten me that promised phone sex."

"Yet. But since I've been remiss about that, how about I make it up to you tonight with in-person sex?" She couldn't keep her eyes off him, with his casually styled hair, dark skin, and tailored shirt. Was he, objectively speaking, really the most handsome, sexy man she'd ever gone out with, or was it pheromones speaking?

He gave that white, rakish grin of his. "That's an offer I won't refuse." Under the table, his foot nudged hers.

Trying to control her racing pulse, Maribeth got the conversation back on track. "So, anyhow, I gather your landladies voted in favor of Caruso?"

"They said they'd give him a chance." He gave a soft laugh. "Which, I think, was pretty much their attitude when they rented to me as well. Anyhow, so there I was Monday night, installing a small-sized pet door."

"Small? Oh, because he's like a cat and can squeeze through small spaces?"

"Yeah, he only needs a space as wide as his face. That's something the ladies found out on the Internet. And the smaller the door, the less cold air comes in with him."

"He's using it?"

"Yeah, he thinks it's fun."

She smiled, liking the dog and the man better all the time. "He sleeps inside at your place at night? Where?"

"A wooden apple crate. My landladies had a couple of old blankets they said they didn't need."

"What are you feeding him?"

"Dog food. Ms. Haldenby told me which kind to get."

"You bought dog food. And you have a doggy bed." She put her elbows on the table, clasped her hands, and rested her chin on them. "Aw, Mo, that's so sweet."

He snorted.

She laughed. It was so cute how Caruso had insinuated his way into Mo's life and how he'd let him. Mo's soft-heartedness gave her hope that inside the self-professed loner lay a man who would one day enjoy having a real home and a family. Because the truth was that in addition to being super hot, Mo was insinuating his own way into her heart.

Whether he wanted to or not.

Chapter Nine

When the attractive Japanese hostess had shown him and Maribeth to their table, Mo had felt a bit like a bull in a china shop—or like an auto mechanic in a refined, classy Japanese tearoom. And yet, sitting across from Maribeth and glancing around, he was starting to feel comfortable.

The elegant simplicity was actually relaxing: the pure notes of the flute music, the vivid purple of the spray of flowers on the table, the painted scroll on the wall portraying mountains and a Japanese woman crossing a bridge. Of course the thing he enjoyed the most was Maribeth's animated face. The deep red of her hair set off the creaminess of her skin, the brightness of her emerald eyes, the rosiness of her full lips. And then there was the tantalizing cleavage revealed by that sexy leopard-print top, making him remember the fullness and softness of her breasts.

Keiko returned to their table, taking small steps within the long, wrapped skirt of her printed kimono. She set their appetizers on the table and said, "Mo-san, would you like me to bring cutlery?"

"Thanks for the offer, but I'm okay with chopsticks." He'd eaten in his share of Chinese restaurants and an occasional sushi bar. He could manage the appetizers, and he assumed that when his steak was served, there'd be a knife and fork.

Keiko dipped her head and moved away.

The plates of salad and dumplings were in the center of the table, along with little bowls of dipping sauce. He and Maribeth had their own small rectangular plates, so he gestured to her to serve herself first. Efficiently, she dished out small portions, and then he did the same, doing okay with the gyoza but being a little clumsy with the edamame and shitake mushrooms.

He sampled both dishes, enjoying the blend of tanginess and sweetness. "Good choices."

"You can't go wrong with anything here." She sipped her flower-scented tea. "Tell me how it went with Brooke."

That called for a long swallow of his fruit drink as he reflected. "Conversation went in fits and starts. She told me more about how she was diagnosed with bipolar disorder and realized she was an alcoholic. And how those discoveries turned her life around."

"It was Brooke who was responsible for turning her life around. Some people would have just used the illness and alcoholism as excuses to keep messing up."

"I know." He shook his head ruefully as they both dished out more food. "Something we said is that it took us both one hell of a long time to grow up. She did it in her late thirties. In the hospital, drying out after an accident, being manic and getting diagnosed."

Maribeth paused with a dumpling halfway to her mouth. "And you?"

"I was roughly the same age, but for me it didn't happen in a dramatic way. No accident, no diagnosis, no sudden revelations. It just got kind of old, that 'rebel without a cause' thing. Kind of dumb when you've passed thirty-five. Getting fired from yet another job, waking up with a nasty hangover and bruised knuckles from a bar fight."

Maribeth's gaze was intent, like listening to him ramble on was the most important thing in her world.

He shook his head. "So, anyhow. I was sick of myself. Did some thinking, did some reading. Went to some A.A. meetings. Figured out I wasn't an alcoholic, but I was just as messed up as the others, and drinking made it worse. One guy said the 'tread lightly' thing. And it made me think about the harm I'd done. Some minor stuff along the way, and some big stuff to Brooke and Evan. I was a shit, and I was sick of being a shit. So I cleaned up my act." He shrugged. "End of story."

"Not the end. You're still writing the story."

Mo wasn't entirely sure what she meant, but there was one thing he knew, so he said it. "Seems like we're always talking about me, and I'm way more interested in knowing about you. You're a good listener, Maribeth. But now it's my turn."

She finished her last bite of salad and placed her chopsticks across a small ceramic crane. Mo had a crane, too, and until now had assumed it was purely decorative. "What do you want to know?" Maribeth asked.

"All of it." He moved his chopsticks from his plate to his crane's back. "Your interests, hobbies. Why you chose to run a thrift shop. What it was like growing up in Caribou Crossing. How you decide where you're going to go for those holidays of yours. What's your—" He broke off to smile at Keiko as she approached the table rather tentatively, like she didn't want to interrupt.

The hostess cleared their appetizer plates, leaving their

chopsticks and saying, "I will be back with your prawns and steak."

She returned quickly, and Mo saw that he wouldn't need a knife and fork after all because the steak had been sliced. It wasn't what he'd expected, yet it looked and smelled delicious, sitting atop a mix of rice and vegetables.

"Is the drink to your liking, Mo-san?" Keiko asked.

"It's great, Keiko. I'll have another, when you get a chance. And the steak looks wonderful. Thank you."

"Maribeth-san, a glass of wine perhaps?"

"Not tonight, thanks, Keiko. I'm happy with the tea."

"I will freshen it up." She whisked the teapot away.

Mo and Maribeth both tasted their meals, proclaimed them good, and exchanged bites. They thanked Keiko when she returned with fresh drinks. Then, with all the little rituals out of the way, he returned to the subject he was most interested in. "Tell me something about you, Maribeth Scott."

"Well, I had a wonderful childhood, right in that same house I live in now. The only thing I was unhappy about was being an only child. I wanted siblings. When I was a little kid I was a pest about it." She sighed. "Until one day my poor mom sat me down and said it wasn't that she and Dad hadn't wanted more children, but they weren't able to have them, and every time I whined about it I hurt them."

He nodded his understanding. "As an only child, were you spoiled rotten?"

"No. My mom and dad were responsible parents. They made sure I had everything I needed plus a few treats, but they didn't overindulge me. They taught me about priorities, the value of money, budgeting. Just because a girlfriend had a new doll or sweater or whatever, or got to buy candy after school or go to the movies whenever she wanted to, that didn't mean I got to do it."

"Did you whine about that, too?" he asked with a grin.

"Sometimes, yeah." She wrinkled her cute turned-up nose. "And they'd tell me I shouldn't have blown through my allowance so quickly. As I got older, I realized they'd done me a huge favor. Their lessons stood me in strong stead when I wanted to open my own business."

"They do sound like good parents. Like they thought about what was right for you rather than what they wanted from you." He wondered how he'd have turned out if he'd been born to parents like hers. And he felt like an utter shit for not doing right by Evan. No wonder his son didn't want to see him ever again.

"Absolutely. They taught me how parenting should be done." She blinked and then looked down at her plate and concentrated on picking up a prawn with her chopsticks.

She'd said she'd like to be married and have kids one day. Was she wondering what she was doing wasting her time with a guy like him? His time with her was limited and would end when some better man came along. That was a sad thought, yet Mo counted himself blessed for each moment he had with this special woman.

Maribeth finished her prawn and then smiled brightly. "I think I mentioned that I got my travel bug from my parents. They both had a yen to explore the world, and watched travel shows in their spare time. They'd decide on a destination then do their research, work out a budget, and save for it. By the time I was sixteen, we'd been to England, France, Italy, and Spain."

She put down her chopsticks. "The next trip was Austria," she said solemnly, "in May of the year I turned nineteen. They said they'd pay my way, but I'd just finished my second year at university in Vancouver and, being the responsible kid they'd raised, I decided I needed to get a summer job instead." She sighed. "They died on that trip, in a bus crash."

"I'm so sorry, Maribeth." He reached across the table and rested his hand atop hers. Thank God she hadn't gone with her parents.

She squeezed her eyes shut for a moment. "It was awful. We were so close, and I was shattered."

"Were there other family around to help?"

"My parents were both only children like me. Dad's parents died when I was little. Mom's are wonderful, though. They have a house in Kitsilano in Vancouver, and I lived with them while I was at university. They helped me so much after my parents died, and I don't know how I'd have survived without them. And my friends as well. I got a lot of practical and emotional support, and I got through the worst of it. Grandma and Granddad were hurting, too, of course, and they helped make me see that what we needed to do was focus on the memories, the good times, the love we'd shared."

Mo thought about Maribeth at nineteen, dealing with the loss of her parents. He, at the same age, had been messing up his life and Brooke's. "You decided to keep the house."

"Yes. Living there made—still makes—me feel close to Mom and Dad." She gave his hand a pat and then lifted her arm, freeing them both to pick up their chopsticks again. "I decided not to go back to university. I'd been studying arts and design, with the idea that I might go into fashion design."

"I bet you'd have been great at it." He picked up another bite of tender steak.

"Thanks. But you know, I've never been that interested in schoolwork, and I'm just not very ambitious. Fashion design is a competitive industry, and it'd be hard to do it in Caribou Crossing. My grandparents wanted me to move to Vancouver. The idea of being with them was really tempting, but after two years in the big city, I knew that the lifestyle wasn't for me. I'm a small-town girl. Anyhow, the mom of one of my friends was a career counselor, and she helped me figure out what I really wanted to do."

Her eyes sparkled as she leaned forward, and he tried to focus on those sparkles rather than look down her cleavage.

"I'd always liked shopping at thrift stores and consignment stores," she said. "Friends came to me for fashion advice. And thanks to my parents' life insurance and everything else I inherited, I could afford to start my own business. Not only that, but it didn't have to be a business where I made a fortune."

"That was a pretty special gift your parents left you."

"I know." Her eyes held affection and sadness. "I kind of named the shop after them."

"How do you mean?"

"Dad, who was several years older than Mom, had this habit of talking about how things were when he was young, and Mom would say, teasingly, 'Oh yes, way back in days of yore.' So I used that, but changed the spelling to y-o-u-r."

"Clever. And a nice tribute to them." He was glad she'd been so close to her parents. It wasn't her fault that each time she raved about how wonderful they'd been, he felt guilty for being such a shitty dad. "Tell me more about the store."

He finished his dinner and drink as she talked enthusiastically, with him interspersing an occasional comment or question but mostly just enjoying listening and watching her expressive face.

When Maribeth finished her meal, Keiko came to remove their plates and ask if they'd care for anything else. She recited the dessert menu and Mo said, "How about you, Maribeth? I could go for that blood orange sorbet, if you want to stay for dessert."

"I love the sour cherry and green tea sorbet," she said. "So yes, please, Keiko. Sorbet for both of us."

"Coffee?" Keiko offered.

"Please," Mo said, but Maribeth said she'd stick with her tea.

When dessert was served, Mo kept the focus of the conversation on his companion. He enjoyed getting to know her better. She sure was rooted in her community, being involved in so many activities and having such a large number of friends.

"We're opposites, aren't we?" he commented as he pushed aside his empty sorbet bowl.

She considered that and then said, "In a lot of ways, I suppose. In the way we grew up and the way we've lived our lives."

Childhood and adulthood. That pretty much covered everything. Except maybe for one or two of the fine things in life. "Do we have anything in common? Except for liking good food and"—he leaned forward, giving her a teasing grin as he murmured—"good sex."

She returned the grin and reached over to weave her fingers through his. "Having a soft spot for stray dogs."

Her words struck a deeper chord than she'd likely intended. He tugged his hand free and crossed his arms over his chest. "Is that what I am to you, Maribeth? A stray like Caruso, and your heart's too soft to leave us out in the cold?"

She gazed evenly at him. "I think you and Caruso have

a lot in common. You're self-sufficient and you're wary of people."

"Uh-huh."

"As for my soft heart, what's wrong with wanting the best for people and for animals? I'd like Caruso to find the kind of home that suits him, where he has protection and affection but also all the freedom he needs. I'd like you to . . ." Her voice faded and there was an inward expression in her eyes.

He uncrossed his arms and leaned toward her. "Yes?"

She blinked. "To find what you're looking for. What you're really, really looking for, deep inside, if you'd let yourself dream. To not only apologize to Brooke and Evan and make whatever amends you can, but to build good relationships with them. And with their families. I'd like you to find a home of your own where, well . . . I guess as with Caruso, you wouldn't feel tied down and bound, but you'd have affection and—" She broke off.

"And?" he prompted.

And intimacy. Love. A real family. A wife and children of his own. Those were all the things that had flitted through Maribeth's head, the things she didn't dare say to him yet. To her, it seemed so obvious what his future should hold, but was she projecting her own dreams on him? Friends occasionally gave her gentle flak for being pushy and trying to impose her views on others, even if her pushiness was well-intentioned.

She made a dismissive gesture, "Oh, people, closeness. Relationships." She found a smile. "Relationships can be nice, or haven't you noticed?"

His lips pressed together and then curved a little. "Have

to admit, this one's pretty nice. But I'm way out of practice." His brow furrowed. "D'you know, I've really never dated."

"Never? Seriously? A hot guy like you?"

"Well, I guess kind of, in my teens. A movie, sneak a drink or a toke together, find a place to have sex. Not all that much talking. Not about anything that wasn't superficial. Then Brooke and I were married, we had a baby, we came to Canada."

"Married couples have date nights. And they talk about important things." Although she knew that not all did—and not all women, much less men, wanted that much closeness.

"For us, it was more arguing than talking. And date night was going to the bar and getting hammered. An evening that could end up with either wild sex or a screaming match."

It was so hard to imagine Brooke and Mo like that. "You two sure weren't good for each other."

He barked out a laugh. "Understatement."

Returning to the subject, she said, "After you'd left and were on your own, you never dated? It was just hookups?" He'd kind of said that before, but it seemed so hard to believe. So lonely.

"That was all I trusted myself with. I knew I sucked at relationships, having blown every single important one in my life. Parents, sister, wife, son."

Yes, lonely. Horribly lonely. Feeling guilty and punishing himself, not trusting himself. "But then things changed," she said quietly. "And once you turned your life around, you started thinking about relationships."

His forehead seemed stuck in a frown. "I thought about the ones I'd blown, and how I wanted to apologize."

"The apology is only the start. What comes after?"

"Amends, the A.A. people say, and I think they're right."

"And after that? A relationship. You and Brooke are starting a new relationship, one where you'll try to understand and support each other rather than fight. And you want to build a relationship with Evan."

His frown deepened.

She plowed on. "You want a relationship with me, too. You knew right from the beginning that this would be more than a hookup, and that's what you wanted. And still want."

"Uh . . ."

"That's okay, Mo, you don't have to say it. Actions speak louder than words." She winked at him. "You need to learn to listen to your own actions. They're trying to tell you something."

He rubbed his fingers over the frown lines in his forehead, pressing hard.

She almost felt sorry for the poor guy. Clearly, she was stressing out his brain. "Did you and Brooke talk about Evan and how he's feeling about seeing you?"

He lowered his hands with a sigh. "When she told him I was in town, he said he didn't want to see me. She gave it a couple of days and tried again, and he said he didn't want to hear any more about it. She said his wife, Jess, is halfway convinced that he should see me, but Jess wants some assurance that I'm a decent guy now. That I'm not going to hurt Evan. Emotionally, I mean." He sighed again. "How can I give her that? All I've got is my word, and why should she trust me?"

Why do I trust you? Thinking about that, Maribeth said, "You need to see Jess."

He cocked his head.

"I trust you because I've listened to you," she told him. "I've heard not just the words but your tone of voice and I've seen your face. You're either a brilliant actor or you're sincere. Jess is a savvy woman." Smart, practical, and also compassionate. "I think she'd see the same thing I do." Hearing her own last words, Maribeth gave a quick smile. "Well, hopefully not *exactly* the same thing, but you know what I mean."

"I could ask Brooke what she thinks," he said slowly.

"Yes. If people are to trust you, you can't be going behind someone's back." She tapped her fingertips against the table, musing. "I have an idea. What if you, Brooke, and Jess came to my house? There'd be less pressure than in a one-on-one with just you and your daughter-in-law." And maybe seeing that Maribeth liked and trusted Mo would help Jess get over her fears.

"That's nice of you, Maribeth."

"Oh, pfft. I love entertaining friends." And she'd love to help Mo and his family come to terms with the past and move forward.

Keiko came over to see if there was anything else they needed. They both said no, and she slid a small folder onto the table, its cover made of rice paper with a design of cherry blossoms.

As soon as she'd gone, Mo reached for it.

"I'll split you," Maribeth offered.

He shook his head. "This one's mine." He glanced at it and slipped some cash into the folder.

"Thank you, Mo. It's been a lovely evening." She shot him a flirtatious look. "So far. And I have a feeling it's only going to get better." After a couple of hours in public and a conversation that had included her parents' death and his estrangement from his son, it was time for some sexy fun.

"I've been looking forward to that."

They rose and, as Maribeth walked toward the door, Mo followed. He didn't touch her, and she was glad. So many men did that thing where they put a hand on a woman's lower back. Some women enjoyed it, but to Maribeth it often felt like possessiveness and control—like she was a doll the guy was steering where he wanted her to go. Mo was close enough, though, that she felt a tingly, almost electric sensation as if sparks were just waiting to fly between their bodies.

Keiko joined them in the entryway and handed them their coats. Mo helped Maribeth on with hers, then pulled on his own jacket and wrapped the jaunty scarf around his neck. Red looked great on him, with his dramatic coloring.

When Mo thanked Keiko and her husband for a delicious meal, the Japanese woman bowed her head and said, "It is our pleasure to have you here, Mo-san. I hope you will come again."

When she said good night to Maribeth, there was a gleam in her black eyes that looked like approval.

Outside, Maribeth slipped her hand through Mo's arm and shivered. "Brrr. No Caruso. I hope he's inside somewhere. Hmm, now that you have a dog, do you have to go home at night?"

He chuckled. "Nope. Remember, that's a self-sufficient beast."

Walking quickly, they covered the short distance to her car and climbed in. She pushed the buttons to activate the seat heaters, then drove the few blocks to her house.

As her headlights illuminated the driveway, Caruso came running from the direction of the house.

"Well," Mo said, "doesn't that beat all? Smart dog. He saw me with you and figured this was where we'd end up."

"There's no way into the house or garage, so he must have been out on the porch in the cold. Mo, I need you to install a pet door in the sunroom."

"You sure about that?"

It was a relationship gesture, she realized. More significant, really, than inviting a man to leave a toothbrush and razor in her bathroom, because it meant a physical change to her house. But it wasn't a major change. "Of course. It's not a big deal." It would be easy enough to buy a new back door and have it installed, if Mo . . . whatever. Left town; broke up with her; ditched the dog—which was, she figured, less likely than either of the first two possibilities.

Caruso's tail was actually wagging when Maribeth and Mo stepped out of the car in the garage. He even voluntarily brushed against Maribeth's leg. And when she opened the door to the house, he barely paused before coming inside.

"I bet you're hungry," she said, heading for the kitchen. "And it just happens that I bought some dog food. I'm not sure it's the kind Ms. Haldenby recommends, but I'm guessing you're not picky."

She and Mo got Caruso set up in the sunroom with his blanket, food and water, and the outside door open a crack. It felt comfortable, doing these simple tasks with Mo. He was easy to be around, and it seemed as if the two of them were attuned to each other. That surprised her, given what he'd said about his inexperience with relationships.

After she closed the door to the sunroom, Mo caught her hand and tugged her close, putting his arms around her. "You look really sexy in leopard skin."

She leaned back against the wall of the hallway. "I did notice you leering at my cleavage a time or two."

"Sorry."

"Don't be. Why d'you think I wore this top?"

His grin flashed. "You don't mind being seen as an object of lust?"

She laughed. "If that was all it was, I wouldn't be

impressed. But I know you like me and you're interested in more than just my body."

"You sound pretty confident about that."

"I am. I've dated a lot of guys, and I've turned down a lot, too. I'm good at reading men."

"If I thought too hard about that, I'd probably be terrified."

No doubt he would. But rather than say so, she joked, "Then don't think, just act."

"I'm way better at that."

He ran a finger over her chest, following the neckline of her top, his deliberate, rough-skinned touch creating shivers of arousal. He went all the way around the neckline and then returned to center front, dipping deep into her cleavage. "Is it warm in your house?" he asked innocently. "You're dewy. But no, it can't be warm." He brushed the back of his other hand across her budded nipple. "Your nipples say it's cold."

Of course cold was the last thing she was feeling, but she could play this game, too. Gazing at him seductively, she asked, "You know the best cure for being cold?"

His irresistible grin flashed. "I have a mighty good idea."

"Then you'll join me?"

"Wouldn't be much fun alone, would it?"

"Oh, I've been known to have a fine time on my own."

When a flush tinted his cheekbones, she knew he was imagining her masturbating.

"But you're definitely welcome to join in," she said. "Fortunately, mine's big enough."

He gaped, and she had to hold back a laugh before delivering her punch line. "My bathtub, that is."

He blinked. "A bath? You were talking about taking a bath?"

With faux innocence, she said, "What on earth else would I have been talking about?" Then, laughing, she captured his hand and led him upstairs.

Maribeth firmly believed that a woman was entitled to the bathroom of her dreams. In her twenties, she'd had the master bath completely redone, treating herself to green-marbled Italian tile, gold and silver taps, a gorgeous vanity, and heated towel rails. The bathroom had a large window that no one could look in, and the combination of light and humidity was ideal for the couple of orchid plants on the vanity.

She reached down to turn on the bathtub taps.

"Wow," Mo said. "This room suits you, but I have to admit, I feel out of place."

It was funny, but until that moment she hadn't realized that her perfect bathroom had been missing something. "No, you're exactly what it needs."

She tugged the hem of her top upward and with slow, seductive motions, peeled off the garment. Her ivory trousers and her knee-high stockings went next, leaving her in a bra and panties. Her lingerie was peach silk with lace trimming, the bra cut low to showcase her breasts and the thong barely covering the essentials.

Mo had watched without moving, so now she urged, "Come on. You're not going to climb into the bathtub with your clothes on."

He shook himself like he was coming out of a trance and quickly undid his shirt buttons, yanking the tail of his shirt out of his pants along the way, and then pulled off the shirt. His pants and socks followed, leaving him in slim-fitting black boxers.

Maribeth was constitutionally incapable of having a bath without tossing some sort of bath salts or bubble bath into the water. The tub's wide marble-tiled surround held an assortment of bottles, jars, and bars of soap, and when she reached among them, Mo said, "I'm not a flowers kind of guy."

"Trust me." She sprinkled bath salts into the water. "This is sandalwood, and it smells the way you look." Steam and a woodsy, slightly spicy scent drifted through the air. That aroma fit him so much better than the scent of the basic brands of soap and shampoo he favored.

He sniffed warily, and then smiled. "I like it."

Of course he did. And so did she.

The mirror was fogging at the edges as Maribeth faced it and said, "Look at us. Such perfect opposites."

He came to stand beside her. "Yeah, we kind of are, aren't we? You're, like, the ideal female and I'm definitely a guy."

She was all curves while he was lean muscles. Her skin was pale and creamy, accented by the peach silk and her red hair. His skin was a blend of coffee, cream, and cinnamon, dramatic against the black of his hair and boxers. "The ideal male," she corrected him. She couldn't help but think what beautiful babies the two of them would make.

While she stayed facing the mirror, he stepped away to turn off the taps. Then he returned, putting his arms around her to palm her breasts. Through her bra, he teased her nipples to tight buds as she watched, the view providing extra titillation. He fingered the front clasp, it slipped open, and he eased her bra away from her body.

"The most beautiful breasts I've ever seen," he said, his rough-edged voice caressing her senses. "The most beautiful body. I swear you're like a fantasy come true, Maribeth."

"I know the feeling." She pushed backward to mold the bare cheeks of her butt to his pelvis. His erection pressed against her through his underwear, and her sex moistened with the desire to have him fill her.

He pumped his hips, thrusting against her, and then to her surprise stepped away. Ah, he was peeling off his boxers. She started to turn, but he caught her by the hips and held her in place, and then her thong was sliding down her legs.

Bending forward, he pressed his lips to the spot where neck met shoulder and, to her surprise, bit her. It was only a gentle nip, but she'd anticipated a kiss, so it startled her. He sucked the tender spot, and she shuddered at the delicious sensation. "Mo, why don't we—" She was about to suggest they climb into the bath, but he interrupted.

"Action. I promised I'd act, not think." He caught her hips again, tugging her backward. "Brace yourself on the counter."

Oh, so that's what he was up to! She could definitely get into that. She leaned forward with her forearms on the vanity, her legs spread, and her butt cocked in his direction.

His finger followed the crease between her buttocks, all the way down to where she was hot and damp. He slicked moisture over her, sliding his finger back and forth but never quite touching her clit. Another finger joined in, and then he thrust both fingers inside her, making her gasp with pleasure.

He pumped and circled, exploring her secret places, dragging whimpers of need from her.

She stared into the mirror at her hectically flushed cheeks and dazzle-bright eyes. "Now," she told him. "Please, Mo, I want you inside me."

His fingers withdrew and she waited, aching with anticipation.

She heard a rustle; knew he was opening a condom and sheathing himself. Her body tensed and she quivered with the waiting.

And then he caught her waist in one hand, urging her to tilt her hips a bit more, and then—

"Oh God," she cried as he thrust deep and hard, all the way into her core. Her body, so primed and on edge, convulsed and a sharp orgasm ripped through her.

She was so caught up in it that Mo's voice barely registered and she didn't catch his words.

"Open your eyes, Maribeth," he said more sharply.

She hadn't realized she'd closed them, but now she obeyed his command and saw their reflections, the creamy-skinned woman and the coffee-brown man, joined together as sultry sandalwood steam drifted around them. One of his arms circled her waist, holding her firmly as he pumped in and out. His head rose above her left shoulder, color riding his cheekbones. As his gaze met and held hers, his eyes, too, were glittery with passion.

This man. He was everything she wanted.

Or at least he could be if he managed to move beyond the shackles of his past and let himself dream of a full, rich future. If he could let himself be the man who she was positive dwelt deep inside him.

Chapter Ten

The next Monday evening, Mo forced down a few bites of a ham sandwich. He had worked at the garage that day. Though it was supposed to be his day off, Hank had been feeling under the weather and Mo'd been happy to fill in. It kept him busy and took his mind off worrying about that night. He'd closed up late after having to tow in a minivan that had broken down as the owner drove home from work. Still, he'd made it back to his apartment with enough time to shower and fix a snack.

He crumbled the rest of his sandwich into Caruso's bowl. "Yeah, I'm nervous," he told the dog. "If Evan's wife doesn't like me, I don't think there's a hope in hell that he will agree to see me." Maribeth had arranged for Jess and Brooke to come over to her place tonight and talk to Mo.

For a man who had, over the past ten years, reduced his life to the basic elements, things sure had become complicated.

After checking his watch for the dozenth time, he pulled his denim jacket on over the good shirt and pants he'd worn when he went out with Maribeth. "However this goes, it'll be a relief to get it over with." He wrapped the red scarf around his neck and stepped outside.

Caruso came with him, falling in step at his left heel. Having taken Maribeth's suggestion, Mo pulled a leash from his pocket and dangled it. Caruso ignored it.

At a brisk pace, they set out for Maribeth's house. Mo went over it all again in his head, the details Maribeth had conveyed to him. Tonight, Evan was scheduled to give a talk on financial management at the community center. Brooke's husband, the RCMP officer, was on duty. Jess's daughter from her first marriage, Robin, was staying with her father and his wife, Dave and Cassidy. Jess and Evan's little boy, who'd be two in December, was there, too, being babysat, as was Brooke and Jake's slightly younger daughter. Brooke and Jess would pick up the toddlers after they left Maribeth's.

All these people were, to varying degrees, related to Mo. How was that possible, from one teenage screwup with birth control?

"I am so out of my depth," he muttered to Caruso.

The dog nudged his gloved hand as if he understood and was offering support.

Mo stroked the animal's head. "Life would be a whole lot simpler if it was just us guys." Now how had that happened, that he'd not only accepted Caruso into his life, but saw the two of them as a team?

When they reached Maribeth's, an SUV was parked in her driveway. It had a logo with riding boots and the words "Riders Boot Camp." Maribeth and Brooke had both mentioned that Jess and Evan owned a residential riding school.

Mo's son, the boy who'd been a klutz when it came

to any physical activity, the kid who'd refused to even consider mounting a horse, was now helping his horse-crazy wife run a riding school. It boggled the mind.

At Maribeth's door, Mo took a deep breath, then rang the bell. A moment later she opened the door, looking soft and feminine in a pink sweater and, for the first time, a skirt. A skirt patterned in bright pink and charcoal gray that brushed the tops of her feet. Instead of her usual puppy-dog slippers, she wore pink flats with sparkly stones. They emphasized how small and cute her feet were.

"Hi, Mo," she said, and then raised up to brush a kiss across his lips.

"Hey, Maribeth. You sure look nice."

"Thanks. Jess and Brooke are both here."

He nodded. Maribeth had suggested that they time things so the women arrived first and got settled and comfortable. Before going inside, he squatted and said to Caruso, "If you want to be inside where it's warm and dry, you can go around back. Okay?" Over the weekend, Mo had installed a pet door, and Caruso had quickly become comfortable with it.

Caruso gave a short warble and then ran off to chase a robin.

Mo stuck the leash in his jacket pocket, squared his shoulders, and stepped through the front door.

"You look nice, too," Maribeth said, taking his coat and scarf. "It's good that you dressed up. It shows this is important to you."

He followed her into the living room. A fire was burning, instrumental music played quietly in the background, and Brooke and a younger woman sat side by side on the sofa.

Evan's wife. Mo's daughter-in-law. He'd met her before,

but only a couple of times, and that was decades back. Though Jess Bly had been Evan's best and only friend when they were kids, Evan—smart boy that he was—had avoided bringing her to his dysfunctional home. The friendship hadn't made sense to Mo. Evan had been all about schoolwork and Jess was totally into horses. But something had drawn them together as kids and, according to Brooke, when Evan had returned to Caribou Crossing as an adult, their paths had crossed again and friendship had bloomed into romance.

As Mo seated himself in one of the chairs, Brooke said unnecessarily, "Mo, this is Jess."

Jess was the slimmest of the three women, and her jeans and flannel shirt made a statement that she wasn't dressing up for him. She was attractive in a natural way, and there was one thing about her that he recognized. "You still have a ponytail."

"And I still look out for the people I care about," she said, chin lifted and a challenge in her voice.

"That's a good quality," he responded.

Her brown eyes, a shade darker than her chestnut hair, narrowed, and he could sense a host of snide comments hovering in her mind.

Before she could decide which one to utter, Maribeth intervened. "What can I get everyone to drink? I have a pot of decaf coffee brewing, and the kettle's on so I can make tea. There's also fruit drinks and soda in the fridge. And beer, Jess, if you'd like one."

"Coffee's good," Jess said. Brooke asked for herbal tea. Mo, feeling a little sweaty from anxiety, asked for a cold drink.

When Maribeth had gone to the kitchen, Mo said, "Jess, thank you for coming and giving me a chance."

"I'm here because I respect Brooke's and Maribeth's

judgment." Her expression was troubled. "And because I think that if you've actually turned into a decent guy, it would be good for Evan to know you. But that's a big *if*."

"I understand. Like I've told Brooke and Maribeth, I was a total shit back then. And I had no excuse, not like Brooke with her bipolar disorder and alcoholism."

"We were both, uh, shits," Brooke said firmly. Clad in a pretty blue blouse and navy pants, she sat upright with her hands folded in her lap and a solemn expression on her face. "My illnesses are no excuse. I should have acknowledged that I had problems and sought help. I just thank God that Evan was so smart and independent, and that he had Jess and her parents to support him."

Mo recalled how, more often than not, Evan had been over at Bly Ranch, doing homework with Jess and staying for dinner. One of her parents would pick the kids up from school and drop Evan back home near bedtime. "Yes, Jess, that was a good thing you and your folks did. And, Brooke, don't be too hard on yourself. At least you stuck by Evan rather than abandoning him."

She gave him a wobbly smile.

"Mo, you should know—" Jess started, then she stopped as Maribeth returned carrying a tray.

They were all silent as Maribeth organized everything. A mug of coffee for Jess; a teapot and mugs of tea for Brooke and herself; a glass of sparkling orange drink for Mo; a plate of chocolate chip cookies on the coffee table. She seated herself in a chair.

Mo took a long swallow of the orange beverage. "What were you going to say, Jess?"

Her chin was up again. "It was my parents who reported you to the RCMP."

He absorbed that information. "I always wondered. I

thought it might have been a teacher." He swallowed. "I'm grateful to them."

"What?" she said, clearly taken by surprise. Then she carried on. "You mean because it gave you an excuse to skip town, right?"

He thought back. "To be honest, yeah, I guess partly so. But it also brought it home to me, what I was doing to Evan. And to Brooke. A slap, a shove, those things didn't seem so bad to me when I was drinking and pissed off with them and the world."

"I did the same things," Brooke said quickly. "It wasn't all Mo."

He gave her a grateful nod. "But when the police officer said I'd been reported for suspected child abuse, I realized that's exactly what it was: abuse. A criminal act and a, well, an immoral, inexcusable act."

"But you didn't face the consequences, admit it, and take your punishment," Jess said. "You didn't change."

"No, I didn't stay and take my punishment. And for years after, I still drank and got riled up sometimes, but I swear, I never again hit a woman or a child."

Brooke's eyes—blue green but a different shade than his, a color that had always made him think of a tropical ocean on a travel poster—were fixed on his face and he thought he read compassion in them. "The police at the door was my wake-up call, too," she said quietly. "I was still a terrible mother, but I never again hit Evan. He was uncoordinated, bumped into things and tripped over his own feet, but from that point on, none of his bruises came from me."

There was a long silence. Near Mo, Maribeth sat back in her chair, sipping from a mug of tea, listening but not intervening. Jess pressed her fingers to her temples as if she was fighting a headache.

Mo took a breath and then addressed Jess again. "Yeah, I ran away, abandoning my wife and son. I had a history of running when things got too tough for me to handle. When I didn't want to face consequences. Did Brooke tell you about the army?"

"Yes. So did her parents and sister, who've been here to visit. You deserted. You skipped the country, you and Brooke had to cut all ties with your families, and you can never return to the States." Jess didn't sound the least bit sympathetic, and there was no reason she should.

Mo found himself quite liking this young woman who was willing to listen to him but wouldn't cut him any slack.

"Actually, I did go back," he said, and told her about the lawyer who'd represented him and how he'd been given an administrative discharge.

Brooke leaned forward. "Mo, I didn't know that."

"Sorry. Guess I should've got in touch and told you. But I figured so much time had passed, and we were divorced, so my, uh, legal status wouldn't really affect yours."

"No, that's not what I meant. Just that . . . well, I'm glad you did it. That you faced up to what you'd done." She took a breath and then said hesitantly, "I asked my parents about your family, but they said they lost touch right after we left."

"I tracked down my sister on the Internet," he told her. "She's married with two children and is co-owner of a catering business. Our mother died fifteen or so years back. Dad remarried—a divorced woman with a couple of kids. He's retired now. I e-mail with my sister now and then, and my dad maybe once a year."

He glanced at Jess and Maribeth. "Sorry for the sidetrack." And then back to Brooke. "I'm glad you've made things up with your family."

"Me, too. Say hi to your sister and dad from me, the next time you're in touch."

"Mo." The firm voice was Jess's, and he turned to look at her.

"A sidetrack?" she said. "Not exactly. Do you realize you're talking about Evan's aunt and grandfather?"

His mouth fell open. "Uh, I hadn't thought about it that way."

"Obviously." Her eyes narrowed again.

Mo didn't think she'd even picked up her coffee mug, she'd been so intent on watching him and listening to him. Now he waited with trepidation to see what she'd say next.

"You ran away from two families," Jess said, "and from the army. Now you've sort of come back. The army discharged you, so you're done with them. You have occasional e-mail contact with your family, and that's it. And now here you are in Caribou Crossing, wanting what? Absolution or something? To turn yourself in, like with the army, and say you're sorry, and then get some official 'it's okay, it's in the past' discharge kind of thing? So you can go away again?"

"Uh . . ." That had been a lot of words, a lot to take in and process. A lot to think about. But those clear brown eyes were fixed on him, expecting an answer. Now.

"You haven't thought it through," Jess said.

The army had been easier to deal with than this one slender woman.

"No, I guess I haven't. What's been in my mind these past years is how badly I treated Evan and Brooke. I didn't—don't—want to mess up their lives any more than I've already done. But I do want them to know that I realize how bad I behaved and that I am truly sorry."

"And I appreciate that," Brooke said, her voice so soft and compassionate after Jess's judgmental tone. "You and I were immature and screwed up and we had an unhealthy dynamic. It's good for me to be able to talk to you about those days and the mistakes we both made, and to know that you've shouldered your share of the blame."

"But Evan doesn't deserve any of the blame," Jess said implacably. "So it's a different situation. How will it help him to talk to you?"

"Maybe it'll give him a chance to vent some anger," Mo said. "And to know how rotten I feel."

Maribeth spoke quietly. "Perhaps Evan would like to know that his father cares about him."

Mo shot her a surprised look. She'd been so quiet up until now. Her understanding smile was a small shaft of warmth and comfort that soothed his frazzled nerves.

Brooke spoke next. "Evan had many things to blame me for, too, Jess. But look how close the two of us are now. And you know that it's largely due to you. You believed in me, and you helped open Evan's mind to giving me a second chance."

"But I knew you, Brooke. I'd seen you turn your life around. I'd seen you stick with A.A., stay on your meds, reinvent yourself as a responsible citizen. Year by year."

"One day at a time," Brooke said. "And those days turned into years. Well, Mo's done the same thing over the past years. It's just that we haven't been around to see it."

"Thanks, Brooke," he said. "It's more than I deserve, having you on my side."

She gave a short laugh. "I wasn't on your side all those years ago—despite the vows I swore when we got married.

Maybe if I'd been supportive rather than bitching all the time, we'd have done better."

Finally, Jess picked up her coffee mug. "I'm so confused." She took a sip and made a face. "And I've let my coffee go cold."

"The pot's still on," Maribeth said. "I'll get you a fresh cup. Brooke, could you pour more tea for us? Mo, another glass of San Pellegrino?"

"Thanks," he said.

As Maribeth left the room, Mo turned again to Jess. "I'm sorry. I wish I could do a better sales pitch for myself, but the truth is that I'm confused, too. But you can believe me when I say I haven't had a drink in years, I never get violent, and I try never to hurt anyone. I would never want to hurt Evan again."

She nodded slowly. "You sound sincere when you say that. But what if Brooke and I can persuade him to talk to you and it doesn't go well? Yeah, he's angry. And hurt. Let's say he does vent all of that, and says he won't forgive you and he never wants to see you again. What then? Will you tell yourself you've given it your best shot, and run away again?"

He considered for a moment. "No. No, I won't. It would be like abandoning him all over again. Even if he tells me to get lost, I'll stick around. Try to be patient, to show him that this—that he—matters to me. I'd try to get him to give me another chance." Mo noticed Maribeth hovering in the doorway, apparently not wanting to step into the room and interrupt the conversation.

Jess nodded slowly. "Okay, let's say that Evan does eventually get there and agrees to having a relationship with you. Then what about the rest of us? How do we fit in?"

"I'm not sure what you mean."

"How about me? What about Evan's and my children,

Robin and little Alex? Then there's Brooke's new husband and their daughter. My parents. Robin's other dad, Dave, and his wife. Robin's other grandparents. We're a"—she glanced at Brooke, and the two women exchanged grins—"big, messy family."

"Yeah," he said slowly. "I'm kind of getting that. It's not something I'd thought about, to be honest. I hurt Evan and Brooke, and they were the two people on my mind. The two people I wanted to . . . well, try to make things right with, if that's possible." Thinking past those two people to all these other circles of family was baffling and overwhelming. He still couldn't get his mind around the idea that he was a grandfather. "There's no reason I need to be part of anyone else's life."

Jess leaned forward. "But don't you want to? Don't you want to know your grandchildren?"

They were simple words, but the concept was too big to comprehend. Gruffly, he said, "I'm no good with kids. They're better off without me."

Maribeth, standing in the doorway listening, almost dropped the mug and glass as a pang stabbed through her. Was that really how Mo felt about children? Or did his comment come from a place of inexperience, a sense of failure, a fear of not measuring up?

Was she crazy to be spending time with him? He'd been telling her pretty clearly how he saw himself—as a man who trod lightly, one who didn't want connections.

She didn't want to believe that he was right. She'd felt that click, both physical and something deeper, the one she'd been waiting for all her life. Mo might not have wanted a connection, but there was one. At least for her. It had led her to champion his cause with Brooke, and to set up this meeting with Jess. It had led her into bed with him, for something that went way further than just great sex.

Although she'd selected a sperm donor, she had postponed getting inseminated in hopes that things would work out between her and Mo. She was emotionally involved with him. More, much more, than with any man before. Was she falling in love?

But if the things he'd said were really true, then he couldn't be the love of her life and she couldn't let herself fall for him. She truly believed there was more to Mo than what he seemed to see in himself. But even if she was right, would he ever be willing to take a deeper look into his own heart? This was all so confusing. If he was her one true love, everything was supposed to fall seamlessly into place, not be such a mess.

Uncertain, moving quietly, she stepped into the room just as Jess pinned Mo with one of her level gazes and said, "Better off without you? Why? Would you hit them?"

Maribeth barely managed to suppress a gasp.

"God, no!" Mo said. "I just meant, I have nothing to offer them."

Steadying herself, Maribeth handed the mug of coffee to Jess.

The younger woman took it absentmindedly, still staring at Mo. "You're a mechanic," Jess said. "Little Alex loves his toy trucks. Play with him and he'd be happy."

Maribeth handed the orange San Pellegrino to Mo and said, "You ride. Robin's as horse-crazy as her mom, and she's an excellent rider."

"Yes," Jess said, "You could go riding with her. She'd love to give you some pointers." She took a sip of coffee. "They're kids, Mo. You don't have to give them a lot, just your time and, um, attention."

Maribeth guessed that Jess had been going to say "love," but stopped herself, figuring—and rightly so—that it would be too much for Mo to deal with.

"I guess I could do that," Mo said slowly. "Yeah, I'd like to. If Evan agrees."

Maribeth let out a slow breath, her body relaxing. No, Mo's reservations about kids weren't absolute. If he got to know his grandchildren, he'd be bound to love them. And that would surely make him more amenable to having another child of his own.

Brooke said, "Maribeth, I poured tea for you. Now, Mo, why not tell Jess what you've been doing since you left Caribou Crossing."

A less emotion-packed topic, and Maribeth was grateful to Brooke for lowering the tension level. She drank peach ginger tea and listened as Mo gave the condensed version, ending with his job as manager of an auto repair shop in Regina.

"Brooke says you're working at Hennessey's?" Jess said.

"I worked for Hank a long time ago, and he was good enough to take me back."

"He can sure use the help," Maribeth chimed in. "He's getting on in years. My parents used to take their car to his garage."

"He told me he had his sixty-fifth birthday a couple months back," Mo said. "And he has cut back on his time since I got here. He says he likes the work and doesn't want to give it up, but yeah, he gets tired. And he's got kids and grandkids he wants to spend time with."

Jess raised her eyebrows at that, but didn't comment.

"Where are you living, Mo?" Brooke asked. "You said you rented a studio apartment?"

He turned to her. "Yeah, it's in a house. My landladies are two retired teachers, Ms. Haldenby and Ms. Peabody."

"Oh, Ms. Haldenby," Jess said. "Man, she was tough. Wasn't she, Maribeth?"

"She sure was. But in a good way. She taught us a lot."

Mo glanced from one to the other. "You two weren't in the same class? I mean, Jess is . . ."

"Yes, considerably younger," Maribeth said dryly. "But we all had Ms. Haldenby for fourth grade."

"Evan was in my class," Jess said. "You're staying in his teacher's house, Mo. Did you realize that? Does Ms. Haldenby know?"

Maribeth's mouth opened. She should have put two and two together, but hadn't until Jess did it for her.

"I didn't realize," Mo said slowly. "I don't think she does either. Kincaid's not that unusual a last name. When I rented the room, I just said I was new in town and working for Hank Hennessey. I didn't say anything about Brooke or Evan. That was, you know, private."

And it could remain private, Maribeth supposed. Mo was seeing Brooke at her house, not out in public. He could do the same with Evan, if his son ever agreed to talk to him. If Mo didn't get involved with their families, no one else really needed to know. But if he did . . .

"Have you told your parents about Mo being back?" she asked Jess.

"Not yet." Her friend looked troubled. "And I don't feel good about it. I also don't feel good that I didn't tell Evan the truth about tonight, only that I was hanging out with you and Brooke."

"Why didn't you?" Maribeth asked.

"Because he'd have asked me not to do it," Jess said. "Oh, I will tell him, because we don't keep secrets. But I wanted to tell him after, once I'd had a chance to listen to Mo." She frowned at Mo. "I deceived my husband because of you."

He gazed steadily at her. "I'm sorry. But I thank you for coming. And Brooke as well. And you, Maribeth, for inviting us here."

Jess turned her penetrating gaze on Maribeth. "Yeah, what's that about, MB? What's your part in all of this?"

They were close friends and had shared lots of girl talk. How much to tell her here, now? "I guess I was pretty much the second person in town that Mo met, after Hank. I was picking up my car and happened to mention Brooke. Mo told me who he was and what he wanted to do, and asked my opinion. He said he didn't want to cause more pain for Brooke or Evan."

"So this is all because of you? You couldn't have just told him to go away?" Fortunately, there was humor in Jess's brown eyes.

Maribeth shook her head. "I thought about Evan and Brooke's reconciliation and all of the wonderful things that have happened with all of you since then."

Jess groaned. "No one's making this easy."

"True," Maribeth said. "But it's because we all want to do the right thing."

Mo cleared his throat. "Speaking of which."

They all turned to him.

"I think Ms. Haldenby has a right to know. Jess, Brooke, do you figure it'd be okay with Evan if I told her and her wife that I'm his father?"

The two women exchanged glances, and both nodded. Jess said, "I think it's the right thing to do, like you said."

He nodded. "The ladies are away right now, down in Vancouver. Ms. Peabody's granddaughter just had a baby. But as soon as they're back, I'll tell them."

Maribeth really hoped his landladies would be understanding and not kick him out.

Jess sipped coffee, a frown line marring her smooth

forehead. Then she said, "I'll talk to Evan. I'll try to persuade him to see you, Mo."

"Thank—" he started.

She stopped him with a raised hand. "Don't thank me yet. I'm going to tell him the truth about you. That you seem to be a decent guy and you have a bunch of regrets. That you want to apologize and you're prepared for his anger. But I'll also tell him that you're still kind of messed up, and you're a loner, and you seem kind of uncertain about the idea of acquiring a family. But the family part is something different from what's between you and Evan. I think it'd be good for him if you two could get that resolved in some fashion."

Mo waited and then said, "You done? Can I thank you now?"

Her lips curved slightly. "Yeah. You can thank me, father-in-law."

Maribeth felt a drop in the tension level in the room. "Now that that's been resolved, would you please try my cookies?"

"Be glad to," Mo said promptly, leaning forward and taking one. He gave her a smile, one so sincere and grateful that it stopped her heart.

She returned it, happy that she'd helped him move a step ahead in his quest to reconnect with his son.

Brooke had leaned forward to take a cookie, but Jess was gazing at Maribeth and Mo. "You two," she said, "know each other pretty well, it seems to me."

"Pretty well," Maribeth said evenly.

Her friend's eyes widened. "Oh my God! You're sleeping with my husband's father!" The words flew out, and then she clapped a hand over her mouth as if she wanted to call them back. She shot an anguished look at Brooke. "I'm so sorry. I mean—"

"It's fine," Brooke said calmly. "Maribeth checked with me before they started dating."

"You knew? You knew and you didn't tell me?"

"Well, I didn't know, um, how far along the relationship had progressed," Brooke said. "And it wasn't my business to be sharing with anyone."

Jess opened her mouth, closed it, opened it again. "I just . . . I mean, it's weird. Isn't it weird? Mo, you're what, late forties?"

"Fifty," he said.

"And MB, you're thirty-nine."

Brooke said, "Jake's eight years younger than me."

"Right, I guess I forget about that," Jess said. "Okay, I suppose age isn't a huge factor, but . . . well, he's Evan's *father*, MB."

"I do know that, Jess," she said, amused. Maribeth had rarely seen her friend so discombobulated.

"But you heard everything he just said," Jess went on, "and only last Friday you were saying—" She stopped herself at the same time both Maribeth and Brooke said, "Jess!"

"I'm sorry." She did look repentant at having almost spilled the sperm donor story. "It's just that the two of you are so different."

"Opposites attract," Brooke pointed out.

Maribeth glanced at Mo, whose expression said he was way out of his depth, not to mention a little horrified. "Look," she said firmly, "we're dating. Jess, how many guys have you seen me date? Some were opposites and some were similar to me. Don't make such a big deal of it."

"No, of course." The younger woman shook her head. "God, I'm sorry. Whack me upside the head now, okay? Better still, I'm going to eat a cookie so I don't stick my foot any farther down my throat." She reached forward, took a cookie, and then grabbed a second one as well.

"Mo," Maribeth said, seeking a less emotionally charged subject, "tell Jess and Brooke about Caruso."

He finished his cookie and told them the story, and for the first time that evening showed them a more relaxed side of himself. Maribeth loved seeing the humor and affection in his eyes as he talked about "that crazy singing dog," and when his white smile flashed, it took her breath away.

Jess took a third cookie and said, "MB, you heard about Ben Traynor, right? At the CFR?"

"Oh God, I forgot that the Canadian Finals Rodeo was this weekend. How did he do?"

"Canadian champion in saddle bronc," Jess said, sounding as proud and smug as if Ben had been her fiancé, not Sally Ryland's. "And he and Dusty came third in team roping. That'll give the fledgling Traynor Rodeo School a nice boost in terms of credibility."

"I'm so thrilled for Ben and Sally." Not to mention a little envious about how wonderfully things were working out for the couple. Sally and Ben were the loves of each other's lives and everything was falling into place—which was exactly how things were supposed to go. Mind you, there'd been that couple of months when they'd gone their separate ways, before they had the sense to confess their true feelings for each other . . .

Brooke glanced at her watch and said, "Jess, we should head over to the Wild Rose and pick up the little ones."

They all stood and walked together to the door. Maribeth took coats from the closet and Mo helped Brooke into hers, though Jess made a point of pulling on her puffy jacket by herself. Maribeth was trying to decide whether to take Mo's denim jacket off its hanger when Jess said wryly, "That horse has already left the barn, MB. You don't have to send him out in the cold only for him to walk around the block and sneak back."

Brooke finished buttoning her coat and glanced at Maribeth, then at Mo. Something passed between the two exes, something a touch rueful, and then Brooke gave a gentle smile and said, "Good night, Mo."

"Good night, Brooke," Mo said. A little gruffly, he added, "And thanks."

The two women stepped outside and Maribeth, hugging her arms around herself to combat the chill air, watched as they walked to the Riders Boot Camp SUV and climbed in. Only after Jess had backed down the driveway and pulled into the street, and Maribeth had given a final wave, did she step inside and close the door.

Turning to Mo, she said, "It's been quite an evening."

"God, yes." He put a hand to his forehead and dragged it through his hair. Then he gave a pale imitation of his rakish grin. "I owe you, Maribeth. Big-time."

"You do. You're seriously in my debt," she teased. "And I know exactly how you can pay me back." She stepped closer, looped her arms around him, and slipped her hands into the back pockets of his black jeans, gripping his firm butt. "A kiss will settle your tab."

"I like the way you think." He smiled down at her. "In fact, I like a whole lot of things about you."

"Same goes," she said softly, wondering if there was any way that his "liking" for her would ever reach the depth of what she was coming to feel for him.

Chapter Eleven

The next Sunday morning, Mo lazed in bed with Maribeth, feeling odd. Odd in a good way. He glanced around her bedroom, which wasn't lacy and fluffy like so many women's, but instead cozy and bright with simple furniture and vivid colors. Sunlight peeked through slits between the venetian blinds.

His gaze returned to the bed, where Maribeth lay next to him. Her shoulders were bare above the pale green sheet, and her red hair tumbled across the pillowcase. Her eyes were closed, her cheeks were flushed, and a smile curved her lips. They'd just made love and she looked satiated and contented.

Yeah, that was how he felt, too. Like there wasn't anywhere he'd rather be or anyone he'd rather be with. Before meeting Maribeth, he'd only ever felt that kind of pleasure after completing a particularly challenging vehicle repair job. The comparison made him chuckle.

Her eyes opened. "What's so funny?"

Somehow he doubted she'd be amused if he told her. Instead, he smoothed a damp curl back from her cheek and said, "Just thinking how nice this is." Which wasn't a lie. "Looks like the weather's going to be good. Want to see if we can rent horses and go riding?" The snow had disappeared over the past few days, and it should be great riding weather.

"I'd love that. And I bet Caruso would enjoy a good long run in the country." She rolled onto her side, facing him. "He's sure an easy-care dog."

"He is." From what his landladies had told him, singing dogs often preferred their own adventures to human company, so Mo was flattered that Caruso so often chose to be with him. "It still ticks me off that someone abandoned him."

"They should have done their research before they got him. They probably thought a New Guinea singing dog sounded distinctive, and they never checked to see if he'd make a good house pet. Though he's sure getting more domestic as he comes to know us."

Mo nodded. "Yeah, he seems happy with domesticity as long as it's his choice and he knows he's free to come and go as he pleases." Caruso had settled in nicely at his apartment. He used the pet door frequently, but seemed happy to sleep inside. The dog had even been fine the night Maribeth had slept over. And at her house, Caruso now ventured into the kitchen. Mo figured it wouldn't be all that long before Caruso would be napping in front of the fire.

"I'm hungry," Maribeth announced. "Let's go down and make breakfast. French toast sound good?"

"I knew there was a reason I like spending the night with you."

"Ha ha."

He dressed in last night's clothes while she pulled on her robe and put on her glasses, and then they went downstairs and fixed breakfast together. Caruso joined them, his reward a couple of the breakfast sausages Mo fried up.

While the humans were drinking second cups of the decaf coffee that Maribeth preferred, she phoned Ryland Riding and reserved horses for later.

As they went up to shower, Mo said, "I need to change into heavier clothes and shoes." She'd given him a new toothbrush the first night he stayed over, but neither of them had suggested that he bring spare clothes with him.

"We can drop by your place on the way," she said as she tidied the sheets and striped duvet.

"The thing is . . . well, Ms. Haldenby and Ms. Peabody got back yesterday afternoon. And Ms. Peabody's grandson and his husband, who live in Caribou Crossing, brought over some groceries and they were all having dinner together. So I didn't get a chance to talk to them about Evan."

Maribeth faced him across the bed. "Do you want to see if the ladies are around today and have time to talk?"

"Yeah, I think so. It feels kind of deceptive, not telling them. Now that I know Ms. Haldenby was Evan's teacher." He sure wasn't looking forward to it, though.

She fluffed a pillow. "Do you want me there, or would you rather do it on your own? I want to call my grandparents, but after that my schedule's clear until we go riding."

"It's my issue, Maribeth. You don't always have to help me out."

Her eyes flashed green fire, a moment's irritation. "Friends help friends. You fixed my porch railing and got the tap in the powder room to stop dripping."

Tiny things, and he liked fixing stuff. But then he guessed Maribeth liked helping people. "I think this is something I need to do by myself. I do appreciate the offer, though."

"I like being appreciated."

"Let's climb into the shower, and I'll show you some appreciation."

She slipped her glasses down her nose and gave him a seductive look over the top of the frames. Then she undid the tie of her bathrobe, peeled it off, and dropped it on the bed. With a sensual saunter she headed for the bathroom, leaving Mo scrambling to tear off his clothes.

Maribeth was already in the shower, and he slid back the curtain to join her. Her glasses were off now. She was creamy-skinned and voluptuous, her hair gathered up in a shower cap, which on her actually looked sexy. She chose a bottle from the assortment set out on the tiled surround and squeezed gel onto a bath sponge.

Mo had never been anywhere near a French country garden, but this was how he guessed one might smell. When he'd first met Maribeth, he'd marveled that her scent was rarely the same. It wasn't perfume, but the shower gels, shampoos, and lotions she used.

He lifted his head to the spray of the shower and then, refreshed, shook water drops every which way. "You sure do like variety," he commented, gesturing to her array of products.

"It makes life interesting."

He picked up a bottle of shampoo, smelled it—too flowery—and tried another. Finding one that reminded him of the ocean, he lathered his hair.

She had more than a dozen scented products to choose from. She wore different clothes every day, using her thrift shop as her personal boutique. When she took a holiday, it was always to somewhere new. And she'd dated lots and lots of men.

She'd said that she'd like to find the right man, marry, and have kids—but it seemed to him that maybe she actually preferred to keep her life "interesting" with a variety of men. She was thirty-nine. Not that he knew a lot about having babies, but wasn't thirty-nine pushing it? Of course, Brooke had been forty-two when she got pregnant for the second time, but that wasn't the way most women chose to have kids, he was pretty sure. Maybe Maribeth was thinking about adopting. Or maybe—yeah, this made more sense—when she got older and was ready to settle down, she planned to marry a man who already had kids.

"I think your hair's clean enough," she said, and Mo realized he'd been rubbing shampoo through his hair while his thoughts drifted.

He rinsed it out, and then took the bath sponge from her. "Just practicing, because next I'm going to get you clean. And I plan to be very, very thorough. Make sure I get in all the nooks and crannies."

"Mister, you've already been in my best nook and cranny," she teased.

"And it was so great, I have to make a return trip." Gazing into her sparkling green eyes, he thought that everything about Maribeth was great. This was one very special woman, and he was damned lucky to be with her.

He dropped the sponge, shoved her wet hair back from her face, and held her head steady, tilted up to his. When he kissed her, it wasn't light and teasing. He showed her all the passion, appreciation, and affection she made him feel.

She made a tiny, surprised sound, and then she was kissing him back. Her hands gripped his ass, tugging him closer, trapping the solid thrust of his erection between their bodies. Breaking the kiss, she came up for air and gasped, "Oh God, Mo."

"Yeah." He captured her mouth again, releasing his grip on her head and stroking up and down her back.

Against his chest, her nipples were budded as if they craved his touch. He couldn't resist them and reached between their bodies to cup and caress her breasts. Water streamed over her shoulders, sliding over her skin and making it slick.

She moaned, throwing her head back and arching into his hands.

"Shit, Maribeth, I want you." He ached with the need to be inside her.

"Me too. Now."

"So glad you said that." He released her and stepped out of the shower to grab a condom from the package on the bathroom counter.

A moment later, he'd sheathed himself, climbed back into the shower, and hoisted her into his arms.

Agile Maribeth hooked her legs around his waist.

He backed her up against the wall of the shower so it supported her shoulders while he clasped her butt. As she raised her arms to loop them around his neck, he lowered his head to kiss the inside of her wrist and tongue the pulse point.

She shuddered. "Mo, please. Now." She freed her hand and reached down between them, grasping his shaft.

He groaned as she guided him to her center. And then, with one powerful thrust, he was exactly where he wanted to be.

She circled his neck with her arms and hung on as, with long, deep strokes, he drove both of them higher and higher.

"Mo," she gasped, "I need to come. Make me come now." She ground herself against him.

His hips tilted, jerked, and somehow he was even

deeper inside her, and he felt her start to come apart. When her orgasm hit, she cried out, high and loud.

Mo let himself go, his own climax ripping through him. He shouted too, a wordless, primitive sound.

He barely managed to support their entwined bodies until she slowly unwound her arms and legs and stood leaning against him, breathing hard. His legs were shaky and he felt weak from the combination of the steamy shower and the steamy sex. And, maybe, from something more. From the strength of his feelings for Maribeth, a generous woman who had given him so much in the short time he'd known her.

Attachments. For the first time in twenty years, he was forming attachments. Suddenly life was filled with possibilities, a prospect that was both scary and amazing.

He dropped a kiss on the top of Maribeth's head and gently pushed her away. Reaching down to find her bath sponge, he said, "Now, where was I?"

Eventually, they finished their shower, dressed, and went downstairs again.

"Well," Mo said, "I'll leave you to phone your grandparents, and head over to my place. I hope my landladies are free to have a chat."

"You should take something with you. If only that orange almond cake had turned out . . ."

"It tasted great." Last night, with the radio playing country tunes and him sitting at the kitchen table watching her, she'd tried out a new recipe for a cake that didn't use flour.

"But it didn't turn out to be a proper cake and I can't slice it. It's just this messy . . . I don't even know what to call it."

When they'd finally sat down to sample the finished product, the "cake" had been so moist and crumbly that she'd ended up serving it in bowls rather than on plates. Still, they'd both eaten sizable portions. He liked that she'd taken the semi-failure in stride, laughing about it and scribbling notes on the recipe for things to try the next time. So many women would have been all fussed, either angry or apologetic, and it might've ruined the evening. From what he'd seen so far, it would take a lot to spoil Maribeth's good temper.

"Maribeth, I can just pick up flowers on the way."

"No, it should be something more personal. How about these?" She took a zipper bag of chocolate chip cookies from the freezer.

He knew better than to protest again. "Your cookies are great. Thank you." He only hoped they were magic cookies that would soften his landladies' hearts, or else he and Caruso would find themselves homeless.

A couple of hours later, Mo and Caruso were waiting at the curb in front of his landladies' house—which, fortunately, was still home for him and the dog.

Maribeth drove up in her Mini, right on time. Caruso actually wagged his tail, and Mo said, "Yeah. Me, too, buddy."

He opened the back door and the dog jumped in willingly, but when Mo went to get into the passenger seat, he found a Stetson sitting there. He picked it up. "Maribeth?"

"I have this fantasy about going riding with a real cowboy," she told him with a wink.

Grinning, he climbed into the car and put the cowboy hat on his lap. "Would that be on horseback or . . . ?" he teased.

"Both," she replied promptly, and leaned over to kiss him.

As she drove away, she said, "I got your text that things went well with your landladies. I'm so glad."

"Yeah. Now Caruso and I don't have to go house-hunting."

"Hah. It's more than that. They're nice women and you don't want them to disapprove of you."

"Okay, you got me." Sometimes it seemed like she knew him better than he knew himself.

"Tell me what they said."

"Ms. Haldenby said Evan did so well in school, he was head and shoulders above the rest, and that's not usually true of children with bad home situations."

"I gather he had a strong drive to leave Caribou Crossing and to create a very different kind of life."

"Yeah. He had big dreams." Mo smiled wryly. "No, it was more than dreams. He had a goal, a focus in life, and he worked hard to achieve it. He was completely unlike me or Brooke. Hard to believe he was our kid."

They were out of town now, on the two-lane road that led to Ryland Riding. The world was dusted with snow, like that icing sugar Maribeth had sifted over the top of her orange cake.

She glanced over at him. "You told the ladies about what you'd been doing since you left town, and why you came back?"

"I told them everything. Including my talks with Brooke and Jess, and how Evan is refusing to see me." He rotated the Stetson, running his fingers along the edge of the brim. "Ms. Haldenby said she thought we were right not to try and force him. She said he was strong-minded, and he'd been badly hurt, and now he likely needs to feel in control. She also said she hopes things work out."

"And she and Ms. Peabody said they were fine with you staying."

He smiled a little. "They said that I'd have trouble

finding another place that would take Caruso. So I said they shouldn't feel obligated because of the dog, and I'd work something out. They said they didn't feel obligated, but they kind of liked Caruso. And then they said they kind of liked me, too, if you can believe it."

"Of course I can." She reached over to touch his hand, then returned hers to the steering wheel.

"Ms. Peabody said that they knew something about mistakes and regrets, about trying to make things right and about happy endings." She'd also said she hoped that Mo would find his own.

A happy ending. Maribeth had asked him, when he first told her about his situation, what he'd like his life to look like. He hadn't had an answer because he'd never let himself think in those terms.

But now he had the glimmering of a dream. His relationship with Brooke would become more comfortable, and he'd slowly build one with Evan as well. Which meant he'd stay in Caribou Crossing. Would he get to know his grandkids? Maybe he'd see if he could buy into Hank's business, keep the shop going as the old guy cut back on his work hours. Perhaps he'd eventually get Caruso to relax about wearing a leash.

And there would be Maribeth. The warmhearted, sexy redhead would be . . . what?

A friend and lover on a casual basis? Until her craving for variety had her thinking it was time to replace him?

That didn't feel like much of a happy ending. But what did he have to offer a woman like Maribeth, long term, that the dozens of guys she'd dated hadn't been able to give her?

Wait. Was he seriously thinking about a long-term relationship? A commitment? He wasn't that kind of guy.

Was he? Even if he might possibly be, it sure didn't seem as if Maribeth was that kind of woman.

The phone rang around eleven on Tuesday morning, and Maribeth answered it with a bright "Good morning. This is Days of Your."

"Maribeth, it's Evan."

"Hi there." She glanced at the two customers, a twenty-something new mother and her mom, who were browsing through baby clothes. With the phone held to her ear, she moved farther away from them. "What's up?"

"The end of the year's approaching, and I thought we should talk about transferring the maximum to your Tax-Free Savings Account."

"Uh, sure." Every year in mid-December, they did that. If the government was going to provide a means of sheltering money from tax consequences, she'd take full advantage. But it was only the twenty-eighth of November, so why was he calling now? Unless it was a pretext for sounding her out about Mo. Even if it wasn't, maybe she could take this opportunity. "What fund would you suggest transferring it from?"

They discussed the issue, reached a decision, and then he said, "I had another reason for calling."

"I thought you might."

"I hear that you're seeing, uh, him."

"Mo. Your father. Yes, I am."

There was silence. She checked that her customers were still happily engrossed and said quietly, "I like him. I didn't know him before, but he's told me how things were with him and Brooke, and what a terrible father he was. I truly believe he's changed, Evan, and that he regrets what he did."

"Regrets?" His tone was bitter. "How nice for him. He wasn't the one who suffered through all that crap."

"He knows that. He's not making any excuses." She took a breath and dared to make a comparison. "Like Brooke, he takes full blame for his behavior. He knows there's nothing he can do to make it right. He just wants an opportunity to talk to you."

"Oh, hell, Maribeth. I have a great life. I don't need this asshole back in it."

"Did you need Brooke back?"

Another silence. And then, "I didn't think so at the time. But . . ."

"But it helped you, being able to talk about your childhood with her, and to know how bad she felt about her mistakes."

"I guess. It was a resolution of sorts."

"And a beginning. You're very happy to have you in her life now, right?"

He snorted. "I don't see that happening with . . . him."

"Maybe not. But you won't know unless you talk to him."

"I hate this."

"I can only imagine. But please give Mo credit for trying, at long last, to be a decent man."

"I'll think about it," he said grudgingly. And then, "Sorry. I meant this to be a business call. Or at least I thought I did."

"Evan, it's okay. I'm glad we had a chance to talk."

"I'll attend to your TFSA right away."

"Thanks." She hung up and, as she went to chat with her customers and hear baby stories, she crossed her fingers that Evan would open his mind, and his heart.

After that, more people came in and the store was hopping. It was one thirty before she had a chance to microwave the homemade cauliflower-and-cheddar soup she'd brought for lunch. She perched on the chair behind the counter and spooned it up hungrily, but was only halfway through eating when—wouldn't you know it?—the shop bell rang again.

This time it was Lark Cantrell, whose face was bright with excitement. She didn't say a word, just strode toward Maribeth and held up her left hand. Light glittered off a lovely engagement ring.

Maribeth squealed, and Lark told her all about Eric's romantic proposal at Zephyr Lake on the weekend.

"I am so, so happy for you," Maribeth said. "And for Jayden and Mary." Lark's ex-husband had run out on her and her son Jayden when, as a baby, the boy was diagnosed with cerebral palsy. Lark's mom Mary, a single parent herself, had moved in and been with them ever since.

"I'd told myself I never wanted to fall in love again," Lark said, "but then along came Eric. He'd told himself he never wanted to have a family, but . . ." She grinned.

"But there you were, the three of you, ready-made, perfect, and totally lovable. It was destiny." And she had to wonder, were she and Mo each other's destiny? If Eric could change his mind about wanting a family, maybe so could Mo.

"Well, it took us a while to figure that out for ourselves, but we got there."

Her words gave Maribeth hope. "You're a lucky woman," she told her friend. In all likelihood, within a couple of years Lark and Eric would be having a baby. Maribeth knew her friend hoped to give Jayden a little brother or sister.

Well, she wasn't going to be envious. She'd have a baby too, whether with Mo, by using the sperm donor, or by adoption if it came down to that. Maybe her and Lark's little ones would become good friends.

Lark moved toward the children's section. "I actually did have another reason for coming in. Jayden needs a new winter jacket. He's a couple of inches taller and a good fifteen pounds heavier than last year."

"That's fantastic." The adorable ten-year-old, who'd been confined to a wheelchair until recently, had always been small and weak for his age. "Let's see what I've got." Maribeth skimmed her fingers along a row of hangers and pulled out a couple of possibilities.

"On the subject of destiny," Lark said as she examined the jackets, "how's it going on the sperm donor front? Did you pick one?"

"The doctor. But, well, I decided to wait—at least until next month."

"To make absolutely sure you want to go ahead? That makes sense."

"Yes, something like that."

Lark glanced up from the jackets. "Something like that? What's going on, MB?"

"I'm dating someone."

Lark's dark brown eyes narrowed. "You're usually dating someone. Men, men, men, right? So what you really mean is, this guy's special."

"Maybe. Kind of. I guess."

Lark's black eyebrows arched. "You said Eric and me meeting was destiny. Is it maybe destiny that you'd meet a special guy just when you'd decided to use a sperm donor?"

Maribeth groaned. "I don't know. Maybe. But what kind of destiny? The kind that tests my resolve about whether I want to go ahead and be a single parent? Or the kind that sends me the right man to make babies with?"

"I'd hope for the latter." By now Lark had put the jackets down. "Wouldn't you?"

"Yes! Obviously. Except I'm not at all sure that's what's happening."

"Why not? You think he's special and you have feelings for him. Doesn't he have feelings for you?"

"He likes me. We have chemistry. But he's—" She broke off as the bell jingled again.

It was one of her regulars, a sixtysomething pensioner who came in at least once a week to see if there was anything new in her size. Maribeth called out, "Hi, Mrs. Appleby. I'll be with you in a minute."

"No rush, dear," came the reply.

"He's what?" Lark prompted quietly.

Her own voice low, Maribeth said, "Brooke's ex."

Lark gaped. "No. Not seriously? Does she know?"

"Yes, of course. I asked her first. She's fine with us dating." Maribeth frowned. "Mind you, dating—the way I've always dated—isn't the same thing as getting seriously involved. I don't know if that would bother her or not . . ." Oh great, another thing to worry about. "But there are other problems. He's ten years older than me, which isn't a biggie, but it's there. He's been a real loner and he's wary about relationships. Worst of all, he says he doesn't want any more kids."

"Wow. That's some big stuff, MB."

"I know," she said glumly. "Believe me, I know."

"But you feel that click you've always said was missing?"

She nodded. "And I think Mo may change his mind about kids. If he meets Robin and Alex, he won't be able to resist them." Mind you, if Evan refused to talk to his father, Mo might never even see his grandkids. But surely Evan would relent. "And once he sees how wonderful children are, surely he'll be more open to having another one or two of his own."

Lark frowned. "MB, I know you get these, uh, strong ideas about how things should be and how people should act. And yes, people do change. But do you think it's realistic to expect Mo to change that much?"

"He's already changed so much! He's not at all like the man he used to be. He's a work in progress, so of course he'll keep changing." Bolstering her argument, she said, "Eric changed, right? He was sure he didn't want a family, but when he met you and examined his heart, he found that he truly did. That was a total turnaround."

"That's true," Lark said thoughtfully. "You said Mo is forty-nine?"

"Fifty, actually."

She cocked her head, reflecting. "That's kind of cool. That someone that age isn't set in his ways, but still evolving."

"I know, right? Mo really is pretty cool in so many ways."

"How fast is he evolving?"

"How do you mean?"

"MB, you're thirty-nine. That's one of the big reasons you decided to get pregnant now, isn't it? If it takes Mo a couple of years to reach the point where he can see having children . . ."

"Women have babies in their early and midforties these days."

"They do." There was sympathy in Lark's eyes, and she obviously felt no need to reiterate a bunch of truths that Maribeth was already well aware of. Like the fact that every year she waited, the chance of getting pregnant grew lower and the risks grew higher.

Chapter Twelve

Tuesday night around 6:20, Mo sat at a small conference table in a meeting room in Evan's office. Evan sat across from him. The tension in the air coming from the two of them was almost tangible, so intense that Mo figured one spark would ignite it.

His son had called that afternoon and said he'd spare Mo a few minutes if he came by at six. Mo had showered after work and walked over. The office of "Evan Kincaid—Financial Counselor" was on the second floor of a two-story historic building on Caribou Crossing's main street. When Mo arrived, the office door was locked, so he knocked.

Evan had come to open the door and he and Mo had stared at each other, and then without a word Evan led the way through the empty reception area and past an office with a desk to this meeting room.

Now, after Mo had recited the same story he'd told everyone else—one he figured Evan would have already heard from both his mother and his wife—Mo was still staring at Evan, fascinated by him and fearful of his judgment. This was his son. A thirty-year-old man. He'd been a scrawny, awkward kid, but now he was a tall, well-put-together man in a lightweight navy turtleneck, navy pants, and a tweedy jacket. A man who in many ways seemed to be a blend of his parents, with skin lighter than Mo's but darker than Brooke's; hair medium brown with the remnants of sunshine streaks; eyes blue green but as unique a shade as each of his parents' eyes were.

Evan hadn't said much. When he'd ushered Mo into the room, he hadn't offered him a drink. He'd simply sat down, his body and face rigid, and said, "Well, you're here. Tell me your story." And as Mo spoke, his son hadn't commented or asked questions. He had, however, huffed, snorted, and scowled.

It pissed Mo off, actually. Not that he wanted his son to be a pushover, nor did he expect forgiveness. But it was damned annoying listening to the sound of his own voice and feeling as if every word he spoke was being rejected out of hand. Still, he held on to his temper. When he finished speaking, he closed his mouth and sat still. The room was so quiet that Mo could hear voices drift up from the sidewalk.

Evan's face was set in harsh lines. Mo wondered what it would look like when he was happy, laughing with his wife and kids. With Brooke.

He thought of one more thing he wanted to say. "You gave your mom a second chance. I hope you'll consider doing the same with me."

"Don't even compare yourself to her." Cold fury colored Evan's voice, and he sprang to his feet like a coil that's been wound too tight.

There was no good response, so Mo didn't even try.

Evan paced over to the window and turned. "You screwed up. Every step of the way."

"I know. And I'm sorry."

"You hurt me and Mom! You were too busy drinking to even put food on the table."

Mo nodded. His son was a contained man. His anger was unmistakable, but he kept it under control. Mo would bet that it would take a lot—probably an attack on his wife, child, or mother—before Evan would use his fists.

His son strode around the table until he was across from Mo again, but he didn't sit. He rested his palms on the flat surface and leaned forward, braced on them, glaring at Mo. "You never cared about me! Not one iota."

"I did, in my own, uh, flawed way. But I didn't want a kid and I sure as hell wasn't mature enough to have one."

"You sure as hell weren't." He straightened and crossed his arms in front of his chest. "You may not have wanted a kid, but I wanted a dad. And I deserved a decent one, but instead I got you."

"I know. You deserved much better. Every child deserves to have two responsible, loving parents."

The anger left Evan's face, replaced by an introspective look. His throat rippled as he swallowed hard, and an expression that looked like regret or maybe guilt crossed his face. It struck Mo as an odd reaction to his own straightforward words.

A moment later, Evan narrowed his eyes and resumed his attack, saying, "The best thing you did for me was to leave."

"I've said the same thing to myself, many times." Mo nodded. "Leaving was the best thing I *did* do, but it wasn't the best I could have done. I should've shaped up. Confessed to my sins, gone to jail, straightened myself out, and been a real father to you. And a real husband to Brooke." Maybe if he'd done that, Brooke would have got herself sorted out, too.

"Ha. Like you were capable of that." The words were

harsh, yet there was a hint of something else in Evan's voice, as if his son was imagining what life might have been like if Mo had cleaned up his act.

"Whether I was or wasn't, I didn't do it. And I'm very sorry for that."

"What good does an apology do now?"

"I don't exactly know. It feels like something I need to do."

"For you!" Evan uncrossed his arms and leaned forward, bracing himself on the table again. "This is all about you. You're getting old and you've got a guilty conscience. It's like you're doing confession in church and you want to be absolved of your sins." His face was tense and his blue-green eyes icy. "But you know what? I don't care if you feel guilty for the rest of your life. I don't care about you."

Despite his son's obvious anger and his harsh words, an unexpected warmth tugged at Mo's heart and he felt a visceral urge to reach out and hug Evan. He wanted to ease his son's pain, but he knew that touching him would be the worst thing to do. Mo wasn't used to expressing, much less experiencing, emotion, but he had to tell Evan the truth. "Well, I care about you," he said gruffly.

Again, Evan was taken aback. It was obvious in the widening of his eyes, the slackening of his taut jaw. He recovered quickly. "I don't believe you."

Mo swallowed, wishing he had a drink to ease his parched throat. "I don't blame you. But it's true. And yeah, this is about me, wanting to apologize. But it's about you, too. I want—"

"I hate you. I wish you hadn't come back to Caribou Crossing."

Was his son even listening to him? Or were his defenses, the ones he'd learned from his parents all those years ago, too firmly entrenched? "Does your mother"—Mo cleared his throat—"does she wish I hadn't come?"

Evan blinked. "She's been upset since you got here. She thought you were long gone. She was happy without you, and now you've upset her."

Mo knew all of that, and was sorry for it. But there was more to this than Evan was letting himself see. "But does she wish I hadn't come? Has she said that?"

"Not in so many words. But it's obvious."

"Ask her." Mo pushed back his chair and rose. "Please, for all our sakes, do that one thing. Ask her." He walked toward the door.

When he reached it, he turned back and again faced his son. "I quit on you and your mother once before, when things got too tough for me to handle. This time, I don't plan on leaving."

Evan, still seated, looked worn out as he asked quietly, "Is that a threat?"

"I don't mean it that way. I'm just saying that it matters to me. You and Brooke matter to me. I'm going to wait while you think about this some more." And then he walked out of Evan's office.

When he was outside on the street, the strength left Mo's legs. Shaky, he leaned against the cold brick wall of the old building. He raised one hand and dragged it through his hair, feeling tension pounding inside his skull. His other hand dangled at his side, and after a few minutes something nudged it.

He jerked, glanced down, and there was Caruso. Again, the dog nudged his hand.

"Hey, buddy," Mo said. "I'm sure glad to see you." He stroked the dog's head. "Come on now, we need to walk. Don't want Evan coming out and finding us lurking here." As Mo forced his legs down the sidewalk, Caruso trotted along with him. Mo remembered to take the leash from his jacket pocket and dangle it from his left hand.

Where to go? He was too keyed up to sit in his tiny apartment, and he wasn't fit company for anyone but the undemanding dog. Calling Maribeth was out of the question. Maybe he and Caruso would walk out of town, hike in the cold for an hour or so until Mo's mind settled down.

In his jeans pocket, his phone vibrated, startling him. He still wasn't used to having a phone, or having anyone who'd want to call him. When he slid it from his pocket, the caller name was displayed: Maribeth. Maybe he shouldn't answer, given his mood, and yet he couldn't resist.

"Hey," he said, the phone to his ear as he carried on down the sidewalk. More and more businesses were putting up Christmas decorations and window displays, which he figured must annoy Maribeth since it was only November 28. The thought brought a hint of a smile to his lips.

"Hi, Mo. Have you eaten?"

"Uh, no." The thought of food hadn't even crossed his mind.

"I stayed at the shop to do some bookkeeping and I have a craving for Chinese food. But it's much better shared, so you can order more things. Interested?"

He was. Mostly in seeing her pretty face, though he did like Chinese food. But he said, "Not tonight, thanks."

"No problem." A pause, and then, "Are you okay? You sound a little . . ."

A little what? Abrupt? Depressed? Pissed off? "I'm okay. Just not, uh, very good company."

Another pause. "Why not?"

He sighed. "I talked to Evan."

"Oh," she said on a long breath of air. "It didn't go well?"

"Nuh-uh."

"I'm sorry. Want to talk about it?"

"There's really nothing to talk about. I said my bit and I'm not sure he even listened. He's determined to be pissed off at me. In the end he said he hated me and didn't want me in his life. End of story."

"Oh, Mo, I'm so sorry."

The compassion in her voice warmed him. "Yeah. Well. I told him that I didn't plan on running away this time, and I'd wait for him to think about it some more."

"Good. I'm sure he will."

Right now, Mo didn't have much hope that it would do any good. In Evan's state of mind, the thinking would likely be about all the past wrongs Mo had done him.

"So," Maribeth said, "how about Chinese takeout and a movie on TV, and we don't have to talk about anything at all?"

Caruso's nose bumped Mo's hand. The dog had acute hearing and had no doubt recognized Maribeth's voice.

It occurred to Mo that Maribeth was doing the human equivalent of Caruso's hand-bump. Offering companionship without making demands. Damn, but he was lucky to have the two of them in his life. Gruffly, he said, "You really do want someone to share that Chinese food, don't you?"

"That's my sole reason," she said cheerfully.

"You're a fine woman, you know that?"

"Oh!" Rare for her, she sounded flustered. "Thank you, Mo."

"Why don't you go home, get the fire going, put on something comfy? I'll stop at the Golden Dragon and pick up some food. What do you like?"

"Everything. I love their chicken chow mein, and

please include something with veggies. Otherwise, I'll leave it to you."

"Be there shortly."

His energy had returned and his step quickened as he and Caruso headed toward the restaurant. Mo had passed by it several times, always thinking it looked tempting, but he'd never been inside before.

When he walked in, telling Caruso to wait outside, he saw that the Golden Dragon was very different from Arigata. This place, which smelled spicy and enticing, wasn't elegant and subdued, but well-lit and casual. Most of the tables were occupied, a couple by family groups.

A teenage girl emerged from the back and hurried toward him with a smile. She had Asian features and wore jeans and a white T-shirt with the logo of a gold dragon outlined in black. "Hi, I'm Emily," she said. "Table for one?"

"Actually, it's takeout for two."

"Sure." She handed him a menu made of a sheet of paper folded in three. "Let me know what you'd like."

He had a quick peruse and said, "How about chicken chow mein, the chop suey with nuts, beef with broccoli and black beans, and Szechuan prawns? Does that sound like a good combination?"

"For sure. And rice, of course."

"You bet."

"I'll put in the order. Have a seat. It won't be long."

He claimed a chair in the entrance area and took a closer look at the menu. On the front was the restaurant's name and logo, and the words, "The oldest restaurant in Caribou Crossing. In continuous operation since the Gold Rush." On the back, he found a blurb and photos. He learned that Yao Men Wu and his wife, Lian, had come to Canada at the beginning of the gold rush when there was a wave of Chinese immigration. They made their way to the primitive camp at Caribou Crossing, put up a tent, and opened a restaurant. As the town grew up, the restaurant moved into more permanent accommodation. The Yaos and their descendants kept it in operation until the present time, making it over a century and a half old.

Emily emerged from the back with two takeout bags, and Mo pulled out his wallet. "Are you part of the family who owns the restaurant?"

"Yes. I'm Emily Yao. My parents run the Golden Dragon. They say that one day it'll be me and my brother's turn, but I don't really think I want to stay in Caribou Crossing. It's, like, so small, you know?"

"Yeah. But there's something to be said for that." When he used to live here, he, too, had disparaged the town. But it had changed and so had he, and at the moment there was no place he'd rather be. Unless, of course, his son continued to shun him.

"I guess," she said doubtfully. "Well, enjoy the food. Hope you come back again."

"Thanks."

Outside, Caruso sniffed the bags and did a head toss.

"It's human food," Mo told him. "But I bet Maribeth has some dog food in her pantry. Come on, let's hurry so this stuff doesn't get cold."

When they arrived at Maribeth's welcoming house, Caruso came to the front door with Mo rather than beating a retreat around back. Maribeth, in a turquoise sweater and stretchy black pants, gave Mo a warm hug and Caruso a scratch behind the ears.

"I set the coffee table in the living room," she said, ushering them in. "Just bring the bags in there and we'll dish out the food. Oh, how much do I owe you?"

"I've got it," he said as he followed her.

"No, really, Mo, it was my idea."

"Maribeth, I'm not hard up, okay?" He put the bags on the table. "Hank's paying me decent money. Besides, I have a fair bit saved up from my previous jobs."

"If you're sure." She turned toward the door to the hall. "Come on, Caruso. There's food for you in the kitchen. Mo, what would you like to drink?"

"I'll have a glass of that orange drink, if you've got it."

"Coming up."

After she disappeared down the hall, he set the covered containers on the round cork pads she'd laid on the table, checked the fire, and then sat down on the couch.

When she came back with his drink and a mug of tea, she said, "You want to watch a movie?"

"I'd like that. I don't feel much like talking."

"I wonder if we can agree on something." She sat beside him, picked up the remote, and navigated to the movie menu. "Oh, how about this? It's ages since I've seen *Raiders of the Lost Ark*."

"Indiana Jones? Yeah, I could go for that." He leaned forward and began removing the tops from the containers. Delicious aromas mingled in the air.

As the movie titles began to play, he and Maribeth dished out food, and then he covered the containers again and sat back to eat.

This was good. Instead of roaming the chilly countryside or sitting in his small apartment alone with Caruso, he had tasty food, an engaging movie, and a lovely woman at his side. A woman who, amazingly, knew when to let a guy alone to nurse his wounds.

The way she treated him made him feel as if he were special. When he'd come to Caribou Crossing, he'd figured that the best he could be in life was a man who trod lightly and didn't cause harm. Now he found himself wondering if he could be more than that, and if he and Maribeth might . . . Might what?

This was the woman who'd been dating for more than twenty-five years. The woman who loved variety in all things. If she had a knack for making a man feel special, it was because she had lots of experience. He had to remember that she'd one day tire of him, just as she had of all the men who'd come before.

What he needed to do was enjoy the moment, not worry about the future.

On Sunday, Maribeth woke alone and found that her period had started. She felt a little crampy, not to mention depressed, because only a couple of weeks ago she'd optimistically thought that she might be pregnant by now. Still, she reminded herself that she'd postponed insemination for a good reason. If things worked out with her and Mo, she'd have a real father for her child.

In better spirits, she did a long yoga session, which eased the cramps. After a leisurely breakfast and a lengthy Skype call with her grandparents, she prepared food for that night as well as some to stock up her freezer for the week to come. It was a familiar and satisfying Sunday routine, and yet today she found herself missing Mo. He hadn't come over the previous night because Hank Hennessey and his wife had invited him to dine with them.

She hadn't seen Mo since Thursday when he'd asked her over to his place for dinner. She'd expected takeout or something from a can, but he'd surprised her with an excellent home-made chili accompanied by a tossed salad. Dessert had been apple crisp, which he admitted his landladies had supplied in exchange for a portion of his chili. She was happy to see how well he was getting along with the retired schoolteachers, and that he was in better spirits than on Tuesday night—even though he hadn't heard anything further from Evan.

Maribeth had spent the night at his place. It was cozy in the studio apartment with Mo and Caruso, but she did feel a little odd about having sex in the same house as her fourth-grade teacher. When Mo pointed out that her teacher might well also be having sex, it hadn't helped one bit.

Smiling at the memory, she changed into her outdoor clothes: heavy pants, thick sweater, and socks. She was on her way downstairs when she heard noises on her front porch. Mo said something she couldn't make out, and just when she was expecting her doorbell to ring, she instead heard Caruso's warble.

Laughing, she hurried down the remaining stairs and flung open the door. "Hi, guys."

It had started to snow, not heavily but with soft, light flakes. Mo's black hair and the shoulders of his jacket were dusted with white, his cheeks were almost as rosy as his red scarf, and he was smiling. Her heart flooded with warmth. It was amazing how just seeing him could make her so happy.

She bent to greet his companion, whose thick cinnamon coat was also decorated with snowflakes. "Caruso, you sound much nicer than my doorbell." She stroked his damp head and was pleased when he wagged his tail.

Then she unbuttoned Mo's jacket, slipped her arms inside, and hugged him. "It's good to see you." Should she tell him how much she'd missed him? No, it might make him feel like she was getting possessive. And she wasn't; she wasn't the clingy sort. She had her own life, her friends, lots of activities that kept her busy. It was just that if a day went by without seeing Mo, life seemed a little flat.

"Good to see you, too." His arms were warm and firm

around her, and when she tipped her head up to his, he gave her a long, thorough kiss. Then he pushed her away. "Better stop now, if you want to get those lights up."

With some regret, she said, "Yes, I really do. It's the third of December, so it's officially Christmas month."

"By Maribeth's rules," he teased.

"Which are the only rules that count at this house." She put on her jacket, red knitted hat, and gloves and led the way to the garage. As she and Mo pulled out the boxes containing the outdoor Christmas lights, she said, "How was dinner with Hank and Inga?"

"Nice. Inga is what Hank's like beneath the gruffness. Know what I mean?"

"You mean that Hank's really a softy underneath that macho façade. And Inga's just a softy, through and through."

"That's it. Want to carry a box and I'll bring the ladder?"

Lugging supplies, they went to the front of the house and he set up the ladder while she returned to the garage for the second box. She opened it. "The multicolored lights go along the eaves," she said, "and the twinkly white ones around the windows."

"Got it. I'll start with the eaves. You untangle the strings and pass them up to me."

Once they got a process going, he said, "After we had dinner, Hank and Inga left me in their living room alone for a few minutes. I guess they had a private chat in the kitchen. Anyhow, then they came back and he asked me if I'd be interested in being his partner. And eventually taking over the garage."

"Wow." Gazing up at him, she blinked snowflakes from her lashes. That would mean Mo definitely staying in Caribou Crossing. "What did you tell him?"

"That I'd seriously consider it. He said he wouldn't pressure me, but I think he'd like to get things resolved."

She handed up another loop of colored lights, enjoying the soft kiss of snowflakes on her cheeks. "What does it depend on, for you? How would it work out financially?"

"The financing isn't a problem. He's priced comparable businesses and says his is worth around a hundred thousand. I've got that much and—"

"You do?"

He glanced down at her and laughed. "Thought all I owned was the pack on my back? No, for the last ten or so years I've saved more than I've spent. And done okay with investments."

She'd never thought of footloose Mo as being an investor. The man was full of surprises. "Okay, then I won't feel bad when you buy me dinner."

"Anyhow, Hank says what he'd like to do is have me buy just less than fifty percent, so he's the senior partner for the next year. Over time, I'd increase my share, and when he's eventually ready, I'd buy him out. But he gets to keep working part-time for as long as he wants."

"Sounds like a good deal. What do you think?"

"Yeah, it's a real good deal. But if things never work out with Evan, it could be awkward, me being in the same town as him."

She nodded, understanding but not happy about the uncertainty. Couldn't things just come together for all of them? Why did this have to be so complicated? "I hope tonight's dinner is another step in the right direction."

"Had to bring that up, did you? Here I was relaxing and enjoying the afternoon."

"It'll be fine." Surreptitiously, she crossed her gloved fingers. She and Brooke had been talking and thought it would be a good idea to have a social evening that included Brooke's husband, Jake. The women had persuaded the men.

Maribeth liked Jake a lot, especially when she saw how much he loved Brooke and how he doted on their baby, Nicki. But she had to admit, the police chief, a former undercover cop, could be one awe-inspiring guy. She didn't figure Mo would be intimidated, but she was a little afraid that the guys might face off rather than get along.

"Hey, if you keep daydreaming," Mo said, "we'll never get these lights hung."

"Right. Sorry." She unwound more of the string and fed it up to him.

Across the street, Mr. and Mrs. Gardiner came out, waved, and began to set up their holiday display of reindeer pulling a sleigh with Santa inside. They had a radio on their porch, and snatches of George Strait singing "Jingle Bell Rock" drifted in the snowy air.

"Lucky for them it's December," Mo said, gazing across the street from high up on the ladder, "or they'd be in serious trouble with you." Then he called, "Hey, Caruso! Damn it, Maribeth, can you get him?"

The dog, who'd been happily exploring Maribeth's yard and playing in the snow, had made his way across the street to sniff at the plastic reindeer. Maribeth ran over, clumsy in her boots. "Caruso, leave those alone!"

The dog turned his face up to her in a "what did I do wrong?" expression.

Mrs. Gardiner said, "Oh, isn't he the prettiest boy? I didn't know you had a dog, Maribeth."

"He belongs to my friend, Mo. He's a New Guinea singing dog and a bit of a free spirit."

"Well, as long as he does no harm," she said comfortably. "I never did take with having to put dogs and kids on leashes. Seems to me it's better to just teach them proper behavior."

"I totally agree."

The women watched as Mr. Gardiner arranged the reindeer and Caruso inspected all of them. "Do *not* lift your leg," Maribeth warned the dog and, surprisingly, he didn't. When he'd sniffed to his heart's content, he came to sit at her side, where he lifted his head and sang.

"What in hell?" Mr. Gardiner said, and then he laughed. "If that don't beat all. There you go, Annie, that's the coyote you keep saying you've heard."

Maribeth tapped her leg, saying, "Come on, Caruso, or Mo will never get those lights finished."

They returned to her yard, and she kept an eye on the dog while she and Mo finished stringing lights.

When they were done, she flicked the switch. She and Mo walked out to the sidewalk and gazed at the house, admiring their handiwork. "The snow makes everything prettier," she said. "More holiday-like."

"If you say so," he said tolerantly.

She poked him in the ribs. "Grinch. Come on in. I need to get changed."

Inside, Mo said he'd get the fire going. She made sure the slow cooker was humming away and then hurried upstairs. She took an ibuprofen to ease the slight achiness from her period and then donned semi-dressy jeans and, in keeping with the Christmas lights, a red cashmere sweater and dangly earrings with multicolored stones.

When she came down again, she found Mo in the sitting room with a bottle of San Pellegrino. He had taken off his sweater. Underneath it he wore a nice shirt which, with jeans, looked just right for a casual Sunday night dinner.

"You look pretty," he said, tugging her down beside him on the couch.

She took the bottle from him, had a long swallow, and then he removed the bottle from her hand and put it on the coffee table. He gave her a leisurely kiss and she made small sounds of pleasure as she kissed him back.

She forced herself to pull away before things got too heated. "To be continued," she promised. "They'll be here any minute." She'd barely finished speaking when headlights flashed through the window as a car turned into the driveway.

When she rose, Mo did, too, grumbling, "Life used to be so much easier."

She clasped his hand and held on to it as she opened the door to see Brooke climbing out of the passenger seat of her Toyota and Jake extracting Nicki from the child seat in the back.

"They brought their kid?" Mo said in a low voice, sounding a little horrified.

"They're parents with a young one. Of course they did." She'd never thought to mention it to him because she'd taken Nicki's presence for granted. "Is that a problem?"

"I guess not. When I've gotten together with Brooke, she's had their daughter in another room, and I've never actually seen her before."

They stopped talking as their guests came up the path to the door, with Brooke holding Nicki's hand and Jake toting a bag of toddler stuff.

"The lights look great, MB," Brooke said. "We haven't had a chance to hang ours yet."

"Thanks. We put them up this afternoon." She ushered them in. "Jake, you and Mo have met, haven't you?"

"We have," he said evenly. "Hello, Kincaid." He held out his hand.

"Brannon," Mo said, shaking his hand.

The handshake was more than casual, and Maribeth sensed that the men were, if not challenging each other, at least conveying some kind of testosterone-type message. She studied the pair, both very handsome men, making comparisons. Jake was taller and broader across the shoulders, though Mo was equally fit and muscled. They both had black hair, but Jake's was cut in a short, neat style that showed off his strong features while Mo's was longer and curlier. Mo's hair, together with his dark skin and unusual eyes, gave him a more exotic, dramatic masculine appeal.

Maribeth squatted down in front of Nicki. The toddler, who would turn two in February, looked adorable in a puffy red coat and red gumboots with black lady bugs on them. The little girl had inherited her dad's black hair rather than Brooke's blond, and had smoky blue eyes. "Hi, Nicki," Maribeth said.

"Tee Bee!" she said, opening her arms in a request to be lifted up. The name was her way of saying Auntie MB.

Maribeth hoisted her and planted a big kiss on her nose. "Nicki, this is my friend, Mo."

Mo said awkwardly, "Hi there, Nicki."

The child gazed at him and her forehead puckered. "Ma?" she ventured doubtfully, and glanced toward Brooke, who was taking off her coat. Maribeth knew that Nicki called her mother Mama.

Mo stifled a laugh. "Not quite. Mo," he pronounced clearly, and then repeated it. "Mo."

"Mo-Mo," Nicki said more confidently.

"That'll do fine." He smiled at the girl, and Maribeth thought that it was impossible to resist Nicki's charm.

While Maribeth held the toddler, Mo hung up Brooke's and Jake's coats, and then they all went into the sitting room. Maribeth offered beverages and everyone chose fruit drinks. Jake, who'd often have a beer or two when he was off duty, said he'd pass tonight because he'd be driving home on snowy roads with precious cargo.

Mo went to the kitchen to get the drinks and Maribeth, sitting down in a chair with Nicki on her lap, said, "Jake, thanks for coming."

"It's important to Brooke." He seated himself on the sofa beside his wife and mustered a smile. "Besides, it's always good to see you, and you always have great food. And of course Nicki loves you."

"And I adore her. But wow, every time I see her, she's grown." Right now, the child was squirming to get free, so Maribeth put her down so she could explore. She puttered around the room in her clunky boots.

"She's a smart one," Jake said with pride. "It's hard keeping up with her."

Brooke rose and went over to her daughter. "Her latest thing is toilet training." She took a blanket and a couple of stuffed animals out of the baby bag. "Everyone says to wait until the child shows interest in it, and Nicki definitely has." She got the girl settled with the toys. "Much as I hate to see her grow up, I admit I won't miss the diapers."

Mo had walked into the room as she was speaking and said, "Oh, man, I remember diapers. Bleck." He handed out the drinks and took the other chair.

"Ha," Brooke said, rising from the floor. "Seems to me you always found a way to avoid changing them."

"So did you," he shot back. "When we were living with your parents, you usually managed to get your mom to do it."

There was a snippiness to Brooke's and Mo's banter,

but also a sense of intimacy, a reminder that they'd been married for a number of years.

Brooke wrinkled her nose. "Okay, true enough. Fortunately for both of us, Evan was always ahead of his age when it came to development."

There was an uncomfortable pause and Maribeth hunted for something to say, to shift the focus away from the exes' relationship.

Jake got there first. "I admit," he said, "back before I met Brooke, I sure never figured I'd be changing diapers."

Brooke sat down beside him again and took his hand. "No, the tough old undercover cop on his Harley never planned on being domesticated." The edge was gone, and now her teasing tone was affectionate.

Chapter Thirteen

Mo stared at Jake Brannon. Brooke's husband had been an undercover cop on a Harley? He stifled a snort of laughter. Seemed she hadn't gotten over her taste for bad boys in black leather. "You worked undercover?" Mo said to Jake.

"Yeah, for many years. I pretty much planned on keeping doing that."

"Until he was on an operation in Caribou Crossing," Brooke said, "and crashed his bike through my white picket fence. And no, before he jumps on me for saying that, it's not that he's a bad driver. He'd been shot, lost a lot of blood, and passed out. Which was the only reason"—she leaned her head against his shoulder—"that I forgave him for smashing my fence."

"It was a sign," Jake said, putting his arm around her. "The Harley knew where I belonged even if it took me a while to figure it out."

It was weird seeing Brooke with her husband. When Mo'd been married to her, he hadn't exactly been faithful, yet it had pissed him off when other guys flirted with the pretty blonde. Now it all seemed so long ago. He and

Brooke were different people. Though he was no longer attracted to her in a sexual way, he felt genuine affection, maybe more than he had when they'd been together and both been so miserable. It was pretty clear that Jake made her happy, and Mo was glad for her.

It was also strange seeing her with her daughter. The child had Jake's coloring, but there was something about her face that reminded him of Brooke. As far as he could see, both Nicki's parents lavished her with loving care. Lucky little girl—and poor Evan, who'd been denied that same attention. Mo wondered how his son felt about this decades-younger half sister.

While he'd been reflecting, Maribeth had been trying to coax Brooke and Jake to tell him the rest of the story about how they got together. Mo wouldn't mind hearing it and besides, it would keep the focus off him. "Oh, come on," he said. "I'm interested."

Brooke glanced over to check that Nicki, down on the rug, was absorbed in playing with a stuffed cat and stuffed dog. "There'd been a murder down in Vancouver." She spoke softly. "And it looked like it might be drug-related. Go on, Jake, tell him what brought you up here."

Mo settled back with his drink and listened as Jake told about his undercover operation and how he'd been shot and had his cover blown. After he crashed his bike, Brooke had helped him by supplying a new cover story.

"Yeah, I could see how the excitement would have appealed to you," he said to his ex. In fact, that fit more with his image of her than did the one of a contented small-town wife and mother.

"Yes, but no," Brooke said. "I mean, sure, I used to seek excitement. But since I'd gotten sober and gone on bipolar meds, I'd relegated my adventure to between the pages of books. My life was stable. I had my routines and

I played it safe. I was afraid I couldn't handle anything more, afraid I'd start cycling—you know, manic, then depressed—again."

Oh yeah, he knew what she was talking about. For a moment, he wondered what their lives would have been like if she'd been diagnosed back when they were married.

"But," she said, "there was Jake, and I had to figure out how to deal with him."

Her husband squeezed her shoulders. "She was a lot stronger than she gave herself credit for." He picked up the story again, telling about his investigation and how the killer had been brought to justice. "And all the time," he said, "Brooke and I were growing closer."

"And by then you'd figured out that you liked Brooke and Caribou Crossing, and wanted to stay?" Mo asked.

The married couple exchanged knowing smiles. "Something like that," Brooke said. "But that's a story for another day."

"And right now," Maribeth said, "it's time for dinner. Mo, can you help me in the kitchen? And, Brooke, you and Jake can get Nicki settled in the high chair. The food'll be ready in five minutes."

When she and Mo reached the kitchen, she gave him a quick hug and kiss. "How are you holding up?"

"Okay so far." He had grown more relaxed as Brooke and Jake shared their story. He sniffed the air. "That sure smells good."

"Chicken stew with dumplings. I put the dumpling dough in when I got our drinks."

"You're pretty amazing, you know. What do you need me to do?"

"Could you unplug the slow cooker and take it into the dining room? Set it at one end of the table, on the trivet I put out."

Trivet? A new word to him, but the meaning seemed pretty obvious. When he went into the dining room, he interrupted a hushed conversation between Brooke and Jake, who were getting their toddler settled in a high chair at the table. Mo put the casserole dish on a glazed ceramic tile with a blue, white, and yellow pattern, then left the family alone.

Maribeth was chopping a red-skinned apple. "Would you get me the salad from the fridge?" she asked.

He brought her a bowl of mixed greens and she slid the apple bits into it, then tossed in a handful of raisins. She shook up the contents of a small jar and poured them over. "Mild seasonings tonight," she said, "and food that's easy for Nicki to eat by herself."

"Chicken stew sounds just right for a snowy December night." He picked up the salad and carried it to the dining room, and Maribeth followed.

She got everyone seated: Brooke and Nicki on one side of the table, with Jake at the end beside Nicki. Maribeth placed herself and Mo on the other side of the table with him across from Brooke. That also put him beside the serving dishes.

"Mo," she said, "would you serve the chicken, and then we'll pass the salad around."

"Sure." Glad to have something to do, he stood and dished out portions.

Brooke served salad to herself and Nicki, then passed the bowl to Jake. After that, the talk was casual, about how delicious the food was and how everyone had spent the weekend. Mo kept pretty quiet.

He noted that Nicki was included in the conversation and participated readily, usually managing to make her thoughts clear despite her limited vocabulary. She was also reasonably proficient with a fork and spoon, not spilling much down her chin or onto the bib she wore.

He tried to remember Evan at that age. They'd left L.A. by then and come to Canada. Had Evan turned two when they were living in Red Deer, Lethbridge, or Lillooet? Had Mo been repairing cars, selling motorcycles, or working at a twenty-four-hour convenience store? The months and years blurred together. So many places, so many jobs, so much drinking.

Everyone was on seconds when Jake turned to Mo and asked, "How long are you planning on staying in Caribou Crossing?"

Mo put down his fork. "I'm not sure. Hank Hennessey and I have talked about me buying into the garage, taking it over one day. But . . ." He sighed and glanced across the table at Brooke. "I'm giving Evan time and hoping he'll come around. But if he doesn't, and he really never wants to see me, maybe I should respect that and move away."

His ex pressed her lips together, her tropical ocean eyes looking troubled. "I don't know what to say, Mo. It took him some time before he agreed to see me."

"But he did see me," he pointed out. "And it didn't go well."

"I think maybe when he reconciled with me," Brooke said slowly, "he ended up putting even more blame on you." She leaned forward, gazing straight into his eyes. "I think he still had all the hurt and anger inside, and once he stopped directing some of it toward me, it all went on you. And that was easy for him because you weren't, um, real to him. You were gone and he never expected to see you again. So it was easy to hate you."

Mo swallowed hard, Maribeth's delicious food settling in his gut like oil sludge in a vehicle engine. "That's what he said. That he hates me."

Maribeth's hand snuck over to squeeze his thigh, and he was grateful to her.

"I'm sorry about that," Brooke said. "You were the easy target by not being here. Now you're real, and he has to deal with that, and doing it is painful. He's mad at you for that, as well as for past wrongs."

"Am I causing him more pain by being here?"

"In the short term, yes. But you're like"—her lips curved with a hint of mischief—"a nasty boil, and he's not going to be able to ignore you. Pain is going to drive him to deal with you, and I hope he can lance the wound, and ultimately the infection and pain will drain away."

"A boil." He grinned at his ex, liking the woman she'd become. "I knew I was a sh—" Remembering Nicki, he broke off. He figured the adults knew what he'd been going to say. "But now I'm a boil?"

Brooke laughed, and so did Maribeth.

Mo forced himself to turn to Jake and ask, "What do you think? Evan's your stepson."

Jake's mouth quirked on one side. "We don't really treat it that way since I'm only seven years older than him."

Mo tried not to show his surprise. That made Jake eight years younger than Brooke. Not that there was anything wrong with that, as the saying went.

"But yeah," Jake said, "I've gotten to know Evan. He's a good man. The kind who tries to do the right thing. I think he will this time, too."

"What's the right thing?" Mo asked. Brooke's husband sure had no reason to be on Mo's side.

"For him and for you," Jake said, "the right thing is to reconcile." He gazed levelly at Mo. "I checked you out."

Mo had expected that. "You're RCMP. Of course you would."

"Your story holds up. Everything you told Brooke."

"It's the truth."

Jake pinned him with a steely gaze. "The whole truth? You didn't shade the story to make yourself look better?"

Mo snorted. "What part of 'I'm a sh—uh, a sure-fire loser' sounds like trying to make myself look better?"

Jake nodded, and now his expression was lighter. "Yeah, there's that. I've got good radar when it comes to BS, and I'm not getting that from you."

Maribeth finally spoke. "So what do you think Mo should do, Jake and Brooke? Just keep waiting?"

Jake said thoughtfully, "Working undercover, I know the value of waiting. But it's boring as h—heck." He glanced wryly at Nicki, who seemed less interested in the conversation than in picking raisins out of her salad and eating them. "Little girl, you've sure cleaned up your daddy's speech. Anyhow, here's something I've learned about waiting. If nothing happens after a while, you can often find a way to poke the beast."

"Poke the beast?" Brooke echoed with amusement. "Evan's a beast?"

"Ha ha," her husband said. "You know what I mean. Facilitate some kind of change that stirs up the mix."

They were all quiet, and Mo wondered how he could poke Evan without further raising his ire.

"Here's a thought," Maribeth said. "We watch our speech and behavior around Nicki because she's a child, right? She's impressionable and she needs to be protected. But Evan's a grown-up."

The three adults stared at her, and then Brooke said, "Yes. And?"

"We shouldn't tiptoe around him. We should get on with our own lives, the way we'd normally live them."

"My turn," Jake said. "Yes, and?"

"You know that I have an open house on the day I put

up my Christmas tree, and that's going to be next Sunday." She turned to Mo. "I invite all my friends and their significant others and kids. All my old friends from school and those I've made over the years. I'll be inviting Sally and Ben, Corrie and her boyfriend, Lark and her family, Dave and Cassidy, and of course Robin." She glanced between her two friends. "Brooke and Jake, I hope you can come and bring Nicki."

The spouses exchanged grins. "We'd love to," Brooke said. "It's always a lot of fun. And I see where you're going with this."

So did Mo.

"Of course I'll invite Jess and Evan, and little Alex," Maribeth said. "They almost always come."

Mo wasn't sure if this was a wise idea, but it would definitely shake things up. And not only for Evan. The thought of meeting all those people, and especially Evan's stepdaughter and young son, his grandchildren, made him distinctly jumpy.

Maribeth went on. "Mo, I think this year I'll invite Hank Hennessey and Inga. And Ms. Haldenby and Ms. Peabody."

Now she was stacking the deck with people who seemed, for whatever reason, to support him. The woman truly was amazing. Could her idea possibly work?

"Evan knows you two are dating," Brooke said. "He'll guess Mo will be here and he'll stay away."

Mo's heart sank. So much for that idea.

Maribeth was afraid Brooke was right. She tilted her head, chin up. "Then we'll have a lovely time without Evan. He'll miss out, and so will poor Jess. And he'll miss out at the next social event, and the next one. You've done everything you can do, and he's the one who's being stubborn."

"Maribeth, I'm not sure—" Brooke started tentatively, but Mo's voice, speaking at the same time, was louder and overrode hers.

"Oh, come on," he said. "That's not fair. It took me years to sort myself out and have the guts to come back here and apologize. Why should Evan be expected to suddenly change his mind about me?"

Okay, maybe he was right. She was impressed that Mo thought that way. She gave him a warm smile and squeezed his arm. "You're defending your son. That's so nice, Mo. And I'm sorry. I know you're right and I was being too harsh. I'm just impatient because I know you and Evan are both going to be so much happier when you've worked things out."

"I agree," Brooke said softly.

"And then you can finalize things with Hank," Maribeth said, "because you'll be staying in Caribou Crossing." Mo's new life would fall into place, he'd grow close to his grandkids, and maybe Maribeth's dreams really would come true.

"I think it's worth trying MB's plan for the open house," Brooke said. "If that doesn't work, then we'll consider what to do next. With Christmas coming, there are lots of social events, and I'm certainly not going to put Mo ahead of Evan and his family."

"God, no, Brooke," Mo said.

She smiled at him. "So we'll start with the open house and see how that goes." And then she leveled a rather stern gaze at Maribeth. "I think that's fair, don't you, MB?"

Taking that as a warning to not interfere too much with another family's issues, Maribeth nodded. "It's fair."

"Good," Brooke responded. "So, for the moment, we

have a week to try to get Evan to come to the open house. Tell Jess your plan, MB. She'll quietly lobby with Evan. I'll talk to him, too, and let him know Jake and I had dinner with you and Mo. Jake will put in a word, too. Won't you, sweetheart?"

Her husband shot her a wry look. "If I know what's good for me, right?"

"You catch on quickly," she teased back.

Maribeth drummed her fingernails on the table. "Hmm, I wonder . . ."

"I'm afraid to ask," Jake said.

"Ms. Haldenby. She was Evan's teacher. She has a, um, commanding way about her. Most of her former students are still afraid of her. If she had a word with Evan . . ." She pressed her lips together. "She said he probably needs to feel like he's in control. She could find some way of showing him how coming to my open house would put him in a position of control."

"You wouldn't," Mo said.

She gave him a knowing grin. "When I call to invite her and her wife, maybe I can find a way of sounding her out. Subtly." If she had the nerve. Maribeth had always been more than a little in awe of her fourth-grade teacher, but she was thirty-nine now. It was time to grow up. "I'm on a mission, and woe to anyone who stands in my way." Little did Mo know that her true mission was to find out if he was her destiny, the love of her life, the future father of her children.

"MB's the commander," Jake said, "and she's mustering her troops and soliciting allies."

"I'm, uh, stunned to think I'd have allies," Mo said. "I don't know why people would be on my side."

"Because you shared yourself with them," Maribeth said. "You told the truth and you revealed your vulnerabilities."

"Sh—" Mo cut off the exclamation and changed it to "Sugar."

Jake shot him a sympathetic look. "Yeah. Women spout this stuff all the time, and it wreaks havoc on us guys."

"While Mo's nursing his fragile ego," Maribeth said with a grin, "I'm going to clear the table and fetch dessert."

"I can help," Mo said.

"I go pot-tie now!" Nicki announced in an urgent tone.

Brooke jumped up. "I'll help MB in the kitchen. Jake, if you could look after your daughter, I bet Mo would be willing to assist."

While Mo shot her a horrified look, Maribeth and Jake both laughed. Jake said, "Yeah, if we're going to be his allies, Mo's got to give us something in return." As his wife passed by him, he rose, looped an arm around her waist, and pulled her in for a smooch.

Then, as the two women cleared the table, Jake freed Nicki from her high chair and turned to Mo. "Time to man up. I'll get the supplies. Meet me in the downstairs bathroom." Then, to the little girl, he said, "Mo-Mo's going to carry you to the bathroom, sweetie."

Before Mo could react, Jake had dumped the child into his arms, saying, "Better be quick about it, Mo. Nicki doesn't give a lot of warning."

Maribeth stifled a giggle as Mo hurried out of the room, holding Nicki like she was a bomb that might explode any second.

As Maribeth and Brooke moved comfortably around the kitchen, they refined the details of their plan for winning Evan over. But even as they plotted, Maribeth couldn't help wondering how Mo was doing. She wanted him to become familiar with kids and love them the way she did, but potty training wasn't the way she'd have chosen to break him in. Still, it beat changing diapers.

When Maribeth heard voices in the hallway, she peeked out the kitchen door and saw Mo and Nicki walking from the powder room to the dining room, side by side. The little girl had her fingers curled into the leg of his jeans and was chattering away to him about how she rode horsies with her mama and daddy. Best of all, Mo looked interested and told her that he and Tee Bee also rode horsies.

Grinning, Maribeth pulled her head back into the kitchen. "Too cute."

Brooke studied her. "Oh, Maribeth. Are you getting in too deep with Mo?"

"What? All I said was that he and Nicki looked cute."

"It was your expression. You're falling for him."

Of course she was. Maribeth straightened her shoulders. "If I was, would that be a problem for you?"

"Not in the way you mean. But—"

Eager to defend her budding relationship, Maribeth jumped in. "I know you said you were afraid he might, uh, drag me down because he's kind of a lost soul. But you see how he's changed. Maybe his soul was lost for a while, but he's found it now. He isn't dragging me down, Brooke, he's making me happy. The way no man ever has before."

Her friend's forehead creased. "You want children. More than anything else, you said. Do you really think Mo would buy into that?"

"I hope so." When she smiled, her lips trembled. "In time. Once he sees how wonderful kids are. And believes he could be a good father."

Brooke sighed. "I like the new Mo. I really do. But I wonder if you're asking too much of him."

"I'm not asking it. Not yet. We're still taking things one day at a time."

"But you, my friend, are hoping. And you're thirty-nine. And you want to be pregnant."

"You got pregnant at forty-two."

Her friend gave a reluctant smile. "And unintentionally at that. Yes, it can happen. Oh, Maribeth, I'm not giving advice. I can't because I have no idea what's the right thing here. I just want your dreams to come true. You've been dreaming them a long time, and you're such a good person. You deserve every happiness."

"I'm coming to think Mo can give me that." Maribeth picked up the serving bowl of dessert—a pudding made of yogurt and strawberries, sugar-free because Brooke and Jake were careful about Nicki's sugar intake—and headed for the dining room.

Over dessert, the conversation was relaxed as if, by unspoken agreement, they'd all decided to avoid sensitive subjects. Maribeth was glad because she felt unsettled by Brooke's comments, not to mention her tummy was achy from her period. Although she loved her friends' company, she was almost relieved when Nicki got tired and cranky and her parents said it was time to take her home to bed.

Standing on the porch beside Mo, waving good-bye, Maribeth admired the sparkle of the Christmas lights they'd hung, and the Santa sleigh across the street. What a wonderful time of year—a season best shared with children. Surely next year . . .

She leaned back against Mo with a sigh. "Are you as worn out as I am?"

"A little drained, yeah." He put his arm around her, tugged her inside, and closed the door. "You know, I think that's the first time I've heard you admit to being tired."

She wrinkled her nose. "First day of my period." She'd never been one for pretending to guys that women didn't menstruate. If a man couldn't deal with that basic fact of life, she had no time for him. "No biggie, but I'm a little achy and burned out."

"I'm sorry. Would a bath help?"

"Sounds divine."

"Then go soak, and I'll tidy up down here. Uh, should I go back to my place tonight?"

Was that what he'd prefer? "If you want, but not for my sake. Sometimes I feel pretty horny during my period, and as you well know, there's lots of ways of making love."

His eyes gleamed. "I've heard rumors."

"But," she warned, "it's entirely possible that after a bath, all I'll want to do is snuggle and fall asleep. How do you feel about no sex?"

His expression was almost tender. "I don't want you just for the sex, Maribeth."

Her heart turned over. "Same for me." Maybe it was hormones, but she had a feeling that she was no longer falling in love with Mo. She had fallen. That could be either the best thing that had ever happened to her, or the stupidest.

Leaving him to look after the fire, the dishes, and Caruso, she dragged her weary body upstairs. While water ran in the tub, she took out her contact lenses, removed the small amount of eye makeup she wore, and brushed her teeth. Then she sank gratefully into a bath full of lavender-scented bubbles. Gradually, the aches eased out, her muscles melted, and she drifted off.

She'd left the bathroom door open and woke to the caress of Mo's hand against her cheek. "Hey, now," he said. "There are better places to sleep."

"Don't have the energy to move," she complained.

Chuckling, he reached under her armpits and lifted her upward, not caring that when she clutched him, her dripping body wet his clothing. He supported her as she climbed from the tub.

Clutching the towel rail for support, she stayed more or less upright while he patted her dry with a warm, fluffy towel. He hoisted her into his arms, she snuggled against him—and then she came to her senses and said, "No, wait. Need a new tampon."

He put her down again. "That, you can do on your own."

"Just give me a minute."

When he left the bathroom, she attended to that intimate detail. Yawning widely, she made it to the door and said, "Wouldn't mind that ride now." After all, why walk when you had a strong, hot man like Mo at your disposal?

"Such a princess," he teased as he lifted her again and carried her to the bed, which he'd already turned down.

"You're good at this," she mumbled, as he laid her down and pulled the covers up around her.

"At what?"

Looking after her. Being there. Understanding. Her brain too fuzzy with sleep to figure out the right words, she said, "Everything."

"You keep believing that."

He began to unbutton his damp shirt and she forced her tired eyes to stay open because the view was too fine to miss. Even so, by the time he unfastened his jeans, her lids were at half-mast.

"Let me guess," he said, turning away as he pulled off his remaining clothes. "It's not one of those 'feeling horny' times."

Lids closed now, she made an unintelligible sound, not even knowing what she was trying to say.

She felt the press of a kiss on her forehead.

"Roll over and let me hold you," he said. Gently, he

guided her body into a fetal position and climbed in beside her, curving his body to fit hers.

When his arm came around her and his breath settled warm on her neck, she gave a deep sigh of contentment and surrendered to sleep.

Sometime in the middle of the night, Maribeth woke, crampy and needing to pee. When she came back from the bathroom, she realized that Mo had forgotten to pull the blinds. He'd also left the outside Christmas lights on, either deliberately or unintentionally. Colors glowed through the window, giving a festive touch to the dim bedroom.

He lay sleeping on his side, his black hair tousled on the pillow, one arm curved up over his head.

Her hormones stirred again—this time not the sloppy, sentimental ones but the lustful ones. Besides, an orgasm usually helped with her cramps. Would Mo mind if she woke him up to use him for sex? Somehow, she guessed not.

Rather than slide under the covers, she slowly pulled the duvet and sheet down to reveal his shoulders, chest, hips, and—oh, yes!—his package. A dormant package, just waiting to be stirred to life.

She bent over and puffed air across his penis and balls. His body twitched. She licked him with small, delicate strokes, like a cat lapping up the last of the cream in a bowl. As she did, he grew under her tongue, which had a reciprocal effect on her own arousal.

"Maribeth?" he said, his voice hoarse with sleep.

She lifted her head enough to tease, "Good guess."

"I mean, what are you doing?"

"You really must be out of it if that isn't obvious." His shaft was erect now, and she curved appreciative fingers around it. So strong, pulsing with life.

He pushed up to a sitting position. "I thought you were feeling achy."

"Orgasm helps with cramps."

"Uh . . ." He shuddered as she opened her mouth and took him in. "Not complaining here, but how does my orgasm help with your cramps?"

She laughed, and then released him so she could speak. "I figured we could take turns. Besides, this is foreplay for me."

"God, I'm a lucky man."

He lay back and within a few minutes she'd brought him to climax. After she'd swallowed the last drops and bestowed a kiss, she reclined gingerly. Pain gripped her, a combination of cramps and the intensity of her arousal.

Mo rose on one elbow and brushed hair back from her face. "Tell me what's going to work best for you. Gentle, I'm guessing?"

Grateful that he'd asked, and that he wasn't put off by the idea of sex at this time of month, she said, "Gentle, but fast. And please don't put any weight on my tummy." So much for any semblance of romance, but right now she was too needy to waste time on anything but the essentials.

He slipped a pillow under her butt so that when she bent her knees and spread her legs, her pelvis tipped upward. He stroked her lightly, the roughness of his fingers increasing the stimulation. "You're so wet," he murmured. "So hot and swollen."

Naughty talk. She liked it, as well as the way he firmed his strokes, and how he brushed against her clit.

"So ready." He tapped her clit and she shuddered.

"So close," she whispered. "Please, Mo."

His tongue replaced his fingers, licking her folds, each

long stroke carrying her closer to the edge. Pleasure and pain mingled inextricably, so fierce as to be almost unbearable.

"Please," she begged again.

He sucked her clit between moist lips, flicked it with his tongue. She squirmed against him, moaning as her body tightened. He flicked it again, and her body clenched and then let go hard, sharp, in a shattering burst that hurt yet felt so good. She cried out at the blessed release.

When the spasms finally died, her legs flopped down. From head to toe, she felt boneless, and the pain in her tummy eased slowly away.

Mo came up the bed, smiling, but his smile faded when he saw her face. "Shit, I hurt you." Gently, he touched her cheek, and for the first time she realized that tears had seeped from her eyes.

"No," she assured him, mustering the strength to lift a hand and touch his mouth. "Or yeah, maybe, but the good kind of pain. You gave me exactly what I needed."

As he leaned down to press a soft kiss to her lips, she wondered if this man she'd fallen in love with would be able—or want—to give her the rest of what she so badly craved: love, a baby, a life together.

Chapter Fourteen

Late in the day on Wednesday, Maribeth was still at Days of Your. Mo was going to come by, and they were going to dine with Ms. Haldenby and Ms. Peabody. When Maribeth had called on Monday to invite the two women to her open house, they'd reciprocated with a dinner invitation. Maribeth had accepted with thanks and gladly taken the excuse to defer any discussion of Evan until that time.

After closing the shop at five thirty, she had decided to be productive while she waited for Mo and was changing the window display. The new one featured a woman in sweats holding up a cherry-red party dress, surrounded by rolls of wrapping paper and unwrapped gifts that included a man's leather jacket and little girl's cowboy boots. She hoped it was a tasteful way of saying both "come shop for a new holiday outfit" and "buy Christmas gifts here."

She was just tweaking the final touches when Mo and Caruso came down the sidewalk and stopped outside to peer in at her. She climbed out of the window and opened the shop door. Caruso declined the invitation, but Mo stepped inside, holding a gift bag with a bottle of wine.

Maribeth wrapped her arms around him, under his jacket. “Hi, you.”

He hugged her back and kissed her, his lips and body giving off a chill freshness. There was definitely nothing cool about his kiss, though, nor the heat that flooded through her.

She pulled back in his arms. “You’re in a good mood.”

“I am. I saw Evan today.”

“Oh my gosh! Really? Tell me about it.”

“Best to do it on the way. I’m running behind—why do the emergency repairs always come in at the end of the day?—and we don’t want to be late for dinner. By the way, when you get a chance, would you see if you’ve got a heavy jacket in my size? This one did better in November than December.”

“And it only gets colder from here on in,” she said over her shoulder as she hurried to get her coat and the red poinsettia plant she’d purchased earlier in the day.

Outside, Caruso’s tail wagged when she greeted him. The dog was warming to the humans in his life, just as, it seemed, Evan was slowly coming to accept Mo. Life was on a positive roll.

When the three of them were in her car, heading for Mo’s landladies’ house, she said, “Tell me about Evan.”

“He phoned and asked if I could get away for a little while at lunch. Hank said sure. Evan picked me up and drove to Gold River Park so we’d have privacy. He’d brought sandwiches and coffee, and we sat in his car and talked.”

“What changed his mind about seeing you?”

“He said he was being nagged at, made out to be the bad guy. I said it wasn’t fair of people to do that. He replied that his family’d already told him I’d said that.

Apparently that was the factor that tipped the scale and got him to call."

"Good. How did it go when you talked?"

"Well, there wasn't any great moment of 'I forgive you and absolve you of all sins,' but I never even hoped for that. We talked about many of the same things I'd told him before, but this time he listened. He asked questions, gave his perspective. Made me realize for the first time what it was really like for him, growing up."

"What was it like for him?" she asked quietly, already having a pretty good idea but wanting to hear it in Mo's words.

He sighed. "Evan was so smart, well-behaved, and self-sufficient from such an early age. Brooke and I tended to ignore him and figure he was okay. But of course he wasn't. And it wasn't just the occasional physical injuries or the stress of seeing Brooke and me fight. Ignoring him hurt, too. Not praising him. Not supporting him when other kids teased him for being an egghead or a klutz."

She nodded, again feeling supremely grateful to her parents, who had always been there to support, encourage, and praise her. "The first time you and Evan got together, you said he was really angry. How about this time?"

"Sometimes I'd hear it in his voice, but mostly he was calmer. He said something like, 'I know you can't change any of this now, but I want you to hear it.' And I told him I wanted to, and I listened."

"Often, listening's the best thing, the only thing, you can do." They were nearing the house and she said, "How was it for you, Mo? Sitting there with him, listening to him recite, uh . . ."

"The long list of my sins? Partly, I felt crappy. Like something slimy that had crawled out from under a rock and ought to head straight back. And yet I felt good, too.

My son was there beside me, taking the time, spending the emotional energy to actually communicate with me. The first time we met, his mind seemed so closed and he told me to stay out of his life. This time it was different. It felt more like a door had opened. Maybe just a crack, but it had opened."

She reached over to squeeze his jacketed arm. "I'm so glad. How did the two of you leave it? Did he say anything about Sunday?"

"He said he needed to think some more, but he might be there. Even if he isn't, I feel like I could call him and offer to buy him a coffee one day, and we'll talk some more."

"That's wonderful, Mo. Evan's a good man. He'll come around." It was all going to work out. It might take some time, but in the end Mo was going to be part of his son's large and already complicated family.

And who knew, maybe so would she.

Mo's pleasure at the way things had gone with Evan had given him a boost that went a long way to overriding his nervousness about the upcoming dinner with his landladies. Still, he told Maribeth, "I'm sure glad you're with me."

"They're just people, Mo." She gave a quick splutter of laughter. "Or so I tell myself. Ms. Haldenby was my teacher—the strict kind, not the motherly type—and that's hard to get over. So I'm glad I'm with you." She pulled up to the curb in front of his landladies' house and turned to him. "And of course that's the only reason we're happy to be together, just for the mutual support, right?"

"Oh, totally. For me it has nothing to do with how

pretty you look, how great you smell, or the thought of having sex later on."

"Taking me for granted, are you?"

"Nope. Eternally hopeful." He'd said the words jokingly, but once he'd uttered them he thought that he would never before in his life have used that phrase to describe himself. And yet, here in Caribou Crossing with Maribeth, he did feel hopeful. Not just about the prospect of great sex tonight, but about life in general. A month ago, on that bus approaching Caribou Crossing, he'd never imagined he could feel this way.

He and Maribeth climbed out of her car and he let Caruso out. "Maribeth and I are going in the front," he told the dog. "If you want to go inside, use your own special door." He hadn't figured out whether the dog really understood English or was good at reading his mind, but it didn't surprise him when Caruso ran around the side of the house.

As Maribeth came around the car holding the poinsettia plant she'd bought, Mo reached out his hand to her. When she took it, he drew her toward him and leaned in close to her cheek. "Mmm, yeah, you smell good." Tonight, her scent was spicy, rather like cinnamon.

He captured her lips for a smiling kiss and then they headed up the front walk. "It feels odd coming to this door," he said. "The only other time I did was the day I applied to rent here."

"And now you're a guest. I see you're bringing wine."

He held up the bag. "I happen to know that the ladies have a fondness for a good red. And that dinner is roast beef with Yorkshire pudding." He rang the doorbell.

Ms. Haldenby, tall and straight-backed, tailored in navy pants and a blue-and-white striped blouse, opened the door. Her welcoming smile widened when they handed her the plant and wine. "You shouldn't have."

"Of course we should," Maribeth said. "It's so kind of you and Ms. Peabody to invite us for dinner." To Mo's ear, she sounded a little stiff, not her normal bubbly self.

As Maribeth and Mo hung their coats in the hall closet, Ms. Haldenby said, "I know it's hard for my former students to move past the habits they learned in the classroom, but please call me Daphne. You as well, Mo. And my wife is Irene." With a glint of humor in the blue eyes behind the thick lenses of her glasses, she added, "Irene's teenage granddaughter calls us Ire-nee. And I suppose there is a certain irony to having found your true love in your early twenties but not having the sense to actually get together until you're past eighty."

Irony, or just sadness?

"Now," Daphne Haldenby went on, "come sit down in the front room and let's have a drink and a snack while dinner finishes cooking."

She ushered them to the same rather formally decorated room where she and her wife had interviewed Mo when he'd inquired about renting. Tonight, it seemed more welcoming with the curtains drawn, a gas fire burning cheerfully, a couple of wreaths of holly and pine, and classical music playing in the background. Their hostess put the poinsettia on the mantel, where it added a splash of color.

When Maribeth chose to sit on a blue-and-white striped sofa, Mo sat beside her. He promptly got to his feet again as Ms. Peabody bustled into the room carrying a serving plate with steaming stuffed mushroom caps. She was less tailored than her wife, wearing a red sweater and black pants, her white hair in soft curls around her face.

After another round of greetings, Ms. Haldenby—Daphne—opened the wine and offered it around. Mo declined, and so did Maribeth, choosing instead to have nonalcoholic cider.

He tried one of the mushroom caps, finding that the stuffing was a mixture of shrimp, creamy cheese, and herbs. "These are delicious," he told his hostesses.

"We like to cook together," Ms. Peabody—Irene—said. "We love browsing through cookbooks and trying recipes."

As they all ate appetizers, the women got onto the subject of Christmas decorations and Mo mostly kept quiet. He noticed that it took Maribeth a while to get comfortable and to use the older ladies' first names, but she got there. So did he, when he gave them a summary of his talk with Evan. He was pleased by their encouraging comments.

From time to time, Daphne or Irene excused herself to tend to things in the kitchen, and finally Irene announced that dinner was ready.

As they made their way down the hall, Daphne said, "We'll be eating in the kitchen. Maribeth, this house once had a dining room, but living on my own, I never used it. I converted it, as well as the main floor bathroom, into the flat that Mo rents."

"And that Cassidy used to rent," Maribeth said. "She's a friend of mine, too."

"Of course. I remember seeing you at her and Dave's wedding, though we didn't have an opportunity to talk."

Mo shook his head in amusement. Did everyone in this town know each other?

The kitchen was a spacious, old-fashioned one, and the table was set with an ivory tablecloth, gleaming china, and silverware.

"Mo," Daphne said, "I know that you're good with

engines, snow shovels, and tools." He'd done some minor repairs and yard work around the house. "I imagine you can wield a carving knife quite competently?"

It was something he'd rarely done, but it couldn't be too difficult. "I'd be happy to try."

A platter holding a sizable roast of beef sat on the counter with carving utensils beside it. He washed his hands thoroughly and got to work. As he sliced meat, Irene and Daphne put the rest of the food on the table and Maribeth topped up everyone's glasses.

When they were all seated, Maribeth said, "What a feast!"

Mo agreed. In addition to the beef, there were roasted turnips and carrots, a dish of green peas that smelled of mint, puffy individual Yorkshire puddings, and a big server of rich brown gravy.

After he'd tasted everything and complimented the food, Maribeth chimed in. "Yes, I'm very glad the two of you enjoy cooking, and we get to reap the benefits."

"I'm a little surprised, Daphne," Mo ventured, "that the two of you only got together recently."

"Because we're so old?" the woman asked wryly.

He gave an embarrassed laugh. "Well, kind of. But it's just that you seem so right, so natural together. Of course I did know Irene had a grandson, so obviously . . ." Now he wished he hadn't raised the subject.

Irene didn't seem fussed, though, when she said, "Yes, I was married. For almost twenty years. But it wasn't a very happy marriage, I'm sad to say." She sighed. "My family—which includes a younger brother, two children, five grandchildren, and my brand-new great-granddaughter—has been pretty accepting of my big 'coming out.'" Her fingers put apostrophes around the phrase. "It probably helps that I'm so old. They want me to enjoy the last years of my life, and they're happy I'm with Daphne."

"And so they should be," Maribeth said firmly.

"I wish my ex-husband thought so," Irene said. "He's the person who's had the most trouble with this. He feels betrayed. And he's right. Oh, I didn't mean to do it. I didn't know better at the time. I thought all girls were supposed to marry men and that what I felt for Daphne was . . . some childish passing fancy. Even now, I have no idea if I'm lesbian or bisexual. All I know is that Daphne is the one person in the world I want to be with."

"The love of your life," Maribeth said softly.

"Indeed." Irene smiled at Maribeth. "But when I married my husband, I did betray him, and my own true self. I worked hard at that marriage, and that should have been a clue. When it's right, it shouldn't be so much work."

"No, it shouldn't," Maribeth said. "Things should click into place, shouldn't they?"

"At least the important things," Irene said. "Not that it's ever going to be a total bed of roses"—she winked at her wife—"and disagreements are inevitable."

"But the two of you are happy together," Maribeth said. "You remind me of my mom's parents, who've been married more than sixty years. What's your secret?"

"Love, first and foremost, of course," Daphne said. "And honesty, communication, trust."

Irene smiled at her. "Reminding ourselves how lucky we are. Not getting caught up with the petty things but focusing on the important ones."

"Which is good advice for life in general, isn't it?" Maribeth said.

It probably was, Mo reflected, thinking about the relationships in his life. And what a foreign concept that still seemed: that he actually had relationships that went beyond casual ones with coworkers. His life had changed more in the past month than in the ten years prior. It could feel a little overwhelming—like when he thought about Maribeth's upcoming open house—but it also felt kind of . . . warm. Almost like he'd found a place that he might call home. Home in the true sense of that word, not just a room to come back to at night. A place where he could belong, be accepted, even perhaps be cared about.

Cared about by people he cared for in return. And at the heart of all of it, there was Maribeth. He studied her across the table. She was always such a pleasure to look at, so feminine and pretty with her gleaming red hair and colorful clothing. Tonight she wore a turquoise blouse and had a purple-and-turquoise scarf tied around her neck.

She caught him looking and smiled.

He smiled back, just so damned happy that she was in his life.

A hint of surprise flickered across her face, and then her smile deepened like she was saying the same thing back.

Could it be true? She'd dated so many men, not settling on any one of them. Was it possible that she might see something special in Mo? Feel something special for him? If she did, what the hell would he do about it? He had no experience—except the dysfunctional one with Brooke—when it came to serious relationships.

He realized that Irene was passing him the meat platter, urging him to have seconds. Happy to, he forked a slice of rare meat onto his plate.

After the serving dishes had gone around the table again, Maribeth said, "Daphne, Irene, how do you know? You meet someone, you're attracted to them and get along, but how do you know this is your one and only?"

Was there really such a thing as a one and only? It

sounded like romantic nonsense to Mo, and yet he had to admit that he'd never before felt the way he did with Maribeth.

"We're the wrong ones to ask," Daphne said. "We didn't have the sense to realize it when we were young."

"It took almost sixty years of never being able to forget each other," Irene said. "I don't think a day went by when I didn't think of Daphne. The highs, the lows, I wanted to share them with her. I wanted to ask her advice, seek her comfort. Just be with her."

That was how Mo felt about Maribeth. Surely she couldn't feel that way about a loser like him.

"Exactly," Daphne said. "However, figuring it out over sixty years is not a course of action I'd recommend to anyone."

They all laughed, and then Daphne addressed Maribeth. "I remember teaching you. You weren't the most brilliant student."

Maribeth winced. "True."

That struck Mo as strange. He thought Maribeth was plenty smart, and a good businesswoman.

"Not because you lacked intelligence," Daphne went on, "but because you were more interested in your friends and hobbies. I always asked my children to write an essay about what they wanted to do with their lives. Correct me if I'm wrong, but I believe yours was about wearing pretty clothes and being a wife and mother."

"That sounds like me." She made a face. "And like something out of the fifties. Hopelessly unliberated."

"Well, you turned into a capable businesswoman, so I wouldn't call you too old-fashioned. You even found a career that lets you wear pretty clothes. No husband and children, though. Has that goal changed?"

Maribeth shook her head.

"You're still single, and not for lack of suitors, I would imagine," the older woman continued.

"I've done my share of dating over the years."

"Did any of those men haunt your thoughts? Did you find yourself wanting to be with them, to share your joys and woes with them?"

That was how he felt about Maribeth.

"No," Maribeth said softly, picking up her cider glass and gazing into its depths. "That didn't happen with any of those men."

Of course she wouldn't feel that way about Mo. Sooner or later she'd ditch him, as she had all her previous boyfriends. Would he get over her or would she still be there in his mind? Maybe even in his heart.

"Well then," Daphne said to Maribeth, "at least you know one thing. None of them was your true love."

Chapter Fifteen

After the dinner with Daphne and Irene, and after she and Mo had made love, Maribeth had trouble getting to sleep. Her mind insisted on puzzling over what the women had said. No, none of her previous boyfriends was the love of her life. That, she'd already known. But was Mo?

Yes, he haunted her thoughts and she wanted to share her highs and lows with him. But would that feeling last? And what if he didn't feel the same? Or what if he did, but truly didn't want to have children? If that was the case, he couldn't possibly be the love of her life. Could he? Irene Peabody had confirmed what Maribeth had always believed: if it was true love, both people should agree on the important issues. And no "issue" was more important, in Maribeth's mind, than views on having children.

After Mo left on Thursday morning to go to work, she did her yoga. Usually that settled not only her body but her brain. Not today. She kept mulling.

Her parents had been so right for each other. They said they'd fallen in love at first sight and never had second thoughts. She'd always expected that the same would happen for her.

Many times over the years, Maribeth had wished her mom and dad were still alive, and now she did so again. She'd love to be able to ask their advice. Of course, there were loads of girlfriends she could talk to, and some guy friends as well, but she wanted the wisdom of someone older. Someone whose love had stood the test of time.

What about her grandparents? Her mom's parents were soul mates for life. They lived in Vancouver, but Maribeth visited them at least once a year and spoke to them on the phone or by video chat once or twice a week.

By the time she'd finished her yoga, she knew her grandparents would be at their breakfast table. She poured herself a cup of decaf Lady Grey tea, sat at her own kitchen table, and placed the call. After the usual catching-up chat, she told them about dining with Daphne and Irene and talking about relationships.

"They had great advice about how to sustain a relationship," she said, "but they couldn't tell me how you know when someone's the right person. So I thought I'd ask you."

"You think we can remember that far back?" Granddad's voice rumbled.

"You'd better remember," his wife warned teasingly. Then she said, "You've met someone special, Maribeth." It wasn't a question.

"Yes." Until now, she hadn't mentioned Mo to them, nor her plan to get pregnant via a sperm donor. She'd wanted to wait until she was sure of what she was doing, but now she needed their help. "You know how I always said I was waiting for that click? Well, I feel it for him, physically and emotionally. But there are some problems, and I'm not sure we're right for each other."

"Well," Grandma said slowly, "there's no such thing as a relationship that's problem-free. But some problems are more serious than others, and some prove to be insurmountable. So, dear, tell us what's troubling you about your young man."

Maribeth gave a short laugh. "Young man? Well, let's start there. I'll turn forty next year, and he's fifty."

"Pfft," Grandma said, making Maribeth smile because she, too, used that expression. "Age is a meaningless number."

"You didn't say that when we were dating," Granddad said. "Maribeth, you know she's five years older than me, don't you?"

"Yes, though I never really think about it."

"Nor do we," he responded. "But when I first asked her out, she fussed over it."

"It was a big deal back in those days," his wife said defensively.

"The man was supposed to be older," he said. "Established, able to support the woman. I was just starting out, planning to be a lawyer but with years of education still ahead of me, and Cynthia was already a teacher."

"That was partly it," she said. "But it was more that I felt old and spinsterish compared to the girls you'd been dating." She laughed. "Oh dear, when I look back, it seems like we grew up in the Dark Ages. Anyhow, Maribeth, are you telling me that ten years' difference matters that much to you?"

"No, it really doesn't. Fifty's the new forty, right? And he, Mo, certainly doesn't look like he's fifty." The man exuded hotness. Women of all ages, from their twenties through their eighties, responded to it, and likely that would never change.

"If it's not age, then what's the problem?" Grandma asked.

"He's had a troubled life. He was, to use a cliché, an angry young man. He did some stupid things and some downright bad things. When he grew up and sorted himself out, he was determined to do no harm. Which has meant that, basically, he's wary about getting too close to anyone. Though recently he's been reconnecting with people from his past, apologizing for things he did to hurt them."

"Hmm," Granddad said. "It's not good that he hurt people, but none of us has lived a blameless life. I will note that the easier thing for him would have been to stay away, but that's not what he chose to do. Sounds like the man's moral compass is set on the right course now."

"It is. If it wasn't, we wouldn't be having this conversation."

"Maribeth, you're so warm and outgoing," Grandma said. "You've always been an extrovert. You see the best in people, and you give the best of yourself with great generosity."

Warmed by her approval, Maribeth was about to say "thank you," but her grandmother wasn't finished. "Your Mo is a different kind of person. He has carried a fair bit of negative emotion, am I right?"

"In the past, yes. Even now, I think he's almost afraid to see the good in himself. To believe that he's capable of emotional intimacy. To believe that he deserves to be loved." She added slowly, "And no matter how much I might care about him, I deserve wholehearted love and commitment, not some shadowy halfway thing."

"Of course you do, dear," Grandma said. "But are you putting yourself in his shoes? Can you understand that it may be very difficult for him to achieve the things you want from him? You know I love you dearly, but you're not always the most patient or flexible person when you get your mind fixed on something."

Maribeth winced. She guessed she'd have to work on that, if she was going to be a good mother. "I know it's not easy for Mo."

"So, dear, can you be patient with him? How long have you known this man anyhow?"

"Well . . . a month," she admitted.

Both of her grandparents' laughter came through the phone.

"Okay, okay," Maribeth said. "But you know how badly I want to have children. I can't wait much longer."

Granddad cleared his throat. "From the male perspective, if a woman I'd known for a month told me she wanted to have my baby, I'd likely turn tail and run for the hills."

"You are expecting an awful lot from this man," Grandma said, "in a very short time."

"I know. You're right. And that's partly why I called. I always thought love would happen for me the way it did for Mom and Dad: that magic moment of recognition, like it's destiny, and then everything falling perfectly into place."

"Your parents were extremely lucky," Grandma said. "As were your granddad and I. But there are other paths to true love, and they can be equally valid."

"I know. I see that with my friends and I guess I was naïve to think it would be totally obvious and easy for me. So now I need to figure out whether, despite the difficulties, Mo is the right man. In that case, I'll try to be patient and work things out. But if he isn't, then I need to move ahead, uh, in another direction." If she did choose to get pregnant using the sperm donor, she'd make a trip down to Vancouver and tell her grandparents in person.

"Ask yourself," her grandmother said, "if you're drawn to Mo because he came along when you're nearing forty and running out of time to have a baby. Is he like a last-gasp opportunity?"

"I've dated other men this year and never felt like this." Of course Mo was the only man she'd been with since deciding to have a baby through insemination. Thinking it through, she added slowly, "In all the years I've been dating, I've never been so attracted to a man. It's not just his looks and the, uh, physical side of things." Her grandparents knew she dated a lot and no doubt also knew she'd lost her virginity long ago, but she'd never actually told them she'd had sex. "I also love being with him, talking to him. He has so many good qualities and . . . well, I could list attributes, but it's . . ." She remembered what Irene and Daphne had said. "I think about him. I want to be with him. The idea of going through life without him feels bleak and empty."

There was no response for a few seconds, and then Grandma said, "How does he feel about you?"

"Good question. I'm afraid to ask. Afraid to push him."

"That sounds wise," her grandfather said.

"Well," Grandma said, "pushing isn't wise. But what those retired schoolteachers said was right, about communication. If you don't talk, there are bound to be misunderstandings. And then people get hurt. I don't want to see you get hurt, dear."

"Me either."

"You need to get right down to the nitty-gritty," her grandmother said. "Are your core values compatible? Yes, you say he has a strong moral compass, but how does he feel about the things that are most important to you? You care for others, you believe in equality, you hate prejudice. You support causes you believe in, with your money and your time. You value family, maybe above all else, and want to create one of your own. If your Mo doesn't believe in these things, too, could you really see the two of you being happy together?"

"No," she said quietly. As Grandma had spoken, Maribeth had been ticking off points in her mind. From the way Mo treated his landladies, she was pretty sure he wasn't prejudiced. His behavior with Caruso indicated compassion; he volunteered at soup kitchens at Christmas; and he was generous in doing little fix-up chores for Maribeth and his landladies. As for valuing family—while Mo might not admit it even to himself, Maribeth thought that his attempts to reconcile with Brooke and Evan demonstrated that he did. But could he imagine himself starting a new family? With her? "Thanks for the advice, you two. I love you."

After hanging up, she cradled her mug of tea in both hands. It seemed she and Mo were due for a serious conversation. Now she had to think about how to communicate honestly about her feelings without making him think she was pressuring him—which, as Granddad said, might well make him turn tail and run for the hills.

Mo already knew what her ultimate goal was: a happy marriage and children. But they'd known each other for only a month and had agreed to take things a day at a time. Realistically, a month's dating was too short a foundation to leap into a lifelong commitment, no matter how powerful the attraction. So she wouldn't talk about commitment, only about how her feelings for him were deepening.

And then she'd see how he responded.

Maribeth embraced the whole holiday thing with her characteristic enthusiasm, and so here Mo was on a Saturday evening, wandering around the tree lot that had been set up at one end of Caribou Crossing's town square. It was a fund-raiser for the local Boys & Girls Club, and obviously popular with the townspeople. The place was a bit of a bedlam, with excited kids dragging their parents from tree to tree.

Still, he wasn't about to complain, as he strolled along with Maribeth in the heavy sheepskin jacket he'd bought at her shop. Her hand was tucked through his arm and she was bright-eyed and rosy-cheeked, wearing a candy-cane striped hat and a matching long scarf.

"What do you think of this one?" she asked, pointing to a Douglas fir.

"It's lopsided. There are more symmetrical ones."

"Other people will buy those. I always choose a Charlie Brown tree."

"A what?"

"You know, from *Peanuts*? The poor spindly, neglected tree? If you give it appreciation and love, it can turn into something beautiful."

"Okay." It figured that Maribeth would do something like that. He also had to wonder just how much of a Charlie Brown fixer-upper project he was for the tenderhearted woman. His pride wasn't fond of that notion.

They took another tour around the lot, and she ended up choosing the lopsided fir. As Mo carried it to her car, he said, "Sure does smell good. And it's definitely fresh. The needles are soft and springy."

He'd met her at her house earlier to put the roof rack on her Mini. Now he tied the tree onto the rack, and she drove home. Her house looked nice with the lights they'd strung last weekend, and snow on the roof and in the yard. When they had left earlier, Caruso'd gone off on one of his explorations, but at some point he'd come back and now he pranced down the shoveled walk to greet them. Mo had learned that the dog had amazing hearing, which made it virtually impossible to ever surprise him.

Maribeth parked at the curb. "We'll bring the tree in the front door and into the living room, and put it in the stand," she said. "And we'll put the lights on. I've already checked that none are burned out. Then tomorrow morning, we'll decorate it."

Mo snapped a salute. "Yes, Chief." He climbed out of the car and greeted Caruso with a stroke.

"Sorry." Maribeth came around to join them and patted the dog. "Am I being bossy?"

"Just knowing how you like things done." Mostly, he thought it was cute.

"I should have asked you for input. I haven't even asked if you have any Christmas traditions of your own."

He suppressed a snort. "Nope." He began to untie the tree. And then, because this was Maribeth and he didn't want to hide things from her, he went on. "Christmas has never been that great a time of year for me."

"Oh, Mo, that's terrible. Not even when you were a child?"

Speaking as he worked, he said, "My dad, the Catholic, wanted to celebrate Christmas with all the trappings, and of course, so did my sister and I. But Amma said it wasn't right for Hindus to celebrate Christian holidays. She made some concessions—like, we did have a small tree and get a couple of presents—but she was begrudging, and it took the fun out of it."

He pulled the freed tree off the top of the car and headed up the walk. "When Brooke and I were married . . . Well, I guess now that I know about her bipolar, it makes more sense. Some years she'd kind of go crazy with Christmas stuff and other years she was so depressed she didn't even want to think about it." He held on to the tree while Maribeth unlocked the front door. "Whichever way she was feeling, there was one constant: we drank, fought, and screwed Evan out of an enjoyable holiday."

"How about after you left Caribou Crossing?"

"I pretty much just ignored Christmas."

"You once said that you usually volunteer at a soup kitchen?"

"Yeah. If I'm lucky enough to have a roof over my head and food in the cupboards, I figure it's good to help those who are less fortunate. Didn't you say you help out at a soup kitchen, too?"

"I do. Maybe we can do that together this year."

"I'd like that."

"So how do you feel about the rest of it?" Maribeth asked, leading the way into the living room. "I mean, with the lights and tree and all? Am I pressuring you into doing things you really don't want to?"

"It feels kind of odd, I admit. But I like doing things with you. You're helping me see the holiday in a different light."

He propped the fir in a corner by the window, beside where she'd set a tree stand and a box filled with strings of lights. The dog had followed them in, and now sniffed at the tree and gave a tail wag. Mo brushed a hand over Caruso's back, thinking that for a pair of stray creatures, they were both doing pretty damned well.

As he took off his coat, Maribeth came into the room, coatless herself, and went to turn on music. He didn't pay much attention to the song until the beat picked up and Maribeth dance-stepped over to him. "This one's for you, Mo." She held out her arms in an invitation.

He realized the female singer was urging him to put a little holiday in his heart. It had been a long time since he'd danced with a pretty woman, and he wasn't about to resist Maribeth's arms. He took her in a two-step dance hold and set their bodies in motion. He was a little rusty, but who cared when she was smiling up at him, her whole face alight with pleasure.

That shared pleasure felt just right settling in his heart.

As the catchy tune faded away, Maribeth said, "That song kind of fits with the soup kitchen thing. Being nice to others, not looking down on people. You're like that, aren't you, Mo?"

"Uh, I guess. Not when I was younger, but now, sure."

The next song to play was one that even he recognized: "Silent Night." He and Maribeth stopped dancing and she looped her arms around his neck. He circled his around her waist.

He was thinking it'd be a good time to kiss her, when she said, "You're not prejudiced against people who are different."

Maribeth did raise some odd subjects, but he went along with it. "I sure have no right to think I'm better than anyone else."

"And you'll give your time to help people who are less fortunate. Not to mention a homeless dog."

"Don't make me out to be some kind of saint," he warned, not understanding what she was getting at. "And remember, I've got a lot of sins to make up for."

"Which you're trying to do, especially with Brooke and Evan. They were your family, and you've finally realized what that means and you want to make things right."

"Guess that's true."

Gazing up at him, the sparkle in her eyes became a glow, turning the green from emerald to jade. "Mo, I care about you."

Her words caught him off guard, giving him a sensation

that was pretty much *Oh, wow.* Santa had come early this year, bringing him such a gift. Like the dumbass he was, all he could think of to say was, “You do?”

“Yes. I know we’re taking this one day at a time, no pressure or expectations. But I need you to know that I care. More than I’ve ever cared for another man.”

“Oh, wow.” This time, the words popped out. *More than she’s ever cared for another man?* He felt as if he’d landed in a parallel universe.

A twinkle ignited in those jade eyes. “Took you by surprise, did I?”

“You can say that again.” All those men she’d dated, and he was the one she cared about most? It was too big a concept to get his mind around.

“You’re not running away,” she pointed out.

No, apparently he wasn’t. His arms still circled her supple waist. And that was interesting. His first gut reaction had not been to flee. Casting a feeler into a pond he rarely explored—his emotions—he said, “I’m honored, Maribeth. That a woman like you would care for a guy like me.”

She shook her head. “You. Not a guy like you.”

“I guess that makes me feel even more honored.” He swallowed, knowing that he had to tell her the truth, but finding the unfamiliar words so difficult to say. “I care for you, too.” There, he’d said it, and her radiant smile was his reward, along with a warmth that seeped through every cell of his body. When he went on, the words were no longer hard to find or to say. “My life is so much richer and happier for having you in it.” He gave a rueful laugh. “And yours, I’m guessing, is way more complicated than it was before.”

“True. But in a very good way.”

He studied her lovely face. "Why did you tell me now? Tonight?"

"I thought you had feelings for me, but I needed to know. Before I got in any deeper, I needed to know I wasn't alone. That the one-day-at-a-time thing was heading somewhere, and that we were walking the path side by side."

He swallowed. "All of this is new to me. Heading somewhere . . . I never expected that. Didn't think I wanted it. Never imagined that I'd fall for a woman and contemplate . . ."

"Contemplate what?"

"I don't even know." What did she mean when she said she cared more for him than she'd ever cared for any other man? What did she want? What did he?

"Because you haven't allowed yourself to have dreams. Now it's time to do that."

"Now?" He was too stunned to think straight. "Like, right now?"

Her face crinkled with merriment. "Not this very second, no. But in the quiet times. Let yourself envision the future. Find a dream that feels right to you."

"I can try to do that." She'd once said that she didn't need to be married, but she'd also said that ideally she'd like to marry and have kids. He'd made it clear that he wasn't going to have any more children, and yet she had still come to care deeply for him. Did that mean . . . that it actually didn't matter to her about having a child, and that one day she might want to marry him? Could he contemplate marriage again? He'd failed so miserably the first time—

She tugged on the collar of his plaid shirt. "Not this very second, right?"

He blew out a breath. "Yeah."

"But talk to me while you're thinking about it. Share with me. Okay?"

"I'm not used to doing that." Which wasn't an excuse. "I've talked more to you than to anyone ever before. So I'll try to keep on. But for now, maybe we should get on with the tree." A practical task would be a welcome relief.

"Sounds like a plan." Still in the cradle of his arms, she came up on her toes. "But first, a kiss to seal the deal."

When his lips touched hers, so soft and giving, he thought again, *She cares for me*. It was almost too much to believe. As was the notion that one day he might have a home here in Caribou Crossing with this generous, beautiful, sexy woman at his side, a crazy singing dog, and a decent relationship with Evan and his family.

Could he actually fit himself into that picture or was he the dingy, oddly shaped piece that would never fit the serene, colorful picture on the outside of the jigsaw puzzle box?

Chapter Sixteen

This was going to be the best Christmas ever, Maribeth thought as she gazed around her crowded living room on Sunday afternoon.

Alan Jackson's "Let It Be Christmas," playing quietly in the background, set exactly the right mood. The Charlie Brown tree had undergone a Cinderella-like transformation thanks to her and Mo's efforts. Multicolored lights sparkled off strands of tinsel and highlighted the dozens of ornaments she'd collected over the years. The decorations ranged from the clunky—things she'd made as a child or been gifted by friends' children—to the sublime, such as the stained glass angel she'd bought in Venice. Every single one had a story, and she loved them all.

Even more, though, she loved the collection of people who had gathered to celebrate the beginning of the holiday season. Her Caribou Crossing family—by ties of affection, if not blood. They, too, ranged widely. She'd been friends with two of the women since preschool, gotten to know other folks over the years, and a few were new on-the-way-to-being-friends like Daphne Haldenby and Irene Peabody. The older ladies were currently chatting with

Corrie and her boyfriend, Daniel, who owned one of the arts and crafts stores. He and Maribeth had dated two or three years ago and remained friends afterward, and Maribeth had introduced him and Corrie earlier this fall.

Hank Hennessey and his wife Inga also looked right at home. No surprise since the residents of Caribou Crossing relied on his shop for car repairs.

When the guests had started to arrive in the early afternoon, poor Mo'd had an expression on his face that reminded Maribeth of Caruso when he was feeling trapped. She'd bet Mo would have given anything to be able to run away and climb a tree. But points to him, he'd stuck around, and as people came and circulated, he'd spoken to a number of them.

For the past five or ten minutes, he'd been talking to Evan and Jess. Both of the men's body language broadcast discomfort. Yet there'd been no raised voices; no one had stalked off; she'd even seen tentative smiles from both of them.

Everything was going to work out. She just knew it. Last night, Mo had told her he cared for her. He hadn't pulled back when she talked about the future. Their lovemaking had been so tender and intimate. Ever since, she'd been filled with joy and exhilaration. Now, watching the handsome man, she let herself imagine for the first time what it would truly be like to have his child. To feel a baby they'd created growing inside her. To see the wonder on Mo's face when he felt the baby move and they saw their child on the ultrasound screen. To shop together, assemble a crib, discuss baby names. Yes, she knew she was getting ahead of herself, but she just couldn't help it. The next year was going to be the most incredible one of her life. Happiness bubbled inside her and she wanted to embrace the entire world.

As if to endorse Maribeth's optimism, Jess was now beckoning Robin over. The girl was her daughter from her first marriage, but Robin and her stepdad Evan had hit it off from the moment they met.

Evan was introducing his father to his stepdaughter. What a special moment.

Maribeth sighed with contentment and turned in the direction of the kitchen, needing to get more platters of snacks from the fridge. Her path took her behind the family group, where Robin was saying to Mo, "I have so many grandparents! There's Grandma and Grandpa—those are Dad's parents. And Gran and Gramps are Mom's parents. Evan's mom is Gramma Brooke and her husband is Jake. What am I supposed to call you?"

Maribeth hovered, eavesdropping shamelessly.

"How about we do it like with Jake?" Mo said. "Just call me Mo."

"Nicki says 'Mo-Mo,'" the girl responded. "How about that?"

"I guess I can be Mo-Mo."

"If you marry Maribeth, then she'll be another grandmother. And if you have kids, it'll get really complicated."

Maribeth wouldn't have left at that point if someone had told her there was a fire in her kitchen.

"Hold on, Robin," Mo said. "Marriage is . . . well, let's just say that it'd be a ways off if it was ever going to happen."

She smiled to herself. Mo had admitted in public that he wasn't ruling out the possibility of them marrying.

He shrugged. "But as for kids, I'm definitely not having any more kids."

What? *What?*

Yes, he'd initially said that he didn't want kids, and he'd also said that he avoided relationships and hadn't dated.

But things had changed in the past weeks. Mo was forming relationships with his family. He'd said he cared for Maribeth and that they were walking the path side by side. He hadn't said no when Robin hinted about marriage. And yet he'd just given a categorical no to the idea of having another child.

Maribeth had told him she wanted children. Was he just ignoring that, or lying to her, or what? Did he think she'd changed her mind? Her pulse thrummed fast and light in her throat like a hummingbird's wings, making it hard to draw breath. She was vaguely aware that Elvis was singing "Blue Christmas" and she was terribly afraid that song might be prophetic.

"Maribeth." A hand touched her shoulder, making her jump. It was one of her old friends.

"Oh, Christie. Sorry, I was . . . never mind."

"Nate and I need to leave now, and I just wanted to say thanks so much for inviting us. We look forward to this party every year. It's the launch to the holidays, the signal that we can all start celebrating."

Celebrating. Despite the Christmas decorations and music, and the colorful collection of friends, that was the last thing Maribeth felt like doing just then. Five minutes ago she'd been glowing with happiness, and now she felt like she'd been flattened by a snowplow.

She made the conventional social responses to Christie and Nate, and then tried to focus on the other conversations that came her way, but really all she wanted to do was hustle everyone out of her house. It was wrong to jump to conclusions even if Mo's words had sounded decisive. He was in an unfamiliar situation, one he had little experience or comfort with. Maybe he wasn't really thinking about what he was saying; it was the old

Mo reacting, not the evolving one. She needed to talk to him. Alone.

Until then, for the couple more hours until her open house wound down, she stayed away from him. When she caught him watching her with a puzzled expression, she turned away, pretending she hadn't noticed.

After ushering the last guest out the door, Maribeth realized that Mo, too, had disappeared. Had he slipped away with a group of people? More likely, he'd gone to see if Caruso was in the sunroom. The song playing now was Roger Miller's "Old Toy Trains." Damn it, there would be a toy train under her Christmas tree one year, or a doll or a stuffed pony or all of those things. She would have a child, with or without Mo Kincaid.

Shoulders back, chin up, she walked down the hallway. The closed door to the sunroom still had the "Off-Limits" sign they'd put on it earlier.

When she opened the door, the room was dark. There was barely enough light for her to see Mo slumped bonelessly in a chair with Caruso sitting beside him. The man's arm dangled, his hand resting on the dog's shoulders.

Earlier today she'd thought that the pair might be the beginning of her very own family. Now . . . Well, that was what she needed to find out.

"Tiring afternoon?" she queried, her voice coming out with the same social tone she'd been using with the guests. She leaned her back—achy from too much standing and stress—against the door frame.

"Tiring," Mo echoed. "For you, too? Are you okay?"

She knew he was looking at her, but the light was too dim to see his expression. "Why do you ask?"

"Partway through, you kind of lost your sparkle. It's the first time I've seen that happen. I wondered if you had a headache or something."

"A headache. You might say that." She sighed. "I'd like to talk to you."

For a moment, he didn't respond. "Did I do something wrong? I thought things went pretty well. Evan and Robin—"

"That's not what I want to talk about." Normally, she'd have loved to hear about all his interactions this afternoon, especially the ones with his family. "Would you please come back into the living room?"

Mo stood. Caruso did, too, glancing from the man to Maribeth. He put back his head and warbled. There was a melancholy sound to it, or was that her imagination?

"Is he hungry?" she asked. Just because she felt miserable, that was no reason for the dog to suffer.

"I fed him." Mo walked toward her, paused beside her, and then without speaking again or touching her, he headed down the hall.

In the living room, he took a chair by the window, the chair that happened to be closest to the tree. At any other time, she'd have relished that picture. She sat on the couch, trying to ignore the clutter of glasses, plates, and napkins that covered every surface.

"What's wrong, Maribeth?" Mo asked.

"I overheard you talking to Robin," she said, trying to speak calmly despite her anxiety. "I think I heard you tell her you definitely don't want to have children."

He eyed her warily. "That's right. I told you that before, when we first met."

"You said a lot of things back then. Like that you weren't into serious relationships. Yet last night we started talking like we might have a future."

"I hope we do." His tone was cautious.

Confused, she shook her head. "How can we have a future if you don't want kids and I do?"

He stared at her, swallowed audibly, and then said, "You're really that serious about it?"

"Damn right I am!" She almost never swore, but this situation called for it. "What, you thought I was just fantasizing?"

"I guess I thought," he said slowly, "that since you're thirty-nine and have never been married, it wasn't that big a thing for you. That you liked kids and figured maybe one day you'd get together with a man who had some." He swallowed. "I have grandchildren."

Was he serious? "It's not the same thing. I want to be pregnant, to have a baby, to raise my own child. Or children, preferably."

"Oh," he said heavily. "I didn't realize that." He frowned slightly. "But . . . Look, I don't want to sound rude or insensitive, but aren't you getting a little old for that? I mean"—he added quickly—"not that you're too old to have kids, but that if you hadn't found the right guy by now . . ."

"I thought I might have." She glared at him. "Obviously, I was wrong."

He squeezed his eyes shut and shook his head. "When we first met and you said that down the road you'd like marriage and children, you were already slotting me into that role?"

She heaved a sigh. "No. I'd given up on slotting any man in that role."

He considered that and then said, "You've lost me."

"I'd decided to use a sperm donor. In fact, I've already got one picked out, and the sperm is at the women's clinic, just waiting for me."

His eyes widened as she spoke. "Oh, man."

"I would have already used it, except you came along

and the connection between us felt so strong that I put it off."

"You thought I . . ." He scrubbed his hand through his hair and stared at her, for once almost looking his age. "Maribeth, I had a vasectomy."

"*What? You what?* And you never thought to mention that to me?" Hurt and anger flared and she blinked against the moisture that welled in her eyes.

"When I told you I didn't want more kids, I figured you'd believe me."

The anger dimmed because he had a fair point. She said wryly, "Well, when I told you I wanted them, I thought *you* would believe *me*." She swiped her hand under one eye to flick away an escaping tear and tried to explain. "Mo, you said you didn't want to date, but you changed your mind. You said you weren't good at relationships, but yet you've been working hard at building them with me and Brooke and Evan. I hoped the same thing would happen when it came to your views on kids. That once you met your grandchildren, you'd see that having children is a wonderful thing. If I'd known you'd had a vasectomy, I'd have . . ." She trailed off, not sure how she'd have reacted. Would she have nipped their relationship in the bud despite the click she felt with him?

"Oh, man, Maribeth. I'm sorry. I'm really sorry." He sounded it, which wasn't much consolation.

"I believe you, and I am, too." She swallowed against a lump in her throat. "I guess . . . I mean, I know it's sometimes possible to reverse a vasectomy . . ."

He scrubbed a hand across his jaw. "I had one because I wanted to make sure I never, ever had another child. I'm sorry, but you need to believe me, Maribeth."

"I do," she whispered. Now, finally, she did. And that meant that if she used the sperm donor, Mo would never want to be father to that child. Tears slid down her cheeks. "That thing Irene and Daphne said about communication? I guess we're pretty t-terrible at it." A sob came out like a hiccup.

"I've never been good at it," he said gruffly. "Look, I'm really sorry if I hurt you, Maribeth. But I'm not sorry for what we've had together. I've never, uh, opened up to anyone the way I have with you. I've never cared for someone this way. Even if you want to end things now, I'll always be glad for having had this time with you. For seeing that, even if only for a little while, life could be better."

Life had been better with Mo in it. Until that afternoon—but that was as much her fault as his. She shouldn't have let her faith in the magical click lead her to make assumptions. She shouldn't have let her dreams—and her perhaps desperate desire to fulfill them—overrule her common sense.

"I wanted a sibling and couldn't have one," she said, her voice barely more than a whisper. "But I did have my parents and they were wonderful—and then they were taken away. I thought I'd fall in love and have kids, have the big, happy family I'd always wanted, but years passed and it never happened." Another sob caught in her throat and she forced it back, staring down at her clasped hands rather than letting Mo see her face.

"I'm an optimistic person," she went on, "and I kept telling myself that one day it would happen. But now I'm thirty-nine, and so I thought that even if I hadn't found Mr. Right yet, I could have a child. I could fulfill that dream and start building my family. I was taking action, being positive, con-controlling my l-life." More sobs came out, breaking up her words. "B-but then I met you, fell for you, and I d-didn't realize—didn't let myself truly understand—how you felt. I was b-being optimistic, too optimistic. Unrealistic." She drew a long, shuddering breath, trying to regain control. But it was hopeless. Tears flooded down her cheeks as she wailed, "I thought for once I could have it all. But I can't, can I?"

She raised both hands to cover her face, embarrassed by her outburst. If she'd set out to drive Mo away, she probably couldn't have made a better job of it. "I need a tissue," she said from behind her hands, her voice muffled. She rose and hurried to the downstairs powder room where she blew her nose, splashed her flushed, swollen cheeks and eyes with water, and tried to regain her self-control.

Over the noise she made, she didn't hear sounds of Mo leaving, but she was sure he'd be gone when she returned to the living room a few minutes later.

So it was a surprise to find him still sitting in the same place. She had to give him points for that.

Slowly, she sank into the same seat on the couch that she'd occupied before. "I'm sorry for that meltdown."

"Don't apologize. I can see how much all of this means to you." His expression was pained. "So what are you saying, Maribeth? Do you want to end things now?"

"I . . ." *Want?* No, of course that wasn't what she wanted. But he wasn't going to give her what she wanted. "I don't see how we can stay together," she said slowly, regret shading her voice. "Next time I'm ovulating, I'll be inseminated. Yes, I'm a little old, but I'm in excellent health. My doctor is optimistic that even if it doesn't happen on the first try, I'll get pregnant. I'll have a baby, which is what I most want in the world. You don't want children, so what kind of relationship could we have?"

Her question hung in the air between them. What was

she hoping for? That miraculously he'd find words that would fix everything?

What he did say, again, was, "I'm sorry." He said it heavily, finally. When he pushed himself out of the chair, he moved without his usual agility, like an arthritic man whose movements caused him pain. He walked across the room toward her, stopping on the far side of the littered coffee table. "Does this mean you don't want to see me again? Even as a friend?"

Not see him again. How could she bear it? Tears welled again and she tried to force them back. But how could she bear seeing this man—the only one who'd ever come close to claiming her heart—and not sorrow for what might have been? She dropped her head, staring at the floor rather than at Mo. "I don't know. I need to think about it."

Slow footsteps on the wooden floor told her he was leaving the room. She gazed teary-eyed at the Christmas tree. The lights were blurry, as if she were looking at them through a rain-streaked window.

A door opened down the hall, and then closed.

She loved Mo. What a fool she'd been. The first time she'd met him, she'd felt that tectonic shift she'd been waiting for all her life. She'd told herself she was being sensible, taking time to get to know him, to see if her brain and heart agreed with that first gut instinct. And they did. Everything about Mo: how he'd turned his life around, his connection with the abandoned dog, how hard he worked on reconciling with Brooke and Evan, even the way he'd been so patient with her as she insisted on hanging lights and ornaments in exactly the right spot. The way he made love, so fierce and passionate and yet so tender and reverent.

She loved him, but that hadn't meant that everything

would fall neatly into place. If Mo was the love of her life, then it seemed she'd be living the rest of her life without love.

Farther away, another door shut. He had collected Caruso and left via the sunroom. She was alone.

A sob burst from her. As if that first one had cleared the way, more followed until she was wailing like a child who'd lost her beloved stuffed animal. Or a woman who had lost her one chance at true love.

Monday evening, Maribeth sat in her living room, trying to read. The fire crackled, the Christmas tree sparkled, Anne Murray was singing "O Come All Ye Faithful," the novel was the latest by one of her favorite authors—and Maribeth felt like crap. A sense of loss had settled deep in her bones, in her heart, almost as painful as when her parents had died.

When the phone rang, her heart kicked. Mo? Had he changed his mind?

She rushed to answer and tried not to be disappointed when the caller turned out to be Jess Kincaid.

"Thanks again for yesterday," Jess said. "We all had a terrific time."

"I'm glad you came."

"MB, are you okay? Is Mo there?"

"No." No Mo. Hey, how about that, it rhymed. "We broke up."

"Oh, no. I'm so sorry."

Maribeth's brain wasn't functioning all that efficiently, but now it dawned on her that this wasn't a normal courtesy call. "You suspected, didn't you?"

"Not exactly. But he said something yesterday, and I thought you should know."

"About never wanting kids. I overheard. That's why we broke up."

"I'm so, so sorry. So it's over? Completely?"

"It's pretty black and white. No room for compromise when we want things that are completely opposite." As her grandmother had said, some problems were insurmountable.

"I guess. But you seemed so good together. I didn't expect that in the beginning, but he's a better guy than I thought he'd be, and you complement each other."

"*Did* complement each other. I thought so, too."

On the radio, Kellie Pickler was singing the sassy "Santa Baby." Maribeth muttered, "Oh, shut up," and clicked it off.

"What?" Jess said.

"Not you, the radio. Sorry." Maribeth sighed, feeling about a hundred years old. "Mo asked if we could still be friends, but I don't know if I can do that."

"You've stayed friends with a number of guys you've dated," Jess said neutrally.

Maribeth sighed again. Deliberated. And then decided, because that's what girlfriends were for. "I love him."

"Oh, MB. I thought maybe you did. You had a glow I've never seen before."

"All those years of waiting for the right man, and then he came along. I really thought he'd come along. But obviously I was wrong."

"I sure don't know Mo very well, but it looked to me like he has strong feelings for you, too."

"I think he does. And that would make it even tougher to be friends." She glanced over at the Christmas tree. "I've only known him five weeks, and already so many things remind me of him. Of what might have been. It's depressing."

"Want to have a girls' night? We'll drink too much, commiserate, and call him bad names?"

Maribeth mustered a small laugh. "Tempting. Except I don't want to drink alcohol because I'm going to get inseminated soon." *Get inseminated.* It sure wasn't the most romantic way of creating a new life, but it was the only avenue open to her.

"You're sure about the insemination?"

"Yes, of course. I'd already decided on a sperm donor, and Mo just delayed the process by a month."

"True love versus having a child. That's just so damned unfair, MB, that you have to choose."

"Tell me about it."

"This is really impressive," Mo told Robin on Sunday afternoon, a week after the open house at Maribeth's. A week after they'd broken up. He had a hard time thinking of anything but her, and a hard time mustering enthusiasm, but he gave it his best shot as Robin completed giving him a tour of Riders Boot Camp.

The operation included a big barn, a riding ring, a picturesque lodge, log guest cottages, and a bunkhouse. It was designed for weeklong residential programs aimed at teaching serious riders more about horses and helping them improve their skills. Evan's stepdaughter called it "no frills" and he supposed she was right if you compared it to fancy dude ranches with spas. To him, rustic worked just right in this part of the world.

"It was Mom's dream," Robin said. "And we all made it happen." She directed their steps along the road that led to Evan and Jess's house. A few inches of snow covered the landscape, but the road had been plowed.

"Who's the 'all'?"

"Me, Dad, Evan, all my grandparents, plus this cool couple from New York who're on the board of directors."

"That's nice. All of you working together."

"That's how it is in my family. We've all got, like, different skills and ideas, and when we put them together, we can do anything." She cocked her cowboy-hatted head toward him. "You're part of the family now, Mo-Mo. What do you bring to the table?"

Her question, like the running commentary she'd delivered as she took him around Boots, as she called it, seemed to him a little mature for a twelve-year-old, but what did he know about kids? She'd also caught him off guard, including him as part of the family. He rather doubted that Evan and Jess would want him to be part of the business they'd built from scratch, but he had to admit that the prospect, though foreign to him, had a certain appeal. To be part of a team. A family. Working together toward a common goal. "I can fix anything that has an engine," he told the girl, "but I'm afraid horses aren't my area of expertise. I've got a strong back, though. If you need some manual labor, I'm your guy."

"We *always* need manual labor."

He smiled at her vehemence. Robin was a charmer, not in that precociously flirty way some girls had but in her confidence and enthusiasm.

As they approached the nicely designed wooden house where Evan and Jess lived, Mo noted that Brooke and Jake's Toyota was parked outside. It was the only new addition. Either Miriam and Wade Bly hadn't arrived yet, or they'd walked over from their own ranch house, which was situated down the road on the same huge chunk of property.

He wasn't looking forward to meeting Jess's parents, fearing that they'd hold his past against him. After all, they were the ones who'd been there for young Evan when Mo and Brooke failed as parents, and they were the people who'd reported Mo to the police for suspected child abuse. He'd been glad, last Sunday, when Wade Bly's flu had prevented them from attending Maribeth's open house.

And there he was again, thinking of Maribeth. He hadn't spoken to her in a week. It constantly amazed him how he, a man who'd lived a lone-wolf life for more than twenty years, could miss someone so badly. For a short time, his life had had color, warmth, and a sense of possibility. Much as he told himself how lucky he was to be reconnecting with Brooke and Evan, and getting to know their families, Maribeth's absence left a hole in his heart.

Robin flung open the front door and they entered, shedding their outer clothing. She was faster, already at the entrance to the front room by the time he'd taken off his boots, hung his coat in the hall closet, and put his Stetson—the one Maribeth had given him—on a hook beside Robin's.

"Oh, good," Robin called to him. "Gran and Gramps are here. You haven't met them yet, Mo-Mo."

Jess's parents. "No, I haven't." Another hurdle to cross.

Mo had put some thought to this encounter and knew how he wanted to handle it. "Robin, would you mind asking them to come out into the hall so I can have a word with them privately?"

Her brown eyes round with curiosity, she said, "Okay."

A minute or so later, a man and woman around his age emerged from the front room holding hands. They were ranchers, Mo knew, and were attractive in a natural way. Miriam Bly had the same slim, fit build as her daughter Jess, an attractive face, and shoulder-length sandy hair streaked with silver. Wade, gray-haired, looked rugged, distinguished, and also very fit. Neither was smiling.

Nor did Mo when he said, "I want to thank you for all you did for Evan."

Surprise flickered in Miriam's eyes. Wade said in a rather grim voice, "I'm not sure it's your place to be thanking us. Seems like that's something a parent would do, and you weren't much of a father to that boy."

"I did him more harm than good," Mo said. "But all the same, I am his father and that's something I take seriously now. I'm very grateful that you two were there for him when he was growing up." He squared his shoulders. "And I'm grateful you called the police."

Miriam let out a tiny gasp. Had she figured he didn't know or wouldn't mention that?

Mo went on. "You were the reason I left town, and that was the right thing for Evan. And for Brooke."

"But now you're back," Wade said flatly.

"Wade," Miriam said quickly, warningly. "Jessica and Evan say he's changed, and so does Brooke."

"I have," Mo said. "And I respect that you're still looking out for Evan as well as for your daughter and, I'm sure, your grandkids. I also hope you'll give me a chance. One day, I'd like to sit down with you and tell you the whole story, and then you can see what you think. But this isn't the time or place."

"You're right," Miriam said firmly. "We're guests in Jessica and Evan's house and we don't want things to be awkward. But, Mo, I appreciate what you've said. And I, for one, will take you up on that offer." She tilted her face up to Wade. "Of course, I don't speak for my husband." Again there was a warning tone.

For the first time, the harsh lines of Wade's face relaxed. "Like hell you don't. Everyone knows you're the boss of this family. Mo, we'll set up a time and get together."

Mo heaved the proverbial sigh of relief as he followed

the other couple into the living room. Now all he had to do was survive a couple of hours under Wade Bly's judgmental eyes, interacting with the son and ex he'd abandoned, not to mention their spouses, two toddlers, and clever young Robin. Not a piece of cake by any means.

He wished Maribeth were there at his side. And not only because she had a gift for easing uncomfortable situations, but because he felt like half a person without her.

Or maybe, he thought later, after dinner, when everyone had assembled again in the spacious front room with its huge natural stone fireplace, it wasn't that he felt like half a person, but that he couldn't figure out how to mesh all his new roles into one identity.

He was father to Evan, father-in-law to Jess. To Robin, he was Mo-Mo, her stepdad's father. Evan and Jess's little boy, Alex, called him Mo-Mo as well, and in this case he really was the chestnut-haired child's grandfather—though he hadn't been invited to his second birthday party a few days earlier. Brooke and Jake's toddler Nicki also called him Mo-Mo. He was no relation to her, yet she seemed to have taken a yen to him and kept tugging on his pant leg and begging to be picked up.

Today he'd held toddlers and played with toy trucks and stuffed animals, he'd accepted Robin's invitation to go riding, and he'd promised to take a look at a hay baler that had given Wade some trouble the last time he used it. When Mo had felt compelled to return to Caribou Crossing, the most he'd hoped for was a civil relationship with Brooke and Evan. He'd never imagined being drawn into such a complicated web of relationships.

And these relationships mattered, they really did. It was just that without Maribeth, it was like there was a filter between him and the rest of the world, dulling the experience, turning the colors to shades of gray.

Maybe it was this odd phenomenon that made him wonder if Jess and Brooke were being a little reserved toward him—or perhaps he read them right, and they'd heard about his breakup with Maribeth. She was their friend. Of course they'd take her side.

It seemed that maybe he was right, because when all the guests headed out the front door around eight thirty, Brooke said, "Jake, will you take Nicki home? I'm going to catch a ride with Mo."

Jake slanted him a cool look, but said, "Sure."

Without speaking to Mo, Brooke walked alongside him to the Hennessey Auto Repair truck, and when he opened the passenger door, she climbed in.

He started the engine and waited as the other vehicles pulled out. Miriam and Wade were riding with Jake rather than walk home in the dark.

"Well," Mo said when he put the truck in motion. "You want to talk to me?"

"You and Maribeth broke up," she said accusingly.

"We did."

"Why?"

"Hasn't she already told you?"

"She said she wants a baby, and she's right that it's the most amazing experience in the world. But she said you're adamant about not wanting to have children."

"Yeah." It seemed Maribeth hadn't told her about his vasectomy. He appreciated her discretion.

"Why, Mo?"

"Jesus, Brooke." He glanced over in disbelief. "You of all people shouldn't have to ask that question. You saw what a crappy father I was."

"I was a crappy mother, but I changed and so have you."

"It did surprise me that you'd decided to have another child," he admitted. Then he quickly said, "I mean, seeing you with Nicki, it's obvious you're a great mom. I just wouldn't have thought you'd choose to have a baby."

She gazed out the windshield in silence, and then said, "Okay, here's the truth. I didn't plan to get pregnant."

"Oh, man, Brooke!" He let out a low whistle. "Just like with Evan."

"Yes, you'd think I'd have learned my lesson, wouldn't you? And I admit, when I found out I was pregnant at the age of forty-two, with bipolar disorder, I thought about getting an abortion."

"What did Jake say?"

"He wasn't in the picture then. We'd broken up. I figured that if I did have the baby, I'd be a single parent."

"I had no idea." Her and her husband's love was so obvious, Mo had just assumed things had gone smoothly for them. "What made you decide to have the baby?"

"I started thinking of it as a person and realized I already loved her or him. I knew the thing holding me back was fear. Fear that I wasn't strong enough to go off my meds during my pregnancy, and then to be a single parent. Fear that I wouldn't be a good mother, after the mess I'd made with Evan." She gave a soft laugh. "Fear versus love. Love won out."

"And everything worked out." He'd reached her and Jake's house, which sat on a patch of land situated near where the road to Bly Ranch and Riders Boot Camp joined the two-lane country road. It was a cute, bungalow-style building and, like Maribeth's, had Christmas lights strung along the eaves and around the windows.

"Yes. As a result of luck, hard work, and lots more love."

When Mo turned off the engine, Brooke undid her seat belt and reached over to touch his arm. "Are you so different from me, Mo? Why is it you don't want more children? Is it fear? If so, you'd be a fool to let that stop you. And how do you feel about Maribeth? Do you love her?"

"I, uh . . . Jesus, Brooke."

"No, I don't expect you to share all of that with me. I'm just saying, don't be in a rush to reject the best thing that may ever happen to you."

Maribeth was, most definitely, the best thing that had ever happened to him. But he couldn't give her what she wanted. Could he?

Brooke had opened the passenger door and was now sliding out. She started to close the door, and then leaned inside to say one more thing. "When Jake first proposed to me, I turned him down because I thought he was doing it out of a sense of duty. Because I was pregnant and not because he loved me. Thank God he came back and proposed again, and convinced me his feelings were genuine."

Mo wasn't sure why she was telling him this. "I'm happy for you."

"People make mistakes. Sometimes mistakes can be rectified."

"I get it, that you think I'm making a mistake in saying I can't give Maribeth what she wants."

"I don't know, Mo. Only you can answer that question. Only you know what kind of man you've turned into, what you want, and how you feel. What I will say is, MB's one of the finest people I've ever met, and she's a good friend of mine. Make up your mind what you want, and be honest with her. Don't hurt her any more than you already have."

He'd been honest with Maribeth from day one, but he had to admit that his feelings about a lot of things had changed over the weeks since then. "The last thing in the world I want is to hurt Maribeth."

"Then doesn't that tell you the truth of your feelings for her?" Leaving that thought hanging in the air, she closed the car door firmly.

As Brooke walked toward her house, the front door opened, revealing Jake framed in the doorway. What would that feel like, to have someone to come home to?

Mo pondered that as he drove the nearly deserted road back to town and pulled up in front of Daphne and Irene's house, where golden light came from an upstairs window. Another home shared by two people who loved each other.

Caruso came running down the block to greet Mo, and Mo bent to stroke him. Maybe he didn't have a real home or a woman who loved him, but he had this dog, and it seemed he now had family. He was coping. More than coping—actually enjoying the companionship.

But it was one thing to play with his grandkids for an hour or two, and a whole other thing to imagine taking on responsibility for a new life.

Maribeth had that kind of strength. She'd be a wonderful mother. She deserved a man who was like her, not a deeply flawed one like Mo.

Except it was him she seemed to want.

Chapter Seventeen

When Maribeth turned out the lights at Days of Your on Tuesday, six days before Christmas Day, and stepped outside, Caruso bounded up to her. Even though she hadn't seen Mo in more than a week, the dog had appeared every now and then to say hi, walk with her for a few blocks, or even cadge some food at her house.

She bent to reach out her hand. "Hey, you. It's good to see you." His cold nose met her palm and she stroked his head.

"How about me?" Mo stepped out from the recessed doorway of the neighboring shop.

Her heart skipped. Why was he here? Still, she believed in speaking the truth, so said, "I missed you."

"Me, too. Can we talk? Maybe walk and talk?"

She loved him, and so there was only one possible answer. "Of course." She wrapped her knitted scarf tighter around her neck and took her gloves from her purse. He was wearing the heavy sheepskin jacket he'd bought from her store, and its masculine style suited him perfectly. The red scarf she'd given him set off his black hair.

They strolled in silence for a few minutes, walking

from the side street where her shop was located to the main street of town.

"It's really looking like Christmas," he said, sounding stilted.

"Caribou Crossing does it well." Twinkly lights—colored strands and white ones—were everywhere, casting pretty patterns on the fresh white snow. Each store window had a seasonal display. At the florist, it was poinsettias, holly, and evergreen wreaths; the toy store featured Mr. and Mrs. Claus and the elves wrapping an abundance of toys; at Kleinfeld's Deli a lovely menorah sat in the window, with a new candle lit for each day of Hanukkah.

Maribeth and her companions crossed over to the town square, where a big decorated tree took pride of place. Beneath it, wire-framed caribou had been rigged out as Santa's reindeer pulling a sleigh.

"I don't want to hurt you," Mo said.

She glanced at him to see him staring at the faux reindeer. "I never thought you did. Nor did I want to hurt you. We just didn't communicate very well."

"My fault," he said gruffly. "I'm lousy at it. Don't have much experience."

"Well, I have a lot of experience," she said wryly, "and I didn't do that great a job either. I made assumptions, and that's always a stupid thing to do."

"Want to sit? No, you're probably too cold. You've just finished work, had a long day."

"Mo, I'm not cold. Let's sit." She strode over to a park bench, brushed off a crisp lacework of snow, and plunked down.

He sat beside her, leaving a foot of space between them. Caruso gazed between the two of them and then went off to sniff at the caribou.

Maribeth restrained herself from asking questions. Mo

had initiated this meeting and she'd give him time and space to say what he wanted to say.

Finally, still not looking at her, he spoke. "I don't know anything about love. Except that when I was with you, I felt something I'd never felt before. Like my heart came alive. Like it was warm and beating, and full. Like life might mean more than just passing through and doing no harm."

She blinked against sudden tears. "You did?"

"And when we broke up, all of that died. I mean, I do care about Evan. And his family, and Brooke. But it's . . . pale. It's not like what I feel for you. That's so . . . big. Vivid." Now he did turn to face her. "I think maybe I love you, Maribeth."

A tear slipped free. "I love you, Mo."

"Well, shit." He looked stunned. "I mean, wow."

She scrubbed a gloved finger under her eye, not knowing whether to be happy or sad. "But where does that get us? If we want such different things . . ."

"Maybe I'm rethinking," he said slowly. "I can't promise to suddenly change and say I'd be thrilled to have another kid. But I'm thinking about it. Brooke talked to me, and I've spent more time with the grandkids, and . . ." He shook his head. "I had this idea of what my life was, and now it's all changing."

Heart fluttering, she nodded, encouraging him to go on.

"When we first met, you asked me to envision the future, to dream. That wasn't something I'd ever done. I'm still no good at it because, well, I don't really know who I am. There's this new Mo Kincaid person that I seem to be turning into, and I don't know what he'll end up being."

"I didn't mean to rush you."

"I know. But you had everything figured out. The

whole, uh, sperm donor thing. And then I came along and threw a monkey wrench in the works."

"And you're the mechanic who's supposed to fix stuff, not break it," she teased gently.

"I wish I could." There was no teasing note in his voice, just utter seriousness. "I wish I could turn a magic screw or charge a battery and somehow make everything all right for both of us. But I can't."

The dog chose that moment to run over and glance from Mo to her and back again, clearly impatient. "Not now, Caruso," Mo said, and Maribeth could almost hear the creature let out a huff of frustration as he did one of those odd head tosses and then wandered off to sniff at tracks in the snow.

She turned back to Mo. "So what are you saying? Why did you want to talk?"

"I have no right to ask this, but I'm going to. Because I think I'm in love with you and because I want to be honest. I don't want to give up on something wonderful just because I'm afraid and uncertain. I want us to have another chance, Maribeth. I'm asking if you could be patient with me. If we could keep seeing each other and you could give me a little time to see if I can possibly get to . . . well, to being the man you want me to be."

The man she wanted him to be? Those words rang a bell. Occasionally, Maribeth had been accused of being too pushy in trying to persuade friends to do something that, to her, seemed obviously right, but that they weren't ready for or simply didn't want to do. She touched her gloved fingers to her brow. "Oh, my. Is that what I'm trying to do? Turn you into a different man? That's not right." Guiltily, she remembered, "That's what you said your parents did."

He shrugged awkwardly. "It kind of is."

"I'm sorry, Mo. You have to do what *you* want. I truly don't want you trying to turn yourself from a square peg to a round one, to fill some hole in my life."

He was quiet for a bit and then reached his gloved hand across the bench toward her. "Maybe it'll turn out that I want to be a round peg. But I can't promise that."

She wanted promises. Certainty. A baby. But she also wanted this man, and if their love was ever going to blossom into a happy future, she had to be patient.

She stretched out her hand and met his as it curled upward. "Promise me to be true to yourself. If you aren't, if you pretend—to me or to yourself—then it would never work between us, long term." She'd seen more than one couple break up because one or both were trying to be something they really weren't.

Gazing at the faux caribou, she remembered something Brooke had said when Maribeth had first asked about dating Mo. Brooke had commented that she worried Mo might drag Maribeth down—but then she'd changed her mind. She'd said that, of all those guys Maribeth had gone out with, none had changed her and she wouldn't give a man that power. At the time, something about those words had bothered Maribeth, but then she'd brushed them aside in the excitement of getting together with Mo.

Now she realized that it wasn't right for one person in a relationship to have all the power. It wasn't right to be inflexible.

Thinking about her friends, the ones who were now in happy relationships, she realized that, for most, the path of true love hadn't run smoothly. There'd been obstacles, sometimes ones that seemed insurmountable. Often—almost always—there'd been adjustments and compromises. Not the kind where one person bent themselves out of shape for the other, but the kind where two people who truly loved each other looked deep into their hearts and found a solution they'd both be happy with.

She took a breath. "And I'll promise to think hard as well. Wanting a child—well, that's always been there for me, ever since I was a little girl. But I know life doesn't always give us everything we want, and I know that people make compromises."

He gripped her hand so tightly that if they hadn't been wearing gloves, it would have been painful. "Maribeth, you can't give up a long-held dream for me."

"I'm not saying that I would. I'm just saying we both have a lot of thinking to do." She turned to give him a tremulous smile, and found him watching her. "I have another long-held dream. To find a special man to share my life."

A slow smile warmed his face. "So where do we go from here?"

She felt a little weepy, and for the life of her she didn't know whether it was because she felt a new sense of possibility or because she was afraid she might have to give up on one of her dreams. If she felt that way, she'd bet Mo did as well. They needed a change of scene, of pace. She raised her chin, shoving her concerns to the back of her mind. "Pizza," she said. "Why don't we pick up a pizza, take it back to my place, and eat in front of the fire?"

"Now, that sounds like a fine plan." Still clasping her hand, he stood and pulled her to her feet. "Thank you. For listening. For giving me another chance."

She gazed up at his striking face. "Thank you for coming to me and asking, Mo." Even if he had, once again, thrown her tidy plans for a total loop.

No way could she regret that when his lips, chilly from the winter air, met hers. As warmth sparked between them, she focused on one miraculous thought: Mo Kincaid was falling in love with her.

She held that thought close in her heart as they collected Caruso and walked over to Venezia Pizza, squabbled amiably over the choices, and sat across from each other at a small table with a red-and-white-check tablecloth waiting for their large half-salami, half-margherita pie.

The thought was never far from her mind as they drove back to her place, fed the dog and put him in the sunroom, and then settled on the rug by the fire with the pizza box and a roll of paper towels.

Mo had said he might love her. She'd laid her heart on the line and told him the truth, that she did love him. How would her heart survive if this second chance didn't work out for them?

He rose, and she glanced up. "Stay," he said, moving to the fireplace and adding a new log. "I'm just going to toss out the garbage. Can I bring you anything back? A glass of wine or a liqueur, maybe? I've seen the bottles in your cupboards, Maribeth. I really don't mind if you have a drink."

She would *love* a glass of wine or Grand Marnier, but she said, "No, thanks." They'd promised to be honest and to talk, so she went on. "I'm avoiding alcohol. It was something the doctor at the women's clinic recommended, in preparation for getting pregnant. I'm also staying away from caffeine."

He processed that in silence, and then said, "Tea, maybe?"

"A mug of chamomile tea sounds lovely. Thanks, Mo."

When he'd gone, she glanced over at the lit-up tree and then turned on some Christmas music. It was the same mix she'd played the night they'd danced, starting with "Holiday in Your Heart." A song about the true holiday spirit, about how if each person would reach out and be kind to someone who was down on their luck, the world would be a better place.

She sank down on the rug again, leaning back against the couch. LeAnn Rimes really put things in perspective. Maribeth had so much: a cozy house, a wonderful community, a business she loved, the best grandparents in the world, and a huge collection of friends. An amazing man whom she loved, who seemed to be falling in love with her. How selfish was she being, that she wanted even more? She had always wanted more and been denied it, and now perhaps it was time to give up on another dream. Gazing at the tree she and Mo had put up together, melancholy seeped through her.

He returned to the room and put a warm mug in her hands.

"Thank you." She cradled it, watching the handsome, complicated guy in faded jeans and a black jersey who lowered himself to sit beside her. If she could have Mo and Caruso, did she really need anything more?

He was holding a bottle of lemon-lime soda and took a sip before turning toward her. "Tell me what it means to you, having a baby."

"What?" It was the last thing she'd expected him to say.

"I mean, I guess most women have a maternal instinct, but I don't really understand it."

She frowned and put her mug down. "Not all women want children. And I'd guess that for those who do, it's a bit different for each one. And, I'll point out, a lot of men want children, too."

"Sorry, I didn't mean it the way it came out. What I want to know is how *you* feel about it."

Okay, that was better. In fact, she counted it as a positive step that he'd asked the question. She picked up her mug again and inhaled the familiar, comforting scent of chamomile. "It's like there's a part of me that will never be whole until I have a child. There's a craving I've always felt, and it gets stronger the older I get. But it's not just like a straightforward biological urge, it's this whole complex of things."

"Go on." They weren't touching, but his gaze was fixed on her face as if he was really listening and trying to understand.

"It's wanting to create life and then experience that moment of knowing there's a tiny new life inside me. Of spending all those days carrying that baby as it grows. Feeling it move, talking to it. Singing to it, even though I'm no great singer. Wondering who it's going to be when it finally emerges, and who it'll turn into as it grows up. Knowing it's going to be this incredible, unique human being who's made up of part of me and part of—" She broke off, because of course the ideal was that the baby's biological father would be the man she loved. "Well, of another special person. But the child would be so much more than just the sum of two sets of DNA."

He nodded. "That's so true. Kids are made up of genetics, environment, and something that seems to be uniquely their own."

"Yes! Their spirit or soul or whatever. Anyhow, I even want to go through childbirth. I'm told it's the closest thing to hell a person can experience, and then when you hold your baby for the first time, that's what heaven's like."

"Oh, man. That's . . . big."

"I know." She was sure it hadn't been that way for him when he first held Evan, and likely not for Brooke, either. "And I want it. Then I want to care for that child, raise him or her, teach and play and laugh together. Be so filled with love that . . ." She blinked against her tears. "That it's a bigger thing than I can even imagine. Be protective and scared and proud and . . ." She put her mug down, pulled a tissue from her pocket, and blew her nose.

Mo was frowning slightly. It wasn't denial she saw on his face, more like puzzlement. She drew in a long, cleansing breath and let it out again. Calmer now, she said, "You've spent time with Robin. What's that like for you?"

He tilted his head, obviously thinking about it. The hard, masculine lines of his face softened with affection. "She's a fine girl. Smart, capable, generous." He must know that Maribeth was looking for more than that, because his eyes narrowed. "I enjoy being with her. She makes me feel younger and older, all at the same time."

"How do you mean?"

He took a swallow of soda. "Well, younger because she's so full of spirit and she shares it. Her enthusiasm, her joy in life, they're contagious." He gave Maribeth a soft smile. "Same as with you. But she also makes me feel older because even if she's only Evan's stepdaughter, that does kind of make her my grandchild. I feel responsible, like I want to do right by her."

"Is that a bad feeling?"

"Kind of a scary one. Given my past." His voice firmed. "But I'm different now. I'm up to handling that responsibility."

She was about to ask him about Evan and Jess's little Alex, but Mo went on. "She's a lot like her mom, Robin is. But it's funny, I see Evan in her, too. Almost like he was her biological dad. Little gestures, the way her jaw firms up when she's determined. He's had an influence on her, and I like seeing that. I only met her real dad, Dave, briefly at your open house, but I can see he's a good man. He and Robin are really close, and that's how it should be.

But it's nice to see that she and Evan love each other so much, too."

Maribeth had picked up her mug again and sipped tea as she listened. Now she said, "I know. She's a lucky girl, having such a big, loving family." She tried not to sound sad or envious.

Mo's gaze sharpened and he rested his hand on her thigh. "I'm sorry you didn't have that. Sorry it was just you and your parents, and they died so young."

She appreciated his words, his understanding, the comfort of his touch. "Thanks. I have a great relationship with my grandparents, but they're in Vancouver and it's not the same thing as having family in town. But I've built a really lovely family of my heart, here in Caribou Crossing."

"I've seen that. And I'm not one bit surprised, given the kind of woman you are." He pressed his lips together and then said, almost reluctantly, "You'd make a terrific mother."

She knew that. With every ounce of her being. She also happened to think that Mo had the makings of an excellent father. Curling her hand into his, on her thigh, she asked, "How about Alex? Do you enjoy being with him?"

Mo gave a quick laugh. "Hard not to. He's one spunky little kid. Him and Brooke's Nicki, they're quite the pair." He took a breath. "Yeah, they're fun. Playing with toy trucks and stuffed animals, that's easy. Even dealing with toilet training. But man, they're so vulnerable, kids that age."

"Kids of all ages are vulnerable."

He nodded slowly. "And that's the responsibility side. The fear side. Brooke and I were so stupid when we had Evan. We didn't realize all that stuff."

"And yet he survived."

"In spite of us. But he was damaged. Oh, he did an

amazing job of getting past it all and building a fine life for himself. But we damaged him, and that's wrong."

"It was. But you wouldn't do that again. Not with Robin or Alex."

"Never. Not intentionally. Can't say I won't make mistakes, though." He freed his hand from hers. Strain creased the corners of his blue-green eyes, and suddenly they were no longer talking about him being a grandfather. "What the hell do I know about parenting, Maribeth?"

"You know a lot of things not to do."

"That's for sure."

She caught both his hands in hers. "Mo, do you get it at all? Do you have any notion of how I feel when I think about having a child?"

He blew out air, but didn't pull away from her touch. "Maybe. Maybe I'm starting to." He shrugged his shoulders like he was working out knots. "Feelings. Maribeth, when I was a kid the feelings I had were mostly negative ones. Resentment, anger, a craving for excitement and danger. Later, when I realized what a shit I'd been, I tried not to feel. Just to take each day at a time and, like I said, try to do no harm. It was all shades of gray, my life, for years and years."

Tension radiated not only from his words but from the hands she clasped. He went on, "And then there was you. And Caribou Crossing. Brooke, Evan, those kids. The singing dog. Life's a whole new thing, with lots of colors. And I have feelings, but I don't know what to do with them. Don't even know how to label them."

Her first instinct was to jump in with questions to help him pin down his feelings. But maybe this was a time to step back and not be so pushy. She truly did want Mo to work things out for himself, to be honest with himself and with her, and to not let her persuade him into doing something that he might end up regretting. And so, she said tentatively, "This may not resonate with you at all, but have you thought of seeing a professional? A counselor?"

His jaw dropped. "Talk to a stranger about touchy-feely stuff?" he asked incredulously. "Even at those A.A. meetings I went to, I never talked about my own shit. I learned what I needed by listening to others."

She clasped his hands firmly. "You learned what you needed at the time, and you learned it because those other people were brave enough to share. Now you've got all these new issues and feelings to deal with, and talking might help. And yes, to a stranger. Someone who has no vested interest. Whose only goal is to help you figure out what you feel. What you want."

"Well, huh. I hadn't thought of it that way."

"Consider it."

He nodded slowly. "I'll consider anything that'll help us figure out what to do."

She smiled at him, feeling good about how hard both of them were trying. "I love you, Mo Kincaid."

"Oh, hell," he said softly, his expression suddenly vulnerable. "For all that I don't know much about feelings, I'm pretty sure I love you, too."

Oh, yes! "Then get over here and kiss me."

He did, and the sincerity of that kiss confirmed everything he'd just told her. Maribeth was sinking into it wholeheartedly when he startled her by breaking it off.

"A question," he said, his arms still around her.

"Okay," she replied a little warily.

"You have all these rules about Christmas."

He wanted to talk about Christmas *now*? "Well, kind of," she admitted, leaning back in the circle of his arms.

"Like, there's the right way and wrong way to decorate a Christmas tree."

Was he saying she was too rigid? "I guess I could be more flexible about that." Realizing something, she smiled. "It's been *my* tree for so long. Just mine. But if it's a shared tree, others should have input. I'm sorry I didn't give you that and just bossed you around."

"Well, if I'm going to have input, there is one thing I'd suggest."

He didn't think the tree was perfect? She tried not to be offended as she asked, "What's that?"

His eyes twinkled. "The best way to christen a new tree is to make love under it."

A surprised laugh escaped. "Under it?" She glanced at the low-hanging bottom branches, just perfect for sheltering wrapped gifts but not designed to accommodate two bodies.

"Don't be so literal. Beside it will do." He tugged her closer. "What do you think?"

She gave him a flirtatious grin. "I think that a new rule should be tested out before it's given final approval."

Chapter Eighteen

On Friday evening, Mo stood beside Maribeth outside Caribou Crossing's one cinema—a theater dating back to gold rush days, which had been renovated over the years and was now designed to allow the showing of two different movies. They'd decided to go to an early show, and as they studied the posters for their options, Caruso headed off on his own business. Mo put up a token male effort in favor of the save-the-world thriller but knew they'd end up going to the romantic comedy, and that didn't bother him in the least.

His cell phone rang, startling him. "Good thing," he muttered as he extracted it from his jacket. "I'd have forgotten to turn it off. I'm still not used to having one of these things." Or having people who wanted to talk to him. After checking the caller display, he answered, "Hey, Jess."

"Mo, we have a family emergency." His daughter-in-law, normally so calm and capable, sounded frazzled.

His heart jerked. "An accident? Is someone hurt?" He was barely aware of Maribeth clutching his arm and gazing at him with wide eyes.

"No, sorry, nothing that bad. Just . . . a crisis. Can you come to the house?"

"Now?"

"Yes."

"Of course. Uh, Maribeth is with me."

"Bring her. That's fine. Just come." She hung up.

Heart still racing, he said, "No one's hurt, but there's some kind of crisis. I have to go to Evan and Jess's house. You're invited, but don't feel you have to come. I've no idea what's going on."

Her hand tucked under his elbow. "Of course I'll come. If you want me to."

When did he ever not want her by his side? "Please."

Hurrying, they went to where her car was parked.

Maribeth drove quickly and, rather than speculate on the nature of the crisis, Mo took the opportunity to update her on his news of the day. "I saw that counselor, Karim." She'd asked around and told him that the fiancé of one of her girlfriends recommended this guy. When Maribeth added that the fiancé was ex-army and the counselor had helped him with PTSD, Mo figured it was worth giving Karim a chance.

"Did you find it useful?" she asked.

"I think. He's a pretty laid-back guy, more touchy-feely than I'm comfortable with, but he's persistent. And he says interesting things that make me think. Kind of like you do."

She tossed him a smile. "But like we discussed, he's a stranger, so maybe you'll listen in a different way."

"Yeah." After having so many people in his life who seemed to have a vested interest in what Mo did—even Hank Hennessey, with his proposal about the garage—it had been refreshing to discuss his issues with a stranger.

"So, did he say anything interesting that you'd be willing to share?"

"I guess. When I told him I had trouble identifying or maybe even feeling my emotions, he asked if perhaps I felt so guilty over things I'd done in my past that I figured I didn't deserve to be happy. To be loved, to have a full life."

She glanced over. "Like you're doing penance for past bad behavior. What do you think?"

Once before, when they'd first met, she'd muttered something under her breath about him doing penance. He'd forgotten until now. But if she thought that, and so did Karim, maybe there was something to it. "I dunno. Guess I'll think about it. I'm going to see him again next week."

She reached over to touch his jacketed arm. "Thanks for doing this, Mo."

"I think I may end up thanking you for suggesting it."

They drove past Brooke and Jake's house to the big wooden signs for Bly Ranch and Riders Boot Camp, and Maribeth made the turn. A moment later, another pair of headlights followed.

When she pulled into the driveway of Evan and Jess's house, where four vehicles were already parked, she said, "It looks as if the whole family has come. I hope they don't mind me being here."

"I hope they don't mind *me* being here," he muttered. He was such a recent, and fringe, member of this family. What right did he have to be present during a family crisis? Or was that the kind of notion Karim had been talking about, letting past guilt affect his life today?

As he and Maribeth got out of her Mini, Ken and Sheila Cousins emerged from the car that had been following them. The gray-haired couple, whom he'd met at

Maribeth's open house, were the parents of Dave, who was Robin's father and Jess's ex-husband. "Any idea what's going on?" Ken asked Mo.

"Not a clue."

Sheila linked arms with Maribeth. "It's nice to see you. Thanks again for that wonderful party a couple of weeks ago." The two women led the way toward the front door of the house, with Mo and Ken following.

Sheila knocked twice and then opened the door, and they all went inside.

Boots, coats, hats, and scarves littered the big entrance hall. They added their own to the mess and proceeded toward the front room. As Ken and Sheila walked ahead, Mo took the opportunity to claim Maribeth again, clasping hands with her and drawing comfort from her warm, familiar touch.

Evan and Jess's front room was large, highlighted by the huge stone fireplace and a big, decorated Douglas fir. Mo gazed around, cataloguing the occupants. In one corner of the room Evan and Jess stood side by side, with little Alex fussing in Jess's arms. They were involved in what looked like a rather tense conversation with Dave and his wife, Cassidy. Cassidy had her arms wrapped around herself, and her expression looked defensive.

It seemed that the obvious tension in that small group had caused everyone else to keep their distance. Brooke and Jake sat on a couch, with Nicki sleeping in a sling across Jake's chest. They were chatting with Jess's parents, Miriam and Wade Bly, who sat on a smaller sofa facing them. The four adults all glanced up and exchanged hellos with the newcomers. The only family member who seemed to be missing was Robin. Whatever kind of family crisis this was, it seemed it was for the ears of adults and toddlers only.

Sheila and Ken took the other end of the four-seater, beside Brooke. Mo was about to steer Maribeth to a pair of chairs near the fireplace when Jess glanced around and her troubled gaze lit on him. "Mo, would you take Alex?"

Him? But he hurried over to scoop his grandson from her arms. The poor kid's face was red and scrunched and he was making choky, wailing sounds. Mo cradled him close, rocked him gently, and murmured, "Hey, there, kiddo, it's not so bad."

Amazingly, as Mo crossed the room to sit down, the toddler blinked and stopped crying. "Mo-Mo?" he said. "Play trucks now?"

"It's not a good time for trucks." Mo settled the child on his lap so that they faced each other. "The grown-ups are going to do some boring talking, so you might want to take a little snooze right about now."

Alex's face screwed up with displeasure again. Before he could let out another wail, Maribeth, who'd taken the chair beside Mo, pulled the woven scarf off from around her neck and held it out, catching the boy's attention. She made a couple of folds and knots and said, "Hey, Alex, it's a bunny rabbit. See, here's his head and here's his tail."

The kid must have a lot of trust or a great imagination, because he accepted her word for it and began to play with the improvised toy, a smile on his face.

Mo glanced across the room to see that both Evan and Jess still looked distressed. Dave scowled at Cassidy and she said something, looking earnest and apologetic. He heaved a sigh and put his arm around her. She tensed for a moment and then leaned into him. She said something else, Jess nodded, Dave spoke, and then Jess left the room.

Maribeth rose and said quietly, "I'll get drinks for us."

As she moved to a sideboard, Mo saw that it held a

collection of bottles and cans. She came back with a couple of cans of ginger ale. She cracked them both open, handed him one, and took her seat again. Finding it difficult to juggle his grandson, the scarf toy, and the drink, Mo put the can down on a coaster on a side table.

Evan spoke, his voice cutting through a couple of quiet conversations. "Jess has gone to get Robin. Then we'll explain why we asked you all to come." He sounded as unhappy as he looked.

Did this have something to do with Robin?

Apparently so, because the girl thudded down the stairs and stalked into the room, red-faced, her usual ponytail a scraggly mess. Normally, she was poised and bouncy. It was a shock seeing her so obviously upset. What the hell was going on here?

Jess followed her daughter into the room, a couple of steps back, also flushed. She went to join Evan, Dave, and Cassidy. Robin's parents and stepparents remained standing in their corner of the room, a little apart from the seated grandparents and Maribeth.

Robin paced over to the Christmas tree. She turned, fisted her hands on her hips, glared around the room, and said, "You've all been lying to me!"

Her accusation was met with a collection of gasps, protests, and questions. Mo examined his conscience. In agreement with Robin's parents and Brooke, he hadn't told the girl all the details of his crappy parenting of Evan, but he'd given her the general idea and had never once lied.

Voice taut with anger, Robin said, "I found out who my real dad is."

Her real dad? That was Dave. Wasn't it? Maybe not, from the pained expression on the man's face.

Dave's mother, Sheila, spoke first, gently, sounding puzzled. "Honey, Dave's your dad."

"Yeah, that's what you all wanted me to think, wasn't it? That's the stupid big lie!"

"It's not a lie," Sheila said, the slightest quaver in her voice. She turned to her son. "It's not. Is it?"

Dave squeezed his eyes shut, and when he opened them their hazel was glossed with moisture. "I'm afraid it is, Mom. I'm sorry. And, Robin, you're wrong. Your grandparents didn't lie. They didn't know the truth. None of them did."

What was the truth? Mo felt like he'd gone to a movie and was too dumb to follow the plot. From the puzzled expressions on others' faces, he wasn't the only one.

"How stupid do you think I am?" Robin raged, her cheeks even brighter. "Like I'd never learn about DNA?"

DNA? What was the girl talking about?

Miriam gave a soft gasp. "Your school assignment. You called me to ask about your mother's blood type."

Robin nodded. "Lucky thing I couldn't get Mom, Dad, or Evan on the phone this afternoon, right? If I'd have asked them, they'd have lied. But Cassidy told me the truth when I called her to ask *his*"—she glared at Dave—"blood type. And I realized he couldn't be my real dad."

Cassidy said, "I'm sorry. I'm so sorry. I didn't mean to spill the big secret. I was distracted, in the middle of dealing with a supplier crisis, and when Robin asked I didn't think about the implications."

Dave sighed. "We should've thought about the DNA thing, and that Robin would be studying it in school one day. I guess we figured we had time . . ." He shook his head. "I don't know. Ostriches. Heads in the sand. Stupid."

Mo exchanged glances with Maribeth, who looked as stunned as he felt. Dave really wasn't Robin's biological father. Dave had known that and had obviously told Cassidy, but it seemed that they and Jess had been the only ones who knew the truth. And maybe Evan? Mo studied his son's face, which bore just as tortured an expression as Dave's. Had Evan shared the secret or been just as in the dark as Robin?

Mo had to wonder who had fathered Robin, and what the circumstances had been.

Robin had been echoing Dave, saying "Yeah, stupid, stupid, stupid." She sneered, her pretty face twisting in a far too adult expression. "Like I didn't know I have this really weird blood type."

Weird blood type? Mo had a rare one, inherited from his mother. His son had inherited it from him . . . But no, surely Evan couldn't be the girl's biological father.

Mo had almost forgotten that he was holding little Alex. The child had been happily playing with his makeshift toy, and Mo'd been intent on Robin and the unfolding drama. But now his grandson moved restlessly, as if the tension in the room was getting to him. Mo jiggled the scarf-bunny absently, not wanting to miss a second of the conversation.

"After all," Robin said, "we always stockpile some of my blood so the hospital has it frozen in case I need it. Like when I had the splenectomy three years ago."

Jess's sad gaze met her daughter's. "That night, there wasn't enough blood on hand and there was a storm, so we weren't sure that more could be flown in. So we had to ask"—she paused, and tears slid down her cheeks—"your biological father. It was just sheer blind luck that he happened to be in town."

At the sound of a feminine gasp, Mo's gaze turned to Brooke.

"Evan?" she asked in a squeaky, disbelieving voice.

Mo, along with everyone else, stared at his son. Evan had knocked up teenage Jess and run out on her? Oh shit, the apple didn't fall far from that tree.

A memory flashed into Mo's mind. When he and Evan had first talked, Mo had said that every child deserved to have two responsible, loving parents—and his words had taken his son aback. Now he understood why.

"Yeah," Robin said. "Evan." She spoke the name with disgust. Even so, her voice trembled when she said, "The father who didn't want me."

"He didn't know!" Jess cried. "He never knew. I didn't tell him. Not until the night you needed surgery."

Robin's eyes widened. "Mom! How could you do that?"

"I meant well." Tears rolled freely down Jess's cheeks. "I swear, I honestly meant well. And so did Dave. He loved us, Robin. Dave loved you as his own daughter, from way before you were even born."

"Oh yeah, right!" The girl was crying and almost yelling. "None of you love me. You're all just a bunch of liars!"

Alex twisted in Mo's grip, opened his round little mouth, and began to wail.

Nicki, in the sling across Jake's torso, promptly did the same.

Maribeth rose, gave Mo a tiny, pained smile, and then lifted Alex from his lap and set the toddler on his feet. She took his hand. "Come with me, little one. Tee Bee will find us some toys to play with or read you and Nicki a story." Towing the whimpering little boy, she walked over to Jake as he unbundled Nicki and put her down so Maribeth could take her hand, too. Maribeth glanced around the group of on-edge adults. "We'll be in the playroom."

"Thank you," Jess said fervently.

Mo, realizing his mouth was dry from stress, picked up his can of ginger ale and took a long swallow.

There were a few moments of silence as the threesome left the room, and then Brooke, her voice firm now, said, "Evan, tell us how this happened."

The obvious answer would have been, "In the usual way," but clearly Brooke meant much more than that.

Evan sighed. "It was once. Just once. Right after, I realized it was a big mistake. I felt like I'd betrayed my friendship with Jess, Miriam, and Wade." He glanced warily at Robin, who'd perched on the edge of a chair and was glaring at him. "We did use protection, but it failed. Anyhow, this happened right before I left for university. After that, Jess and I didn't really keep in touch. She didn't tell me and she had good reasons for that. Anyhow, the first I knew was when she came to me the night of Robin's accident, saying they needed blood. I was . . . in shock."

Evan hadn't known. He hadn't run out on Jess and the baby. Mo felt horrible for having imagined that his son might have done such a thing.

"Jessica?" Miriam said in a firm mother-to-daughter voice. "Why didn't you tell Evan? Surely he had a right to know."

"You think?" Robin said sarcastically.

Evan put a supporting arm around his wife as she began to speak. "Maybe he did. But all he'd ever wanted to do was leave Caribou Crossing and make a new life."

"That's true," Brooke said softly, sadly.

Mo caught her eye and gave her a sympathetic half-smile.

Jess went on. "If I'd told him, he'd have done what he thought was the right thing. He'd have married me, been stuck in Caribou Crossing, and been miserable. Which meant I'd have been unhappy, too." She glanced over at her daughter. "And probably so would Robin."

Just as had happened when Mo and Brooke wed. His ex, still gazing at Mo, nodded slightly, confirming that they shared the thought.

Dave coughed, drawing attention. "Jess came to me," he said. "We were good friends and she wanted a guy's opinion."

"Why didn't you come to us, Jessica?" Miriam cried in a hurt tone.

"Oh, Mom," Jess said. "I wanted to, and I knew you and Dad would support me, but I felt so stupid and I was so confused and . . . I don't even remember what I was thinking. Just that Dave was someone I trusted totally."

"People have always taken their problems to our son," Sheila said with both pride and a touch of ruefulness.

"When I thought about Jess's situation," Dave said quietly, "the solution seemed obvious. She and I liked each other a lot and were really compatible. More suited to each other than her and Evan, I thought at the time."

"And that was true," Jess said. "Back then, Ev and I were so different, even though we were such good friends."

"*Friends*," Robin said bitterly.

"When I thought about Jess's baby," Dave said, "I felt something I'd never felt before. Like I could be that child's father, and I wanted to be." He gazed at Robin with her red, tear-streaked face. "I did love you, sweetheart. From before you were born. I have never, not for one moment, loved you anything less than wholeheartedly. And when Evan came back and we had to tell him the truth, it almost broke my heart."

Mo read the truth of that on Dave's face, but he felt sorry for Evan as well. What a shock, to find out that he had a daughter. That Jess, his best friend and onetime lover, had betrayed him, even if her intentions had been good. To learn that another man had raised his child as his own.

"Good," Robin said to Dave. "You deserve it. You all deserve to feel crappy."

"Robin," Dave said warningly. "Language."

"Ha! Like you have any right to order me around. You're not even my real f-father!" Her angry words came out chokily, mixed with sobs. "And Evan doesn't deserve to be my father because he r-ran out! And Mom's a liar, and Cassidy kept this huge, giant secret from me, and everyone else is, is—" She broke off, either crying so hard she couldn't speak or unable to find the words she wanted. The poor kid was obviously heartbroken and looked to be on the verge of an all-out temper tantrum.

Somehow, Mo found himself on his feet, walking over to Robin. His granddaughter in all senses of that word, as proved by the flaky blood she'd inherited.

He kneeled in front of the chair where she sat, not daring to touch her. "Robin, look around this room. Right now, you're really mad at all of us."

"I'm so mad I could, could . . ." Again, it seemed words failed her.

"Look at each person," Mo said. "Every single one is here tonight because of you. Because they—" He took a breath, realizing the truth and finding the courage to speak it. "Because *we* love you so much." He stared into her glazed, bloodshot eyes and realized she was actually paying attention.

"It tears us apart that you're hurt," he said, "but believe me, no one here ever wanted to hurt you. We want to protect you, but that isn't always possible. Right now, we'd do anything to make it better, but things happened in the past that can't be undone. But here's the thing. Because of what happened, you've ended up with even more people who love you and who'd do anything for you. And you know what?"

Her tears had eased, her cheeks were a little less red, and she shook her head slowly.

"In my books, that makes you one very lucky girl."

She frowned. "L-lucky?" It came out hiccupy, but questioning rather than angry.

"Lucky." As he said it, he realized that what he'd told her was, in fact, a little bit true for him, too. He'd gone from being all alone in the world to being connected to everyone in this room. "Robin, you already know that family can be complicated. Remember when you met me and had to figure out what to call me because you already had so many grandparents?"

For the first time since he'd seen her that night, a hint of a smile flickered on her face. "Yeah. I remember, Mo-Mo."

That softening gave him the courage to rest his hand on her arm when he went on. "So, what you learned tonight about Evan is just one more little complication that makes your family even more special. But it doesn't change any of the love. You're a smart girl, Robin. You know that nothing's going to change the love."

"I guess you're right," she said wonderingly. And then she launched herself off the chair and into his arms.

He caught her, awkwardly but firmly. As he hugged his granddaughter, this time it was his eyes that were moist.

Then the others were there, gathering around them hug upon hug, with tears and words of love. Mo's only regret was that Maribeth wasn't there to be part of the family embrace.

Chapter Nineteen

The next evening, Saturday, the friends Maribeth had been babysitting for returned home just after nine. When she climbed into her car, she called Mo. "I'm finished and am heading over to your place. Should I pick up anything on the way?"

"You're the only thing Caruso and I want."

She smiled as she put her phone back in her purse. How lovely that sounded, and she really hoped he meant it.

Last night, she'd been a bit worried. When she and Mo had driven back from Jess and Evan's house, he'd filled her in on what had happened after she'd taken the toddlers to the playroom. She'd been shocked by the evening's revelations, and clearly Mo was feeling stunned, too.

When she'd asked if he wanted to come to her place, he'd said, "Not tonight, thanks. I need some time to process everything. Besides, I have to get up early because I promised Hank I'd be at the garage at six. We've got a bunch of jobs to finish up before the holidays."

His kiss had been perfunctory when she dropped him off, and she'd tried to tell herself he was just distracted and she shouldn't take it personally. Like Caruso, Mo was a creature who needed space and freedom.

Earlier today, Mo had called to ask if she was free tonight, and she'd immediately hoped that he really wanted to see her, not that he was having third thoughts about their involvement. She had told him she'd promised friends she'd babysit while they went to the wife's office party—and also said that the couple hated the obligatory event and planned to be home early. Mo had invited her to his place when she was finished, saying, "I'll sweeten the pot with a Sunday brunch invitation from Daphne and Irene."

"As if the pot needed any sweetening," she'd told him sincerely, relieved that it seemed he had no intention of breaking up.

And now here she was, pulling up in front of his house and reaching for her bulging tote bag. In it were a change of clothes, a few toiletries and cosmetics, and her contribution to tomorrow's brunch: the makings for nonalcoholic mimosas.

At the front of his landladies' house, the curtains were closed and the outside Christmas lights lit. As she walked around the side, Caruso came running to greet her with a warble. She squatted to greet him and was delighted to receive his latest gesture of affection: a cheek rub.

By the time the two of them had reached Mo's door, it was open and he stood there, lean and handsome in jeans and a gray Henley. Smiling a welcome.

Barely pausing to put down her heavy tote, she stepped into his arms and clung tight as he wrapped her in a warm hug. "I missed you," she said. "Last night was so strange."

He eased her away, gestured for Caruso to come inside, and closed the door. As she unbuttoned her coat, he said, "You can say that again. I was overwhelmed. Sorry, I didn't mean to shove you away, but I guess I'm still a bit of the lone wolf. Sometimes I need to process stuff on my own."

"It's fine. I understand, Mo. Believe it or not, I even do that myself sometimes." After all, she'd been alone since her late teens. As great as her grandparents were, they lived so far away. And her friends might be a "family of the heart," people to call on for support and to provide support to in return, but she didn't want to burden them with every woe, setback, or doubt.

Mo had slipped her coat off her shoulders and was hanging it up while she bent to unzip her boots. When she straightened, he was studying her with an appreciative smile. "You are always such a treat for my eyes," he said.

"Same goes for you, Mr. Kincaid."

"Me?"

She snorted. "Don't give me that. You have to know that you're serious eye candy."

"Maribeth, I'm fifty."

"And some things get better with age."

"Flatterer. You must want something from me." He said it teasingly, unthinkingly, and then his face sobered.

He knew what she wanted. Everything.

"Right now, a nice cup of tea or hot chocolate would be perfect," she said, to take the pressure off.

"I think I've learned how to make decent hot chocolate."

She could have made it herself, and probably more efficiently, but she liked that he was waiting on her. So, after she put the nonalcoholic bubbly wine and the organic orange juice in the small fridge, she settled herself on the comfortable couch that unfolded into a less comfortable but acceptable bed. With a sigh of relief, she put her sock-clad feet up on the coffee table. Her friends' three kids had been little monsters tonight. With only two days to go until Christmas, they'd been hyped up.

She glanced over to watch Mo as he heated milk on the hot plate. Aside from a small bathroom with a shower and no tub, the apartment was a single room. The kitchen had a little fridge, a sink, a microwave, and a two-burner hot plate. The rest of the room held the couch, a coffee table and end table, a small table with a couple of chairs, and a TV. The furniture was simple and the decor gender neutral. If Maribeth lived here, she'd add books, knickknacks, colored pillows and throws, and some art on the walls. Now the only personal touches were Mo's tablet on the coffee table, and the box with an old blanket where Caruso now curled up.

Still, the very fact of the man's and dog's presence, not to mention the scent of chocolate as Mo stirred cocoa into the hot milk, made the place feel homey.

She smiled gratefully up at Mo as he brought her a steaming mug. "This is just what I needed. Thank you." Did he know she meant much more than just the beverage?

"Long day?" he asked as he seated himself beside her, put his own sock-clad feet on the coffee table, and reached for her free hand.

She twined her fingers with his and squeezed. "Oh, yes. The store was crazy busy, lots of last-minute shopping happening. And the babysitting—well, let's just say I've seen those kids on better days." She blew on the hot beverage and took a tentative sip.

"Seems to be the weekend for kids in bad moods."

"I wonder how Robin's doing."

"I called her. She's settled down some and seems to be putting things in better perspective." He turned to Maribeth. "She asked me to go riding with her tomorrow afternoon. Just the two of us. I hope you don't mind."

"No, of course not. Mo, that's great. I'm glad you two are growing close."

"So am I." He released her hand, dropped his feet to the floor, and sat forward in the couch, elbows resting on his thighs and both hands curving around his mug. "When I thought over everything that happened last night, I realized that, well, I have a family. That's not what I expected when I came to Caribou Crossing, but it's what has happened."

She nodded. "How do you feel about that?"

His face relaxed and he smiled, the kind of smile that turned the lines running between his nose and lips into dimpled clefts. "Good. That's what I realized last night. I like it. And I think maybe I can do it." His blue-green eyes twinkled. "What I saw at Evan and Jess's is that all those people who are great parents and grandparents can get thrown for a loop. They don't always make the right decisions or know the best thing to do."

She smiled back. "Of course not, because they're human."

"Just like me. I think I, well, did okay with Robin last night. I found things to say that maybe actually helped her." Wonder lit his face. "She hugged me, Maribeth. She kind of launched herself into my arms. Like she needed me. Like she was glad I was there."

"Oh, Mo. That's wonderful." She was sorry for the girl's trauma, but so happy that Mo had found the internal resources to help—and that he was able to give himself credit for it.

"So . . ." He put his mug on the coffee table and swung around to face her, his knee bumping hers. "Maybe I wouldn't be such an awful parent. If I were, uh, to do it again."

Fizzy bubbles rose in her blood and she forced herself

to take a calming breath before saying, "You could be an amazing father. If you decided, with all your heart, that it's what you truly want to do. Not something you're doing just to make me happy."

He nodded, soberly and reflectively. "I hear you, Maribeth. But I need more time."

"I know. Take whatever time you need." Still, she felt encouraged that he was heading in the right direction—not just one that was right for her, but for him as well.

She finished the last couple of mouthfuls of cocoa and sat up to put her mug on the coffee table. "Unfold this couch, Mo, and take me to bed."

As Mo ushered Maribeth down the hall of his landladies' home, he put his arm around her shoulders, wishing he never had to let go. There was one thing he was sure of: he wanted this woman. He loved her and, as much as he was capable of imagining the future, he knew he wanted to spend it with her. But did he deserve her? Was he the right man for her? She said she loved him, but could he give her what she wanted most?

One moment, he'd think yes, all optimistic that they could have a child, maybe children, and be happy. But the next moment, he'd have second thoughts. He'd remember his past; focus on his guilt and his flaws; worry that he couldn't possibly deserve happiness and he shouldn't drag this wonderful woman down with him.

As always, Daphne and Irene's kitchen was bright and attractive and smelled wonderful. The two women looked festive. The usually tailored Daphne wore a holiday sweater, black with snowflakes the same silvery white as her short hair. Irene's sweater was red with a big snowman, a little incongruous on an eightysomething-year-old and yet it went perfectly with her rosy cheeks and sparkling eyes. Both women's smiles were warm and welcoming, with no hint in their expressions that they saw him as a deeply flawed man.

Maribeth gave their hostesses her offerings, and the couple promptly set her and Mo to work. He took graceful flute glasses from a high shelf and Maribeth filled them half-full of orange juice while he uncorked the non-alcoholic sparkling wine. Pouring carefully, she topped up the glasses so the bubbles rose boisterously but didn't overflow.

Irene poured coffee—decaf for Maribeth—and put a bowl of sliced fruit, including jewel-red pomegranate seeds, on the kitchen table. Daphne took a casserole from the oven, saying, "It's a breakfast strata and I'm afraid you're guinea pigs."

Mo didn't know what a breakfast strata was, but once the white-haired woman had put a sizable serving on his plate, he saw that there were layers of all sorts of good things: onions, potatoes, sausage, eggs, cheese, mushrooms, and who knew what else.

Once the four of them had all taken chairs, Maribeth, seated to Mo's right, lifted her flute glass and said, "To a happy and memorable holiday season."

They all drank the toast and then Mo dug into the strata. "Mmm, that's good. This guinea pig says don't change a thing."

"I agree," Maribeth said. "When you get a chance, I'd love the recipe." She helped herself to fruit and passed the bowl to Mo, who did the same before sending it on.

"Good," Daphne said. "This is one of the dishes we want to serve for Christmas breakfast. Everyone's coming over here."

"Andrew and Terry want to host the turkey dinner," Irene said. "The first one in their new house."

Mo had met Andrew, Irene's son, and his husband Terry. "Did your daughter and her family get here as well?" he asked the woman.

"Yes, they drove up from Vancouver on Friday," she said. "My daughter and her husband along with my granddaughter, her partner, and the new baby. They're all staying with Andrew and Terry."

"They'll love Christmas in Caribou Crossing," Maribeth said. "It's the best, and way more fun than being in a big city."

Mo had been in all sorts of places during the holidays and had never paid attention to the differences because it had never mattered. Now, as he'd seen this small town deck itself out with lights, ornaments, trees, menorahs, and holiday cheer, he had a pretty good idea what Maribeth meant. And it wasn't just the decorations—ranging from spiritual to humorously tacky—it was the cheerful, generous spirit of the residents.

Daphne rose and made fresh mimosas for them. When she sat down again, across from Mo, she said, "I truly regret not having had children. I had my students, of course. A new class each year. I wanted the best for them and did my best, but it wasn't like having my own children. I didn't let myself care deeply. Or, rather, I couldn't. My heart locked itself up when I said good-bye to Irene after teachers college."

"You were an excellent teacher," Maribeth said.

"Thank you. I was certainly never the most popular one. I wasn't a warm person."

"Your students respected you," Maribeth said. "We learned a lot from you. You got us at an impressionable age in fourth grade. Those who were paying attention learned good work habits, goal-setting, discipline, morality."

The older woman smiled at her. "It's kind of you to say that. Looking back, I see that there's more I could have given, but sadly I didn't have it in me."

"Oh, now, love," Irene said.

Daphne took her hand. "No pity, please. I had a fulfilling, busy life and I had colleagues and friends who offered companionship and stimulating conversation. If I lacked for more, it was my own damned fault. I didn't have the guts to be the woman I was meant to be." She tilted her head to study Maribeth. "Do you know when my heart opened up again?"

She gave the same answer Mo would have. "When you got back with Irene?"

"Before that. When your friend Cassidy came to stay here. She has a way about her."

Maribeth laughed. "Yes, she does." She turned to him. "Mo, you don't know her well yet, but Cassidy's special. She's frank, generous, smart, free-spirited."

"Somehow," Daphne said, "that young woman managed to see through all my guff and realize there was a rather tender heart lurking within me. I came to care for her, and she was the catalyst who urged me to follow my heart and go looking for Irene." She glanced at Mo. "When another person sees the good in you, or at least sees the special person you could be, somehow it makes you want to be that person, doesn't it? And helps you find the courage to do it."

Thoughtfully, he said, "Somehow it does."

Now the question was: was he capable of it?

Chapter Twenty

This was how Christmas morning should start. Lying on her side in bed, Maribeth gazed at a still-sleeping Mo. It was past nine, late for both of them to sleep in, but they'd gone to midnight Mass with old friends of hers last night—another of her holiday traditions—and by the time they'd curled up after making love, it had been almost two.

Earlier on Christmas Eve, they'd eaten nachos at the crowded, boisterous Wild Rose bar, danced to a few country tunes, and then joined a group of carol singers who meandered around town. Who'd have expected that Mo, with his rough-edged voice, would be a good singer? But he was, though he relied on a carol sheet for the words.

Now he lay on his side facing her, his features relaxed so that she could see the man he'd been in his twenties and thirties. Such a multifaceted guy he was turning out to be. He'd been a good sport, the self-professed loner spending an entire evening immersed in crowds. She'd loved being at his side, their bodies almost always touching, whether it was in their close embrace as they'd shuffle stepped to Martina McBride's moving "O Holy Night" or the simplicity of interlocked gloved hands as they stood among other carol singers while delicate snowflakes brushed their shoulders.

This morning, however, was just for the two of them. That was the way they both wanted it. Later, she'd Skype her grandparents and introduce them to Mo, and then she and Mo would go to a soup kitchen to help out. After that, they'd dress up for a big Cousins-Kincaid-Bly-Brannon turkey dinner. The family took turns hosting, and this year's dinner was at Miriam and Wade Bly's house.

While Maribeth loved being included and starting to feel part of such a large and wonderful family, she couldn't help the occasional worry. What if she and Mo couldn't work things out in a manner that let them both be true to themselves? The more she invested emotionally, the more she had to lose if it all fell apart. She knew Mo would never be deliberately cruel to her, but if he honestly couldn't find it in his heart to tackle fatherhood again, she'd be faced with a "love versus baby" decision, and either choice would break her heart.

But those were no thoughts for an optimist on Christmas morning when her amazing lover slept beside her, naked and warm.

She reached out to wrap a wavy strand of his silver-threaded hair around her finger and tugged gently.

His hand came up like he was swatting at a mosquito.

She pulled harder.

His lips curved and he said sleepily, "Trying to tell me something?"

"Merry Christmas."

His thick lashes fluttered and he opened his eyes. "Oh, yeah. I forgot." The smile bloomed wider and his eyes gleamed, as excited as a child's on Christmas morning. "Merry Christmas, Maribeth." He gave her a quick, hard kiss and then, all energy now, rolled out of bed.

"Are you coming back?"

"Breakfast." He was pulling on the jeans he'd tossed on a chair last night. "Let's feed Caruso, have breakfast, and open presents."

Her eyebrows rose. "No morning sex?" They didn't make love every morning, but this was Christmas, and what better way to start the day?

"Later," he said over his shoulder as he strode toward the bathroom. He muttered something else that she didn't quite catch, though it might have been "I hope."

Well, that was weird. She shook her head, then ran her fingers through her tangled hair. Maybe he was making up for all the years he'd never had a proper Christmas with presents under a tree.

By the time she'd risen, Mo was out of the bathroom and hurrying downstairs.

And by the time she made it down to the kitchen herself, in her robe and glasses, the scent of frying bacon greeted her along with Caruso's happy warble. "And Merry Christmas to you, too," she said, squatting down and exchanging cheek rubs with him.

Mo was at the stove, bacon sizzling in one pan and pancakes in another. She'd assembled two bowls of pancake ingredients yesterday, one wet and one dry, all ready to mix this morning. She had also set the table, so now she poured two glasses of orange juice and sat down to watch her man cook. It wasn't sex, but it wasn't a bad start to the day.

He had the meal plated quickly, and while she was inclined to linger and enjoy the combined flavors of oatmeal pancakes, bacon, and maple syrup, Mo seemed in a rush to eat and get on to the next stage of the day. He almost flung the dishes into the dishwasher and barely let her pour a second mug of decaf coffee before urging her into the living room.

There, she found that he'd turned on the tree lights and was hunkered down getting a fire started. She clicked on the radio to hear Bing Crosby dreaming of a white Christmas—and sure enough, outside the window sun shone brightly on a fresh layer of snow. A handful of neighborhood kids were happily engaged in a snowball fight.

If Mo was eager to get to the gift-giving, Maribeth wouldn't stand in his way. The collection of wrapped presents under the tree was huge, but most would be going along with them to the turkey dinner. The two largest, however, were the ones she really hoped would work out.

"Caruso," she called, and a moment later the dog trotted into the room. Maribeth plunked down on the rug by the fire and urged Caruso to sit next to her. "Mo, I think we should start with his present."

Mo gave the fire a final poke. "Sure." He hauled out the big box wrapped in reindeer-printed paper and dropped to the rug, too. "If he hates the gift, at least he'll have some paper to play with. You open it for him, Maribeth."

She did so, to reveal the cushy new wicker bed and green-and-red plaid blanket she and Mo had bought. "Caruso," she said as the dog sniffed tentatively at the gifts, "we figure you deserve something new and fancy, not the makeshift beds we've been giving you." She spread the blanket out, fluffing it to make a nest.

Caruso stepped into the bed, circled, pawed the blanket into a more satisfying shape, and then curled up with his head on his paws, watching them.

"The stamp of approval," Mo said.

"Yours next," she said, and extracted the gift she'd

stashed behind the tree. The parcel, wrapped in gold paper with silver snowflakes, was about two feet by a foot and a half, and quite narrow. "This is from Caruso and me."

"Interesting," Mo said, hefting it. "It looks and feels like something framed. Artwork? A photograph?" He undid the tape, unfolded the paper, and pulled out the painting. The expression that slipped across his face looked like wonder, and Maribeth relaxed.

"It's us," he said. "Us, painted by Mary Cantrell."

A few weeks ago, they'd walked by a gallery and Mo had admired a cluster of paintings in the window. Maribeth had told him that the painter was a friend of hers, and she'd introduced the two of them at her Sunday open house earlier in the month.

This watercolor was a scenic, set in early winter. Tree branches bore a light kiss of snow and the sun gleamed palely through clouds. The painting was impressionist more than true-to-life, and it had the artist's distinctive Native Canadian flair, but there was no mistaking the threesome. The man on the palomino had black hair under his Stetson and a red scarf around his neck. The woman rode a bay horse and her red hair spilled from beneath a red knitted cap. Ranging along beside them was a cinnamon-colored dog.

"I asked Mary to do it," Maribeth said, "and I gave her the photos I took with my cell the last time we went riding." Her request had been a last-minute one and she'd been ecstatic when Mary fit her in.

"Wow. I'm stunned. It's a memory *and* a work of art. I've never owned anything so amazing. Maribeth, thank you. It's such a thoughtful gift."

It was also too big to fit in his backpack, but the man who'd previously toted all his possessions on his back didn't comment on that.

"Okay," he said, sounding nervous. "It's my turn. And it's not so much a gift as kind of a story."

"A story? That sounds intriguing."

"First, go look out the window."

She rose and obeyed, seeing a similar scene to the last time she'd looked, except now a couple of girls were making snow angels in a neighboring yard. Behind her, she heard a jangle, and Mo came up beside her.

"See that silver minivan?" he asked.

"The one parked in front of my house?" She'd noticed it last night and assumed it belonged to someone who was staying with one of her neighbors. "It's hard to miss." She turned to him. "Mo?"

He pressed a key ring into her hand. "No, I'm not giving you a minivan, just a spare set of keys to the one I bought yesterday."

"I didn't know you were planning on buying a car."

"It's time I stopped borrowing Hank's truck from the garage. I need my own wheels. One of Hank's clients brought in the minivan to get it all tuned up because he planned to sell it, and he gave me a good deal."

"That's great. Though I'd have taken you for more of a Jeep man—or of course a motorcycle in summer."

"Yeah, well . . ." He caught her hand and pulled her back to their seats in front of the fire. "Like I said, it's a story. Here's the second chapter." He reached under the tree and handed her an envelope.

She was expecting a greeting card, but instead found an appointment slip. For the women's clinic. In Mo's name, for right after New Year's. "Mo, I don't understand."

He licked his lips as if they were dry. "If you want to go the sperm donor route, that's okay. But I thought we could look into options, so I did some research. My vasectomy was so long ago, they may not be able to reverse it."

What? Was he actually thinking that—

Heart fluttering, she listened as he went on. "There's this other process where they can extract a guy's sperm"—he winced slightly, but went on—"even after he's had a vasectomy and fertilize the woman's egg. They fertilize it outside the body and then implant it in the uterus, and there's a pretty good chance of it working."

"M-Mo?" Her voice quivered. "Are you thinking . . . I mean, have you decided . . . ?"

"Guess it's time for chapter three of the story." He stared into her eyes, his blue-green gaze mesmerizing. "Maribeth, I've thought long and hard. Something Daphne said on Sunday was the final piece of the puzzle. She talked about when someone sees you for the person you're really meant to be, the one who's hiding inside because you don't have the guts to let them out. And how that can give you the courage to be that person. Maribeth, I've been afraid, guilty, just downright messed up."

"Lost," she whispered. "A lost soul."

He nodded. "That's who I was. But I'm not that man anymore. You've helped me find my way to being the real Mo." He took a breath and gazed steadily into her eyes. "The real Mo wants it all, and I will spend the rest of my life making sure I deserve it."

"A-all?" she stammered.

"This," he said.

She hadn't been able to look away from his eyes, which was why it took her a moment to realize that he was holding something else out to her. When she finally glanced down and saw the ring box, she let out a squeak. Her eyes felt so wide they could pop out of her head, and her heart pounded so fast she couldn't think straight. "Mo?"

"Will you marry me, Maribeth Scott? I love you, I want you, and I want our babies, however they're created. I want to be part of your life, to meet your grandparents and all your friends. I want you to be part of my big, messy family. I want us to build a future together and I want us to be happy."

Was this really happening? It was all she'd dreamed of, so maybe she was still asleep.

He gave a rough laugh. "And that's a whole lot of 'I wants.' What do you want, Maribeth?"

Whether this was a dream or reality, there was only one possible answer. "You! I want you, Mo."

"I am the luckiest bugger in the entire world," he said gruffly as he opened the box to reveal a lovely ring—an emerald set off with sparkly little diamonds.

As Mo slipped the ring on her finger, Caruso sat up, lifted his head, and sang them a long, warbly ballad.

Maribeth stared at her finger, tears of joy glazing her vision. It seemed like she'd waited for this moment all her life. It was every dream come true, to be engaged to a man she loved deeply, a man with whom she'd create a family. "Oh my God, I can't wait to tell my grandparents!" The words burst out.

Mo looked a little startled, and she hurried to explain. "They're my only family and they'll understand how much this means to me. I want them to be the first to know, and I want to introduce them to you. This is going to give them such a happy Christmas, too. And oh, Mo, just imagine the expressions on the faces of your family when we walk in this afternoon and I flash this ring!"

He shook his head, giving her an amused smile. "You want to tell the world?"

"I do! The whole entire world. I'm so happy, so excited, I just can't believe it." Euphoria, that's what this feeling was. "I'm the happiest woman in the world!"

"D'you think there's maybe a couple of things you could do before you call your grandparents?"

"Like what?"

"Say, 'Yes, I'll marry you, Mo,' and then kiss me."

Laughter bubbled out. She couldn't complain about her man's priorities. "Oh yes, Mo, I will most definitely marry you." Kneeling, she captured his head between her palms and leaned forward to kiss him. In her enthusiasm, she lost her balance and tumbled him down to the rug, landing on top of him.

Gazing into his stunning eyes—knowing she'd be seeing those eyes every day for the rest of her life—she said, "I love you, Mo, and we're going to have the most amazing life together."

Epilogue

A year later, on Christmas afternoon, Maribeth dropped onto the couch beside her grandmother. "Best Christmas ever," she told the elderly woman with deep satisfaction.

"It is a special one," Grandma said with a smile, and her husband, seated in a chair on her other side said, "It sure is." They were in the big living room at Evan and Jess's, since it was that couple's turn to host the turkey dinner.

"I am so, so glad the two of you moved to Caribou Crossing," Maribeth said. It had been almost four months since her grandparents had sold their house in North Vancouver—the one they'd bought half a century earlier—making a huge profit that would ensure they lived in comfort for the rest of their lives. They had rented the studio apartment at Daphne and Irene's house, figuring on taking their time looking for a new home. The four eighty-somethings had hit it off immediately, and so far Maribeth's grandparents hadn't kept the Realtor very busy.

"We should have done it years ago," Granddad said. "Don't know why we felt so rooted in Vancouver."

"It's always been our home," his wife said, "and change is hard, especially when you're older. We had our clubs, activities, and friends there, though fewer friends as the years went by. But all those things can't compete with the charms of our first great-granddaughter." She hugged month-old Joy, who was sleeping in her arms.

"Speaking of whom," Maribeth said, "can I borrow her back? I can only go so long without holding her."

As she happily took custody of her daughter, Joy stirred, blinked, and then fell back asleep. Maribeth gazed down at her, endlessly fascinated by this small, warm miracle. Joy's wispy hair was as black as her dad's, her skin was a gorgeous light caramel, and Maribeth really hoped her blue eyes would end up the same shade as Mo's. Joy was clothed in an adorable red onesie with snowflakes on it, a gift from Mo's sister. The wedding and pregnancy were forging a closer relationship with her and even with Mo's dad, and that made Maribeth very happy.

Feeling the warmth of her husband's gaze, Maribeth glanced across the room to where he sat on the floor playing trucks with Alex, who had turned three a couple of weeks earlier. Mo rose and headed over, trailed by Alex. Maribeth moved closer to her grandmother, letting Mo squeeze in on her other side.

He put his arm around Maribeth and trailed a gentle finger over Joy's delicate cheek. "How's our little bundle of joy holding up?" It was the baby's first big family outing.

"Hi, Bundle," Alex said, reaching his own less gentle pudgy fingers toward the baby's face.

"Careful now," Mo said, seizing the boy's hand and guiding it into a caress. "And her name's Joy."

"She's Bundle," Alex announced firmly. "Tee Bee and

Mo-Mo's baby is Bundle." He turned away. "I go play with Nicki now!" and off he raced.

"The Bundle thing is my fault," Grandma said ruefully. When Maribeth and Mo had found out she was pregnant with a girl, they'd agreed on the name Joy, because it so perfectly expressed their emotions. The day Joy was born, when Grandma first saw her in the hospital, she'd cried and called her their bundle of joy. Maribeth and Mo had started doing it, too, and Alex, with the persistence of a three-year-old, had glommed onto the Bundle part and refused to budge.

"You look more rested," Grandma said to Maribeth. "Is Joy sleeping better now?"

Maribeth grinned at her husband. "Mo found the perfect lullaby for her."

"You're singing to the baby?" Grandma asked him.

"Sometimes," he admitted. "But there's a voice she prefers. Caruso's, if you can believe it. We realized that whenever he sings, she settles right down. So we made a tape of his songs, repeating over and over."

After her grandparents chuckled, Granddad said, "That dog's good with children, isn't he? I admit, when you first told us what breed he was, I looked it up and was worried. I thought he'd be too wild and unpredictable."

"Amazingly," Mo said, squeezing Maribeth's shoulders, "some wild things actually enjoy being domesticated, in the right circumstances."

She snuggled closer into the curve of his arm, knowing he was talking about himself as well as Caruso. There was still a touch of wildness in both the man and the singing dog, a craving that sent them out together for two-hour walks in the country once or twice a week. But she didn't mind it one bit. She had her own cravings, like for time with girlfriends—lunches and the occasional ladies' evening out at a pub or at one of their homes. It was good for her and Mo to be different. They complemented each other—and on the truly important things, like the value of family, they were in total agreement.

Grandma took her husband's hand and squared her shoulders. "We have a question for you two."

"Okay," Maribeth said, a little wary of this lead-up.

"Now that Joy's settling in," Grandma said, "when are the pair of you planning to give her a baby brother or sister?"

Maribeth's mouth fell open. Yes, she and Mo had talked in general terms about having more than one child. He knew how she'd regretted being an only. But Joy was barely a month old.

Granddad spoke next. "It's not like any of us is getting any younger."

Mo gave a soft laugh. "The man has a point, my love."

She gazed from her beloved grandparents, down to beautiful little Joy, whose rosebud mouth was pursed in her sleep, and then to the handsome face of the man she loved.

His grin flashed, the slow, dazzling one that carved dimples into his cheeks.

She smiled back. "Yes, Granddad has an excellent point."

If you enjoyed HOLIDAY IN YOUR HEART,
be sure not to miss Susan Fox's

RING OF FIRE

No one is a stranger in Caribou Crossing,
a small Western town
made for healing and second chances . . .

She's raising her son on her own, but that's just fine with Lark Cantrell. Caribou Crossing's fire chief comes from a long line of strong, independent women—who have lousy luck with men. Lark's ex-husband walked out when Jayden was born with cerebral palsy. No matter—Jayden, now ten, is a bright, terrific kid, and the love of her life. When it comes to men, Lark is content with the occasional casual hookup; there's no room in her heart for more disappointment.

Major Eric Weaver is in Caribou Crossing for one reason: to complete his rehabilitation so he can return to active service. Haunted by what went down in Afghanistan, his wounded soul isn't healing as quickly as his body. But it's almost impossible to resist the appeal of the sexy, feisty fire chief and her plucky son—not to mention the friendly, caring small town way of life. In Lark's loving arms, the scarred soldier begins to believe he may finally have found his true home . . .

A Zebra mass-market paperback
and eBook on sale now.

Turn the page for a special look!

Lark Cantrell snapped awake at the familiar bleep of her pager and grabbed the device from the bedside table. A residential structure fire on Tannen Road; occupancy undetermined.

In a flash she responded and jumped out of bed. She ran down the hall, clad in her checked cotton sleep pants and blue tank top. Tannen was out in the country, ten or more minutes' drive from the town of Caribou Crossing.

She shoved her feet into a pair of sandals that sat by the front door. No need to leave a note for her family. Lark's ten-year-old son and mom were used to the unpredictable schedule of a firefighter. As for a man, there hadn't been a significant guy in Lark's life since Jayden's dad walked out on them when he was a baby, and she intended to keep it that way.

She sprinted next door to the fire hall, the mid-July air warm on her skin. As chief, she worked regular weekday hours and didn't have to respond to after-hours callouts. Although no one staffed the fire hall at night, she trusted her volunteers to show up when paged. But she lived beside the station, and with the fire so far outside town, every second counted.

Besides, firefighting was way more exhilarating than sleeping.

She raced into the apparatus bay, kicked off her sandals, and jumped into her boots and turnout pants. By that time, Javi Sanchez had joined her, and moments later Daniels and Mason ran in. As the volunteers dressed, Lark contacted dispatch to report their status, and learned that Captain Tom Weston, tonight's on-call duty officer, was on his way to the scene in the duty vehicle. He'd likely arrive five minutes before Lark's team, but he wouldn't have a mask and breathing apparatus so he couldn't enter the structure. Still, he'd provide valuable information while the other firefighters were en route, so they could plan their strategy.

Usually, Lark took the command role, but tonight she wanted the adrenaline buzz of active firefighting. Besides, it was good to give learning opportunities to some of the others. As she gathered her balaclava, mask, and breathing apparatus, she called out, "Engine 4. Daniels, you're driving."

"Yes, Chief." Sharon Daniels raced for the pumper truck. As driver, the volunteer would also be responsible for operating the pump once they were on-scene.

"Sanchez, you're Command," Lark continued. He was a great firefighter and he'd relish the chance to be in charge. "Mason, you and I are the attack team." She and Mason would be the first team into the structure, assuming it was safe to enter when they arrived. Cal Mason was only a couple of months out of training and Lark wanted to work with him, help him out.

More firefighters were arriving, including Manny Singh. Captain Singh was one of the paid personnel; like her, he worked regular weekday hours but also often responded to after-hours callouts. "Engine 3," she told him. His team would follow Engine 4, bringing the additional water supply that could be needed out in the country where there were no hydrants.

Lark jumped into the back of Engine 4, joining Mason. Daniels drove the truck out the open doors with flashing lights and a whoop of the siren. Sanchez, beside Daniels up front, was on the radio. He relayed information to the firefighters. "Dispatch says a guy was driving home after a late shift at work. Saw flickering lights in a back window of a two-story residence. Said it looked to him like fire, maybe in the kitchen. The house is owned by the Hoppingtons, an elderly couple. The guy thinks they moved into an assisted living facility two or three months back, but he's not positive."

The engine raced through the residential outskirts of the small town, and onto a country road leading northeast. One good thing about night callouts: the roads were virtually empty.

"Even if the couple did move," Lark said, "there might be family staying there, or they could've rented it out."

She checked her watch. They'd made excellent time. It had been only five minutes since she'd received the page. "Wonder how old the house is?" Older houses burned more slowly and cleanly. With a new home, once it had been burning for twenty minutes, it often wasn't safe to enter.

They were five, maybe six minutes from their destination, driving through ranch land where there was only an occasional building. She and Mason pulled on their balaclavas, and then donned their masks and breathing apparatuses.

Weston's voice crackled over the radio. "I'm just arriving.

Jeep parked in front. No one outside. Smoke and flames pouring out the back of the house."

Damn. It seemed the house was occupied, and the residents hadn't managed to get out. Lark leaned forward, readying herself to leap out of the truck the moment it stopped.

Major Eric Weaver eased through the doorway and stepped over a broken piece of wood, careful to walk in the boot prints of Sergeant Danny Peller. Their unit was on a training mission with the Afghan local police, searching an abandoned compound after receiving a tip that insurgents had a weapons cache there.

The vacated room was a mess of broken furniture and equipment. Peller stopped to assess the situation, and Eric glanced over his shoulder to make sure Sharif, the Afghan police officer who was following Eric, held back. Sharif was young and eager, and could be too impetuous.

Peller moved forward. Eric started to follow and—

The world exploded. He was flung into the air, crashing against the wooden wall. For a moment, he was too stunned to move, even to think.

Then . . . *fuck. Where's my weapon?* In the explosion, it had flown out of his hand. *What the fuck happened?* Was it an IED? A grenade? A truck bomb? Were they under attack? When he sucked in a breath, it carried the scent of smoke. Was the building on fire?

Where were Peller and Sharif?

He managed to sit up, blinking against grit in his eyes. His gaze landed first on the Afghan, who'd been blown back out the doorway and lay on the ground, either unconscious or dead. *Fuck.* Through a haze of dust and smoke, Eric searched for Peller and found him sprawled on the floor a few yards away with—oh, shit—his fucking right leg blown away from above the knee. Peller's gaze, wide-eyed with shock, was fixed on Eric.

A tourniquet. Gotta get a tourniquet on him or he'll bleed out before the medics get here.

Automatically, Eric made to rise, but his legs didn't work. For the first time, he looked down at his body. His legs were there, but from his knees down, both of them were a mess of torn flesh, blood, and—oh, fuck—even shattered bone.

And then the pain came. Agonizing pain.

But he couldn't surrender to it. Eric pulled himself onto his side and, using the strength of his arms, torso, and hip, dragged himself toward Peller.

Where were the other men? Were they taking fire, unable to reach him, Peller, and Sharif? Or were they dead, or injured? What the hell was going on out there? His ears rang, making it hard to distinguish sounds. One thing he knew: the building was on fire. Smoke scratched his throat and flames licked the closest wall, spreading quickly. At least the Afghan officer—alive or dead—was outside and should be safe from the fire.

Peller's gaze was fixed on Eric like he was his salvation. This morning, the kid had been joking about how he'd have to quit smoking before he went home, or his pregnant wife wouldn't let him back in the house. And that homecoming was only a couple of weeks away. Canada had almost finished pulling out of Afghanistan. Back on home soil, Peller would finish out the few months left on his Terms of Service contract, and then he planned to leave the army and find a job where he could be home with his wife and baby. As for Eric, he was a career soldier with no obligations other than to the army. After Afghanistan, he'd have a new posting.

As Eric dragged himself toward Peller, the sergeant's lips moved. Eric shook his head, trying to clear the ringing. With the aid of a little lip-reading, he made out Peller's next words. "It's bad, Major." There was blood on the kid's face; he'd been cut by debris. Peller twisted in pain. He coughed and choked out, "Real bad."

Yeah, it was bad, but agreeing with the kid wasn't going to help. "Hang on, Peller." Fighting against his own pain, Eric reached the sergeant, pulled out the tourniquet that all soldiers carried, and wrapped it around what remained of Peller's right leg. The left leg was in bad shape, too, and he got Peller's tourniquet on it.

As for his own legs, they'd have to wait. The fire was a hungry crackle, a rush of flames relentlessly consuming the derelict building. Smoke clogged his throat and lungs. His brain, on overload from shock, pain, smoke, and urgency, struggled to form a plan of action.

No one's gonna get here in time. Have to get Peller out before this place burns down with us in it.

The kid shouldn't be moved, not without a stretcher, but what choice did Eric have? He needed to drag him, and hope the fire didn't cut off their path to the exit. "Gonna get you out now, Danny-Boy. Get you to a medic."

"Wish I could see Ellie," Peller mumbled, his face white and sweaty, streaked with dirt and blood.

"You'll be home before you know it." It was hard to concentrate on anything but the excruciating pain in his own legs.

"Not g-going home, Nails." He forced the words out.

"Sure you are." And if Eric had anything to say about it, it wouldn't be in a body bag. His nickname was Nails because, when he was green, he'd been so dumb that he'd said he was tough enough to eat nails. Well, he was a hell of a lot older now, and damned tough, but the task ahead of him was formidable.

Damn it, where were the others? He could sure use a little help in here. Even though his hearing had improved, he still couldn't make out any sounds from outside—not above the noise of the fire. He maneuvered his body into a position where he could try to drag Danny by the back collar of his uniform.

Soldier up, boy, and get your man out of there! This time the harsh command ringing inside his skull was in his father's voice. The Brigadier-General had no patience with wimps.

Eric grabbed on to Danny's uniform and braced himself to tug, but then the sergeant's mouth opened again. Eric leaned closer as words came out slowly and clumsily.

"Tell El-lie . . ." The life faded from Danny's voice before he could finish the sentence. It was fading from his blue eyes, too, yet Eric saw the plea in them and knew exactly what Danny had wanted to say.

Shit. The cocky young sergeant was SOL. He was one of Eric's men, and Eric had sent him into danger. He'd failed to protect him, and now he couldn't save him. Couldn't send him home to his wife and unborn kid. All he could do was respect this dying wish.

"I'll tell her you love her and the baby," he said gruffly, resting his hand on Danny's shoulder. *I'll tell her—if I don't burn to death or die of blood loss myself.* "She loves you, too, Danny-Boy. You know that." But as he spoke the last words, he realized he was talking to a dead man.

Eric lifted his hand from his sergeant's lifeless body and raised clenched fists as he let out a howl of fury. And then—

He fell, landing hard, fierce pain in his right leg jolting him to awareness.

What the hell? What now? Another explosion?

Smoke burned his eyes and clogged his throat, making him cough. Everything was dark, but doing a quick assessment of the situation, he felt a rough texture under his hand. Not concrete, wood, or dirt, but . . . carpet?

Gradually, he came to his senses. He'd had another nightmare. A flashback to the IED explosion that had taken Danny Peller's life.

Eric used the tricks he'd been taught for coping with PTSD flashbacks. Ground himself; orient himself in the present.

"I'm Eric Weaver and I'm not in Afghanistan. This is not the f'ing sandbox. I'm in British Columbia, in Caribou Crossing."

Repeating those words didn't make the smoke go away. He coughed as he rubbed the floor again and felt the well-worn carpet. "I'm in the master bedroom of the farmhouse I rented." And, damn it, he'd fallen out of bed again.

His right leg hurt fiercely. "It's phantom limb pain," he muttered, coughing. "That leg's long gone." Was there some kind of justice or divine irony in the fact that he, the major who hadn't been able to save Danny after the sergeant's right leg was blown off, had lost his own right leg? Eric curled his body so he could massage the stump where his leg ended midthigh. Sometimes that helped ease the pain. His left leg, which had undergone multiple surgeries, didn't feel a hell of a lot better than his phantom limb.

Smoke still choked his nose and filled his lungs, and he coughed again, struggling to expel it. "There's no smoke. I'm not in Afghanistan. It was a nightmare." Except . . .

Oh, fuck, that smoke was no dream; it was real. So was the roar and crackle of flames. The house was on fire.

And had been for some time, he realized, while his fucked-up brain had been back in Afghanistan.

Call 9-1-1.

Damn it, he'd left his phone downstairs in the kitchen. Besides, from the noise and smell, he wasn't sure the Caribou Crossing fire department would be able to reach the remote farmhouse in time. Might any distant neighbors be awake in the middle of the night and have seen the glow of flames in the sky? He sure as hell wasn't going to wait around and see if rescue came.

Disoriented by the darkness, smoke, and the lingering effects of the flashback, he tried to get his bearings. Reaching out, he found the side of the bed. He'd thrashed around so much in his sleep that he'd fallen out on the side farthest from the door.

His T-shirt was at the foot of the bed, where he'd tossed it when he racked out. He grabbed it and held it to his face, trying to block the smoke. He'd already inhaled so much while caught up in his flashback that his burning lungs and throat kept him coughing, and his eyes watered.

He did a quick situation analysis. The bedroom was on the second floor. If he shut the door—that sturdy wooden door—it'd hold the fire back. But there was no fire escape outside the window. Though the bedroom was on the second floor, the way the house was situated atop a hill meant that it was a three-story drop from the window to a concrete patio. He was strong enough to pull himself up onto the roof, but the fire could trap him there if rescue didn't arrive soon. If he donned his prosthesis, maybe he could find a way to climb down, or he could take his chances on jumping. No, wait. Shit. The batteries that operated his high-tech leg were in the charger.

He was running out of time.

The only other exit was down the hall and stairs to the

front door—if the fire didn't block his path. Deciding on that course of action, Eric crawled lopsidedly around the bed, using his good knee, his stump, and one hand. Clad only in cotton boxer briefs, he kept his head low, using his other hand to hold his tee to his nose, but smoke filtered through the cotton. Deep, wrenching coughs racked his body. There was crap in this house, toxic crap. Smoke inhalation messed with your body and your brain. He didn't have a moment to spare.

He made it to the door into the hall. The smoke was even thicker, and orangey-yellow flames engulfed the end of the hall directly above the kitchen. How the hell had the fire started? Faulty wiring in the kitchen, maybe? It was an old house; when he rented it, he hadn't cared that it was run-down.

The fire ate its way toward him, but didn't cut off his escape route to the top of the staircase. Coughing into his T-shirt, he crawled as fast as he could. His coordination was getting worse, a side effect of smoke inhalation.

Stairs were good exercise. He'd been drilling himself running up and down them, getting used to his fancy prosthesis, building his strength, striving for a balanced gait. Improving every day. Now, without that leg, he'd have to "bum it down" as patients referred to it in rehab—plopping on his ass and bumping down step by step the way a toddler would. It'd only take a few seconds, and then the door would be right in front of him.

He forced himself onward. Both his legs—the one that had been seriously injured and the missing one—hurt fiercely. What with the smoke and his coughing, he could barely catch his breath. His head ached so badly he had trouble thinking, and he was dizzy, disoriented, and nauseous. Did he hear a siren, or was he hallucinating?

At the top of the stairs, a coughing fit brought him to a stop. It was so severe he couldn't catch his breath.

Mind over matter, soldier.

Yeah, Dad, I know.

Peering downstairs through burning, watering eyes, he saw that it was less smoky there, but that flames and smoke were spreading down the hallway from the kitchen. He'd left the heavy kitchen door closed and it had blocked the fire for a while, but now the monster had breached it. He had to get to the first floor before fire blocked the front door.

Goddamn it, he'd survived an IED in Afghanistan. He wasn't going to die in a house fire out in the middle of the Cariboo. Dizzy, fighting nausea, he struggled to stop coughing, to breathe shallowly through the protective barrier of his cotton tee, to focus, to push onward.

Downstairs, there was a crash. Breaking glass. Had the fire blown out a window? An instant later, the front door slammed open and two firefighters dashed into the smoky hallway. "Fire Department," a voice yelled. "Call out!"

He tried to respond, but instead coughed like he was hacking up a lung. A haze swam across his eyes, through his brain. He was fading, losing consciousness.

But one of them had seen him. A figure clad in bulky turnout gear raced up the stairs. The other manned a hose, aiming a powerful stream of water down the hallway, attempting to hold back the fire.

The first firefighter knelt beside Eric, reaching for something in the pocket of his turnout pants. "You're okay," he said, his voice muffled and distorted by the face mask. "Is there anyone else in the house? Nod or shake your head."

Eric, still hacking, shook his head while the firefighter pulled out a strap.

"Got an adult male," the firefighter reported to someone. "He says that's all."

Through the visor of the mask, dark brown eyes stared into Eric's. "We'll get you out," the man said. Despite his wonky vision, Eric read confidence and reassurance. A sense of peace stole over him. The hand that held the tee to his nose dropped away. He began to fade . . . His last conscious thought was, *I'm safe*.

His lapse in consciousness didn't last long. When he came to, he was being pulled headfirst down the stairs. The firefighter had wrapped the strap under his armpits and was tugging him, supporting his head and neck. Eric's lower body bumped each step. Pain jabbed him. His body struggled to expel smoke, but he tried to hold still, to not make the rescue more difficult. He hated being helpless, being somebody's burden. Making this other man risk his life to rescue him. Eric was the soldier, the one who was supposed to be tough and self-sufficient.

He was aware of the second firefighter still spraying water, and then his rescuer was pulling him through the open front door. Other hands were there, ready to take him. Fresh air touched his skin. Red and blue lights swirled; water arced from a hose pointed at the house; voices called out.

He was on a stretcher, an oxygen mask being hooked over his face. Needily but cautiously, he sucked air through his scorched airway. Someone draped a blanket over him and fingers checked his pulse. Paramedics, he realized. A man and a woman in blue uniforms.

His rescuer was still there, too, addressing him. "You said there's no one else in the house. Nod if that's correct."

He nodded confirmation.

"Any pets?"

He shook his head. Damn it, his prosthesis was in there.

The high-tech one designed for soldiers to help them be fully functional—and to return to active service if they chose to do so. It was his mobility, his freedom; it was his chance to reclaim his career, his life. But he couldn't ask firefighters to risk their own lives for a damned leg. The prosthetist would make him a new one, but it would take time. Another setback. It was the fucking story of his life these days.

Dimly, he was aware that his rescuer was relaying Eric's report to the other firefighters. Oddly, the man's confident voice had an almost feminine sound.

Eric wanted to lift the oxygen mask and thank the guy, but the firefighter was hurrying away to help the others who were trying to control the blaze.

"You're going to be okay," the female paramedic, youngish, with blond hair pulled back from her face, said calmly. "We'll get you to the hospital and they'll treat you for smoke inhalation."

He nodded his understanding.

She glanced toward the house. "It's fully involved. You're a lucky man. Lark got you just in time."

Lark? An unusual name, especially for a guy.

The other paramedic, a stocky guy with graying hair, said, "Caribou Crossing's sure lucky to have her."

Her? Well, shit. He'd been rescued by a woman.

He had nothing against women. He'd served with a few; they were as capable as the men. But now, for whatever reason, discovering that he'd been saved by a woman felt like the final blow to his ego. Grateful as he was to be alive, could he be any more humiliated?